THE SIGIL BLADE

By Jeff Wilson

The Sigil Blade
By Jeff Wilson

Contents

TITH

SELLENS

DOMIRIA

KADIA

THE TRAELS

LORREL

ORTOL

HERIK

TEK

OSSIA

SERIDOR

CALLIS

NAR
EDOR

AN
INNIS

NAMEK
TOR

Prologue

The ship altered course to investigate after lookouts spotted rising smoke in the early hours of the morning, and the source became apparent a few hours later. They were now quickly closing the distance on the still smoldering vessel, and Fleet Navarch Aelsian watched from the bow of the *Interdiction*, straining his eyes to make out details, as they approached the moderately sized, double masted boat. It was a narrow hulled ship, of a type commonly used by smugglers, built to run in shallow waters and sacrifice cargo space in favor of speed.

The cabin had been reduced to a pile of smoking timbers and most of the ship's railings were similarly destroyed. The deck, though thoroughly charred, was largely in-tact. The sails and the rigging were completely gone, but the double masts, too thick to have burned through completely, still remained, a pair of lonely blackened spires guarding a small, solitary, indistinct object in the middle of the deck.

As the ships drew nearer, the object gradually resolved into a recognizable shape. It was a man, seated unmoving on the deck, covered head to toe in soot and balancing an oversized sword across his legs. On close approach, Aelsian realized that some of what he had taken for soot was instead clothing stained with blood. As they drew nearer still, he saw the man's face. The man, who remained perfectly still as he took in slow silent breaths, was deliberately staring, calm and unperturbed, in Aelsian's direction. The *Interdiction* came into position alongside the doomed ship, and the crew connected the two vessels with a boarding plank. The man rose in response, ash and soot falling from his cloak and swirling in the ocean wind around him as he stood.

Aelsian felt something catch in his throat as recognition struck him. He knew this man. This was Lord Aisen—son of Aedan Elduryn, a captain in the Sigil Corps, and the heir of House Edorin. The young nobleman shouldn't be here; he was supposed to be in Nar Edor resisting an attempt by their king to seize his family's land. Aisen surrendered his sword without resistance to the group of boarders, none of whom showed any hint of recognition. The navarch watched as Aisen allowed the men to escort him over to the *Interdiction*. First Aisen crossed, then two of the crew behind him. What Aelsian saw next, made his heart freeze in his chest. Crossing behind the men, an unseen creature, whose weight was bowing the plank sharply, silently made its way onto the *Interdiction*.

Chapter 1

An Innis

Obscured by steady rains, which fell from a sullen evening sky, a cloaked figure moved along a deteriorating causeway. The tide was out, but substantial portions of the crumbling stonework remained submerged, and the figure, seen from afar, resembled an otherworldly apparition crossing over the surface of the sea on its way toward the tidal island. It hesitated upon reaching the island, taking a moment to evaluate the footing. In that brief pause, the figure seemed to morph into something altogether more solid, revealed now as nothing more than the simple, plainly dressed young man that he was.

His coarse leather boots were entirely soaked through, and with the land before him drenched by the unrelenting weather, the shallow depth of water above the bed of stone and gravel in which he now stood might well have seemed a preferable surface to the muddy earth along the shoreline. Determined to continue onward, the man resumed a steady forward progression, and as he stepped up onto the island from out of the coastal waters, he ignored the dark grey clay which began accumulating on his feet.

Broken walls and left over remnants from the foundations of ancient, ruined buildings lined the shore. Stones had been pillaged from these structures, but enough remained in places to give cover. No one lived on this edge of the island. It was too close to the dense forests which enshrouded the abandoned remains of a forgotten civilization that had flourished throughout the expansive lands to the east, of which this rediscovered island had only been a small part. The mainland on the other side of the causeway, where all attempts to revive any lasting settlements had ended badly, was a dark wilderness, avoided entirely by the current population living here now.

The man glanced nervously towards some of the crumbling walls as he travelled, concerned that someone could be watching from concealment, but he could not afford to divert much of his attention. In the growing darkness, it took considerable concentration to hold to the little used trail he was following. Occasionally, paved stones broke to the surface, but before long the path would revert back to its usual condition, which was nothing more than a narrow band of loosely packed mud. The intermittent exceptional areas, which suggested that the trail might once have been a well maintained roadway, were but tired echoes of a bygone age.

The unmaintained path continued on around the southern edge of the island, skirting its central feature, a steep uplift of rock and earth which extended to the north before it ended in a precipitous drop. A palatial stone structure, more an enormous home than a castle or fortress, crowned the peak of the mountain.

Over the course the evening the man passed by a few damaged buildings and a single isolated cottage, but he saw little else until he arrived at the top of a hill that overlooked a settlement founded on the western edge of the island. He could vaguely see the position of the setting sun, and under the veiled light that it imparted to the turbulent sky, he surveyed a continuous collection of buildings.

Built against a graduated slope on which it had grown in stages, the town extended all of the way from the western shoreline to the island's mountainous peak. Large broad storehouses and repositories dominated the shore beside the town's two stone piers, which projected straight out into the waters beyond the island where they serviced a crowded complement of vessels. A number of other large buildings dotted the curving paths that headed up the mountain.

Less impressive dwellings haphazardly crowded the intervening areas. Some of the smaller homes looked recently built and had been poorly constructed from scavenged stones and rough wooden timbers. Judging by the neglect evident in their condition, it was clear that the majority of these humble structures had been recently abandoned. The buildings that were inhabited could easily be differentiated from the others by the light that escaped through the cracks in their shuttered windows, which were all closed tight against the ongoing storm.

Because of the late hour and the poor weather, the streets were empty and the cloaked figure met no other travelers on his way through the town. Eventually, as he neared the shoreline, he found himself on a cobbled street in what appeared to be the town's commercial section. It was lined with shops and other business establishments, few of which showed signs of use, and only one of what had once been several large inns and taverns remained open. The sign board, affixed beneath the overhanging second floor of the inn, displayed a carved and decorated image of a tarnished sword hilt.

Stepping onto the porch of the inn, he looked for a place to scrape his boots, but he could not find a section of the paving that was free of mud. It took some determined digging with the toe of his boot to expose the top of the stone surface that lay buried beneath the grime in the entryway. Giving up, he took a quick look inside the establishment and saw that his efforts had been pointless. The floors were already covered in layers of wet earth and old dirt throughout; there was more filth trailing out than there was being tracked in.

Upon entering, he was assaulted by a collection of odors: mold, tobacco smoke, and alcohol, all mixed in with the pungent smell of rendered animal fat. None of these would have been terrible in isolation from the others, and a couple would even have been quite welcoming, but when experienced together the combination was very unpleasant. Two drinking rooms were situated to his left, one empty and the other occupied by a group of ragged looking men immersed in a game of dice. They gambled with piles of pale white oblong shells that were used for money. He watched them for a moment, observing their game as one of the men replenished his dwindling pile of shells by pulling them, a couple at a time, from a string that was secured to his belt and threaded into a pouch at his side.

The entrance to a kitchen could be seen at the back of the inn, and the rest of the lower floor was taken up by the large hearth hall. A group of men, several of whom appeared quite old in comparison to the youngest of their friends, were conversing with each other around the fireplace. If any of them took an interest in the stranger or his late evening arrival, they gave no outward indication.

He lowered the hood on his cloak and unfastened a brass clasp before removing the woolen overcoat from where it hung upon his shoulders. He proceeded then to shake it free of the beads of water that had collected on its surface. A number of small emblems, pinned along the edge of the cloak, disappeared into the folds of the damp cloth when he arranged and neatly divided it over his arm. He stood for a moment in the doorway, dimly lit against the backdrop of the darkened rain-soaked street. The doorframe, which served as useful point of reference, measured him a man of less than average height. He was slender to a degree, but physically strong in appearance.

He took deliberate steps inside and made his way to the back of the inn, where he draped his cloak over a chair in an empty corner of the hearth hall. A couple of the silver emblems that were pinned upon the coat made muffled metallic sounds as they struck against the others, serving as an unintentional but audible claim to the table he had selected.

The stranger had intense grey eyes, which were the color of spent charcoal, and a dark sun-weathered complexion. His calm resolute expression carried echoes of a hardness that came from defeat, causing him to seem older and possessed of more experience than his otherwise youthful appearance would have suggested. Sweeping stiff fingers through his dark, damp hair, he eased himself into a chair and took silent stock of the interior surroundings. Lacking any semblance of appropriately deferential behavior, he began to study the other men in the room.

Without exception, they wore unwashed and poorly tailored clothes, but they were all dry, suggesting the men had arrived hours ago before the storm had started, and had ventured nowhere since. Two of them were clearly drunk, and the rest seemed to be working their way into that condition. One of the patrons, a thin man with sharp eyes, turned around after stirring the wood fuel in the hearth. He met the stranger's gaze for a moment, but quickly looked away. Returning to his chair, he whispered something to his neighbor, a nervous balding man with slumping shoulders, who after a couple of short unavailing glances in the direction of the stranger, took, in acquiescence to a sense of caution that was ingrained deeply into his character, great pains to avoid doing so again.

In the kitchen, behind a greasy apron wrapped around his bulging waist, the innkeeper noticed these two customers, but from where he stood he could not see the corner of the hearth hall where their distracted attentions had been directed. Setting aside the plate he had been scraping, he exited the kitchen, a space that he kept much cleaner than the communal hearth hall, and wiped his hands on a towel that was slotted through the cords of his apron. Upon catching sight of his new guest, the innkeeper hurried over to the corner. He was years past what could be called young, but he retained a healthy vigor in spite of his age.

"I wasn't aware someone had come in, or I would have greeted you properly," the innkeeper said. "Welcome to the Broken Oath. I'm Greven, the owner," he recited.

"Edryd," the stranger returned politely.

"I won't be able to offer much in the way of food," Greven apologized. "Pies and bread were finished off hours ago, but I do have some stew left."

"I'm afraid I don't have any kind of coinage that could be easily converted," Edryd cautioned.

"No matter," the innkeeper said, dismissing the issue, "there won't be a charge. It would only go to waste otherwise."

Edryd started to protest, but Greven was already on his way back to the Kitchen. He returned a short while later carrying a wooden bowl and a stone vessel. The mug was filled with ale and the bowl gave off a savory aroma.

"I can't pay for this," Edryd repeated, holding his hands outward in an attempt to decline the offered meal.

"You needn't worry," laughed one of the men, speaking out from across the room, "he's only giving you what no one else was willing to pay for to begin with." Several of the men nodded in agreement.

"I don't want to sound ungrateful, and I do appreciate your generosity, but I wouldn't want to take advantage," Edryd continued to protest, now worried over what exactly it was he was being offered.

Greven proceeded to set the bowl and mug down on the table, refusing to accept Edryd's attempt to decline them.

"You won't convince me that you aren't hungry," Greven said, guessing that Edryd had not eaten for a while. "And I expect," Greven continued, "that we will discover that you have arrived here in An Innis under some set of unusual circumstances, or so I would hope. Any news you may have brought with you will answer your debt for these poor scrapings."

Edryd looked down at the bowl of food, discomforted by Greven's disparagement of the contents as a collection of poor scrapings. It was filled with a thick broth containing bits of potatoes, leeks, and cooked pieces of some sort of animal, the identity of which he could not have given with any confidence. Feeling uncertain about the quality of the meat, Edryd hesitantly inhaled the aroma given off by the stew.

"Made daily," Greven explained, noticing Edryd's unease. "Would ordinarily be mutton, specially prepared and seasoned, but it hasn't been easy to come by of late, so some reworking of the recipe was required." Greven had given this description proudly, but Edryd continued to look tentatively at the stew. "Local game birds," Greven finally offered, declining to be more specific.

Driven by hunger, Edryd tried a bit of the cloudy broth, avoiding the sparse chunks of meat. There was a strong mineral taste, whether from the pot it was stewed in or from the ingredients, Edryd could not be sure, but it was pleasant overall. Satisfied that it was safe, Edryd took several more bites. The meat included pieces from more than one kind of bird, one of which was definitely the source of the strong flavor. Greven looked on expectantly, as did several of the other men in the room.

"I haven't any real news, but you might regard the circumstances that brought me here as being of some interest," Edryd conceded, confirming the innkeeper's earlier supposition that there was a story to be told.

"Go on," prodded Greven, who was, with good reason, curious about this very subject. There hadn't been any newly arrived ships in the port for at least a week, which made Edryd's arrival an obvious point of interest.

Edryd did not wish to tell them who he was or where he had come from, but he couldn't refuse to give an explanation. That would only make them curious. Having worked out the details in advance, and not caring whether anyone believed what he told them, Edryd signaled that he was ready to start. What would matter, in the end, would be whether or not he could forge an identity that was sufficiently dissimilar from the truth and compelling enough to satisfy them.

"Until four days ago, I was on a square rigged freighter of Domirian make, called the *Royal Accrual*," Edryd began.

Greven's eyes darkened. "Your ship was built in one of the countries in the Ossian League," he said. "You don't look at all like someone from Domiria, and I would hope you are not an Ossian."

"No, no of course I'm not," said Edryd. He didn't seem particularly troubled by Greven's assumptions, but he made an effort to dispel them, without volunteering any information about where it was he was actually from. "I was a part of the crew, but not as a matter of choice, you understand."

"I don't," said Greven.

"Before I ended up on the *Accrual*, I was a passenger on a small boat making its way up the Ossian Coast. There were three of us—the owner of the boat, his son, and myself. We were in an inlet replenishing our fresh water when we were met onshore by a landing party from the *Accrual*."

"I'm going to guess that your encounter did not go well?" someone suggested smartly from across the room.

"The captain of the *Accrual* declared our ship a wreck and claimed the salvage rights on our cargo. Well, as you might imagine, the owner of the boat didn't agree."

"Rightly so," insisted Greven.

"There was quite a bit of shouting, and even though there was nothing worth taking, just provisions, nets, dried fish, and a bit of oil, they proceeded to ransack the boat anyway. I don't think they were too happy with any of it, because they left it all on the beach. The only thing they wanted to take in the end was us. They ordered us to board the *Accrual*, and when we refused, they busted holes in the old man's boat."

"Bastards," muttered a dark haired man who had twisted around in his chair at the next nearest table to the one at which Edryd and Greven were sitting. It was becoming clear that more than a few of the people in the room were taking an interest in the conversation.

"I hope you won't judge me for this, but I didn't know the old man. I had paid him for passage up the coast, and that was the extent of our association," Edryd said. He stopped then, as if not wanting to continue.

"What happened?" Greven asked.

"I left them there. I watched from the deck of the *Accrual* as they stranded the man and his son."

"You should have done something," demanded the dark haired man from the nearby table, turning his chair to more directly face Edryd and Greven.

"What could he have done, Ivor?" said a second man, who sat cross from the one who had just spoken. "Apart from staying behind with a broken boat, or making some sort of useless protest, I don't see as he had many options."

"I would like to think they may have been able to repair the boat," Edryd rationalized, moving the story along. "And while I do regret abandoning those two, I regret it more for my own sake than I do for theirs. Things did not go well for me after that."

Greven and his customers were all paying close attention now, and everything Edryd said increased their desire to learn more.

"Domiria being a League state, I had no fears that that I would be made into a slave, but to my misfortune, the captain had novel interpretations on more than just salvage laws."

The room grew quiet.

"Ossians," Ivor spat angrily, interrupting the silence. "The League only banned the sale of slaves as a means to attack the wealth and power of Seridor and her allies!" he declared vehemently. Ivor's allegiance in the long running conflict between the Ossian League states and Seridor seemed clear enough.

"There is no love here in An Innis for Ossians or for the League," Greven explained. "I am sure you must already know that this island was once a prospering slave market."

Edryd would have liked to object, and insist that there was no such thing as a prospering slave market. The benefit realized by those who profited in such a trade, was necessarily more than offset by the suffering of those who were being transacted. But that wouldn't have made Edryd any friends in this crowd, so instead he nodded agreeably, all the while filtering out much of what Greven had to say in reference to the "better days" that might never come again.

"... between that and a trade in Edoric metals," Greven went on, "and assorted valuables taken from captured Ossian merchant ships, we did quite well, but of late, League influence and expansion is making things difficult for us."

"Well, I'm not taking sides," Edryd said, although in his heart he did feel something bordering on sincere disdain towards these unprincipled men of An Innis, and by extension the people of Seridor, where he suspected many of them were from. "But I would agree," Edryd said with feigned sympathy, "given my recent experiences on the *Accrual*, that as Ivor said only a moment ago, tactical rather than moral concerns motivated the League to ban slavery. If Captain Vaedres was in any way typical, and if Ossians are anything like the men of Domiria, then they wield their laws and codes primarily as weapons against enemies, and as tools for obtaining leverage in matters of trade."

Edryd's description was greeted with broad agreement. Ivor, in particular, seemed to appreciate Edryd's support of his earlier comment and regarded him approvingly.

"The captain offered me a rate of six strand per month if I would agree to a yearlong contract as part of his crew," said Edryd, calling everyone's attention back to the story.

"Six strand," groaned Greven, "that is hardly a competitive wage for that kind of work."

"In other circumstances, I would never have entertained the offer had it been twice that amount," Edryd agreed, "but I wasn't given a choice as simple as that. He claimed that I owed twenty strand for passage to the nearest port, and said that unless I had the means to pay right away, which he well knew I did not, I would have to remain until I paid the debt."

"That would never hold up," Ivor's friend said. "At least not under the laws that govern League ships it wouldn't. What you are describing, it amounts to being forced into involuntary service under a threat of imprisonment. Couldn't you report the captain?"

Ivor's friend seemed to be far more educated than the others, and Edryd wondered about that, but for now, he simply took note of it and moved on. "I made it clear that I intended to do exactly that," Edryd said, "but the captain only laughed and reminded me that on board the *Accrual*, he was the arbiter of Domirian law. I was told in very specific terms, that I was bound to his ship for as long as he remained unsatisfied with the balance of my service."

"Sounds like slavery to me," said Ivor.

"Technically it wasn't," disagreed Ivor's friend, "even if the only differences are a matter of the words chosen when describing the arrangement."

"What did you do?" Greven asked.

"I agreed to the contract, and three days on we made the next port. As I was leaving the ship, Captain Vaedres advanced me thirty strand in copper coins, which represented several months of wages."

"I'm not sure your captain was as bad as you are making out," said Greven. "He showed a good deal of trust to someone so recently taken into employment. A generous amount if you ask me."

"Well I didn't ask," Edryd said disagreeably, pausing afterward for a moment in an effort to soften the edge in his voice before he continued. "Anyway, I puzzled over that a little bit myself, but it was not long before I discovered that the captain's motives were anything but generous."

Greven hadn't taken offense to Edryd's tone, but he did look confused. "What was there to stop you from simply leaving with all of that money and never going back?" he asked.

"The advance," Edryd answered. "The contract that he was holding over my head was a weak thing at best. But with a mutually agreed upon sum of borrowed money, accepted in front of witnesses, the captain had gained a more legitimate means to control me. He could, in theory, threaten me with imprisonment if it was not repaid."

Sudden comprehension spread across the faces of the men listening to Edryd's story. "That's an intelligent captain, to be sure," Greven said with a hint of admiration.

"You still should have left," Ivor insisted.

"I would have done that if I could have," Edryd agreed. "As I sat in a tavern deciding what to do, I was joined by some of the crew. A few of them began actively encouraging me with helpful tips on how to best make use of my wages, and I was having trouble trying to politely refuse the advice. I excused myself by saying that I was returning to the ship, but one of my new friends said that he would join me."

"He was following you," Greven surmised.

"I was certain that he was," Edryd confirmed. "All I could think to do was to return the advance as soon as possible. We were not allowed to keep personal coin while on the ship, so I turned it in as soon as I returned to the *Accrual*. Once back on board though, I was no longer permitted to leave without consent from the captain. At the next port we made, after I declined to accept an advance on my wages while going ashore, Vaedres made me stay aboard with the portion of the crew that was protecting the ship, and that pattern continued everywhere we went."

He had a crowd now, many of whom were showing intense interest. Edryd wondered why no one appeared to suspect that some, if not all of the details, were being embellished, but he continued to invent with confidence as he created more layers and added them to the story.

"Months later, when I was finally allowed leave," Edryd said, "I began testing how far I could get from the ship and was surprised when no one followed me. I had just escaped. I couldn't believe my luck. That is until I realized it was not luck at all. It hit me then, all at once, that I had not been paid a single coin for four months of work." Everyone laughed at this part.

"Embarrassed and angry," Edryd continued, "I stormed back to the *Accrual* and demanded my wages. Vaedres offered to pay me a tiny fraction of what I was owed. A wiser man, or even just a less uniquely stupid and petty one, would have cut his losses and left with whatever he could get. Instead, I insisted that I would never leave until I was paid in full."

"I would have done the same!" Ivor approved. "I wouldn't allow myself to be taken advantage of either."

Ivor's friends laughed quietly at his outburst. Greven smiled in amusement as well.

"What?" Ivor demanded.

"You have, Ivor, by your own admission, proclaimed yourself as being both stupid and petty," the other man at Ivor's table explained.

Ivor, his face expressing a mixture of anger and embarrassment, did not understand the logic behind the insult, and he was struggling in vain to think of a suitable retort. All he could come up with was, "you would do well, Vannin, to be silent when no one has asked your opinion." This only made everyone laugh at Ivor a little harder.

"Don't take this wrong, Ivor, but it's a comfort to know that I am not alone in being too proud and foolish for my own good," Edryd said.

"I should think you were a fool because you stood up to that captain?" Ivor complained.

"If you did you wouldn't be wrong," Edryd responded. "Confronting him nearly cost me my life."

Edryd was getting to the crux of his story now, and everyone could sense it.

"The contract, I could have broken," Edryd said, "but the money the captain owed to me, that kept me bound more securely than anything else ever could. The captain would have been only too happy if I chose to walk away from what I was owed, but he was no less pleased at keeping me on at just six strand a month."

"He was never going to honor the debt," Greven pointed out. "You must have realized that."

"I did," Edryd agreed.

"So why did you stay?"

"I was angry. I had wasted part of an entire year of my life with nothing to show for it, and so I resolved then to take the ship from him, no matter what it cost me."

"Now even I will call you something short of wise," marveled Ivor.

"We should all agree on that," Edryd replied with a sigh.

"I do at least respect your courage," Greven said, as the rest of the men in the room stared expectantly at Edryd and waited for him to continue.

"I had been, up to that point, making a highly successful effort to be of as little value during my term of involuntary employment as possible. I knew hardly any of the crew and almost nothing about the ship or its captain. But from that moment, I began to learn everything I could about every shipmate, every piece of cargo we moved between ports, and every merchant, lord, or monarch we transacted with. I intended to use that information to make sure that the captain would never again command a ship, or obtain any income from the contacts he had spent a lifetime cultivating."

"Remind me not to do anything to ever offend you," Greven said with amusement.

Edryd went on to tell of his role in organizing a mutiny on the ship, which, at its peak, had drawn in a quarter of the crew. He also described how his name had surfaced during an investigation by the captain, which had begun when one of the conspirators, incautious in his attempts to bring more men to their side, had been caught.

"Not a winning position given the circumstances," Vannin remarked. "You may have been in as much immediate danger of being killed by a disloyal crewmember seeking to prevent you from talking, as you were of being forced into revealing your role in the plot."

"Best served then to keep your mouth shut, the captain had no real evidence with which to accuse you," Ivor asserted.

"Perhaps," acknowledged Edryd, "but I doubted that I would have withstood the interrogation; keeping silent is not a skill I have much practice with."

"And yet you are here in front of us, healthy and unharmed," remarked Vannin, "you must have come up with something."

"I made a confession," Edryd said.

Vannin looked unsatisfied, Ivor seemed upset, and Greven was clearly disappointed.

"Not a real confession," Edryd amended, "I could have gained nothing from that."

"I don't see what you stood to gain from any confession, real or false," said Vannin.

Ignoring the objection, Edryd continued the story, emphasizing how he had bravely refused to divulge the names of any of the crew who were involved. That is of course until properly threatened with physical harm, at which point he then grudgingly let the names of a few conspirators slip out. Slowly, and with purpose, he continued to give the name of a crewman each time he was questioned, at first only people who were not actually involved, but in the end, just randomly naming a new crew member with no pattern at all to whom he chose.

If Ivor had been angry before, he seemed more so now. Edryd had lost Greven's sympathies as well. Vannin, on the other hand, was impressed.

"He was promoting conditions which would trigger the eventual mutiny," Vannin offered helpfully to Ivor and Greven, admiring Edryd's strategy. "By making the captain paranoid, to the point where he would suspect everyone, more men were pushed into the conspiracy, and it gave all of the crew members an urgent incentive to act before they could be accused."

"I don't care about the reasons. What he did was contemptible," Ivor insisted. "I can't respect someone who accused others to save himself."

Vannin looked to Edryd, seeking support as the others waited for the explanation.

"I think it's best if I just tell you what happened," Edryd responded. "I had been a prisoner for three days with no food, and I was subjected to some fairly rough treatment, but at the end of that, I am not exaggerating when I say the captain looked more distressed than I did."

"I'm sure he would have," Vannin said. "After questioning everyone you named, and in turn everyone they named, he had to have run into as much false information as truth. He would have learned that some of his officers were also involved, and it would have become hopeless trying to unravel it all."

"He had a few choice words for me," Edryd said, and then, speaking in a rough approximation of the voice of the captain from his story, "I gather you think I have not treated you well. If you only wanted to leave, you could have done so at any time." Returning to his own voice, Edryd continued. "Why, he wanted to know, had I instead tried to agitate dissension and upset the peaceful operation of his ship and his crew?"

Edryd paused for effect before he related his answer. "I could have said a lot right then—that I had been a virtual prisoner for most of my time aboard his ship, that he had not dealt fairly with his men, or that the disloyalty in his crew was a product of his own making not mine. But, with my life in jeopardy, I couldn't think of anything so brave or noble as any of that."

"What did you say?" Ivor asked.

"I told him that I would have left long ago if he had only been willing to pay me what I was owed. It didn't seem like I had been understood, so I made my point as clearly as I could: 'You still owe me for eight months of work on this ship!' It was the wrong thing to say. He dragged me up on deck, had a couple of his men toss me over, and threw in a coin purse after me. The captain then shouted from where he stood on the deck 'There, I believe that fully satisfies what you are owed,' much to the amusement of his crew. They clustered at the rail, every one of them, laughing at me. The ship pulled anchor, and it sailed away."

Edryd watched for reactions, and he was pleased to see that everyone was listening intently. Deciding that it was time to wrap things up, Edryd finished the story. "Thinking that I would soon die, I watched the ship fade from sight. What I hadn't realized, until I turned around, was that the shoreline could be seen from where I was. In the state of deprivation I was in after days of imprisonment, I was not sure of my prospects, but I began to swim. Aided by the current, I made it to shore just after nightfall four days ago. After recuperating for a day, I spent three more traveling inland, up onto the cliffs and going south through the forests, before crossing the causeway and ending up here on the island tonight."

At the conclusion of Edryd's story his listeners exchanged uncomfortable looks.

"You travelled three days through the forest?" said Vannin.

Edryd was confused. "That was the part that you find hard to believe?" he replied. "You do know that there's a road through the forest, don't you? Ancient and overgrown, but it was definitely a roadway of some kind. There were ruined buildings here and there along the way and probably a city further inland."

The mood darkened further, and Greven offered up a cryptic explanation, "We do not go into those forests, not for any reason."

Edryd wanted to know why, but the three men were growing increasingly unsettled. He asked them anyway. "What is it about the forest that frightens you?"

"A topic best left for the morning, with the sun high above," Greven said with finality.

"I can't begin to understand why he didn't kill you outright," Ivor said, changing the subject.

"Neither do I," admitted Edryd, "perhaps he hoped that I would drown."

"No, the captain thought things through quite carefully," Vannin disagreed. "He knew that there was a risk that the crew might do to him what he had just done to you."

"So he lets them off, as if nothing happened?" Ivor objected.

"Even if he could separate the disloyal crewmen from the innocent ones, which he could not, they would have been too numerous to confront," Vannin explained. "By getting Edryd off the ship and pretending to dismiss the idea of an ongoing plot against him, he took away any immediate pressure on the crew to act."

"That does make sense," Edryd replied. "He must be praying he can make it to the next port without mishap."

"And discharge the crew and hire on an entirely new one the moment they get there," Greven added.

His story finished, Edryd took advantage of a lull in the conversation and drained what was left of his mug of ale.

Vannin finished his drink as well, and then he briefly tilted his head, listening intently. "Storm seems to have let up," he commented before rising to his feet. "I think I will see if I can make it home before it starts again."

"Live well and in good health," Edryd said rather formally, inspiring a couple of curious looks.

"It was good to meet you," Vannin said in response.

Vannin left quietly, followed shortly afterwards by Ivor and several others, leaving only Greven, who remained sitting on the other side of the table. Noticing the empty bowl and mug, Greven offered to refill them. When Edryd declined, Greven thanked him for the story. "That was interesting," Greven said. "I have to say though, I am not sure I should believe most of it."

"No, you probably shouldn't," Edryd agreed, almost relieved to see that someone had the sense to doubt him. He had resisted the urge to tell some of the more incredible lies that he had considered and rejected, but even so, he had assumed that someone would eventually challenge some part of the poorly crafted tale he had spun. He just couldn't say that he had expected that Greven would end up being the one to do so.

"Doesn't matter, it was well told... for something made up on the spot," Greven said cheerfully. Greven placed his hands on the table, preparing to rise and collect the empty bowl and cup, but he suddenly eased himself back down and leaned forward. "Was any of it true, though?" he asked.

"The eight months of wages are real enough," Edryd acknowledged as he placed a coin purse on the table.

"I thought you said you didn't have any money," Greven complained with an injured look.

"What I actually said, was that I didn't have anything easily convertible," Edryd corrected. "I want to pay for the meal, as well as a room, but I am going to need to find a way to exchange these."

Edryd removed the contents of the bag and then flattened the purse onto the table, placing it strategically between the two of them. With Greven's thick frame effectively shielding that part of the table from the few remaining people in the inn, Edryd proceeded to casually place two large gold coins on top of the cloth pouch.

Greven's eyes widened. "Are those sovereigns?" he asked in a hoarse whisper, his gaze lingering on the two coins which were brightly reflecting the lantern light.

"Yes," confirmed Edryd, "but rather excessive in terms of value for paying for things like lodging and food."

"You could say that," agreed Greven. "This is a good deal more than eight months of wages. If I offered you room and board for an entire year for just one of those, you would be getting a very poor bargain."

"I do need a room, but just for a night or two," Edryd responded. "If there is a place in town where I could get some local currency, I will be able to pay you after I exchange one of these for some smaller denominations."

Greven didn't respond immediately. He seemed to be doing mental arithmetic in his head, never taking his eyes from the two coins.

"Master Innkeep," Edryd prodded.

Greven jerked his head up, slightly startled. "Sorry, lost in thought," he apologized. "You would need to go to one of the four harbormasters down on the pier. No, that probably wouldn't be any good at all. You might want to see the Ard Ri, Lord Esivh Rhol."

"Ard Ri?" Edryd said with skepticism. "That's rarified nobility for a rather smallish island."

Greven cringed at hearing this description, and he gave a quick look around before answering. "I know it's ridiculous, but he makes us call him that. He runs a business, of an immoral and ill reputed nature, out of the palace atop the island, and he dictates terms to everyone else in An Innis."

"Let's say I would just as soon not draw attention. Is seeking an audience with the self-styled High King of An Innis just to get local coins really a good idea? There must be a merchant or two who would be able to handle this."

"The harbormasters I mentioned before, or one of their agents, would surely have the means," Greven admitted, "but you have to understand, they are smugglers, swindlers, and villains of one kind or another, each and every last one of them. If you were to meet with any of those thieves, alone and unprotected, and you decided to play out those coins like you just did for me, they would take them alright, and not see any reason to give you anything in return."

"Lord Esivh is a more legitimate sort then?" Edryd asked.

"No!" Greven said. "He is worse than any of them, and it is no close contest. Only, two gold sovereigns would not be a particularly large sum of money to him. Not so much at least that he would tarnish his image by taking coins from you like a common thief. He would spare no effort in prying them from you by other means though."

"You group them all together, the Ard Ri included," Edryd commented.

"There is good reason for that. They came from similar places and used similar means to take hold of what they could. Esivh has merely been the most successful recent example of a black market profiteer advancing his own interests."

"I take your point about not tempting anyone. Perhaps I would be better off borrowing money instead."

"That might come with another set of complications, but it probably would be safer," Greven agreed.

"For something like that, I expect I will be better off dealing with one of your town's less successful merchants, lower class notwithstanding. If you could give me a room for the night, and recommend someone appropriate, I will make sure to compensate you properly when I can."

Greven, appearing apologetic, took a moment to respond. "I haven't been successful enough of late to hire any help, so things here are in a bit of a neglected state. The few rooms I have that are fit to live in are already taken."

"I would be happy for anything at all," Edryd pressed. "Even a bare spot on the floor in a hallway would suit me fine if it will keep me dry."

Greven's brow furrowed in thought for a moment. He had begun to shake his head, when the corners of his mouth suddenly tightened into an odd sort of self-satisfied grin. "Wait one minute," he said. "I think I have a solution."

With no more comment than that, the innkeeper hurried up a nearby set of stairs. He was gone for several minutes and Edryd began to grow a little impatient before he finally saw Greven coming back down. The innkeeper was carrying a small brass ring, dangling from which, were two long iron keys. Setting the keys on the table, Greven settled back into his seat across from Edryd.

"There is a house on the other side of the courtyard behind this inn. Belonged to a friend of mine who asked me to look after the place for him," Greven explained. "He has been gone for years now, so I don't know that there is much risk that he has returned suddenly and will be in need of it tonight."

Collecting the keys eagerly, Edryd rose from his chair. "I appreciate this Master Greven," he said. "If you can think on it tonight, when I return these in the morning I will get your recommendation regarding whom I ought to see for credit on reasonable terms. I will make certain that all of this will have been well worth your time."

Thanking the innkeeper one more time from the rear entrance to the inn, Edryd stepped out into the dark night air.

Chapter 2

Aed Seoras

With his cloak swept back, hanging freely from where it was secured over his shoulders, Edryd took a deep breath and walked out into the courtyard behind the inn. The rain had stopped, but the air remained damp and fragrant with the smell of wet stones and moistened earth. An easterly wind carried a hint of the ocean, feeling cool against the skin on his neck as he made his way across the smooth cobbles beneath his feet. Twenty yards from the inn, with a low wall around its circular edge, a large community well stood in the center of the courtyard.

Choosing an angle that would skirt the edges of the wall around the well, Edryd made his way across the open space. The area was roughly squared by the boundaries of several large residential properties. Houses on each site, built two or three levels high with fine quarried granite blocks, overlooked the square. Most, including the home Greven had mentioned, were in various stages of progressing deterioration. Edryd could not connect the knowledge with anything which he had heard or seen, but he was aware that someone had followed him out of the inn and settled into the shadows against the establishment's back wall. Edryd could feel the man looking at his back, waiting for the right moment to advance. Warding off a natural impulse to pause in response to his discernment of the threat, Edryd constrained his reaction and took care to maintain an uninterrupted bearing and manner.

As Edryd approached the center of the courtyard, the man pulled away from his position against the back wall of the Broken Oath. It was then that Edryd noticed, hidden behind the far side of the well, a partner to man who was at this moment slowly closing in on his back. This second man, who lay in wait behind the well, wasn't in view now, but some movement made in anticipation of his approaching target must have alerted Edryd to his presence. Not willing to oblige his attackers by crossing into the range of whoever was skulking behind the well, Edryd turned to confront the man behind him, who was still about thirty feet away.

Edryd could not clearly see the man's face, which was broad and flat with no resemblance to any of the men he had seen inside, but his intentions were clear from his aggressive posture. He, along with his partner hiding behind the well, intended to ambush a lone unsuspecting victim. Edryd was alone, but he was not the sort of prey these men would have chosen if they had known him better. "Close enough," Edryd commanded, freezing the man in his tracks.

Under the faint light of the stars, and a moon which was nearly full, Edryd could see surprise and frustration on the man's bearded face. Taking advantage of the pause his warning had created, Edryd evaluated the threat. The attacker was broadly built and stood several inches taller than Edryd. Looking for escape routes, Edryd's attention was drawn to a passage that lay between the inn and an adjacent merchant's shop. He peered intently for a moment into that narrow alleyway. It was completely dark and revealed nothing, but Edryd could feel a presence there. Thinking about this third attacker and wondering how much worse things could get, Edryd reflected with regret upon the decisions that had led him here. It had clearly been a serious mistake on his part to enter this town unarmed.

Returning his attention to the bearded attacker who had followed him out of the inn, Edryd did his best to match the man's menacing stare. The broadly built thief appeared unwashed and poorly groomed, but his black woolen coat and simple belted pants were remarkably well maintained and clean. Edryd decided it was reasonable to believe that the freshly laundered clothes were probably stolen. Then again, how this giant of a man had found someone else's clothes, which were so well-tailored for such a large frame, Edryd couldn't imagine.

The big man's eyes shifted, drawn towards something over Edryd's right shoulder for a brief moment, before returning to focus on Edryd. His partner has left his cover Edryd realized. Continuing to look forward and pretending to be oblivious to anything but the heavyset man in front, he focused his concentration on the enemy creeping up behind him, listening carefully for the soft muted scrape of leather boots against damp paving stones. Struggling against the urge to tense up, Edryd waited until he could all but feel the man standing behind him in preparation to deliver an attack.

Holding a heavy rock in his right hand, the man swung it downward with great force, hoping to take Edryd down without a struggle. Timing his move for this moment, Edryd turned on his right foot, and bent his knees sharply, bringing his body into a low crouch. The blow, which had been aimed at the back of his head, missed high, leaving his attacker off balance. Edryd grabbed hold of the man's coat with both of his hands and surged back up into a standing potion, lifting his attacker slightly as he did so before slamming the startled man back to the ground. The man landed square on his back with a soft grunt as air was knocked from his lungs, followed by a dull thud when the back of his head struck hard on the stone paving.

Edryd had no time to make sure that his downed opponent would not get back up. The other attacker had already closed the distance between them, moving with more speed than he reasonably could have given such a large man credit for. It was too late to evade the reckless charge, too late to do anything but turn and brace against the unavoidable collision. Trying to ward against the impact, shock surged through every joint in Edryd's frame as he met the crash. His upraised arms absorbed very little of the overwhelming force from his more massive adversary, but Edryd maintained his footing, desperate to not end up on the ground beneath his opponent.

The large man's momentum had not been stopped though, and he now had a firm grip on Edryd's shirt as he continued to surge forward. The smell of old stale sweat, subdued in a small measure by a fragrant herbal scent, permeated the air around the man who had seized hold of him. Edryd tried to lean into his opponent and redirect him, but his feet could not gain any sort of purchase on the slick cobbled stones beneath his boots. He was being driven backwards into the center of the courtyard.

With what little leverage Edryd could manage, he struck a sharp blow aimed at the center of the man's torso just below his ribs. This did not stop the foul smelling man, but it did cause his grip on Edryd's shirt to weaken. Edryd, still being driven backward, tore free and got as low as he could before spinning on his left leg until he was facing in the same direction as his attacker, with only the leg on which he had pivoted still overlapping the man's continued trajectory. Raising his foot from the ground, Edryd caught the crook of the man's ankle with the heel of his boot, sending him into an uncontrolled dive. The wall of stone that encircled the well was only a few feet away, which fortunate for Edryd, but not so convenient for his attacker. The man flew forward, striking the wall first with his head and then his left shoulder. A large section of well gave way, dust from the crumbling mortar clouding the air as the wall collapsed. The falling stones made distorted sounds as they collided back and forth down the sides of the well before splashing loudly in the water below.

Edryd turned back around, intending to locate his original opponent. The man no longer lay where he had fallen. His enemy, an older wiry man not much shorter than Edryd, stood only a dozen feet away, eyes glazed over but still filled with angry intent as he slowly pulled a short thin blade from a sheath that had been concealed somewhere in the recesses of his coat. Unconsciously, Edryd started to reach for the hilt of a sword at his side that wasn't there, muttering a silent curse as he remembered that he was not armed. For now, his enemy made no advancing movement. The earlier exchange had taught him caution.

"Get up, Hagan!" the older man ordered, yelling at his partner who lay in a heap beneath a pile of rocks beside the well. "That can't have been enough to hurt you."

Edryd risked a quick look back at Hagan. If the other man did not think Hagan was hurt, he must have lacked capacity for sympathy. To Edryd's amazement though, Hagan was actually stirring and might be back up on his feet in another minute. Do I have to kill one of them to end this? he wondered silently to himself.

"Yelling out the name of your partner... in the middle of a robbery?" Edryd said, mocking his attacker as he returned his focus to the older man. "I'm sure that's breaking a pretty basic rule in your profession."

If Edryd's comments bothered the man, he wasn't showing it. If anything, it helped the man regain some focus. It occurred to Edryd then, a little too late, that aggravating an armed attacker probably hadn't been the best possible idea. The glazed look in his opponent's eyes seemed to be diminishing, but still he did not attack. Apparently a knife was not advantage enough. He also wanted support from Hagan.

"Get up!" the knife-wielding man shouted again at Hagan.

"Sorry... Cecht," Hagan apologized, struggling to speak clearly. "I... I'm getting up."

"He's barely any smarter than you are," Edryd said to Cecht while shaking his head derisively, forgetting that he had, only just a moment ago, decided against the wisdom of provoking the man who was holding a very dangerous looking double-edged knife.

Edryd was not about to wait for Hagan to recover. It would have been a good time to run, but Edryd chose to attack. A couple of quick strides brought him into striking range. Using his left arm, Edryd deftly knocked away a knife thrust aimed at his chest, deflecting the knife hand inward and up, partially turning his opponent and leaving the side of his ribs and stomach open. Edryd moved as if to strike the exposed area, causing Cecht to instinctively bring his arm down, his forearm tightly pulled in to shield against the feigned attack.

This was what Edryd had hoped for, and he struck down as hard as he could with his fist on the rounded upper edge of Cecht's forearm just below his elbow. Surprise registered on the man's face as his arm straightened, having lost all sensation, and the knife fell from his hand. Edryd took hold of the man's arm at the wrist, thinking to twist his enemy and force him to the ground, but now it was his turn to be surprised. Edryd felt like he was making a futile attempt to hang onto a runaway mount as Cecht tore his arm free with an unbelievable surge of strength that unbalanced Edryd and almost sent him to the ground.

Edryd recovered, collecting Cecht's blade from off of the ground as he rose back up. Hagan was just now struggling to his feet. Edryd couldn't quite get his head around the speed and strength his opponents had surprised him with, but with a weapon in his hand, he was comfortable that there was no longer any serious risk. Even attacking together, Edryd was confident they would be no match for him. His sole concern now was determining the best way to stop the attack without inflicting serious injuries to one or both of them.

"Hagan and Cecht," Edryd said, "a pair of incompetents; each one dumber than the other."

Edryd's previous insults, which he had resorted to in a misconceived effort to project an aura of intimidation, had done more to provoke the attackers than deter them. The results this time were even worse. Cecht produced a small throwing knife in each hand from the sleeves of his coat, and Hagan pulled a small wooden cudgel from inside of his jacket. Forget injuring them, Edryd thought to himself, I really might have to kill these two. It was then that he noticed that both of their coats, though different in size, were made from the same cloth, and cut in the same fashion.

"If you leave now, I promise a day's head start before I begin hunting," Edryd threatened, hoping that an uncomplicated warning would work where his impulsive insults had not.

Both men (wisely) seemed reluctant to initiate anything, but neither of them showed signs of giving up. Convinced there was no avoiding it, Edryd began to formulate an attack strategy. He would need to take Cecht out first; he had to respect those throwing knives. He wouldn't risk turning his back to Cecht without knowing whether the man had the skill to use them effectively. Believing that a delay would not work in his favor, Edryd almost started forward, but he realized that he had been forgetting something important: the man in the alley.

Feeling a twinge of panic, Edryd looked past Cecht toward the darkened passage, where he knew a third enemy remained hidden from view. He could not see anyone, but he was no less certain that there was someone there, someone who had been observing everything.

Edryd was looking directly into the alleyway when the shadows began to shift and move, coalescing into a robed figure in a dark grey cloak. As the figure emerged, his black clothing seemed to shed wisps of darkness. The intimidating man kept a hand on the hilt of a long sword, a weapon which was seated in a wooden scabbard, coated with black lacquer and worked with simple metal embellishments. This was a more dangerous enemy than either Hagan or Cecht. Edryd could recognize a skilled swordsman, and traces of dark strength and power could be seen in every one of this man's deliberate movements. This opponent warranted respect, and Edryd realized that it would be unwise to engage him without a better weapon of his own to even the odds.

"Seoras!" said Hagan, surprise and fear threading through the pitch in his voice as he gave a name to the robed figure.

Hagan was behind him, so Edryd could not see the face that matched the obvious alarm in the big man's voice. Edryd could, in contrast, see plain dismay in Cecht's eyes at the mere mention of the name Seoras. Edryd had thought the man would be a third attacker, tipping the balance in favor of his opponents. The reactions Seoras had

inspired in both Hagan and Cecht though, gave Edryd a reason to hope
that he had gotten this wrong.

The man stepped further into the courtyard, eyes surveying the
scene with his hand still on his sword, ready to draw it out. "What are
you doing?" he demanded.

The knives in Cecht's hands disappeared back into the sleeves of
his coat. Edryd kept his knife in a ready position, but relaxed his
posture. Hagan, still a little staggered by his collision with a stone wall,
was slow to remember that he was holding the cudgel, but he dropped
it to ground in response to an angry look from the swordsman.

"Miserable idiots," Seoras said, looking at the damage to the well.
"I am of a mind to..." he started to say but did not finish, shaking his
head in irritation. "Anyone unwilling to surrender themselves into my
custody to answer for this—should leave now."

Hagan and Cecht did not wait to hear the end of this offer. They
fled, disappearing down an alley opposite the one from which Seoras
had first appeared. Edryd wanted to feel relieved, only he suspected
that he was now in an even worse predicament.

"Are you an authority?" Edryd asked. The man was not dressed like
a guard. Apart from the sword, he looked more like a lord or estate
holder in fine, if somewhat unusual, clothing. Cecht and Hagan would
have done a better job at passing as guardsmen.

"Technically speaking? No," Seoras replied.

"They certainly seemed to treat you as though you were," Edryd
pointed out.

"In a less than official sense, I do occasionally find myself invoking a
semblance of order on this forsaken place," Seoras admitted. "Far too
often for my liking," he added as an afterthought.

"Those men are thieves. I want to report them to whoever might
handle such things," Edryd began to explain.

"Start by telling me your name," Seoras said.

"My name is Edryd. I can give you their names as well. The larger
man went by Hagan and the smaller man was called Cecht. I had never
seen either of them before tonight."

"I am Aed Seoras," the man said, more relaxed now but with his
hand still casually gripping the hilt of his sword. "There is nothing to be
done tonight in the dark, but I have a property a short walk from here.
If you will put your knife away, we can discuss things on the way there.

You can tell me everything from the beginning once we are out of the damp and cold."

Edryd was uneasy. He wasn't really sure whether he was being invited as a guest, or whether Seoras intended to hold him for questioning as he had threatened to do earlier. Edryd shouldn't have needed to describe what had happened. He knew that Aed Seoras had watched the entire encounter. The man's motives were far from clear, and deliberately so it would appear. Hagan and Cecht, despite receiving serious damage, had not shown much fear in that fight, yet they had been terrified of Seoras. With a knife at the ready, Edryd might have had an advantage if he used it to attack now, but Seoras had given him no reason to act. Reluctantly, Edryd handed the weapon, hilt first, to Seoras. He was putting himself at the mercy of the other man, but he wanted to signal that he had no desire cause any trouble.

Seoras almost looked disappointed. Had he wanted to fight? "You don't need to hand over the weapon, just put it away," Seoras clarified.

"This is not mine. I took it from Cecht," Edryd explained. "I do not carry a weapon."

Seoras accepted the knife and motioned for Edryd to follow as he began to cross the courtyard heading east. "You will want to reconsider going about unarmed if you intend to spend any time unescorted in the streets of An Innis," Seoras remarked. "Carrying a sword at your side will deter the sort of people who are willing to do you harm. It might have prevented a situation like the one you found yourself in tonight."

"Sound advice," Edryd agreed, "though I don't know that I will come by a decent weapon so easily."

"I own several. You are welcome to choose one that suits you," Seoras offered. With no trace of humility, Seoras then added, "I am accounted by some a blade master. I wouldn't mind offering some training in the morning if you feel you could benefit from instruction."

Seoras had a flat expression, but his eyes betrayed eager confidence. Edryd had not been wrong; the man did want to fight. "I might take you up on that," Edryd replied. We will see who is instructed, he added silently to himself, restraining an impulse to smile as he followed Seoras up the darkened city streets.

***

His vision was improving, and objects were no longer blurring together, but Cecht was still feeling effects from the encounter. It was difficult to concentrate. His thoughts wouldn't hold together for long before they slipped away, shifting in and out of focus like the damp mists which were swirling through the streets of An Innis. He remembered what had happened, or thought that he did, but there were gaps that he could not account for. Cecht could for example, recall closing in on Edryd while Hagan had held his attention, and he could also remember somehow missing completely when he swung a blow at the base of the man's scalp, but Cecht had no memory to explain how he had ended up being the one who had acquired a painful bruise on the back of his own head. It had gone so horribly wrong, and would have gotten worse, if Seoras had not intervened unexpectedly.

His partner, Hagan, had been precious little help. The stolid man had come out of the fight remembering even less than Cecht, and had returned to his room at the Broken Oath, nursing an injured left shoulder and complaining of a headache. For Hagan to be complaining, it meant that he had been seriously hurt. At some point they would both be made to account to Aed Seoras for their failure tonight, but this was not Cecht's current concern. Getting to Esivh Rhol and making a report took precedence. Aed Seoras was his acknowledged master, demanding complete obedience, where Esivh Rhol was only an occasional employer, who provided a supply of money and other compensations. Cecht cared far more for the latter, at least to the extent to which he could get away with it.

It was not as if Seoras did not know about his double dealings. It was just that his master didn't seem to care, so long as Cecht remembered his place. Still, he took the precaution of entering Esivh Rhol's palace through a hidden side entrance where he would not be seen. It was one thing to split one's services, but it would have been something else entirely to tempt fate by being indiscreet about it.

Cecht, who was well known by the guards providing Esivh Rhol's security, came and went about freely, having long ago become familiar with the layout of the palace. He could expect that Esivh Rhol, who generally slept late into the day and remained up late into the evenings, would still be awake, but he could not be as certain about other aspects of the man's unusual schedule. He had learned the hard way that entering the wrong room unannounced risked interrupting things he didn't need to see. The Ard Ri was a puerile deviant with an assortment of disreputable interests. Tonight though, the Ard Ri was spending a quiet evening poring through a collection of business ledgers.

"Do you know, I haven't brokered a single placement for a Hetaera in over six months?" Esivh Rhol said to Cecht as he entered the room.

"An unenviable state of affairs," Cecht said.

"I'm glad you appreciate the seriousness of the situation. I have other sources of income of course, but none of those are nearly so profitable."

"I would buy one from you," said Cecht, "only with what you pay me, generous as it is, no matter how many jobs I might take I doubt I would ever be able to afford her."

Esivh Rhol was pleased with that comment, so he didn't feel the need to point out that Cecht spent his pay just as fast as he could earn it, all of it typically ending right back up in Esivh Rhol's coffers. Cecht was right after all. If the man were to save every coin he earned, it would remain beyond his means. "We might be able to work something out, if you could find a way to sort out Seoras," The Ard Ri said instead.

Cecht shook his head. "You have no idea what he would do to me if he even thought for a second that I discussed such a thing."

"You will have to content yourself then with lesser women in my employ whose services you do have the means to afford." The Ard Ri said. He had spoken as if Cecht were to be sincerely pitied for being so close to something he would never experience. Esivh Rhol returned his attentions back to the numbers in the books set out before him, as though Cecht was no longer there.

Cecht let out a long sigh. He would not have actually wanted to own one of Esivh Rhol's trained consorts, but having something like that placed forever out of reach, made the companions Esivh Rhol sold to those who could afford them, seem infinitely desirable. He recovered his thoughts with a struggle and gave Esivh Rhol the information he had come to report.

"Someone showed up on the island tonight. He told a room full of people at the Broken Oath that he had been stranded ashore a few days ago north of the island. Hagan and I cornered him alone in the courtyard behind the inn, and we were going to deliver him to Seoras, but we couldn't manage it. He defeated us." Cecht left the part out where they had intended to deliver him minus two gold Ossian sovereigns that the man had so unwisely shown to the innkeeper.

"Both of you... one after the other?" said Esivh Rhol. He was clearly skeptical.

"Both of us at once," corrected Cecht. He was annoyed that the Ard Ri would doubt him. He hardly would have openly admitted such a thing if it hadn't happened.

"And where is he now?"

"Seoras intervened before the fight was finished. Made it seem like he was coming to the rescue. They left together after that. I think we can be certain that Seoras will want to train him."

Esivh Rhol thought for a moment. There would be ways to use this information to his advantage. "Does this man have a name?" he asked.

"He said it was Edryd."

"And you think this Edryd could challenge Seoras?"

"No," said Cecht, who was very sure of that much.

Esivh Rhol hadn't expected any other response, supposing it would have been too much to have hoped for. He had yet to encounter anyone who could contend with that monster. If he had really taken on both Hagan and Cecht and come out ahead though, this Edryd was going to be worth consideration. Esivh Rhol decided then that he would do well to get his hooks into the man early and sink them in deep.

Chapter 3

The Art of a Blade Master

Sunlight flowed in from the window and crept across Edryd's bed coverings, warming areas that were shaped in light by the outlines of the framing in the wooden shutters, which had been left open to admit the morning air. Despite the excitement of the previous night and the unfamiliar surroundings, he had enjoyed pleasant uninterrupted sleep and had awoken with a feeling of deep contentment. That changed when Edryd remembered where he was.

He had spent the late evening hours drinking with Seoras, during which time he had repeated the same story that he had told in the inn, or at least he was pretty sure that he had gotten many of the details nearly the same. Vaguely, Edryd recalled something about a sparring session and tensed with regret, remembering a foolish boast that he would enjoy measuring Seoras's claim of expertise with a sword. It would be a bad idea to demonstrate too much mastery or skill. That would lead to awkward questions, attract far too much notice, and give clues to the truth about who he really was.

Shifting into a seated position on the edge of the bed, Edryd looked for the clothing that he had left draped over a chair the night before. The chair remained where it had been, next to a table positioned near the window, but his clothes were gone. His leather boots were at the side of the bed, not far from where he had removed them, and his belt lay on the table, but his pants, shirt, and cloak were all missing. Bending down, he took in a deep breath as he picked up his left shoe, and exhaled despairingly when he discovered that his coin purse was no longer tucked in the toe of the boot where he had left it. Mud had been cleaned off and someone had treated the leather with oil, but that someone had rewarded themselves exceptionally well for those efforts. "An expensive bit of service that," Edryd muttered in disgust. The knowledge that he had been asleep and vulnerable while someone had gone through the room was more troubling than the missing money.

Edryd threw his bedding aside and stalked barefoot across the stone floor towards a small dresser in the corner. Searching through it quickly, he discovered that all of the drawers were empty, though a folded pile of fresh clothing had been placed on top of the chest. Carefully, he unfolded a pair of woolen trousers and a plain white linen tunic, and examined each in turn. The cloth was of good quality, and if not quite new, neither item showed significant signs of wear. Both had been recently washed and they effused a muted but persistent herbal scent of orris root and fresh lavender. There was something very specific and familiar about the smell, but Edryd could not place it.

Lacking a reasonable alternative, Edryd dressed himself in the provided attire and was surprised at how near a fit the clothing was. They were a bit baggy and loose on his compact frame, but the lengths were nearly perfect and the shirt fit his shoulders well. He was forced to admit that it was a decided improvement over what he had been wearing yesterday. He ran his belt through loops on the pants and cinched it tightly around his waist. Pausing briefly to give the room one last good look, Edryd headed for the door and exited the room, stepping out onto the grounds of the estate, where a thin mist was clinging low to the ground.

He found himself looking out at a fountained courtyard, enclosed on three sides by long single-story buildings with simple living quarters that resembled the one he had slept in. On the open side to the east lay a large square, which was surfaced with reddish-brown crushed stones, and had the appearance of a formal military practice yard. The square was bordered on the north by a single row of marble benches, which were positioned in front of a short boxwood hedge that marked the transition between the practice yard and a beautiful but overgrown and neglected garden. A broken row of trees partially hid the sloping grass-covered field that led up to the manor house further to the east. Stables, filled with crates and supplies instead of horses, lay to the south beside the entrance to the estate. Bracketed by a couple of small towers, and protected by an empty gatehouse, a set of wood and iron gates lay open on their hinges. Low walls, constructed from cemented fieldstones, surrounded the entire property.

He had not appreciated the size of the place when arriving in the dark the night before, but Edryd marveled now at the finely spaced buildings, built using quarried bedrock and topped with flat grey and brown tiled roofing. The manor used less space than the barracks buildings, which included the room Edryd has slept in, but positioned up the slope and standing three stories high, with two separate wings that were decorated with dozens of sculpted stone reliefs, it loomed over everything.

Smoke rose in the air a short distance away, coming from a building nearest to the practice yard. The pleasant smell of warmed bread led him in that direction and then into the interior of the building, which was brightly lit by several open windows and filled with a pair of long wooden tables suitable for communal meals. As Edryd shifted a heavy bench and began to sit down, a uniformed man with close-cropped grey hair, reacting to the noise, peeked out from a back room. The man ducked his head and disappeared without a word before returning a minute later with a stone bowl and a small dark loaf of toasted bread resting atop a rectangular wooden tray.

"Lord Seoras has instructed me to see to anything you might need, Young Master," recited the servant politely as he set the tray down upon the table. Steam rose from the bowl, which was filled with a thin watery soup that would make excellent sop for the dark hard bread that rested beside it. Edryd eyed the food eagerly.

"If you have not eaten yet, you should bring a portion for yourself as well," Edryd suggested. "It feels a little awkward eating in such a large room as this without any company or conversation," he added by way of explanation.

The elderly man hesitated, but his expression soon changed, pleased at having received this invitation. "Very well. With the Young Master's leave, I will be back," he said.

Edryd decided that he liked the man, and ignoring his hunger, he politely waited until the servant returned. Gesturing to the seat opposite his position, he invited the man to sit. "I do not claim any sort of social elevation, nor do I aspire to any, so dispense with the 'Young Master' nonsense; my name is Edryd," he instructed. The man looked as if he were about to object, but Edryd did not allow the pause that would have been needed for him to do so. "How should I call you?" Edryd asked quickly.

"Giric Tolvanes. You may call me Tolvanes, Young Master."

Tolvanes it seemed, as a product of a social structure that insisted upon adhering to entrenched customs, was not going to agree to address Edryd informally, and it could be assumed that he would accord any free man with at least an equal level of respect.

"I am grateful for your company, Tolvanes," Edryd said, before proceeding to dip a broken piece of bread into the soup and shove it into his mouth. The soaked bread, filling him with warmth, was rapidly alleviating the hunger he had been feeling. Between bites, Edryd tried to make casual friendly comments. Eventually he directed the conversation to the subject he was most interested in.

"When I woke this morning, I found someone had gone to the trouble of restoring the condition of my boots. Quality work and expertly done, but I don't know who to thank."

"Why I did that, Young Master," Tolvanes said, brightly responding to the acknowledgement.

The nature of the response was telling. If Tolvanes had taken the coins, he could hardly have managed such a show of foolish pride over the faint praise. If he were guilty, Edryd would have expected it to be more likely that Tolvanes would not have admitted any involvement at all, denying having even touched the boots.

"You did not notice, by chance, a small cloth coin bag in the toe of the left boot did you?"

"No there wasn't any...." Tolvanes suddenly stopped in mid-sentence as he realized the implications. "There wasn't anything in either boot, and nothing on them but three layers of caked mud," he insisted urgently.

"I am not making an accusation," Edryd reassured him. "Only someone went through my room last night, and it would be a great relief to know that the belongings that were taken are safe."

"I haven't been inside of your room at all," Tolvanes pled earnestly. "Mistress Rohvarin arrived shortly after first light and handed me your boots. She collected them not an hour later and returned them to your room. I am certain she would not have taken anything either. It must still be in your room somewhere."

"It must be," Edryd agreed, despite deep misgivings to the contrary.

Their conversation was interrupted by the arrival of a woman. She wore a simple undyed grey woolen dress, cinched loosely in the middle with a dark blue strip of cloth that was joined end to end in the front in an overlapping diamond shape and weighed down by a small ornamented silver buckle. Her dark brown hair was loosely pulled back, revealing deep green eyes and a smooth unwrinkled face. She must have been older than Edryd, but still young and at least a year or two short of thirty. Edryd wondered if this would be Mistress Rohvarin, and whether she had heard any part of the conversation, but as soon as he turned to face her, and before he could ask anything, she began to speak.

"Lord Seoras requests your presence, Master Edryd. He is waiting in the square." Without waiting for a response she turned and left, revealing neatly arranged hair that fell past her shoulders and down her back.

Edryd turned to Tolvanes, who in anticipation of the as yet unasked question, nodded and said, "That was Irial Rohvarin, but I am sure she would never have taken your money."

"I will make a search of my room before I broach the subject," Edryd promised.

This response seemed to sooth Tolvanes, who had obviously been offended by the notion that he could have been involved with taking the money. It would make sense to avoid risking further offense to others without first being certain that it had in fact been stolen, and not simply placed somewhere else in his room. On the chance that Tolvanes had taken the coins, this would also provide an opportunity for him to return them.

Looking down at the table, Edryd saw that his bowl was already empty, but he still had half of the loaf of bread. Reluctantly leaving the leftover food behind, Edryd stood up to go outside. Before he left the room, Tolvanes offered a parting piece of advice.

"Don't take Seoras lightly. And do not anger him," Tolvanes admonished. "He is a dangerous man."

"It won't be the first time I have held a sword," Edryd replied, "and I know enough to yield if I find myself outmatched," he added, feigning a nervous smile.

In the time Edryd had spent inside, the sun had risen a little higher and burnt away what had been left of the morning mist. He spotted Aed Seoras in a corner of the practice yard. Behind Seoras rested a collection of bladed weapons, laid out flat in an evenly spaced row across the white marble surface of one of the benches, with the hilts butted up against and projecting from the front edge. Most of the weapons had scabbards standing propped up at the back of the bench next to the matching swords.

"Choose whichever one you are most comfortable with," Seoras offered with disinterest.

Edryd did not look to the swords. Instead he took a moment to study Aed Seoras. The tall man appeared calm and stone-faced, but his blue eyes betrayed aggression and an eagerness to fight as he met Edryd's appraising stare. Seoras was dressed as he had been the night before, wearing a dark grey cloak over black clothing. Seoras was not young, but Edryd found he couldn't estimate how old he might be. There was no gray in his dark black unkempt hair, but age and experience were evident in the lines of his face. Seoras appeared fit and healthy, but Edryd reasoned that whatever advantages Seoras held in height and reach, it would be possible to more than make up for them with what he felt would be his own advantage in physical strength.

Turning his attention back to the weapons displayed on the marble bench, Edryd tried to represent a lack of competence. "I can't say I am familiar with some of these," Edryd said, gesturing towards the weapons. "Can you make a recommendation?"

"I can only suggest the one weapon with which you are the most familiar," Seoras responded with a trace of impatient sarcasm, as if pained by the obvious nature of the answer to the question. "These are all fine examples so you will only go wrong if you choose something you don't know how to use correctly."

Edryd began a close inspection of each weapon, counting six in total. The first was a slender dueling sword, the type of weapon a wealthy merchant or landowner might carry. It was no soldier's weapon. While it would have been a poor choice to take into battle against armored opponents, it would be ideal for the type of contest that Seoras had proposed. Edryd dismissed it immediately.

The second and third weapons were long double-edged arming swords, the first of which had a blade a little more than thirty inches in length and the other a good three to four inches longer. Beside these rested a falchion, a heavy single edged weapon with a forward curving spine and a recurved edge, slightly concave where it emerged from a jewel capped ivory hilt before swelling into a broader convex section that ended in a menacing angular point. Next was a broad-bladed thrusting backsword with a basket hilt to protect the wielder's hand.

Nearest the end was a great long sword with a hilt that could easily accommodate two hands. Impractical in a duel, it would be nearly impossible to use to any good effect if your opponent could force you into close quarters combat. Overcome by a curious and irrational urge, Edryd almost chose this last weapon before rejecting the idea. Taking a handicap was one thing, but he did not want to come off looking foolish.

If he had opted to accept Seoras's advice, he would have selected one of the two arming swords. He had extensive experience with all of these weapons, but it was to a knight's blade that he had without question devoted the most training and study. Instead of choosing one of these simple straight-bladed battlefield weapons, or the dueling sword or back sword, any of which were ideal single combat weapons, Edryd settled on the falchion. Seoras would think he chose it because it was the most expensive looking sword, jeweled and finely gilded, with a greater weight in steel than some of the others in combination. However, the curved blade gave it poor defensive characteristics and also made it weak as a thrusting weapon. Functioning less like a sword and more like a long edged axe, the heavy blade would make you tire quickly. It was a mounted soldier's battlefield weapon, good at splitting armor or a helm, and it was of an exceptional quality that would have been fit for a general, but it was not something suited for use on foot in a contest of skill.

All those weaknesses aside, Edryd felt confident that he could use it in combination with his superior strength to good advantage. It was simple to wield, requiring no mastery of any particular technique, so he could use it well without revealing the extent of his combat training. If Seoras could be taken off guard, or if he lacked a fraction of the skill he had claimed, he was going to be under pressure. If not, Seoras was going to have an easier time of it, which was fine, given that Edryd intended to allow the man to have a clear victory.

The reassuring weight felt good in his hand as Edryd claimed the curved weapon and took a few experimental swings. It was a well-designed sword that could bring to bear a tremendous amount force on the cutting edge.

"I find that the quality of a contest often benefits if there is a compelling source of motivation," Seoras commented. "Care for a wager?"

"I don't have money," Edryd said, rejecting the suggestion.

"These wouldn't belong to you then," Seoras countered, producing two large gold coins from a pocket somewhere in his dark black robe.

Edryd's face flushed. That answered what had happened to the coins, if not when or how Seoras had come into their possession. "I would appreciate your giving those back to me, now," Edryd said, demanding the return of his property with poorly restrained anger in his voice.

"These coins represent a small fortune. An Innis is not the sort of place where you can expect to safely carry such things around in your pockets. I would feel badly if something happened." Seoras said all this as if he were not doing just that himself, carrying around Edryd's 'small fortune' in his pocket.

"I can take care of myself," Edryd insisted, passing over the fact that the two coins now sitting in this man's hands clearly demonstrated otherwise.

The contradiction between Edryd's words and his present circumstances was obvious, and Seoras said as much. "Were you as capable as you claim, you would never have been so easily dispossessed of all your money within a few short hours of your arrival on this island."

Edryd was in a weak position to argue, but it wasn't the sort of correction that you took evenly from the person who had stolen your property. Seoras had wanted a motivated opponent. Now he had one.

"I won't wager, but I will be taking those back," Edryd said.

Seoras smiled. By his estimation things were going well. "I understand not wanting to stake your money," he relented. "How about something else—if you defeat me, I return your money and acknowledge the better man, submitting to whatever punishment you would like to impose. If you lose, I accept you as a student, and you will then remain here until such time as I have taught you all that I can."

"That isn't going to happen," Edryd refused. He had no desire to have anything more to do with Seoras once he recovered the money. "I will settle for taking back what belongs to me. Stand ready," he ordered.

Seoras stepped back and grasped the top of the sheath where it hung at his right hip as he brought his free sword hand up to undo the clasp on his cloak, letting it fall completely to the ground before grabbing onto the hilt of his weapon. He pulled the hilt upward revealing a few thin sharp inches of bright oiled steel beneath a dull grey steel crossguard, and then, watching cautiously for any reaction, he slowly continued to expose more of the blade. The steel looked exceptionally hard and sharp, but Edryd suspected it would also prove to be quite fragile.

Irritated by his opponent's slow approach, Edryd became impatient. Without waiting for Seoras to finish clearing the weapon from its sheath, Edryd stepped forward with his sword in a raised position ready to strike. He wasn't seeking an unfair advantage, he was just anxious to force the issue and make Seoras finish drawing his weapon. It was a less than honorable tactic though, which did grant to Edryd, who needed to take and keep the initiative, an early edge with which to achieve a dominant positon.

Seoras had his weapon free in an instant, quickly raising and positioning the blade on an almost level plane, ready to shield the imminent attack. Edryd aimed his downward vertical strike to connect near the end of his opponent's weapon, where it would generate leverage that would maximize the stress on the blade as well as on the opposing combatant's grip. If the blade were as hard and brittle as Edryd guessed, it might just break.

Seoras took a half step back as he absorbed the impact of the strike. As soon as the momentum of his swing was stopped, Edryd raised the heavy sword and hammered down again and again in a succession of heavy blows. Seoras's sword held up to the onslaught, but he was being pressed back with each impact. Edryd continued his simple unrelenting attack, delivering quick powerful strikes that Seoras would be able to block but not deflect. He had Seoras completely on his heels, blunting the attacks but unable to manage any sort of counter. Soon, Edryd would pull one of the strikes and bring his blade in down under his opponent's guard and... and do what? No conditions had been set. He could tap Seoras with the flat of his blade, unfasten the man's coat with a precision cut, or even draw blood by inflicting some sort of superficial injury. He was certainly angry enough to do the latter without feeling any remorse, but would that even end the fight?

Edryd was intently focused on Seoras as he continued to strike, trying to pick the right moment, when he caught something in the man's expression. Seoras was on the defensive and giving ground with each attack, but he was not under pressure. He actually looked distant and bored, calmly watching Edryd expend energy, analyzing the attack with near indifference, and waiting on an inevitable feint from his opponent. Edryd chose a new strategy. There was only one sure way to end a sword fight; well, there were many ways, but only one of those didn't involve injuring the enemy.

Edryd shifted the angle of his follow-through as his next strike impacted Seoras's weapon, rasping the falchion down the length of his opponent's long blade with as much strength as he could bring to bear. Seoras was genuinely surprised. Performed with a lighter blade, or by a weaker opponent, the technique would have been ineffective. It would be blocked harmlessly by the other sword's crossguard. It was going to work here though; Seoras would not be strong enough to maintain his grip when the hilt of his sword was struck directly with this much force.

Seoras made a quick decision. It could not have been one born from training or past experience. No school of swordsmanship would have ever taught an adherent to drop his only weapon in a fight. Seoras did though, as if he had never trusted the blade to begin with. With the resistance suddenly gone, Edryd's swing leapt wildly out to the side. Seoras stepped in close on his left leg and trapped Edryd's sword arm as he tried to return it into position. Seoras immediately followed this by striking Edryd in the chest with the palm of his hand. The impact doubled Edryd over, forced him off his feet, and sent him sliding backward in the gravel.

Edryd, eyes shut tightly, gasped in pain where he lay as he tried to refill his lungs. He was not unused to taking punishment from strong opponents, but he had never felt something like this. Had he thought that he had an advantage in strength over Seoras? The man was impossibly strong. Edryd opened his eyes but he could not focus. His head was spinning. A dark shape advanced toward him. The shape, now standing over him, seemed to pause for a moment. Edryd could feel something in that pause, something he had also experienced when Seoras had struck him a moment ago. Acting on an unconscious compulsion, Edryd rolled to his side, out of the way of an attack he had not actually seen.

Scrambling onto his knees while ignoring the pain in his body, Edryd tried to locate Seoras. His vision was still blurry. He could make out two indistinct figures at the edges of the square, but he could not see Seoras at all. As his vision began to clear, his eyes resolved upon on an object a couple of feet away. It was the falchion, with its blade buried a foot and a half deep in the earth where Edryd's head had just been only a moment before. Seoras stood a few paces away, his pale face almost as calm as ever, yet not quite able to hide a dwindling measure of unspent fury still smoldering in his dark azure eyes.

"I yield," Edryd managed weakly.

"Not yet, I am not satisfied," Seoras responded, refusing to accept the concession.

"I am done," Edryd protested as firmly as he could.

"You have not shown me what you are capable of," Seoras insisted. Edryd was not sure whether this meant that Seoras thought he had untapped potential, or whether he had recognized that Edryd had been holding back. Clarification came soon enough.

"We will continue until I am persuaded you have treated this seriously. If you fight with anything less than your full ability, I will leave you with a mark that will remind you that you should not have taken me so lightly."

Edryd stood up and walked slowly over to his weapon, and began gently levering the sword loose, thinking Seoras had already kept that promise. He could feel the damage from the impact he had taken in the chest, and he knew that it was going to bruise badly. Taking a moment to examine the sword once he freed it, Edryd discovered soft gouges scarring much of the length of the weapon where it had contacted the gravel when it had been plunged into the ground. The blade bore stains from the moistened earth and dozens of small notches where it had struck the hardened metal of Seoras's weapon. It was going to need a great deal of skilled work to restore the edge and recondition the surface of the metal.

Tactically, nothing had changed. The best approach remained a focused aggressive attack, but Edryd could not bring himself to charge in again. Any anger over the stolen money had disappeared. He had been properly unsettled by the last exchange and was no longer sure he could secure any success or guarantee his own safety. The curved sword he was using was weak in defense, and given the superior reach of his opponent's weapon it was unwise to do anything other than remain close in and on the attack, but Edryd was unable to contemplate doing this, and so he chose to stay back.

It was a failing he had never overcome. Whenever he was pressured or made to feel vulnerable, he relied too much on reading the movements of his opponent, all but reducing his options to responding in a reactionary mode. Falling into a defensive counter-attacking stance, Edryd waited on Seoras to resume the fight.

Seoras gave Edryd a suspicious, considering look. He seemed to think he was being baited, crediting Edryd for employing some form of deceptive mock defense. But he soon dismissed the need for caution, and when it became clear that his opponent would not engage, Seoras drove forward with a flurry of strikes aimed first at one quarter and then alternating to another.

The attacks were delivered with more speed than Edryd could keep up with. His solution was simple. Ignoring the pain each time he twisted his torso, Edryd moved fluidly and constantly to keep his body well out of the range of Seoras's strikes. If Seoras could not reach him, he couldn't connect. This placed Seoras even further from Edryd's much shorter reach, but that didn't matter. If he could study the man's attack, Edryd was certain he could find a weakness to exploit.

Dodging most of the attacks altogether, Edryd avoided directly blocking any of the strikes. Instead, he would knock one aside intermittently, disrupting his opponent's rhythm and interfering with his technique. Even better, by representing a block and then withdrawing it before Seoras's blade could connect, Edryd could induce his opponent to overextend. Seoras was talented, not to mention shockingly strong and fast, but his technique was, by Edryd's standard, almost sloppy, and he left an occasional obvious opening.

If Edryd thought he was beginning to stabilize, Seoras did not seem to notice. Once seemingly bored and then angry, Seoras now seemed exhilarated, enjoying the unfettered opportunity to engage freely against a competent foe. At this range, Edryd would need to close a great deal of ground to deliver a strike, while remaining mindful of the need to use the length of his own weapon to prevent Seoras from delivering another counter with his free hand. There had been something out of the ordinary about that simple physical attack, and Edryd knew he could not withstand another.

Edryd grew tired as the fight progressed, his sword arm feeling heavy and sluggish, but he continued to patiently ignore minor openings in his opponent's defenses. Seoras too was beginning to pay the price for the furious pace he was imposing on the duel, breathing hard and sweating freely. With fatigue setting in on his opponent, the attacks were certain to grow less controlled, until eventually the openings would grow wider and be recovered from less easily. Edryd would wait until the moment Seoras began to wear down and make the most of it.

An overly ambitious cross-strike from Seoras missed, causing his shoulder to dip down and inward, pulled in the direction of the wild swing. Edryd reacted immediately, stepping around his unbalanced opponent and into place at the side of Seoras's sword arm. From this position Seoras could not possibly make any good use of the point or the edge of his blade. Edryd, on the other hand, had a clear chance to deliver a strike to Seoras's exposed back: a chance that vanished in an instant as Seoras reversed like a tightened spring, aiming the pommel of his weapon at Edryd's head.

The whirlwind stroke left almost no time to react, but Edryd, quickly abandoning any notion of absorbing the attack and delivering a simultaneous strike of his own, managed to collapse in an uncontrolled fall. The awkward tactic just barely caused the attack to miss. It left Seoras wildly off balance, but it left Edryd sprawled on the ground. Rolling quickly into a crouch, Edryd raised his sword, supporting it with both hands just in time to block the next attack. There was a loud reverberating clang as Seoras slammed his weapon into the falchion. The heavy weapon pulsed violently in Edryd's hand, forces travelling through the weapon and painfully jolting the bones in his arm and shoulders as he fought to keep his grip.

Edryd stared at his sword in astonishment, noting the beginnings of a fracture starting a third of the way down the blade and travelling to within a few inches of the hilt. Seoras's next strike shattered the blade into two large pieces and one small splinter that left a laceration on Edryd's scalp when it flew out and struck him just above his right ear.

Edryd looked up, expecting to see a stroke that would end his life, but Seoras had stopped. The man's eyes were closed and he was taking and releasing deep measured breaths as Edryd looked on in stunned silence. The dark man's weapon, coated loosely with dust, no longer shone as brightly, but it did not bear even a hint of damage. It should not have been possible. Suddenly, Seoras opened his eyes and returned

Edryd's attention with a fixed stare that was a model of calm indifferent tranquility.

"Now you may yield," he offered. "And next time, use something you are trained to use," Seoras said before walking away. Exhausted, Edryd sank to the ground in distress, uselessly gripping the hilt of his broken weapon, failing to understand what had just happened.

Chapter 4

Giric Tolvanes

Giric Tolvanes shook Edryd's shoulder lightly in an effort to rouse him. "Young Master, Lord Seoras has gone," he said, trying to reassure him that the fight was over.

Edryd didn't respond. Seoras had left him a damaged and beaten man. His clothing was filthy from rolling on the ground while damp with sweat, and the right side of his head had an unfortunate appearance, covered as it was in a disordered mess of plastered hair gathered together in crusts of drying blood.

"We need to get you cleaned up," Giric suggested.

Edryd allowed himself to be helped to his feet by the thin elderly man, and he followed as Tolvanes led him towards a small stone building situated behind the barracks at the northwestern edge of the property. Through an open archway in the building, which served as the entrance, Edryd saw a shallow pool lined with flat stones. At its far end, the bath was fed with clear water poured through an overturned vase, which was cradled in the arms of a woman gracefully rendered in dark grey stone. The ceiling had a large opening through which afternoon sunlight filled the space, bouncing off of the rippled surfaces of the pool to create shifting patterns of woven illumination. Perforated stone, shaped into intricate branching sylvan latticework, gave privacy while permitting a fresh breeze to flow through the walls.

Edryd removed his clothes and formed them into a loose pile against one of the walls. Welcoming the relief that he felt from the cold water as he entered the basin, Edryd submerged his bruised ribs below the surface. He closed his eyes for a moment and tried to forget where he was, but violent images of the trauma he had faced that morning kept surfacing, and he couldn't keep them shut. Upon reopening his eyes, Edryd gave an involuntary start when he saw that the old man was collecting his discarded clothing. Noticing the reaction, Tolvanes reassured Edryd that there was a robe in a cabinet in the corner and that a clean set of clothing would also be ready in the Young Master's living quarters.

Edryd lingered in the cold water, unsuccessfully trying to sort out how he had been so thoroughly beaten. The bruise was expanding all the way across his chest instead of concentrated near the point of impact where Seoras had struck him with his palm. Concluding that he should just count himself fortunate that none of his ribs were broken, Edryd gave up on the puzzle. Reluctantly, he exited the pool and found a finely woven linen robe in the cabinet Tolvanes had indicated. He wrapped himself in the soft cloth before heading back to the barracks buildings.

Noticing Seoras headed in the direction of his room, with Irial at his side carrying a black coat draped over one arm, Edryd began walking faster to arrive well ahead of them. He had time to ease himself into one of the room's two wooden chairs before he heard a perfunctory knock at the door. Aed Seoras turned the latch on the door, pushing his way in without allowing Edryd the opportunity to invite them to enter, and speaking before Edryd could offer up a protest at the intrusion.

"You came out the worse for wear, but you are a little cleaner now," Seoras remarked. Irial followed him into the room without bothering to close the door behind them.

"I didn't make a good accounting for myself," Edryd responded. "I may have rearranged your hair some, but other than that it seems I gave you no trouble at all."

Seoras reflexively ran fingers through loose strands of his disheveled dark hair in reaction to the comment and laughed. He then remembered the laceration which Edryd had acquired during their fight, hidden now beneath his freshly washed hair. "Inspect that cut on his head," he said to Irial, instructing her to attend to Edryd.

Complying with the order, Irial positioned herself beside Edryd, and carefully placing her soft fingertips on his scalp, she pulled loose strands of his hair out of the way to expose the injury.

"Well?" questioned Seoras.

"Deep, but not wide, or very long," Irial answered. "It will heal on its own, but it needs to be kept clean."

"You understand that was an accident," Seoras said, addressing Edryd. "I thought that falchion would break more cleanly than it did."

"You have plenty of other swords, and it's no business of mine to become angry if you choose to ruin them," Edryd responded, suppressing amazement at Seoras's claim of having deliberately broken the sword. The hard, slender steel blade Seoras carried should have given out and shattered several times over, long before it ever could have placed any stress on the heavy weapon Edryd had borrowed. What had happened shouldn't have been possible.

"It looks like you were hit pretty hard," Irial said, wanting to check the bruise on his chest.

Still sitting down, and ignoring the pain it caused, Edryd awkwardly pulled an arm inside the robe and brought it out of the front opening, allowing the robe to fall from his other shoulder as well. A wide scar, which had not yet fully healed, traversed Edryd's left side from front to back. That older injury looked serious, and a few hours earlier would certainly have inspired a question or two, but it was minor beside the more immediate damage inflicted during the fight with Seoras. Irial made a startled sound, an expression of sympathy in response to seeing the mottled mix of intense red and blue bruising that extended across his entire chest.

"I am sorry for that as well," Seoras said. He didn't seem remorseful towards Edryd or truly sorry for the harm that he had done, so much as he was generally embarrassed at seeing evidence of his lack of control.

"I must look terrible," Edryd replied in response to the show of contrition. "This was an accident too then?" he added, trying to act untroubled, but managing to sound bitter and sarcastic instead.

"No, not an accident," confessed Seoras, "just a lapse in judgment for which I can offer no good excuse."

Edryd did not know what to make of this explanation, but he took it as a sincere apology. "In a month's time, I'm sure I will have forgotten altogether that I ever had my chest nearly crushed in," Edryd joked.

"It will be at least three months before the bruising disappears completely," Seoras responded seriously. "If you rest though, you will be ready to go again in two or three days."

"Another go... at fighting with you?" Edryd cried out. "Any questions in regard to strength or skill have been settled. I don't know how you did those things, but I was completely outmatched. There would be no purpose to doing this again."

"Those things," Seoras remarked, and then paused for emphasis before continuing, "are techniques that can be taught." Thinking Edryd may have missed the implied suggestion, Seoras tried to make his meaning even more clear. "I am prepared to teach you. I want you to be my student."

"You said as much before we began, but please, find another pupil. I don't intend to remain detained under your care," Edryd declared. He would have liked to learn what Seoras was offering to teach him, but he was sensible enough to be frightened, and he was not about to willingly place himself under this darkly enigmatic man's influence and control.

"This estate is not a prison, Edryd," Seoras objected. "Let me know when you want to go into the city, and you can leave the grounds whenever you wish. You are free to go wherever you like, anywhere in An Innis."

Edryd, feeling discomforted by these instructions, was struck by the importance of what Seoras had not said. He had not denied that Edryd was being detained; he had only denied that the manor grounds were the boundaries of his prison. And although Seoras had given Edryd leave to explore the town, he had done so in a manner which emphasized that he had needed permission. The freedom Seoras had then promised to Edryd, allowing him to go anywhere in An Innis, also implied (in somewhat uncertain terms) that Edryd was not so free that he would be permitted to actually leave the island. Deciding it was best not to ask for clarification, Edryd remained quiet, hoping he was overreacting and reading too much into what Seoras had just said.

Seeing the worry on Edryd's face and misinterpreting it, Seoras tried to reassure his would-be student that he was not asking him to leave the property. "You are welcome to remain here while you recover. Stay even longer if you would like." Edryd still looked uneasy, so Seoras continued, making it plain that he was not placing any demands upon Edryd. "I am not asking anything in return, you are here as a guest."

Appreciating the need to get away now more than ever, Edryd pulled his arms back inside the robe and fought to suppress the cold shudder working through his body. "If you return my money, holding back an appropriate amount for expenses and for the broken weapon, I will be on my way now. I wouldn't want to impose any more than I already have," Edryd said. He tried to say this all politely, but there were undercurrents of both anger and fear in his voice.

"That sword is worth as much broken as it ever was whole," Seoras said dismissively. "A blacksmith of even modest skill could use that steel to forge a much better weapon, and the precious stone adornments can be put to better uses as well. You owe me nothing for the damage."

"I would say you were being too generous, except you have my gold sovereigns, and you seem unwilling to return them," Edryd pointed out.

Seoras laughed. He was not bothered at all. Far from it, he was enjoying Edryd's irritation. Edryd's face reddened in response to the laughter, but the rising wellspring of anger agitating his blood was perfectly useless at the moment, for there was nothing he could do.

"I'm sorry," Seoras replied, no longer laughing at Edryd, but still outwardly no less amused. "I insist that you stay until you have healed. Your care will be seen to. Irial manages the housekeeping and Tolvanes prepares morning and evening meals. If there is anything we do not have here, you can send Tolvanes out for it, as he also manages and oversees all of the supplies."

Edryd's face tightened with resentment, his reaction plain and unconcealed. He didn't want to be looked after. He wanted to be somewhere else, far away from Seoras and his hospitality.

"As to your money, I can't allow you to keep that unsecured. I will instead provide you with a letter of deposit, promising to honor any of your debts," Seoras offered. "It should be safer than carrying gold coins around."

Edryd started to complain but stumbled. This was not so different from what he had settled on trying to do after talking with the innkeeper last night. It was exactly what he needed, but it was going to make it very easy for Seoras to learn the exact nature of any transactions made against the note.

"Do that," Edryd accepted grudgingly. It was better than nothing. If he left An Innis, the letter of deposit wasn't going to be worth anything wherever it was he ended up, but that would matter very little to Edryd if he could use it to successfully buy passage off of this island.

"I will draw it up and have it ready when I see you again," Seoras agreed. "I would stay a little longer, but I have business with the Ard Ri," he said, excusing himself as he left.

Tension drained visibly from Edryd as Aed Seoras exited the room. Irial, still holding the black woolen coat over one arm, trailed Seoras to the doorway but did not follow him through. Instead she waited for a few seconds, took a brief look out into the courtyard, and closed the door.

"I need some measurements," Irial said as she turned around and offered the coat to Edryd.

Compliantly, Edryd stood and put the coat on over his robe. It fit his shoulders, but it was loose around the stomach and the sleeves were too long. Waiting patiently as Irial made a series of marks on the fabric, he was struck by a familiar fresh lavender scent coming from the soft wool, presumably from treated water Irial used in laundering the clothing. It all hit him. It had been too dark to say for sure, but this coat differed little from the coats that both Hagan and Cecht had been wearing last night. He also now knew where he recognized the scent from. He had noticed it on Hagan's clothing when they had grappled near the well.

"What's wrong?" Irial asked, noticing the sudden tension.

"Hagan and Cecht work for Seoras," Edryd said. When Irial, who had no knowledge of what had taken place last knight, didn't deny their connection to Seoras, Edryd pressed further. "They are guardsmen, or something of the sort, and this coat is part of a Uniform," Edryd said in a reproachful and accusing tone.

"Underling and sycophant maybe," Irial admitted, "but I object in principle to crediting either of those two with being proper guardsmen."

It wasn't as if he had not previously considered a possible connection between Seoras and the attackers, he had even started out with that assumption last night, but Irial's admission now confirmed what he had so far only imagined. Seoras had probably ordered the attack, and now he was fitting Edryd for a uniform that would mark him as one of them.

"I won't wear this," Edryd declared, removing the coat and insisting that Irial take it back.

"I don't blame you," said Irial as she accepted it. "I will make you a new coat. You can choose the fabric and the cut."

"The coat and cloak I came here with will be just fine," Edryd responded firmly.

Irial drew back, worry spreading across her face. "I can find suitable replacements," she offered.

"What's wrong with what I arrived in?"

Irial straightened and braced before answering. "It was all burned this morning, your coat, your cloak, and the rest of your clothing as well."

Edryd sat back down and slumped forward in his chair in resignation. The whole situation made him feel powerless. "Why?" he finally managed.

"I was instructed to destroy them," Irial answered meekly.

"That isn't what I was really asking," Edryd protested.

"You travelled here through the forests on the mainland," Irial responded. It seemed he was meant to understand that this explained everything.

"I don't understand."

"An Innis has been plagued by some dark events," explained Irial. "People think the forests on the continent are tainted, haunted by spirits which have returned from the dead. The lands across from the causeway are considered to be especially dangerous. Destroying the clothes you were wearing is a precaution against contagion."

Edryd shook his head. He still didn't understand, but he didn't want a history lesson. "You don't believe that, and I'm sure Seoras doesn't either," Edryd guessed. "So the question remains: why?"

"You're right, but you met with others yesterday who do believe those things," Irial answered. Edryd suspected there were other reasons, but he didn't voice his opinion and he let the subject drop. Putting him in borrowed clothing was another subtle way for Seoras to gain a measure of control.

"You were the one who took my coins as well?" Edryd asked.

"Not knowingly," Irial replied, "I had no idea they were in your shoe."

"But you would have taken them, even if you had known," Edryd accused.

Remorse flashed across Irial's face. "I was told to gather your things so that he could look through them," she admitted.

Edryd began to feel guilty. There was little cause to hold her responsible. The true blame lay with Seoras. "I'm sorry, none of this is your fault," Edryd apologized.

"Maybe," Irial agreed, "but I should still arrange replacements for some of your clothing."

"I may not stick around long enough to give you the chance," Edryd said. "After this morning, as you can probably imagine, I have developed some apprehensions about staying here. I suppose though, that I could use a place to heal up for a few days, if it wouldn't be unwise to do so."

Irial hesitated, clearly uncomfortable with the implied question. "I can't decide that for you," she said, unable to commit to offering any useful advice.

"Do you know much about him?" Edryd asked.

"I have worked for him for several years, so I suppose I know him better than most," she replied.

"Was he serious in his offer to teach me?"

Irial placed the coat on the bed and looked to the door as if to reassure herself that it was firmly shut before taking a seat in the chair opposite Edryd.

"Do you know what Seoras does?" she asked in a low discreet tone. Edryd shook his head and Irial continued. "He takes men, usually slaves who have no choice but to serve, and he trains them to become soldiers. You are obviously already a competent soldier, so I don't know how much he could teach you, but if you stay he will force you to serve him."

"He could do that?!" Edryd asked.

"Make you a slave? I don't know, maybe, but you have captured his interest, and he is not going to let you out of his grasp."

"Clear enough of an answer," replied Edryd with unshielded dismay.

"You should leave as soon as you can... right now, if you are up to it," Irial suggested.

"He has my money, among other things," Edryd said.

Irial pulled a set of keys from her pocket, the ones which Greven had given to him last night, and set them on the table. Beside the two keys she placed a clasp along with three metal emblems that had originally been pinned to his cloak. He had assumed these pins might have been destroyed along with his old coat, and it gave Edryd a momentary feeling of hope to see that they were not gone. His coins were the only thing missing now. "I know that what he took was not a small sum, but is it worth risking your freedom?" she asked.

"You don't understand. How will I be able leave if I can't hire passage on a ship?"

Irial did not respond immediately. She seemed to be considering something. "If you want to leave now, I might have a way to help you," she said.

In his misguided pride, which he could ill-afford, Edryd faltered through a confused attempt to refuse, realizing only halfway through that he was not sure if she was offering money, or if it was some other kind of help. The chance to seek clarification was taken away by a sudden knock at the door.

Startled, Irial quickly got to her feet. "Do not tell anyone what we spoke about," she cautioned as she retrieved the coat from the bed. Taking a brief moment to collect herself, Irial strode to the door and opened it admit Tolvanes, who was holding a wooden serving tray that held a freshly prepared meal. Irial motioned him in, and then she left the room, closing the door behind her.

Tolvanes approached and set the tray, which was loaded with two cups of mead, fragrant with the musty smell of fermented honey, and more bread, meat, and cheese than Edryd could possibly eat alone in a single sitting, down upon the table. "If you are feeling well enough, please eat what you can," he said.

Edryd could see that there was obviously food for both of them. "We can talk as we share the meal," he replied, motioning towards the open chair and inviting Tolvanes to stay.

"I am grateful, Young Master," Tolvanes said as he took a seat.

"It turns out Irial took the coins without knowing it," Edryd said once they began to eat. "She hadn't realized that they were in the boot. It was Seoras that actually removed and kept them. I am very sorry if I caused you to feel like I suspected you in any way."

"Of course not," Tolvanes replied. "In any case, it was wrong for Lord Seoras to take what belongs to you," he added, surprisingly earnest in his sympathies.

"He says he will give me a letter of deposit, but I'm not sure how long I will be waiting for that. If he does follow through, it should be useful once he does."

"He will if he said he would," the old man responded. "But you will have no need of it. I can get you anything you need."

"Reassuring, but I don't intend to stay," Edryd replied.

Tolvanes looked suddenly troubled. "You can't go now," he cried.

"I can't?" Edryd said, caught off guard by the surprising urgency in the man's voice.

"Well you can, but I was hoping you wouldn't," Tolvanes responded in a more even tone, having rediscovered his lost composure.

"You warned me that Seoras was dangerous. I have learned through direct experience now how dangerous he really is."

"You are a dangerous man as well I think," Tolvanes countered. "I have never seen anyone who held up half so well against him."

"You think I did well?" Edryd asked with incredulity. "He destroyed me, Tolvanes. He toyed with me."

"You're wrong," Tolvanes insisted. "You disarmed him."

"He dropped the sword intentionally," Edryd disagreed, "and you saw what followed." The pain in Edryd's chest seemed to flare even thinking about it.

"That doesn't matter. You made him drop his sword. People don't do things like that to him. He was furious. And after that, you still managed to get behind him. You could have run him through right then and would have had good cause to have done so. You should have done it."

Edryd was surprised to hear Tolvanes speak this way. The violent impulses that had taken hold of the old man contrasted with and ran counter to the warm regard he had shown towards Edryd, a complete stranger.

"Maybe," Edryd acknowledged, thinking that perhaps things had not been as uneven as he had imagined them. "But I don't think I would have survived it if I had tried. He is too fast. And I'm not so sure I would agree that two stolen coins would be cause to end a man's life."

"Two gold coins? You think that is all that man has taken?" Tolvanes demanded. "This estate, it isn't his. It's mine, or at least it was, and now I serve him as if I were some worthless slave. He has killed countless others for less, taking what he wants from whomever he wishes."

Edryd could see the hatred in Tolvanes' eyes, and took a moment before responding. "I don't want to become one of those 'countless others' Tolvanes," Edryd said, trying to remain calm.

"Oh, he won't kill you." Tolvanes insisted. "He will want to teach you to fight the way he can. Let him. You will become just as fast and strong as he is, and then you will be able to stop him."

Edryd remembered how Seoras had pushed and provoked him. He wondered now whether this speech was just another part of a plan that would ensure that he would give Seoras another spirited fight. The old man's anger seemed real enough though that Edryd had to doubt that Tolvanes was acting in his master's interests.

"He could have ended me ten times over in that fight," Edryd said. "What is it you think I can possibly do?"

"I want you to train with him," Tolvanes replied, "and when the right moment comes, I want you to kill him."

Chapter 5

Ruach

Ruach kept watch atop a tall stone tower, a decaying remnant of Old Vidreigard's broken defenses, and looked out over the ruined fortifications which surrounded the city. He had not chosen the tallest tower. He had instead picked a relatively modest one with an open view of the northward approach, where it commanded an unobstructed position that benefited from a rise in the terrain along the western walls. This area, covered in the resilient remains of scorched marble buildings and tall granite towers and walls, was an expected waypoint for the king's armies and a potential battle site if the king ever moved his forces closer to House Edorin lands. Ruach's presence was meant to provide an advance warning to the Sigil Corps if that should happen.

He was careful to keep his posture low, and despite the intensity of the day's midafternoon warmth, Ruach kept the hood of his cloak drawn over his head. His bright red hair would work against his efforts to remain hidden if left uncovered, and he was tall enough that he would have been exposed to anyone else in the area if he were careless enough to stand and stretch his legs. He took quite seriously his orders to remain as near to invisible as could be managed, despite the complete absence of anyone from whom to remain hidden. He was alone in the keeping this temporary vigil over a city in which there were no longer any living inhabitants.

Vidreigard had once been important, rivaling even the capital, Eidstadt. If you believed in ancient myths, this had once been a land inhabited by an ancient race of men, claimed by some to have been Dwarves, famous for their skill in forging metal and in shaping stone. More recently, Vidreigard had been the home of the Ascetics, a community of sorcerers bound by strict oaths which forbade many of the more dangerous practices to which the arcane subjects they studied could be put to use.

Ruach did not know whether to believe all of these stories, and so he could not say who had had built the city, but he knew that it had been men who had been responsible for its destruction. Five hundred years ago, Vidreigard had been the site of the final battle between the remnants of the Sigil Order and the armies of the dark sorcerer, Ulensorl.

The Ascetics, whose entire population had lived here in this city, were massacred in the earliest stages of an all-encompassing conflict, in which neither Ulensorl nor the Knights of the Sigil Order had lived to see the final conclusion. The leaders of the Sigil Order had died in battle at the hands of Ulensorl. The great sorcerer had fallen too, in the end, when his dark powers broke free from his control. Though their forces ultimately achieved victory over the armies of Ulensorl, all of the sigil knights had been lost, with the sole exception of Trass Edorin, founder of the Edorin line and half-brother to the leader of the Sigil Knight forces, a man known famously as Tem Edor.

The great city of Eidstadt remained, and it was now the capital of what the survivors of those battles had named the Kingdom of Nar Edor, in honor of their fallen commander, Tem Edor. Tem's brother Trass Edorin, on the other hand, was variously regarded either with awe, as the last of the Sigil Knights, or reviled for not having been counted on the battlefield among his brothers when they had fallen.

Ruach was of course among those who were fiercely loyal to the Edorin line. An officer within the attempted revival of the Sigil Order by Trass Edorin's descendant, the late Duke Kyreth Edorin, Ruach's attitude edged closer to worship than it did mere respect. The duke's grandson, Aisen, was Ruach's immediate superior in the Sigil Corps and Ruach felt, as did all of the men of Aisen's command, a deep affection for his captain.

Watching for scouting parties from the king's armies, which had come and gone twice before, Ruach sighted a distant group of mounted men. But these men were approaching from the east, coming from lands under the control of House Edorin. They wore basic grey uniforms, which included light leather armor, marking them as a patrol of Sigil Corps Rangers. One of these men, his stiff posture and straight back making him appear taller than the others, sat uncomfortably on his horse, apparently unaccustomed to riding. His coat was different from the rest. It was a deeper shade of grey and was topped by an even darker collar upon which were affixed, four golden pins that indicated his rank and authority. Streaks of bright white mixed into his grey hair, suggesting his age and giving away his Identity. It was Commander Ledrin, Ruach's superior by two steps in grade.

This was no chance meeting. Ledrin had not come upon this location by accident, crossing through the lone patrol of a subordinate in the course of other business. Ruach frowned, trying to understand why Ledrin was here. He watched as the group of soldiers casually broke apart after passing through the eastern gates, fanning out on predetermined patrols within the abandoned city, before he finally descended from his tower. Estimating the path he had seen Ledrin taking, Ruach moved to intercept.

When they met, sheltered in the shadows between rows of large buildings, the Sigil Corps commander showed recognition, but not surprise, as he looked down at Ruach from atop his horse. Ledrin did look around out of an abundance of caution, but once he was convinced they were very much alone, he began to speak, his voice low and hushed so that the sounds would not travel as they were prone to do in these empty streets. "Have you or any of the others heard from him?" he asked, in reference to Captain Aisen, the man who stood in rank immediately between Ruach and Commander Ledrin.

"Nothing in the last three weeks," Ruach replied.

Ledrin appeared troubled. Ruach felt the same, only perhaps more intently. If Commander Ledrin did not know Lord Aisen's whereabouts, nobody would. Ruach almost hoped that Ledrin had taken Aisen by force and hidden him away somewhere to keep him safe. The alternatives were that Aisen might be dead, or that he was hiding of his own accord in fear. Ruach did not want to imagine the latter. He would have been more willing to accept that Captain Aisen was dead than he was to think that he might be a coward. But none of these scenarios appeared to hold an answer. Aisen was simply missing, and speculation as to what this meant had begun spreading throughout the lands of Nar Edor.

"I don't believe he is anywhere in the kingdom," Ledrin said.

"How is that possible? Where would he have gone? And why?" Ruach said. He had not once considered the possibility that Aisen had left Nar Edor altogether. Thinking about it now, it still seemed very improbable to Ruach.

"Ossia would seem the most obvious choice," Ledrin replied. "That is where his father was from. Aisen would have resources there, people he could rely on, though he may not know it."

"But why leave Nar Edor?" Ruach said, wanting more of an answer, certain that there was something Ledrin had not revealed.

"He thinks that I betrayed him, and blames me for what happened," Ledrin said, looking pained as he openly acknowledged his role in Aisen's disappearance.

"For what happened to his brother... how can Aisen blame you for that?"

"He has reasons, and they are all good ones," Ledrin said. "If I had taken him into confidence, shared my plans, if I had just trusted him, it could have been prevented."

Ruach waited for Ledrin to say more, but the commander remained silent. "If I am going to be of help to you in this, I need to know," Ruach said, urging Ledrin to tell him the full truth.

"I kept things from him, important things," Ledrin said, hesitant about being more specific. Ruach kept silent and waited for Ledrin to continue. "Among other mistakes, I interfered with a messenger from Lord Pendren, who was trying to warn Aisen about what Beonen was planning," Ledrin finally explained.

It was a startling revelation. Aisen had been kept from learning that his younger brother had been planning to murder him. Ruach reacted as could be expected. He could not hide his disapproval as he looked on at his commander in stunned silence.

"I didn't know what the message was," Ledrin quickly qualified. "The messenger refused to speak with me or anyone else. I believed that Lord Pendren was trying to persuade Aisen to cede his claim. I knew he had been leading a group that was advocating for Beonen to inherit."

"That might have been for the best," said Ruach, struggling to figure out what this new information meant. "Beonen did not need to kill Aisen in order to inherit. In truth, I think Aisen would have preferred to remain in the Sigil Corps if he could, and let his brother run the House."

"That is precisely the thing that I feared most. I could not let it happen, and for that reason, I kept your captain out on patrols where no one would be able to find him."

This was making more sense to Ruach now. He had been with Aisen on those patrols along unpopulated reaches of the northern coasts, for months at a time, lasting right up until Aisen left them when he received word that Kyreth Edorin had died.

"If you had let Pendren's messenger speak with Aisen, none of this would have happened," Ruach summarized.

"I didn't trust Pendren," said Ledrin, "but worse than that, I didn't trust Aisen."

Ruach could better understand now why his captain would have had reason to leave. Aisen had many more enemies than friends in Nar Edor, and his allies had now failed his trust as well. "He really is gone then," Ruach said. "But there are not many ways a man can leave Nar Edor. How would he have gotten away without anyone knowing?"

"That is what you need to figure out," said Ledrin. "Go to the Rendish districts and the dockside areas and learn what you can, but absolutely no one can know why you are there."

It was going to be difficult to investigate when he couldn't ask any questions that would betray his purpose, or seek help from friends within the Sigil Corps. Ruach understood, though, why the circumstances required exceptional caution. It would weaken the position of the Sigil Corps if it were confirmed that they were defending the succession claims of a man who had abandoned them.

"There are foreigners recently arrived in the districts," Ledrin continued. "Drab looking men, asking questions about Aisen. One would assume their interests may be to his detriment, but we aren't sure who they are or what their purpose is. If you learn anything, I need to know as much as I can."

"And if I learn where it is that Aisen has gone?"

"Then take your friend Oren with you, and go after him," said Ledrin.

"Why Oren?" wondered Ruach, "and why me for that matter?"

"Aisen will still trust you Ruach, and if it comes to it, Oren is the only man among your company who could equal Aisen in a fight," Ledrin explained.

"If Aisen refuses, you're saying we should force him to return?" Ruach asked. The situation might be desperate, but Ruach was surprised that Ledrin would suggest this. Aisen wasn't going to be of much use if he did not return willingly. Quite the opposite, he might even become a hindrance to Ledrin's ambitions.

"No, I don't want to provoke him further," Ledrin clarified, "but it might aid your cause if he believes that you are capable of making him do so."

The domineering approach that Ledrin was suggesting, did not strike Ruach as being the best way to restore Aisen's faith in the Sigil Corps. Then again, Ruach realized, Ledrin was entrusting him with this matter, and that at least, demonstrated his commander's reputation for wisdom.

Chapter 6

The Blood Prince

After two days spent resting in bed, interrupted only by regular cold baths, the swelling and pain had eased, but the prolonged inactivity left Edryd restive and in need of an excuse to work out the soreness in his muscles. Though the pain was subsiding, the bruising looked even worse than before, with black regions fading into expanding edges of yellow and green. His range of motion was returning, but Edryd often felt cold and weak to a point where he would begin to shake.

Irial, calling his condition of form of dyscrasia, said it was an imbalance of black bile building up in his body, and had suggested switching to heated baths, extra bed coverings at night, and a regiment of exercise to help speed his recovery. She had refused to further discuss what they had talked about on that first day, and remained unwilling to elaborate on how she had meant to aid him in his desire to leave An Innis. That was all he could think about, finding some way to get away from this place. He could feel his past catching up to him, and he needed to stay ahead of it.

Seoras, seeing him actively moving around this morning, had suggested a light sparring session. Edryd declined the invitation, but his host insisted that they would resume tomorrow. Tolvanes appeared not long afterwards with the shorter of the two arming swords. Seoras, it seemed, presumed to know what kind of weapon Edryd was most accustomed to and was picking the sword for him this time. Though Edryd was looking for an activity to get his blood moving, he wasn't ready to fight Seoras. He was lightheaded just from walking around the barracks buildings.

Insisting that he was not sufficiently recovered, Edryd stressed his doubts about the wisdom of fighting Seoras again so soon, and made an effort at persuading Tolvanes to help make the case to Seoras for a delay. This accomplished nothing, aside from prompting the older man to offer unwanted advice. "He will be easier on you going forward,"

Tolvanes reassured. In an attempt at encouragement and praise, Tolvanes then followed this up with a compliment. "You are actually the more technically skilled fighter," he said. Edryd could not tell if the man was being sincere.

These expressions of faith and confidence in his abilities did not make Edryd believe he could win, though after the debasing defeat he had suffered, he desperately wanted to believe that he could. As the day faded into evening, and the time in which to prepare continued to shrink, Edryd began to feel trapped under the unpleasant knowledge that fate was pulling him in a direction that he could not control.

Edryd would have liked to dismiss this mood as the ordinary anxious apprehension that naturally came before an impending conflict, but he understood himself better than that. He knew it for what was—a rational and well placed terror at the prospect of facing Seoras. In this ominous frame of mind, he went to bed and unsuccessfully tried to get some sleep, feeling weaker now than ever. Before even the first hints of light crept over the mountains to the East, Edryd dressed silently. He secured the keys which Irial had returned to him between his hip and his belt, and pocketed the emblems that he had once worn on his cloak. Leaving the sword behind, he slipped away, feeling relieved but also more than a little ashamed.

His linen shirt held in little heat, so Edryd felt rather exposed while walking through the cold morning air. He had not been willing to wear the soldier's coat that had been given to him, and Irial had not made good on her promise to procure a replacement for the one that had been burned. He could only shiver and bear it a while longer as he waited for the sun to rise and warm the earth. He did have the deposit note from Seoras, which would help in negotiating the purchase of a good inconspicuous cloak, which he could hope would serve to keep him warm and also help him blend in. It was too early for that now. He was going to have to wait a while before anyone would be opening up a shop for the day.

Heading west through the curving streets of An Innis, Edryd had no specific destination in mind. He watched as the sun began to brighten the skies while leaving An Innis covered in shadow, blanketed beneath outlines of the forested mountains which rose up on the mainland, across the causeway to the east. Gradually, the palace high atop the island became a point of solitary illumination. Bathed in bright light, its white walls and towers stood alone above the darkness, which at this early hour extended out for miles over the open water beyond the island.

When Edryd reached the western shore he felt disappointed. The two piers, composed of massive stones which had been concreted together, were crowded with aging vessels in varying states of disrepair, but in something of an oddity, there was almost no human activity anywhere along this sea-side anchorage. This time of morning would have prompted a bustle of fishing crews anywhere else, but An Innis had little in common with other places in the world, and its inhabitants were not fishermen. The earliest intervals of the morning were not prime operating hours for swindlers, marauders, and clandestine markets.

With one basic goal foremost in his thoughts, Edryd went looking, hoping to find someone, anyone really, who might be connected to one of the docked vessels. He needed to find a ship that would take him somewhere far away from An Innis, but the deserted condition of the waterfront was making it a challenge to acquire the information that he needed. He had passed no one on his way here, and if not for a scattered handful of men out on the piers, the entire town might have been a deserted ruin.

When he made his way out beyond the shore and onto the northernmost of the two flat stonework pilings, Edryd quickly learned from the workers that there were no independently captained ships in An Innis. Everything was under the power of the Ard Ri and the four harbormasters. In what was, at times, a conflicting combination of coordination and competition, these men controlled the city and dominated its criminal enterprises. They owned all of the moorings and all of the local seagoing ships, all of the seafront warehouses, and most of the businesses that could be found in the city.

It was these men that Greven had warned him about, but there was no other means to arrange travel off of An Innis. Making a decision based on proximity, Edryd headed for a large building built out of rough cut stone, positioned directly opposite the northernmost pier. This building unofficially housed, in something of an open secret, the offices for one of the four harbormasters, a man named Sidrin Eildach.

While speaking to the attendant manning the desk just inside the front of the building, as part of his enquiries into securing passage on a ship, Edryd made a hushed reference to the letter of deposit Seoras had given him. This man, looking a little frightened, told him in quite definite terms that there were no ships leaving An Innis, and that it would be quite impossible to arrange anything. He hadn't said so directly, but the attendant didn't seem to care much for the resident blade master of An Innis, and had become visibly anxious from the moment Edryd first whispered the name Aed Seoras. Sidrin Eildach's organization apparently wanted no involvement with him, and Edryd was quietly but firmly ushered out of the office.

Edryd wasted no time in covering the distance some few blocks away to the headquarters of the next harbormaster. It was the home of Kedwyn Saivelle. The man owned many of the town's local businesses, and he exerted pressure on and influence over the few establishments that he did not control outright. Saivelle had accomplished this through the ruthless use of a loyal mob of laborers and extortionists who answered directly to him. Edryd, who knew very little of this, guessed by the appearance of their respective buildings and the men who frequented them, that Eildach might have had more wealth, but Saivelle seemed to be the more powerful of the two.

At Saivelle's home, he met with a man named Deneg, one of Saivelle's several lieutenants. Edryd had learned the wisdom of concealing his connections to Seoras, but this left him without anything to offer as payment for arranging travel aboard one of Saivelle's ships. To get around this, Edryd tried to find a position working his way onto a departing ship's crew, but Eildach's attendant had spoken not so far from the truth when he had said that there were no ships leaving An Innis. Ships that braved the waters near An Innis were consistently raided by local marauders. When a ship did leave, it did so in secret. Hiring on an unreferenced stranger onto a crew was too much of a risk.

In the interest of establishing his reputation, and ultimately working his way onto a crew, or at least obtaining a more complete understanding of the power structures in the town, Edryd accepted an offer for work as a longshoreman at a complex of warehouses adjacent to the southern pier. If nothing else it would provide reliable income to get by on while he worked out a way to leave An Innis.

Edryd was put to work beside another man, who with the use of a crudely constructed cart, was consolidating stockpiles of oil from two small cellars into more secure storage in a larger guarded building. He hadn't met many people in his time here, so Edryd was surprised when he recognized the man that he would be working with.

"I was wondering about you," Ivor remarked. "Couldn't figure out where it was you ended up."

"I'm still wondering myself," Edryd deflected, not wanting to give Ivor an accounting of the past several days. Assuming Ivor didn't know already, one less person who could make an association between him and Seoras would be for the best.

"I'm glad to have help," Ivor said. "It isn't what you would call desirable work, but it is honest. Well by An Innis standards, leastways," he qualified.

"Should I be concerned?" Edryd asked, not at all sure how moving jars of oil was in any way a suspect activity.

"I don't ask questions, you understand, but I expect this here once belonged to someone who wasn't never compensated for it. Same would go for everything in An Innis, I suppose."

Taking Ivor's meaning, Edryd chose not to explore the subject further, and he set about doing the task for which he was being paid. It was mindless and tiring work, for which Edryd was particularly ill-suited in his present weakened condition. When Edryd questioned the purpose for moving the jars, Ivor just shrugged and cryptically offered what must have passed for a bit of local wisdom: you owned anything of value only by virtue of having the means to forcibly secure and protect it. That was a general truth, and a rather obvious one, but nowhere more so than An Innis. The cellars were vulnerable, and the oil stores were valuable enough to be a tempting target. Together, Ivor and Edryd worked to fill the cart, loading it up with a couple dozen jars from one of the cellars, and once it could hold no more, they proceeded to pull it to a large structure a few streets over.

There were a rough dozen men at the wooden warehouse. Not one of them made an effort to assist in any way. Two men in the front of the building had swords at their sides. Three others on the roof were equipped with crossbows. All of them had long knives on their belts. This was Kedwyn Saivelle's solution for securing things he had taken. No one challenged Edryd or Ivor as they pulled the cart into the building, and no one acknowledged them either. They were expected, and beneath notice.

Passing through a wide set of doors, Edryd was impressed by what he saw when he crossed into the interior. The cavernous space was loaded with stacked crates, barrels, and sacks of varied shapes and sizes, often piled right up to the ceiling. The accumulation in this building alone far exceeded the local population's possible needs for the kinds of items Edryd could see. There were stores of food, bales of wool, carpets, animal skins, and who knew what luxury items secured away in endless rows of wooden containers.

"This is incredible," Edryd marveled. "It has to be worth a fortune."

"Would be if it were saleable," Ivor agreed. "Trouble is, there's no real market here for much of it—there being an overabundance. Without some means by which to transport the stuff, it isn't worth what you might think. Not much ever leaves so it just piles up."

The look Edryd gave Ivor suggested he thought him a little dim. "There are a dozen or more merchant ships docked in the port," Edryd objected, "how can you suggest there isn't a way to move the goods for sale elsewhere?"

"You are not taking the Ash Men, the Ascomanni, into account," Ivor explained. "They attack everything that leaves."

Edryd had in fact learned this much earlier that day, but he hadn't given it much thought. "It's really that bad then?" he asked.

"Merchants stopped coming for slaves and cheap trade goods long ago. Leaving An Innis with a loaded ship usually means losing both ship and cargo to the Ascomanni. We don't even have slaves to sell anymore. It's too expensive to feed and maintain what you can't hope to sell in a reasonable amount of time."

"The Ascomanni can't target every ship," Edryd protested.

"Years ago, when they started out, they were a minor but painful nuisance. There are more of them now though, and in the last couple of years they have become well-coordinated. As of late last winter we are as near cut off from the rest of the world as it can get."

Edryd wanted to know more, but he did not want to appear too curious, and Ivor was already becoming heated as he discussed the situation. After unloading the contents of the cart, they headed back and continued to work without rest, making steady progress on the first of the two cellars. Three trips later, on their way back to the warehouse with a fourth load in the cart, it began to rain. The work became quite miserable then, with sharp droplets of water blowing in against their backs from the direction of the ocean.

"It won't do letting you succumb to a chill," Ivor muttered, eyeing Edryd's wet clothing with concern as they finished stacking the most recent collection next to the other ceramic jars that they had previously unloaded inside the warehouse. "I'll have to finish by myself if you give out," he complained.

"A bit of damp isn't going to do me in," Edryd said dismissively. "I'll be fine."

"You don't look fine. You look terrible, if I'm to be truthful about it," Ivor disagreed, showing real concern. Edryd had been getting weaker and slower on each successive trip, and there was definitely something wrong with him. "I can find you something," Ivor said in a hushed tone, motioning to Edryd to indicate that he should follow him.

Ivor led the way through a maze of stacked crates, deep into the back of the building. Reaching the area he was searching for, Ivor took a quick look around before taking out a thick heavy knife which he used to pry open a crate made of pine slats. Stored inside of the container, were long canvas coats, stained a deep dark color from being treated in a mixture of oil and pitch that was used for waterproofing.

Edryd removed one of the coats and tried it on. It was tight, so he dug through the crate looking for something bigger, but gave up when he discovered that they all appeared to be roughly the same. The cloth was durable and stiff, and the length matched his height well enough, trailing down to about an inch below the top of his boots. The coat produced a strong unavoidable odor from the waterproofing, concentrated by having been packed in a crate with the other coats, but it felt comfortable enough to Edryd if he left it loose and didn't try to tie it shut. It would do well enough for now, and he was very glad to have it.

Satisfied as well, Ivor led them back to the cart, and he and Edryd began pulling it towards the front of the building. "Won't the guards notice?" Edryd asked as they approached the entrance to the warehouse.

"No, and they wouldn't care if they did," Ivor said. Edryd was not so sure, but he was not about to go and return what he had taken, so he didn't say anything else. "Just the same, don't go out of your way to draw any attention as we leave," Ivor said, hedging just a little, while not actually retreating from his earlier assurances.

The two men made their way back without incident, and were nearly done clearing out the remainder of the first of the two cellars when a group of men arrived. There were four of them. The leader of the group was Deneg, the man who had hired Edryd. Edryd had never seen the man standing right beside Deneg, but he recognized the two men in the back as guards from the warehouse.

"Your service is no longer needed," Deneg said once he was sure he had their attention. It was a reasonable assumption that he was speaking only to Edryd.

Edryd almost offered up an apology for taking the coat, but Ivor shot him a look and took the opportunity to intervene. "I need his help to finish this," Ivor complained.

"Don't get involved, Ivor," Deneg warned. "Best if you get back to your work."

Realizing this was not about the coat, Edryd decided against demanding an explanation. He wasn't much interested in continuing the work anyway. "Give me a day's wage, and I will be on my way," he said.

Deneg, looking relieved, began to reach into his coat for a coin, but the man beside him placed a hand on his wrist and stopped him. "He won't need payment," the man said firmly. Edryd noticed the man was wearing a black woolen coat, cut in a familiar design. Things were becoming clear.

Realizing that he would cause Ivor trouble if he remained, without avoiding it himself, Edryd apologized to his partner for leaving him to finish on his own. Offering an insincere farewell to the men confronting him, Edryd tried to remain calm as he turned away from the group and made his way back into the heart of town. Seoras obviously had sent men out after him. They were not forcing him to go back, but they were not about to let him leave the island either. It would do him no good to contact any of the other harbormasters. If they hadn't been informed already, they soon would be, and would know not to offer him any help.

The afternoon's efforts had not been entirely wasted though. Edryd hadn't received payment for the partial day of work, but he was walking away with a coat that would have cost him a week's worth of wages. Whatever small satisfaction Edryd felt as a result of this victory, it departed quickly enough when he began to focus on a growing list of problems. Most immediate among them were finding a place to stay and securing some provisions.

Shelter would have to be his first priority. The day had grown warmer, and he now had a coat, but he felt even colder than he had this morning, and gentle tremors circulated throughout his body whenever he stopped to rest. Edryd suddenly remembered the set of keys Greven had given to him a few days earlier, which could be used to gain access to the home back behind the inn.

As he transferred these keys from his belt into a pocket in his new coat, Edryd began to seriously consider the property which Greven had made available. It would be a place to shelter for the night, but he was already long overdue on his promise to return the keys. He could also assume that Seoras, who had gone through his belongings and had certainly seen the keys, would know what they were as well as who had given them to him. There were more than a few abandoned buildings in this city. It would be better to make use of one of those for the night. Determined to return the keys as soon as possible and be done with them, Edryd hurried on and quickly arrived at the Broken Oath.

There was a regular exchange of people entering and exiting the inn, and Edryd didn't attract particular notice from any of the patrons as he made his way inside. The inn was crowded in comparison to his previous visit, but still far from full, and he had no trouble finding a free spot on a bench at an almost empty table. Greven was busy with the evening crowd, so Edryd decided to settle in and relax. He could wait until people began to leave before disrupting the already overstretched innkeeper.

Pieces of conversations filtered through to Edryd's ears from groups at nearby tables. A great deal of the talk centered on happenings to the west in Nar Edor. One rather animated fellow in particular was managing to out-compete the volume from the rest of the room. "The noble houses are in chaos over the succession of House Edorin," the man pronounced excitedly. "When Duke Edorin died, his young grandsons fought. Intending to remove a rival claim, the oldest one, Aisen, lured the younger brother, Beonen, into his grandfather's crypt and secured the doors behind them."

"Trapping him, along with the oldest son from each of the major families sworn to House Edorin, with no way to escape," someone else said, adding a detail the original speaker had overlooked.

"It doesn't seem likely," argued a woman who was sitting across the table from the speaker. "A weak plan on Aisen's part I should think, luring a group of trained swordsmen into a confined space where he would be outnumbered by them." Everyone knew that Edoric nobles were obsessed with dueling, so no one challenged the point that the men in the crypt would all have been skilled swordsmen.

"I heard it differently," someone else chimed in, apparently in agreement with the woman who had just spoken. "It was Beonen, the younger son, who ambushed Aisen with help from those houses who wanted to see Beonen win the succession." Everyone other than the original speaker, who still believed he had the right of it, agreed that this made more sense.

"Depending on who you believe, there are conflicting versions as to who plotted against whom," the man admitted. "But there is no disagreement about how it ended. Aisen killed every last one of them. When the slaughter was over, Aisen, making no effort to hide what he had done, pushed the doors open, and with total indifference marched straight through the gathered mourners who were there to pay their respects to the duke."

"Aisen's once golden armor was coated red with blood from head to toe, and they all shook in fear as he forced them to move aside to let him pass," the woman added, eager to supply what seemed like an exaggerated detail to a story that continued to grow with each retelling.

"That is why they have taken to calling him the Blood Prince," someone else said excitedly.

Apparently, everyone already knew the story; they were simply repeating popular arguments regarding the particulars in the sequence of events. Edryd's attentions were distracted away when he was bumped by an unkempt stranger who was in the process of sitting down beside Edryd at the table. The man looked thoroughly inebriated, and he smelled even more convincingly the part of an inveterate drunk, but Edryd suspected it was an act, or at least mostly one.

As the rather large man settled onto the bench, his hand skimmed deftly in and out of the leather money pouch attached to Edryd's belt.

It was a quick, much practiced maneuver that might have gone unnoticed if Edryd had not been expecting it. He grabbed the man's arm and forced it up onto the table. Frightened at having been caught, the disheveled man stuttered a momentary protest before smoothly easing back into his drunken pretense. Fortunately for Edryd, as well as for the would-be thief, the pouch had been empty, so nothing had been taken.

"You targeted an empty coin purse," Edryd said, letting go of the man's arm as he locked his eyes on the startled pickpocket, "or this would be a less pleasant conversation than the one we are now having. I'm sure you'll understand, though, if I ask that you find yourself another seat." Muttering nervous apologies, the man turned and quickly fled the establishment. Edryd sat back and began to listen again. He had lost all sense of who was who among the group, but he managed to catch back up to their conversation after a few moments.

"It will be an open war before long," the man at the next table emphasized in serious tones. "The king has refused Aisen's claim to succession and he is raising an army to capture him and confiscate his land and property."

"The Sigil Corps have gathered ranks and they are defending Aisen's claim," the woman said. "They outnumber the king's army for the moment. Until that reverses nothing is likely to happen."

"What of Aisen then? Where is the Blood Prince in all of this with House Edorin's warriors?" asked one of the other men at the table.

The original speaker, still loud and aggressive, gave an answer. "That's just it, no one knows. Not out killing more family members at least, not that he has any left. For three weeks no one has seen him, and nobody seems to know more than what I have already told you. The popular speculation circulating in Nar Edor is that the Blood Prince left to raise an army of Rendish raiding parties and that he intends to conquer all of Nar Edor."

"That doesn't even make the least bit of sense," argued an older man with sharp eyes. "Aisen's father was Aedan Elduryn. He killed Beodred and broke our alliance twenty years ago, forcefully expelling us from Nar Edor, along with every single man woman or child in that land who, like ourselves, could be called a Rend. None of our warriors would look too kindly on his son. Where would Aisen be able to recruit? Not Seridor and certainly not here in An Innis. I can't imagine it."

"The Ossians?" suggested another man doubtfully. "Aedan Elduryn was an Ossian after all. They would have a vested interest in supporting his son, and they are going to want to protect their control over Edoric trade goods and their position of influence over the other League states."

"I'm sure they would eagerly fund an army, but those self-satisfied moralists could hardly raise one."

The group all agreed on that last point and no one gave any credence to the idea that Aisen would, or even could, recruit any sort of useful Rendish support. But because of his descent from an Ossian father, everyone in Nar Edor probably thought Aisen a part of some Rendish plot to conquer their country, so the idea that he was raising a Rendish army would have made sense to them at least. King Eivendr, the monarch of Nar Edor, certainly wouldn't be doing anything to discourage belief in that notion among his people. The more men who believed such things, the easier it would be to gain the support he needed to take control of House Edorin.

The conversation continued, but yielded little additional information. The Sigil Corps controlled the defenses of the Port Citadel on Aisen's behalf, and the king's army had not yet grown to the point where it was ready to start a confrontation. As things stood, Edoric exports were severely diminished, but there was still a steady stream of ships from Ossian League states supplying the region around the country's only major port, which was presently controlled by House Edorin and the Sigil Corps.

Listening in on other groups, Edryd gathered bits and pieces of more local news, which all confirmed that An Innis was in crisis. Cargo carrying vessels leaving An Innis were getting hit by Ascomanni from a base somewhere to the south. Ships coming in or out of An Innis did so late at night hoping to slip past. Commerce had slowed to a point where you could be forgiven if you thought it had stopped entirely.

Mostly this was all news that Edryd had already learned from Ivor, but he did learn why the raiders were called Ash Men. If you believed such things, as many in An Innis apparently did, the Ascomanni were sickened. As a direct consequence of living near the ruins on the mainland, they were caught in a spell which condemned them to wander in an existence somewhere between life and death. This condition granted inhuman powers and left them deathly grey in appearance. It was no wonder that ships were no longer calling here. Add such stories of death and disease into the risk of being attacked by raiding parties, and An Innis was going to be a port you avoided.

The symmetry was not lost on Edryd. An economy built around raiding merchant ships travelling to or from Nar Edor was now being destroyed by a group of raiders that were in turn attacking the ships of An Innis. It was an example of the inherent risk that came with choosing to employ such tactics against an enemy. Success is often brief and short-lived, and inevitably, methods used to good effect against others are just as easily imitated and turned back upon those who first employed them. Those who live by the sword are not immune to dying by the same and should be prepared to defend against it.

As the evening hours progressed, people began making their way out of the establishment. There were still several fragmenting groups distributed unevenly at several of the tables, but Greven was nowhere to be seen. In fact, he hadn't popped out of the kitchen for some time. Looking around at the other groups, one person stood out. Flanked on either side by guards who were wearing tightly fitted blue coats, a graceful woman, wearing a beautiful high-collared green dress made of fine silk, stood up near the other end of the hearth hall. She was of a different class entirely, and looked completely out of place amongst the people in the inn. At first, Edryd failed to register that she was headed in his direction. A moment later she sat down, settling in tightly beside him with her hips and shoulders making contact against his own. The two guards remained standing behind her, arms crossed behind their backs.

Edryd had rarely felt less certain of himself. He was at a loss as to what he should do. Rather stupidly, he continued to stare straight across the table at nothing in particular, as if he could pretend that he had not noticed the woman. He might have gone on doing so, but she reached out and lightly touched him on the arm with a soft hand. Edryd's eyes were pulled towards the contact. There was no jewelry on her smooth fingers or her pale thin wrist, but the fabric of her delicately embroidered clothing was evidence enough to suggest extraordinary wealth.

"You would be Edryd?" she asked him.

Edryd turned to look at her face for the first time. She did not look Edoric or Rendish. Her skin was not dark enough for either. Her deep brown hair had been made up in an elaborate pattern that left a few curling strands of loose hair over her brow, falling down past beautiful hazel eyes. Her pale face was a mask of practiced adoration, and looked as though it had never once been subjected to the indignity of unfiltered sunlight. She had at first appeared fully mature, an illusion brought about by the modest but flattering style of clothing and her formal hairstyle, but now that he was seeing her up close, this woman was plainly still a young girl. She could not possibly be more than fifteen years old.

Though many of them were trying to hide it, most of the eyes in the room were looking in Edryd's direction. Less circumspect individuals, of whom there were quite a few, openly leered at the girl, cautious of the two guards and resentful towards Edryd for what they felt was his good fortune.

"I'm sorry, I don't know who you are," Edryd said.

"My name is Lineue," she answered. "Esivh Rhol has invited you to accompany me and visit him at his home."

Edryd knew by now the sort of business interests that Esivh Rhol trafficked in, so he also now knew what he should have guessed long before. Lineue was one of the women owned by Esivh Rhol, who were sold out of the palace built upon the mountainous peak at the top of An Innis. Conservative by upbringing, in the typical fashion of his homeland, Edryd was repelled by the inappropriate nature of what was implied in the offer that she was delivering to him.

"You like an older woman," she said upon seeing his reaction. There was a look of relief on her face.

Her guess was correct as far as it went, but this accounted for only part of his discomfort. He was about to say that he preferred a woman who wasn't someone's property, but thought better of it.

"You will forgive me for being impolite," Edryd said, "but please tell the Ard Ri that I have no interest in his invitation."

Lineue's guards both shifted in their stances behind her, reacting to the stern tone Edryd had used, and feeling surprised by his refusal. Lineue took it more evenly, though it was plain to Edryd that she was also troubled by his response. She might have been relieved at his disinterest with her personally, but his complete rejection of Esivh Rhol's invitation was a problem for her, representing a failure for which she would not be forgiven.

"You do not refuse an invitation from the Ard Ri," one of the two guards said from behind Edryd.

Edryd turned to face the man. "Clearly you wouldn't, or I should say didn't decline the man, but I have no business with him."

The well-dressed guard went red as his partner resisted an urge to laugh. He wasn't sure what it was that Edryd had meant, and if he had asked, Edryd would have had to admit that it had not been anything specific, but there were plenty of wrong ways to interpret the comment, and the guard had obviously chosen one of them.

Obstructed on one side by Lineue, and also corralled by her two guards standing behind the bench, there would be no easy way to quickly get up from the table in the event his ill-considered approach to this situation triggered a disagreement as seemed increasingly likely with each moment that passed.

Lineue diffused the situation by getting up and telling her guards that she was ready to leave. "You will find yourself in trouble with the Ard Ri if he thinks you made things worse," she said to the guard whom Edryd had offended. Reluctantly, he turned away from Edryd and began escorting Lineue away. Edryd watched until they disappeared out the front door.

Edryd did not need to look to know that everyone was staring at him. It had been a bad idea to come here. Edryd decided not to waste any more time and went looking for Greven.

Leaving the common room and entering Greven's kitchen through a simple archway, he found the space to be a good deal cleaner than the rest of the inn. It would have seemed an impossible task considering the state of the common room, but Greven had managed to keep the floor swept clean of the dirt and mud that surely was getting tracked around with trips in and out of the kitchen to serve the customers. There were a few pots being kept warm on an iron stand set atop the coals in the kitchen fireplace, but otherwise the room showed no sign of activity.

Wondering where Greven could have gone, Edryd spotted a partially opened door that led into a stepped passageway that led down to an underground storage room. As he approached, Edryd began to make out two low unintelligible voices. One of the voices rose in pitch suddenly and could be heard clearly.

"I didn't know he was here!" the voice insisted. It was Greven's voice. Edryd crept closer and settled in next to the wall beside the doorway, trying to make out more of the conversation.

"Now that you do know," the other voice said, trying to calm the innkeeper, "you are in a position to provide a useful service." The voice sounded like it could have been Vannin, a man Edryd had met in this inn that first night here.

"What would you have me do?" Greven asked.

"He has rejected the hospitality of Lord Seoras's estate, and it seems like Seoras would just as soon not make him return by force if it isn't necessary," the man explained. "Offer him a place here, and convince him to stay. Gain his trust if you can."

"It wasn't a week ago Seoras insisted that I refuse him a room, now you are telling me to give him one?"

"Whatever the source of Seoras's peculiar interest in this Edryd, I don't know the reasons. I expect he wants the man to believe he can go about his business unhindered. I am just trying to learn what I can of the man, and relaying to you my orders as they were given."

"I imagine it goes without saying that I am expected to keep track of when he comes or goes?" Greven queried sullenly.

"And report on it."

"I don't suppose I have a choice in the matter?"

"No," Vannin confirmed.

Edryd, deciding it was time to leave, backed away from the doorway. He deposited the set of keys atop the table in the middle of the kitchen, and forgetting that he had no money, absentmindedly began fishing into the leather case at his belt looking for a coin to leave behind in appreciation. In doing so, he discovered that the purse was not empty. It held a single bronze coin of local currency that he was sure he had never seen before. With no time to ponder how it got there, Edryd secured the cold metal coin in a closed fist and headed towards the archway that led into the common room.

Belatedly, Edryd stopped, hit with the realization that leaving the keys behind was a terrible mistake. They would be plain evidence that he had been in the room, and a clear signal that he had possibly overheard the conversation between Greven and Vannin. At the sound of booted feet on the bottom step of the stone stairway, Edryd silently darted back to the kitchen table, and before he could be seen, he snatched up the set of keys and hurried back through the archway and into the common room. Edryd worked his way to the entrance, mindful now of the people in the inn, trying to pick out anyone who might be trying to watch him. He had only been here for a few days, he thought to himself, and could not begin to understand how he had attracted so much attention from so many people.

As soon as he was outside, Edryd made for an alleyway opposite the entrance to the Inn. Once he was out of sight, hidden by the shadows between the two buildings across the street, he accelerated his pace and began to put distance between himself and the businesses in the mercantile section of the town. Pausing occasionally to make sure no one was following him, for he couldn't shake the feeling that someone was, Edryd kept moving at a rapid speed that left him breathing hard and feeling hot in spite of the cold night air. Reaching an empty corner made by two abutting buildings, where he felt confident he could not be observed, Edryd set his back against one of the stone buildings and took a moment to rest while he assessed his situation. The bronze coin was still pressed tightly in his hand and had become warm through the influence of a dissipating heat that was seeping rapidly from his body.

Edryd took the coin between his fingers and held it out under the moonlight. The coin appeared to have been recently struck. The obverse side of the coin bore the image of a crowned figure with subscript identifying the man as Lord Esivh Rhol. The face had been marred with a sharp implement in a manner that obscured Esivh Rhol's eyes under a mess of deep scratches. Near the bottom edge of the coin, through part of Esivh Rhol's throat, was a small hole punched straight through the coin. The previous owner of the coin must have thought none too highly of the self-proclaimed Ard Ri of An Innis.

Edryd shifted the coin in his fingers. An outline of An Innis decorated the other side. The island's two piers were marked at the western shoreline, beside a stylized symbol stamped closer to the center of the coin that approximated the form of the palace at the island's peak, making it a sort of simple but functional map. There was only one other remarkable feature. The hole in the coin cleanly pierced the outline of An Innis at a specific point near the southernmost edge of the island. The placement of the puncture did not appear accidental. Edryd rotated the coin, orienting it so that it matched up with the actual island, and located the direction of the spot marked by the piercing. It wouldn't take half an hour to reach the location.

He was nearing exhaustion, but unable to subdue his curiosity, Edryd began picking his way through the city, angling slowly southward, intent on investigating the area marked by the hole on the coin that had been so strangely placed into his pocket. Thinking about the mysterious pickpocket, Edryd wondered at the possible motivations the man might have had for slipping him the coin. Surely it had not been an accident. If he was being lured to the location on the coin, Edryd had to consider the possibility that he might be walking into an ambush. He was in no shape to deal with something like that.

It seemed far too elaborate a method for a simple robbery though, one that required you slip a coin into instead of out of the target's pocket. Edryd didn't doubt that it was more likely that he would find himself standing alone on an empty shoreline feeling foolish, than set upon by a band of over-thinking criminals. With his recent poor luck though, it made sense to anticipate the possibility of more serious complications, and he continued to be alert to anything that might signal that he was being followed.

The borders of the town soon receded behind him, and Edryd found himself on a sparse and unobstructed rock strewn plain that continued on to a series of crumbling cliffs at the southwestern edge of the island of An Innis. Looking back he saw nothing out of place. There was plenty of moonlight and no cover in which someone could have hidden. If anyone was following him, they had stopped at the edge of the town. Checking the coin once more to be sure of the direction, Edryd headed straight for the location designated upon it. It led to a barren place where an inlet from the ocean had carved out a deep fissure in the cliffs, from which rose currents of damp air that were heavy with the smell of brine.

Passing through a thicket of low shrubs as he arrived near the edge, Edryd surveyed the narrow ocean canyon walls. It was difficult to see, but after some searching he spotted traces of a faintly worn footpath that descended down one side of the crevice before it disappeared into darkness. It took time to find the top of the footpath, which was well hidden by a maze of tall plants, but Edryd soon found himself taking slow careful steps in the dark along the canyon wall. In the dim light that reached into this place, Edryd was able to make out traces of recent travel going both up and down on the pathway. It was persuasive confirmation that the placement of the hole in the coin had not been random.

After making it to the bottom safely, Edryd walked along a footpath that traversed a narrow muddy shoreline along the face of the westernmost canyon wall. Immediately beyond a sharp corner, he noticed traces of lantern light leaking out from an encampment a little further down the path. Edging silently along the cliffside, Edryd spied the source of the light. It was coming from a lantern which cast a wavering light that revealed the shape of a landing craft, a large boat with a furled sail and three sets of retracted oars. The boat was secured in place with a length of corded hemp, tied up against a large stone which protruded above the surface of the water. One man lay sleeping on the shoreline. Another was resting inside the boat. A third sat with his back to the overhanging canyon wall, standing watch for the rest of the men. The boat could easily have carried at least ten more men, so Edryd had to assume that these three did not constitute the entire group. Others were likely in town or elsewhere in An Innis.

The lookout, whose night vision had been weakened by the light, gave no sign that he had seen anything. Edryd could not move closer without stepping into the light, but he wanted to avoid causing undue surprise or alarm anyway. It made sense to greet them from a safe reassuring distance. Edryd straightened and took a single step forward. The movement caught the eye of the man who was standing guard, and he began to lean forward in an unsuccessful effort to better see the dark figure at the edge of the lamplight.

"Krin?" the man asked nervously.

Edryd took another step forward with his hands extended out a little ways from his body.

The lookout's eyes widened. He began kicking the man lying asleep along the shore to wake him, and began to cry out in alarm to the man in the boat. "Wake up Maldrin, someone's here," he shouted. Maldrin bolted upright, looking frightened and confused.

Edryd took one more step forward, placing himself well within the circle of light cast by the lantern on the boat. The man who had been sleeping on the shore slowly raised himself into a sitting position. Propped up on one arm, he looked up from where he rested, apparently angry at having been kicked awake.

Edryd studied the man, whose plain features had few distinguishing characteristics. He might have been just a little taller than Edryd was, with dark hair and brown eyes, and a thin beard spread across a narrow face. He couldn't have appeared less concerned by Edryd's sudden appearance, but wheels were spinning in the man's head, calculating which moves to make and when. By outward appearances, he was altogether unimpressive, yet Edryd felt certain that he must be the leader of this group.

"Was that necessary, Bram?" the man demanded with annoyance, rubbing his shoulder where it had been kicked.

"I had to, Logaeir," Bram explained. "It materialized right out of the mist. It must be a spirit."

Logaeir gave Edryd a once over, and made a quick appraisal. "That's no apparition, it's a man," Logaeir concluded.

"How can you tell?" Bram asked, reassured but not yet convinced.

"Look at the light from our lantern, he's casting a shadow," Logaeir replied.

"A draugr then," countered the lookout.

Logaeir laughed. "You've never encountered one, or you wouldn't say that," he said.

"How am I to know?" Bram protested. There was an injured look on his face.

"You would know a draugr if you ever saw one. It wouldn't stand at the edge of the light waiting for you to invite it into your camp either."

"Well I can't see so clearly. It's all the way out there, and I don't want it coming no closer in," Bram replied, looking over to Maldrin, the man in the boat, for his support.

"I don't know that it's a draugr, but that doesn't mean it doesn't intend us harm," Maldrin agreed.

Logaeir let out an exasperated sigh and beckoned Edryd closer. "Tell us your name, spirit," he invited. "Bram and Maldrin won't relax until you do."

Edryd wasn't sure about the wisdom of approaching, but it was too late to turn around now, and he had questions that needed answers. "My name is Edryd. I didn't mean to frighten anyone," he said as he took a few more steps toward the men.

"I told you he was just a man," Logaeir said. "Draugar don't speak, not in any normal kind of human speech at least." In trying to demonstrate his superiority by criticizing the ignorance of his two companions, Logaeir sounded somehow more naive and foolish than either of them. Yet there was something behind it, as if Logaeir were trying to appear to be something less than what he was. It would be easy to underestimate him.

Maldrin did appear to relax a great deal. Bram did not. "A draugr or a spirit would make more sense traipsing around out here in the middle of the night. If he is just a man, he didn't randomly happen upon us."

"You don't look like Ascomanni," Edryd Interjected. "I assume that is who you are, even if you don't have diseased grey skin, and I see no apparent evidence that you have any unnatural powers."

Maldrin broke the silence caused by this accusation. "We aren't diseased. We only smear that ashen paint on before a raid. It terrifies people like you can't imagine."

Bram and Logaeir stiffened slightly at Maldrin's admission, and shot warning looks in his direction.

"Just what is your purpose for coming here?" Logaeir asked suddenly, returning his attention to Edryd and taking on a more serious tone.

"I believe I was invited," Edryd replied. He retrieved the bronze coin from his pocket and tossed it to Logaeir.

Logaeir took a moment inspecting the coin. "It seems you were," he said.

"You could tell me more about my purpose here than I can," said Edryd. "A man in town slipped this coin into my pocket."

Bram shifted his feet uncomfortably. "Is this really him?" he asked.

Maldrin, sharing Bram's misgivings, decided to give voice to them. "How do we know Krin wasn't caught? He should be here if everything had gone to plan. This could be one of the Ard Ri's men."

"No," Logaeir insisted, "this is him, this is the Red Prince."

Chapter 7

Logaeir

Logaeir, wanting a private conversation, had left Bram and Maldrin behind with the boat while he and Edryd walked a hundred feet back up the shoreline to the where the narrow path began heading back up the cliffside.

"I wanted to ask," Logaeir started to fumble, before choosing a more direct tact. "We need your help, Aisen."

Edryd didn't hide his discomfort over the use of this name, and it must have read plainly on his face even in the darkness. Logaeir quickly reacted. "I can call you Edryd if you prefer, but I know who you are."

"Setting aside whether I am who you think," Edryd responded, "It's my understanding that the Ascomanni have this place under siege. I don't see what I could do for a group that is already so obviously succeeding."

"We have been a little too successful," Logaeir answered. When Edryd didn't seem to comprehend, Logaeir expanded his explanation. "We have grown large, and so effective that trade in An Innis has slowed to almost nothing. It is a problem for them to be sure, but it might just be worse for us. Our men are not soldiers. Most of them are undisciplined and opportunistic, loyal only to the promise of quick wealth. Even if we capture every last bit of cargo going in or out of An Innis it isn't nearly enough. We are beginning to see divisions among the men."

"I'm so sorry to hear that you have run out of things to take," Edryd remarked. It was hard for him to empathize with the troubles of men who took what they wanted by force. He wasn't about to waste any effort trying.

"There isn't a thing connected to An Innis that isn't already five times removed from its proper owner," Logaeir responded in pointed justification. "I have no cause to answer an accusation of supposed wrong for appropriating what was already stolen to begin with."

"Perhaps not," Edryd allowed diplomatically. "I suppose if there is no reasonable way to restore anything, you haven't done new harm in dispossessing those who did not come by the wealth through legitimate means to begin with."

"I'm glad you can see my side," Logaeir agreed. "If it means anything, I would like you to understand that I do mean to restore what I can. There are things yet that are not altogether irretrievable."

Edryd could sense that Logaeir was now talking about something less tangible than captured cargo, but given how little he knew of this man and his history, Edryd was unable to accurately interpret the meaning behind his last comment. He was about to ask Logaeir to say more, when a sudden idea, an apparently obvious solution to the problems Logaeir had described, pushed that impulse aside.

"There might not be much to target on the sea, but I was inside Kedwyn Saivelle's warehouse. That stockpile alone would satisfy the ambitions of no small number of Ascomanni." Edryd offered helpfully, surprised to hear this suggestion spoken in his own voice. He hadn't intended to be getting involved so directly in the affairs of these men.

"Very true," Logaeir replied. "And the building that you visited was only one amongst five others owned by Saivelle. The other three harbormasters control twice that number between them." Logaeir's response implied that he was well aware of Edryd's movements, and knew exactly which warehouse he had been talking about.

Edryd started extrapolating figures based on what he had seen in the warehouse, multiplying that by more than a dozen. It was staggering to say the least. "You mean to raid the town," Edryd asserted confidently, putting the pieces together.

"No," Logaeir laughed. "While I did say we had grown too large, there are not enough of us to pull that off. We would need to take and hold at least one of the piers for a day or more to carry much away with us. Besides, my men would be running the moment Seoras showed his face. That is of course, if they don't fall out with each other over dividing the spoils long before that." Clearly, Logaeir had been running these scenarios through his mind for a while now.

"So you are too many to hold together unless you pull off something of scale, but still too few for a successful raid on An Innis?" Edryd summarized.

"Near to a fair assessment," Logaeir agreed.

"I'm not sure I see a future for myself as an Ascomanni," Edryd responded. "I don't want to say you have done a poor job in selling the offer, but if I were to come around to the notion of mixing with criminals, I think I would pick a group with better prospects."

"But that is where you come in to the equation," Logaeir countered, speaking as though he were solving a complex set of predictions. "The only thing we lack is a leader with credibility, and you have a reputation that commands real fear and respect. I don't need more men. I need better men. And I need someone who will stand up against Seoras when the time comes."

Edryd was speechless, and completely unprepared for what Logaeir was suggesting.

"I am not planning a raid," Logaeir continued. "I want you to plan a battle, and lead the Ascomanni in the taking of An Innis."

Edryd's legs felt like they might give out, and all of the blood drained from his face.

"I am not who you think I am," Edryd finally managed in a weak but steady voice. "I cannot stand against Seoras. I believe you already know that I am running from him. Even if I were this wandering prince, I still would not be who you think I am."

"I know exactly who you are. You are Aisen, son of the hero Aedan Elduryn, and you are a captain in the Sigil Corps, the best soldiers in the world." Logaeir insisted.

"If you place such hopes on me, I will disappoint you," Edryd replied sadly. "I can't help, and I wouldn't if I could."

Logaeir was crestfallen. Edryd was embarrassed. He was also more than a little angry. How could someone ask so much of someone he had met just minutes ago? Too late, Edryd realized he might have irreparably destroyed any chance of using Logaeir to get off of the island. Having flatly refused to help the man, it didn't seem like a good time to ask a favor, but he most likely would never get another chance.

"I am sorry I can't help you in the way that you wanted," Edryd apologized. "I hope you understand."

"I know it was no small thing to ask," Logaeir responded, "but I offer as much in return. After An Innis falls, my men are at your disposal. We can support you and the Sigil Corps against the King of Nar Edor in your claim to your lands. An Innis would recognize you as its ruler and it would become part of your holdings."

"I don't want any of that," Edryd replied sharply, groaning inwardly in frustration. More calmly he added, "I just want to get off of An Innis and away from Aed Seoras."

Logaeir reacted with disappointment, but a small light of hope remained in his eyes. "Spend one month training our men. If after that you still want to leave, I will take you back to Nar Edor or to any destination along the Ossian coast."

Edryd considered the offer. He considered it carefully. He liked to think of himself as an honest man. He once had been. And though he had done nothing but lie from the moment he had arrived on An Innis, he hadn't yet sunk to a point where he could accept the thought of joining or even helping the Ascomanni. These were men who were supporting themselves on the misery of others. They were actively attacking and murdering the people of An Innis. It didn't matter that there were no innocent parties, and that the men of An Innis were quite possibly worse than the Ascomanni. Edryd wanted no part of either side.

"I can't help you, Logaeir, I have no place in this."

Logaeir looked like he was struggling against the urge to say something more, but he had shared far more than was safe already. Edryd was not sure that he was going to be allowed to walk away.

"I am sorry to hear that," Logaeir eventually responded. "I understand your reasons, but I think in the coming days you will find your options are limited. Circumstances will force you to choose a side."

They parted ways at the bottom of the path. Edryd made his way carefully up through the darkness. Distressingly, he found he had to stop and rest several times, his breath coming with unusual effort and his legs protesting each step. Edryd took pride in his strength and stamina so none of this seemed right. It wasn't an easy climb, but it should not have been this difficult.

Emerging from the thick vegetation near the cliff's edge after making his way back to the top of the trail, Edryd found a suitable perch in the form of a large smooth rock on which to take another rest. Looking back towards the town, he noticed the orange glow of a campfire that was illuminating a crude shelter dug into a low hill. The location was protected from the winds by two short irregular walls that extended from the hillside. These were constructed from moss covered stones placed together in an almost haphazard fashion that created a look that felt like a natural extensions of the terrain. Edryd had not seen this hovel on his way out, but the hill that made up the northern wall of the shelter, in combination with the two stone walls, shielded both the encampment and the small fire from being viewed from any direction but south.

Feeling cold and exhausted, Edryd shed any thoughts of caution. He never even considered the idea of skirting around the camp as he made his way back. Instead he went straight for the inviting warmth promised by the light. As he approached the makeshift shelter, he could see the figure of a man tending to the fire. As he drew near, he could see the man's face which was illuminated by the flickering light emanating from the low flames. It was the man who had slipped him the coin. He had apparently trailed Edryd and then stayed up on the cliff to keep watch and give warning if anyone managed to follow him to the meeting.

"You would be Krin?" Edryd asked.

Krin smiled and nodded. He was no longer the drunken oaf he had pretended to be that evening in the inn. Krin invited Edryd to sit on one of the stone seats arranged near the fire. "You've met with Logaeir and the others," Krin stated. "It would seem you must have turned him down."

Edryd nodded his head in confirmation.

"I don't blame you," Krin sympathized. "It would have been foolish to throw in with us. Logaeir has some questionable ideas, and from what I know of his plans, they would have ended up getting you killed. They might yet end up getting me and most of the Ascomanni killed for that matter."

"Logaeir is your leader?" Edryd asked.

"No," Krin answered. "The Ascomanni don't have a leader, or at least not any single leader."

"How does that work?" Edryd wondered.

"Crews choose their own captain. The captains have an informal hierarchy, but no one can give orders to the others. If we act in concert, all of the captains have to agree."

"But Logaeir is one of your leaders," Edryd posited. Logaeir had on several occasions referred to the Ascomanni as 'his' men, and the grand plans he had outlined for Edryd suggested he was in a position to set things in motion. Clearly he had considerable authority in the group.

"No, not as a captain," Krin answered, correcting Edryd's assumption. "I'm a captain for whatever that is worth," Krin continued, "but Logaeir is... Logaeir is something else altogether."

"He doesn't have any authority then?" Edryd protested doubtfully.

"No, none at all," Krin declared. "He has his ideas, and there is no doubt he is very smart, but he is no leader. He would admit as much. He never stays in one place. Not long enough to gain much real trust from any single crew. You don't rise in the ranks that way."

"So he is no one then? Why was I meeting with him and not you?"

"He might not have any formal authority, but that is not to say he is without influence. As proof of that you need only consider that he persuaded me to come here to recruit you. In case you can't tell, that went against my better judgment." Krin grinned in bemused wonder as he admitted having been moved about by Logaeir like a piece on a game board. "It's to your credit that you had the sense to reject what he was asking."

"And what he offered. He was going to give me a place of prominence within the Ascomanni," Edryd said. "I can't imagine he could have been authorized to honor a promise like that."

"No, he wouldn't be," agreed Krin. "For that matter, no one in the Ascomanni could make that offer."

"He lied then?"

"No, I wouldn't say that. You have something of a fearsome reputation, much more than you realize, I'm guessing. You have skill and experience in combat, and you have claims as the master of multiple respected houses. If you joined the Ascomanni, many would follow you. It isn't that Logaeir was offering you leadership, rather he knows what would naturally follow the moment you were accepted among us."

"You believe I made the right decision?" Edryd asked.

"I do," Krin answered. "Captures are falling off too fast and we are already fraying at the edges. It is only a matter of time. Adding the Blood Prince to our ranks would delay things, but it won't stop the inevitable disintegration. You have something to offer, but nothing to gain."

"That is why Logaeir said he plans to take An Innis," Edryd said.

Krin looked completely taken aback.

"You think he said too much about the plan," Edryd said in response to Krin's startled reaction.

"Well, yes, I suppose so, but what's troubling me the most is that there is no 'the plan'. Or if there is, he never bothered to include me in his deliberations. He said he is going to take An Innis? I can't say I'm pleased, though I don't know why I am surprised." Krin looked frustrated, and ready to exact some sort of punishment to reign in the reckless Logaeir.

"You think it is a bad idea then?" Edryd asked, trying to get Krin's take on the feasibility of Logaeir's intentions.

"A bad idea... no, it's a terrible one! If someone could neutralize Seoras, I might give it some thought..." Krin, making a mental connection, stopped his rant short. "You fought Seoras a few days ago. If you had to, do you think you match him?"

"If you know I fought with him, you must also know how it ended. No, I am no match for that man."

Krin did know what had happened. He was disappointed by Edryd's response, but not especially so. He leveled an insult at Edryd anyway. "I understand Logaeir's thinking now. It is a shame that you measure so short of your reputation, and that you are so easily defeated. A man Seoras broke in less than a week wouldn't be any good to us."

Edryd flushed with heat at the remark. He knew Krin was trying to provoke him, but that didn't make Edryd any less angry or Krin any less correct. "This is not my fight," he said.

"No, it isn't," Krin agreed, "and the last thing we need is a man who doesn't want to fight." Krin stood up, gave a short goodbye, and strode away from the camp, shrinking into the darkened night.

The momentary heat from the agitation Krin had kindled faded quickly as cold air sapped the warmth from Edryd's body. Seeking to stay warm, he pulled the ends of his too small coat tight around his body, and having no strength left to do anything else, Edryd curled up on the ground next to the fire and promptly fell asleep.

Edryd slept late into mid-morning the following day, when he was roused by the warmth of the sunlight reaching him through his blanket. It did not immediately occur to him, but eventually he remembered he had not had a blanket with him when he fell asleep. Bolting upright, he looked around in confusion. There were coals still smoldering in what was left of last night's fire. Someone had tended to it in the night or it would have gone cold long ago. Whoever his visitor had been, he had covered Edryd in the blanket. A quick glance around the camp site revealed a full water skin and a half dozen hard biscuits wrapped in a piece of cloth. Beside the supplies was a note, weighted down with a heavy bronze coin.

Edryd took the coin in one hand and held the letter out in the other as he read the note.

I hope this finds you well – I couldn't stay longer and I didn't want to wake you (you look like you needed rest) so this note will have to suffice. Our offer is an open ended one. If you change your mind, or you ever need help, you can find us in the same manner as you did before. – L

It seemed clear who his benefactor was, if you could call him that. Edryd examined the coin. It was similar to the one from the night before, only this one, though it must have been from a much older mintage, was still bright and clean and had no scratches on it. The design of the coin was similar but it did not bear Esivh Rhol's image. Instead there was a family crest inscribed with the motto: wisdom is strength. None of it meant anything to Edryd. However, as with the coin from last night, this one also had a thin piercing. Flipping the coin over he could see the same rough map of the island found on the Esivh Rhol coin. This time the piercing ran through a spot Edryd judged to be just south of the roadway he had travelled upon on his way towards town the night he had first arrived in An Innis. The meaning was obvious enough. He could make contact with the Ascomanni at the marked location.

Edryd nibbled on one of the biscuits but felt sick the moment he swallowed the first few crumbs. Realizing he had eaten nothing the previous day, he forced himself to eat a few more pieces. He also managed a few swallows of water, and felt better for it. Edryd stood, brushing away the small pieces of cold bread that had crumbled into his lap, but feeling dizzy, quickly sat back down.

Taking it slow, he stood up once more. Tying the biscuits into a bundle with the cloth and tucking them into his coat, Edryd grabbed the water and dropped Logaeir's letter into the coals of the fire. He placed the coin into a coat pocket and proceeded to stumble out of the shelter and around the low hill that hid it from view. As he began working his way back towards town, he felt his face and found it burning hot to the touch but completely dry and free of perspiration. Edryd loosened his shirt, hoping that it would help to cool him down.

He tried another swallow of water but it made him cough and caused his throat to tighten up. He had been feeling sick for days, ever since he had been hit by Seoras. The damage was far more serious than anyone realized. Seoras had put Edryd in this fragile state, but the exertions Edryd had taken upon himself over the past day and a half had made things much worse.

As Edryd made his way into the town, true to form, An Innis was predictably quiet at this time of the morning. The few people he encountered all seemed startled, and filled with a fear caused by his sudden appearance, they hurried away. At an intersection of two wide streets, Edryd came to a clear pool, whose surface was broken by slow ripples which extended out from the source that fed its shallow depths with clean water. Seeing his reflection in the pool, he now understood the strange reactions. His open shirt revealed the mottled mass of unsightly bruising. It had a foreboding appearance. His undamaged skin alternated between tones, appearing sickly pale wherever it wasn't faintly pulsing red with blood and heat.

The stories he had heard about the Ascomanni and the contagion that left them looking almost dead, with flesh colored to reveal their accursed state, didn't quite match his appearance, but it did call them to mind. Edryd knew there was no truth to any of it, but that didn't mean the people he encountered would dismiss such fears as easily as he had, especially if they had known of his contact with the feared Ash Men, or knew that he had recently spent time on the mainland within the forests.

Edryd pulled his shirt closed, tried futilely to fasten his coat, and continued on, taking great care to avoid being seen. He did not realize at first that he was headed in the direction of Greven's inn. He couldn't go there, not if he wanted to stay hidden from Seoras. Feeling inside of his coat for the set of iron keys, Edryd was comforted when he discovered that they were still there. He had previously decided against it, but it was his best option for now. He didn't have the strength to go wandering around looking for something both abandoned and unsecured, and he certainly was in no condition to try kicking down any doors.

Edryd travelled slowly, pausing frequently so as not to exhaust his remaining strength. He took an indirect route through narrow alleyways in order to limit the risk of being seen. Arriving at the back of the property, Edryd crawled through an opening in one of the overgrown hedges. He tried both keys at a side door and discovered with frustration that they wouldn't engage. The locking mechanism seemed to be broken or rusted shut. Almost as an afterthought, he placed the palm of his right hand on the rough surface of the wooden door and pushed. The thick heavy oak door swung smoothly inward several inches. The lock wasn't broken, it just wasn't locked. Edryd pushed harder and the door opened the rest of the way.

It was immediately apparent that the home was not altogether abandoned. The interior was empty, completely without furniture, and the floors were layered thick with dust, but that dust had been recently disturbed. There were foot trails going in and out of all of the rooms, and several others that led up and down a wide stairway near the main entrance. Edryd knew he shouldn't stay, but he was past the limits of his strength. He found a comfortable corner away from any windows, and wrapping his coat around him, he slumped into an inert pile. A moment later he was sleeping deeply, oblivious to everything.

He woke twice. Once just at the onset of the evening and again late that night. When he woke the second time he found that someone else had come and gone, disturbing the dust on the floor. This was evidenced by a fresh set of booted impressions going in and out of the room, which led to a spot on the floor beside Edryd where someone had lingered for a while, crouching down beside his sleeping form.

Whoever had been there, it seemed they had been hungry. The bundle of cakes had been taken, but thankfully the water skin had been left untouched. Edryd took a long swallow of water and began shaking. He could not stop the trembling. He felt numb with cold, but when he touched his face, Edryd could feel that his skin was fevered and flushed with heat. It occurred to him then, without much understanding, that he might be about to die.

He wondered if he had been poisoned, but if Logaeir had wanted him dead he would have just killed him while he slept, and Edryd knew that he had been ill long before he had actually encountered any of the

Ascomanni. It had been foolish of him to leave the estate, and even more foolish not to leave with Logaeir. Certainly his situation would have been much improved in either case. It was too late now. Sleep overtook him, mercifully deadening his conscious suffering.

Edryd was aware of nothing else until the next afternoon. He wasn't even sure if he was awake or not, but someone seemed to be leaning over him, taking a close look. The man seemed to be worried about him. Edryd's heart ached with the hope that this person was here to help him. He struggled to concentrate, trying to bring the man into focus. Gradually his vision did improve and he realized that it was Aed Seoras. It was not worry that he saw on the man's face, it was irritation.

"You understand your current condition is entirely your own fault," Seoras insisted.

Edryd might have tried to argue that he had never healed from the damage he received during their fight. Seoras was directly responsible and deserved most if not all of the blame that could be assigned. Weak as Edryd was though, he couldn't manage to speak.

"You should have just stayed at the estate," he continued, and then added more to himself than to Edryd, "You are all but dead where you lay... such a damned waste."

***

Aelsian felt troubled. He had not enjoyed a single night of sound sleep since parting company with the man who had called himself Edryd. The navarch knew the man to actually be Captain Aisen of the Sigil Corps. As the heir of House Edorin, Aisen had holdings in Nar Edor as well as others in Ossia as the son and heir of Aedan Elduryn. The latter was of particular importance to Aelsian.

Aelsian was influential in Ossia, and that influence was in large part owed to his connections with the Elduryn family. His position administering the Elduryn properties and business interests made Aelsian important in political and commercial arenas. His position as Navarch of the Ossian First Fleet made him important in military ones. Aelsian's friend and master, Aedan Elduryn, absent for more than a decade now, was probably dead. If so, Aisen was his friend's only living legacy. For Aedan's sake, Aelsian owed to Aisen whatever faithful service he could hope to offer.

He had wanted to take Aisen back to Ossia, to the family estate, but it was perhaps for the best that he had not succeeded in that ambition. Preparations were necessary before Aisen could assume a role in Ossia without provoking those who would certainly fear him. It had not, in any case, been possible. Edryd had not admitted to his identity as Aisen, and Aelsian had chosen not to force the issue. Now that Aelsian was back in Ossia, there were men in whom he would need to confide.

One of those men was Ludin Kar. He needed the scholar's advice. Ludin Kar had spent a lifetime researching and preserving the history of the last age. He had concentrated especially on those matters related to the now long dead, but once nearly omnipotent, Sigil Order. The ongoing and still evolving attempt to revive this ancient order, in the form of a military fraternity in Nar Edor, was being closely watched, as it was sure to have some very interesting and potentially far reaching implications.

Ludin had proven only too eager to meet, so that had been straight forward enough. Implementing precautions that would guarantee a private environment while also obscuring the importance of the meeting, had been a more delicate problem, but Aelsian had come up with a simple solution. He had invited Ludin to use a cottage on the Elduryn estate as a stopover point on a trip from his home at the site of what remained of an old Sigil Order Temple, to the capital a dozen miles up the coast to the north. It didn't matter that Ludin had not been planning such a trip since it didn't take much imagination to come up with things that the scholar could accomplish while in the city that would provide a cover, and it didn't matter if it was noted that he stayed at the Elduryn estate on his way there.

What Aelsian wanted to avoid, if he could, was confirmation that the two of them had met, and at all costs he had to ensure that no part of their conversation would be overheard. Towards that purpose, he had left his residence in the Elduryn family home, and set out on his own in the early morning hours. To anyone else's knowledge, he had gone on a hunting trip alone. Instead he had spent the day in and around the secluded cottage, spending most of his time studying the sword that he carried with him. It was awkwardly long, with no adornment or markings of any kind, but it had a beautiful clean form. It was pristine, as if newly forged and freshly polished, with no outward indication of what Aelsian knew to be its ancient age and history of use in violent conflicts.

Ludin Kar did not recognize the weapon for what it was when he finally arrived. He showed no interest in it at all. The navarch didn't know whether he should have been surprised, but he was. Ludin was the foremost expert in such things after all. Not for the first time, it struck Aelsian that the man's lanky build and nervous mannerisms did not quite match the image of a sedentary individual who spent his days buried in books.

"Aelsian," the scholar said as he entered. "I have to say, I have been tormented by curiosity these past couple of days. This was arranged in such an ordinary fashion. I wasn't sure you didn't think that I really intended a trip into the city. That you are here waiting, confirms there is more to it."

Aelsian didn't answer right away. Instead he took a quick look out the door and surveyed the perimeter of the property. Satisfied, he went back inside, and seeing that Ludin Kar was already seated at the table, he took the seat opposite his friend.

"I am sure I wasn't followed," if that is what you are concerned about, Ludin offered helpfully. "I barely passed three people on the road all day."

"I'm not so worried about anyone who you would have been able to see, as much as something that you couldn't. I've been having troubles with a very persistent draugr, so precautions seemed appropriate," Aelsian explained.

Ludin went white with fear. After an awkward pause, Ludin gave a nervous laugh and suggested hopefully, "You must be having some fun at my expense."

"No, I only wish that were so," Aelsian answered darkly.

"What would such a creature want with you? Certainly it couldn't have the least interest in me, could it?" Ludin was speaking quickly now, trying to reassure himself. "We're in the middle of an overgrown meadow, plants everywhere—a draugr wouldn't much like that."

"That makes this a good location, but I don't know, I think it would bear all that easily enough if its purpose were important. You might have noticed the loosened earth around the perimeter of the cottage and the layer of fine sand on top of it."

Ludin hadn't noticed, but he understood. "I have heard that those foul creatures cannot be seen if they don't wish to be, but by all accounts they remain heavy, much heavier than a living man. Over softened earth, it wouldn't be able to disguise its path."

Aelsian smiled. "Simple, but efficient," he said, congratulating himself.

"What is to stop it from closing in while we are talking?" Ludin asked.

"Nothing," Aelsian admitted. "However, I lost it some time ago, and I'm hoping it has not picked my trail up again. I will check the perimeter once more when we leave. If anything is disturbed, I will at least know we were observed."

Ludin noticed for the first time how tired the navarch appeared. "You have looked better, my friend," he said with concern.

"I have not been getting much rest," Aelsian admitted.

"I suppose encountering a draugr would interfere with my ability to sleep comfortably as well," Ludin sympathized.

"It isn't the thought of draugar that troubles my sleep," Aelsian disagreed. "Well, not just draugar. What is really keeping me up nights is this," he said as he placed the naked blade in the center of the table.

Ludin was slow to react. He studied the weapon with interest and curiosity but it was a good half a minute before he began to understand.

"This isn't...?" he began.

"That is exactly what it is," Aelsian confirmed.

"The sword of House Edorin, a true sigil sword," Ludin gaped in wonder and excitement. "How can you be sure?"

"I'm sure," Aelsian said. "I know the sword. I saw it more than once when Aedan Elduryn carried it. That was years ago. I was entrusted with it two weeks ago by his son, Aisen. It is the Edorin Sigil Blade."

"I have never seen one," Ludin exclaimed. "A good many rich and powerful men the world over claim to possess one, but invariably they have only a fake. There might be another in Nar Edor of course. I know of maybe two in the league cities that might, just might, be legitimate, but this is the first true sigil sword I have ever seen with my own eyes."

Ludin glanced up at Aelsian, seeking permission to handle the weapon. The navarch nodded his head in assent. Carefully, the aging scholar cradled the long blade and pulled it in close, hands trembling slightly as he inspected the weapon with an air of awe and respect. Aelsian could not remember seeing the man so excited.

"You say it was given to you by Aisen?" Ludin Kar asked, his eyebrows rising at an angle. "There has to be more to tell on that point," he insisted.

"I came across him alone on the burning hulk of a wave breaker two weeks ago. He surrendered the sword to our boarding party before he came aboard. He did not admit his identity to my crew, but I knew him. He is very much his father's son."

"What was he doing, apart from slowly sinking into the ocean?"

"He was calling himself Edryd. He told me that he was taken captive by the men on that ship. He claimed that most of them escaped the fire by getting on a boat they were towing, but there were also signs of a fight. For all I know he killed the crew and put their bodies over the side."

"That might be altogether possible. Rumor of Aisen's conflict with his brother in Nar Edor arrived ahead of your return, and by the sound of it, he's a very dangerous man. It is even being said that he activated the sigil sword."

"I can confirm those rumors," Aelsian acknowledged. "Men had gathered outside the closed doors of the crypt at the sounds of swords clashing. They all saw bright white light streaming from gaps at the edges of the doorway towards the end of the fight. There was also a witness inside the crypt. He was the sole nobleman of the four with Beonen that survived. He told a Commander Ledrin of the Sigil Corps that the sword came to life in Aisen's hand, and that it nearly cut Beonen in half in a single stroke."

"You should have returned the sword to Aisen," Ludin commented reprovingly. "It is his by right. You could not hope to wield it."

"I tried to," Aelsian protested, injured by the implied accusation that he had desired the weapon for himself. "Tried to give it back that is, not wield it myself," he clarified. "Aisen wanted nothing to do with it. He suggested that he would throw it over the side if I left it up to him, and I feared he would have made good on the threat."

"I don't understand," Ludin responded.

"I am not sure I do either," Aelsian agreed. "But I was able to use it to trick the draugr into following me."

"What?" Ludin said, a little shocked, and quite certain that Aelsian had skipped a few things.

"I mentioned I was having trouble with a draugr didn't I?" the navarch laughed.

"You didn't say you actively encouraged it to chase you," Ludin countered, voicing his disapproval for such a foolish act.

"When Aisen made his way onto the *Interdiction*, I saw the draugr cross over with him," Aelsian began to explain.

Ludin arched an eyebrow in skepticism.

"By saw, I mean that I saw the boarding plank bow under the weight of the draugr as it followed behind Aisen," the navarch clarified. "It was following him, to what purpose I do not know. Aisen seemed to have been vaguely aware that he was being watched and followed, but had not known what it was."

Ludin shuddered involuntarily.

"I had to help him shake the creature. Together we devised a plan. We met up with another ship, the *Windfall*. Dressed in Aisen's cloak and clothing and with his sword belted at my side, I tried to sneak across just as we were parting. It all went to plan and the creature followed me across."

"Brave, but stupid," Ludin remarked.

"I remained in one of the ship's cabins for several days before making a second transfer to another ship," the navarch continued. "This time we tried to drop the boarding plank before the creature could cross over. The hope was to either trap it on the other ship or maybe even drop the foul thing into the sea."

"Did it work?" Ludin asked anxiously.

"No," replied Aelsian, "it leapt from one ship to the other."

"How could you tell?" Ludin asked. It was a reasonable question to ask; the creature being discussed should have been impossible to see.

"It wasn't a small vessel, but I am not exaggerating when I tell you it rocked to one side when the creature landed on the deck," Aelsian explained.

There was a moment of disbelief, followed by fear, as Ludin realized that his friend was telling the truth. "That thing didn't follow you all the way here did it?" Ludin asked.

"It wouldn't have become the first time Ossia was visited by one of these monsters, but no, I made one more move to another ship,"

Aelsian said. "I think by then it must have known who I was, but unable to follow Aisen, it was instead following me. I kept up the pretense anyway, and still dressed as Aisen, I transferred over in a small boat. Halfway between the ships, I broke open a hole in the bottom of the boat, and jumped over the side into the ocean. I swam like mad until I made it safely over."

"The draugr couldn't follow?"

"I don't think it did. It's said that they can't float. I don't know that you can drown the undead, but with any luck it is trapped at the bottom of a very deep part of the ocean."

"What of Aisen? Where is he now, did you get him back to Nar Edor?"

"He wanted off at the first opportunity at any destination other than Nar Edor. To the best of my knowledge he went ashore just north of the island of An Innis."

"You left him?" Ludin objected reprovingly. "That is no safe place, especially if anyone were to learn who he was."

"Before I left the *Interdiction*, I made contact with Logaeir," Aelsian said defending himself. "He is going to watch out for him."

"Logaeir?" challenged Ludin even more reprovingly. "He won't protect Aisen; he will try to use him."

"Logaeir is a smart man, he knows better than that," Aelsian disagreed.

"You don't need to tell me how smart he is," Ludin countered, "you will remember he was my pupil for a time."

"You agree he is in good hands then," Aelsian argued.

"Competent hands to be sure, yes, but I would not have entrusted Aisen to him. That man has a singular obsession. He means to take An Innis at any cost, and you have dropped a very powerful pawn right into his lap. Logaeir would be able to make use of him in a number of ways."

The navarch's face tightened in concern as he realized that Ludin was right. "It is done and there is no undoing it," Aelsian said unapologetically.

"The question is what to do now," Ludin discerned. "I suppose that is why I am here."

"I need to know more about this weapon, and you know more about these things than anyone else," Aelsian said. "I have not been able to sleep since I left the *Interdiction*, and it is not because of fear of encountering another draugr or anything else. I could almost swear the sword is pushing me to return it to Aisen."

Ludin paused, considering what Aelsian had just suggested. "I suppose it could be possible. From what I have studied, it has been noted that a sigil knight gained a sort of focusing connection channeled by these weapons. It was something that went past a simple reliance on the object. A portion of the warrior's spiritual strength was actually invested within the weapon. The sword, could want to be reunited with its master."

"You're suggesting the weapon is alive?" Aelsian asked in surprise.

"No, you are the one that suggested that," Ludin disagreed. "I'm saying that the sword may be connected to Aisen in such a way that he is not complete when separated from it."

Aelsian was not so sure. Aisen had seemed more eager to be rid of the sword than he had been to free himself from the draugr. The sword might want to be returned to Aisen, but the feeling was not mutual.

"I can tell you one thing for certain, you need to bring this back to Aisen as soon as possible," Ludin said, leaving no room for any other options.

"I mean to return it to him, but I am not sure he will take it back, and I am afraid that I might put a draugr back on his trail if I do," Aelsian said, outlining the intractable situation.

Realizing what Aelsian was about to ask, Ludin interrupted. "Do not trust this weapon with anyone else, myself included."

"I have to trust someone, I can't leave Ossia just yet."

"Then you will have to keep it safe until you can, and then take it back to him directly," Ludin Kar insisted.

"If I can't convince you to do this for me, can I ask you to come with me when the time comes? I would like you to meet him."

There was a long quiet moment as Ludin took in the gravity of the request. "I would be honored," he responded with deep reverence.

Chapter 8

Eithne

Edryd drifted through a wash of invented recollections and half remembered experiences as he surfaced from a prolonged languor. He saw Irial's concerned face more strongly than anything else, covering his head with a cold cloth, worrying over him, and begging him to recover. He imagined Logaeir talking with Irial. They argued, discussing something in serious tones. Edryd also remembered the voice of an old man, speaking in hushed tones as he described an infection that had tainted the suffering man's blood and might soon claim his life. He told Irial that he had done what he could.

Opening his eyes slowly as these impressions faded, Edryd was unprepared for what was about to happen. A young girl, with long black hair and intense blue eyes, stood leaning over his face studying him silently from just mere inches away. He was not half so startled or shocked as she was. She released a pitched shriek that assaulted his eardrums and set his head reeling with pain. Her cries continued, but declined in volume, as she turned and ran from the room. The little banshee had more than thoroughly woken him all of the way up.

Edryd felt out of place as his thoughts began to clear, disconnected from the expected and the familiar, lying flat on his back resting in a soft bed. He tried to sit up, but his efforts failed completely and he felt full of sudden fear, believing that he had been restrained. He had been, in a sense, if you counted being tucked into a bed and being so weak that he was unable to pull the sheets loose. Slowly, and with exhausting effort, he rolled his shoulder and twisted until he was positioned on his side. It took repeated kicks from his bare feet before he eventually freed himself from the cocoon of coverings. He could now move, but he waited, resting from his efforts, before lowering his feet off of the bed. He allowed the weight of his legs to assist in raising the rest of his body into an upright posture as his feet came down upon a smooth stone floor.

Supporting himself with one hand on the rounded end of an oaken post on the bed's headboard, Edryd made a study of his surroundings, searching for clues that might tell him where he was. The doorway through which the young girl had fled moments earlier still hung open, but revealed nothing other than a hallway decorated with a brightly embroidered wall hanging. Turning his focus to the interior of the room, he found it reasonably large but sparsely furnished. He knew that the room was in the corner of a larger structure, for there were two exterior walls, both of which consisted of plaster covered infilling between large wooden timbers that were joined to a solid oak sill atop a stone plinth that formed the lowest section of the walls. One of the two interior walls, which he guessed separated this room from another right beside it, was basic wood paneling. The other, contained the entrance to the bedroom, and had been built primarily out of roughly squared stones.

The low ceiling was made of wooden planking. There were small cracks and fissures between the boards, which allowed in a little light from the loft above the room. The stone wall, against which was set the bed he had been sleeping in, radiated diffuse heat into the room from carefully placed granite blocks, which were made warm through the influence of a fireplace on the other side. A simple wardrobe constructed from pine planks stood in one of the corners, and against the far wall opposite the bed, a small mirror on a simple stand rested atop a narrow table.

Made careful by the weakness that he felt when he stood, as well as the pain that came with each movement he made, Edryd slowly walked across the stone floor towards the wardrobe. He hoped to find something else to wear other than the basic linen nightshirt he was clothed in, but he found only well cared for dresses and an assortment of women's clothing. Edryd realized he had seen someone wearing some of the items before. This was Irial's clothing. Impulse drove Edryd to close the wardrobe out of a sense of propriety.

He moved away and walked over to the front of the table he had noticed earlier. Ignoring assorted combs and a few pieces of modest jewelry, he looked at his image in the mirror and loosened the strings at the top of his shirt. He began to examine the blighted skin across his chest, but saw only faint traces of the bruising, outlined in lingering areas of faded discoloration. The apparent improvement would have been a welcome sight, if it were not for the startling appearance of his emaciated body. To have lost this much weight, he must have been starving for an extended period. Edryd sank at the sight of his atrophied flesh and sickly thin frame, seeing muscles conditioned through years of training now weakened and wasted. The cause of the pain and the fatigue that he was feeling was only too apparent in the reflection staring back at him. Fighting with despair, he shook himself and turned away from the frail image in the mirror. Using what strength he had left, Edryd returned to the bed and collapsed with relief onto the soft mattress.

***

Eithne shivered, not from the cold air outside on the road above the cottage, but from the fright she had taken. She normally enjoyed being outside, listening to the songbirds in the trees and tracking them as they flew through the sky, and she liked nothing more than the feel of the wind coursing over her and the warmth of sunshine on her face. She couldn't enjoy any of this now though. She was in a panic. If something should happen—if the man got worse or if he hurt himself—it would be her fault.

Other than bouts of incoherence early on, which Irial had monitored closely even though the sporadic utterances were impossible to piece together, the man had been silent in his time at the cottage while under Irial's care, lying near to death and completely still. Eithne had observed nothing else in all the countless hours she herself had spent watching the man sleep, as she had taken to doing with Irial's encouragement. Eithne hadn't believed that the man was going to die, as nearly everyone else did, at least not yet; he was too important for that.

Something had felt different to her this morning though, and she had looked in on him, getting close enough to check his breathing. She had often done this before, sitting at his bedside for hours and making up stories about the important things that she imagined he would do in the future, but there had never been any signs that he was recovering, and so she had not imagined that he could actually have been awake.

She was in awe of the poor man, and with no one else there at the cottage, she had been afraid. She had not known what his eyes looked like until that moment when he first opened them. They had been dark and grey, and deeply frightening, and Eithne had not known what she should do. Having had some time now to calm down and think, Eithne knew that she needed to either go and get her sister, or go back home and watch over the man. Irial was in town though, where Eithne was not permitted to go, and Eithne was not yet over her fright; she could not bring herself to return to the cottage.

She would have forced herself to go back now if she could, but nothing seemed to lend her the courage that she needed to do so. Instead, Eithne sat down in the grass beside a high point atop a hill along one side of the old dusty road and looked out to the west, waiting for Irial to return. Thinking of the blame she would face for having left the sickened man alone, and believing that she would be in serious trouble for which she would not be easily forgiven, Eithne began to cry, still not knowing what she could do.

***

It was a long sleepless hour before anyone came. Irial knocked on the wood panel wall to get his attention as she stepped into the room. The dark haired girl who had been there before stood behind Irial. She stared at Edryd darkly from just outside the room, sheltering behind the doorframe. The older woman evaluated Edryd from the entrance, her short height standing only a few inches taller than her young companion.

Edryd turned in the bed and sat so that he could speak. His voice, unused for so long, did not come easily at first, and the words that he could produce were spoken with a dry, faltering inflection.

"Where am I?" he managed to ask.

"You have been sick, Edryd," Irial answered, her concern easing, and showing visible relief upon seeing her patient awake and talking. "You still are. Eithne and I have been taking care of you."

"Who's Eithne?" Edryd asked. Before Irial could give an answer, Edryd thought of the little banshee, whose earsplitting greeting had frightened him and welcomed his waking soul back into the world of the living. Surely that was the answer to his question.

"Eithne is my sister," Irial replied, confirming Edryd's guess by turning to look in the direction of the young, dark haired girl.

Eithne shrunk further behind the doorframe.

"She is a little nervous of you, but don't expect that to last," Irial said.

"I need to go home," Edryd replied without thinking, his throat loosening and the words coming a little more easily now.

"You don't have a home, not here in An Innis," Irial said, her voice soft and gentle. "You have to remain where you are for a while. It is going to take some time for you to recover."

As if taking those words to be a challenge, Edryd stood and tried to head towards the doorway. Eithne disappeared in a flash at his approach, receding even further into the hallway, but Irial cut Edryd off, and grabbing hold of his arms, awkwardly walked him backwards to the bed and sat him down. He felt doubly humiliated when he discovered that Irial was more than strong enough to counter his attempts to stand back up. She kept him in a seated position and turned back to the doorway where the young girl had now reappeared.

"Eithne, bring a bowl of broth from the cook pot," she ordered.

Eithne, who had yet to speak in front of Edryd, or even make a sound apart from the one very high pitched shriek, left without a word. She returned less than a minute later. The cook pot must have been nearby.

Drawing a chair up beside the bed and collecting the bowl from Eithne, Irial took a seat and prepared to help Edryd eat. He wanted to protest that he was not so weak that he couldn't hold a spoon, but he didn't. Instead he allowed her to portion the warm broth and place it to his lips. He hadn't felt hungry, but as the soup hit his stomach he reacted immediately. His weakened body trembled, as if in response to being summoned from out of its long inert state. It made him all the more aware of his pitiable condition, and he felt intensely vulnerable, but the sensation of warmth in his stomach was wonderful. He wanted more but he was embarrassed at being fed like an infant. Sensing the discomfort, and understanding its source, Irial offered the bowl to Edryd.

"Do you think you can hold it steady?" she asked.

Edryd remained weak, but the trembling was subsiding, allowing him to load up the spoon without difficulty. He carefully moved it into his mouth to prove that he was capable. Greedily, he shoveled in several more spoonfuls, each one faster than the last.

"Not so quickly," Irial admonished. "We need to go slowly, or you will make yourself worse."

Obediently, Edryd took a more measured pace and began to savor the warm soup, noticing its flavors for the first time. There were no vegetable pieces or chunks of meat, but he could clearly taste the wild celery and the rich duck fat that flavored the broth. There had been only an inch of liquid in the bowl and he finished that quickly. Edryd wanted another helping, but he was too proud to ask for more.

"I have to go back to the estate, but I will be back for good sometime midafternoon," Irial said as she collected the empty bowl from Edryd.

"Does Seoras know I'm here?" Edryd asked. It was a stupid question. Edryd didn't know where 'here' was exactly, but Seoras wouldn't have been uninformed on his whereabouts. He remembered enough to know that Seoras was the last person he had seen before he collapsed.

"You are here with his permission," Irial answered, in a tone which suggested the semblance of an apology.

Edryd wondered why he wasn't kept in a room at the estate. It would have been easier for Irial and others to have cared for him there. Deciding not to rush an answer to that question, Edryd instead took what comfort there was in knowing he had some distance from his captor. Irial's home was preferable to the dark empty estate that Seoras dominated, so he could count himself lucky to be here.

Irial placed her hands on her knees, preparing to get up. Edryd didn't know why but he did not want Irial to go. He tried, but could think of no objection that would justify asking her to stay.

"Eithne will be here if you need anything before I get back." Irial said before leaving.

Alone in his room he overheard Irial talking to Eithne out in the hallway. "In an hour, bring him milk. If he wants it you can give him more broth, but under no circumstances let him have anything solid to eat," she said.

"I will make sure," Eithne answered, her voice nervous but determined.

With his eyes closed, Edryd listened to Irial's booted footfalls on the stone floor, and then the sounds of iron latches moving on a door as Irial exited the cottage. He did not hear Eithne when she entered, softly stepping into the room on leather soled shoes, but he sensed her movement from the air she disturbed as she took up a position in the chair beside his bed, attentively warding over him.

Edryd opened his eyes with trepidation, anxious about a possible repeat of the frightened performance Eithne had given before. She wasn't frightened this time. Rather, she had on a mothering look that might have been mimicked from the one Irial had displayed earlier. Realizing that Edryd had noticed her, Eithne's entire demeanor changed. Her dark eyebrows narrowed, and her face tightened in a look of annoyed malice and disapproval. She hadn't mastered this expression. It was all very serious on the surface, but beneath it all she was barely hiding and restraining a feeling of profound self-amusement. Though the whole effect was vaguely uncomfortable, it made Edryd want to laugh. He couldn't tell what Eithne was thinking, but her fear of him was fading, and it was being replaced by something else.

"Did I do something wrong?" Edryd asked, playing along.

Eithne shook her head, but said nothing.

"I am sure I did something," Edryd insisted, "or you wouldn't look so upset."

Eithne refused to react to the comment.

"I suppose you are not going to tell me then," Edryd sighed.

"You're supposed to be dangerous," Eithne finally responded. "But you're not. You can't do anything."

Her words were meant to sound mean, but there was no meanness in them. She was curious, and she was clearly gaining confidence through mocking and provoking him. She had, however, quite neatly summarized precisely how Edryd saw himself in that moment.

"You probably can't even hold a sword," she continued.

"I can do much more than that," Edryd reacted automatically. Thinking about it though, right at this moment he wasn't at all sure that he could. Her comment probably wasn't random. Irial had told her that he was a swordsman.

Eithne eyed him with skepticism.

"Get me a stick or a long branch," Edryd offered, "we can practice right here and I will show you a trick or two."

Eithne eyed him with even more skepticism.

"Get one for yourself as well, and I can show you how to hold it."

"I don't want one. Girls don't fight," Eithne said, insisting upon this point as if it was the most obvious thing in the world and Edryd was a complete idiot.

"Then what do they do?" Edryd asked

The question momentarily confounded Eithne as she struggled for an answer. Now she really was a little bit angry with him. A satisfied smile broke across her face as she found her response. "A woman uses knowledge and intelligence," she declared.

"And you are a woman then?" Edryd asked, showing amusement at her comment. Eithne didn't look like she was any older than ten.

Eithne was well and truly mad now, and she forgot what little was left of her fear of, and her respect for, this man who had insulted her. Mentally, Eithne was intelligent beyond her age. Emotionally and physically though, she was even more immature than she looked, and owing to the one, she was highly sensitive about the other.

"I'm eleven years old," she said with emphasis on the eleven. This was quite old in her estimation. She clearly was taking great pride in all the wisdom that those eleven years had conveyed upon her.

"That is a long time," Edryd agreed.

Eithne couldn't tell if Edryd was being sarcastic or not, but she began to calm down. "A woman studies things, and uses persuasion and reason to achieve what she wants," she continued, elaborating on her previous thought.

Edryd smiled. He found he could easily agree with most of that. "So in other words, with blackmail and by means of other devious manipulations," Edryd teased.

Eithne's mouth fell open in surprise. Closing it tight, she turned on her heel and made an exaggerated march out of the room to show her disdain. For a moment, Edryd wondered how badly he had upset her, but that notion was dispelled when he heard Eithne vainly trying to stifle a fit of laughter out in the hallway.

A few hours and five confrontations later, Eithne was getting better at her mask of malice and disapproval, improving rapidly with practice. It was all good humored and playful, but still pretty perplexing to Edryd. He didn't understand the game, but somehow it was fun to play along. Each conversation had been profitable as well, yielding something new each time.

He learned that she and her sister took care of six goats, seventeen chickens, an herb garden, and a plot of vegetables that included carrots, potatoes, and onions. Added to all of that now was one fairly useless and enfeebled stranger who was more trouble to care for than any other part of the small farm.

He learned more useful things as well. He had been nearly dead to the world for over three weeks, and he had indeed been taken for one of the dreaded Ash Men by people who had seen him stumbling through the town on the day he had collapsed. He was most certainly considered a source of contagion. No one apart from Irial, Eithne, and Seoras was to know where he was. Irial it seemed, was risking a lot. Seoras had acquiesced to Irial's suggestion that he should be cared for in her home, but that had only been because he was convinced that Edryd would not survive. If Edryd was not going to live, just as well that he died quietly somewhere else. Now that he was awake, it wasn't clear what would happen.

Eithne had also let it slip that her sister had plans for Edryd, but Eithne didn't seem to know what was involved. This was hardly an unfamiliar experience. It seemed to Edryd like everyone he met wanted to use him in one way or another. Ordinarily, Edryd would have been frustrated, but he found that he was instead anxiously hoping that he could be useful. He certainly owed a debt, and would do whatever he could to help Irial.

Irial's return interrupted the middle of yet another mini confrontation. It was only as she heard Irial approaching the house that Eithne realized she had never brought Edryd any milk. In a blur of motion, she was gone and back again with an earthen pitcher and a cup made out of a hollowed-out stone. Pouring quickly, she then extended the cup toward Edryd.

"Drink it," she whined urgently, "do it quickly."

Edryd wanted to tell her that it didn't really matter, but Eithne looked so sincerely worried that he took the milk and began to drink. The milk was warm and not quite fresh either, and though it was immensely satisfying to his starved body, he was having trouble finishing it.

"Do it faster," she pled as he tried to swallow, causing him to choke.

Recovering, Edryd drained the contents of the cup and dried his mouth on his sleeve just as Irial was entering the room.

"Oh good, you gave him the milk," Irial said. She was pleased to see Edryd doing well.

"This is his second cup," Eithne lied, "I brought him another right after you left."

Edryd nearly coughed up what was left of a last swallow of milk that he had not gotten completely down.

"We mustn't give him too much, Eithne," Irial cautioned. "He needs to build up slowly."

"Don't worry, I took good care of him," she replied. She flashed Edryd a subtle warning look as if to say he shouldn't dare try and contradict her.

"She certainly did," Edryd agreed. "I can't say I wouldn't have preferred a good piece of roasted meat, but the spiced chicken dumplings she made me were delicious."

Remembering Irial's strict warning that she was not to give him anything solid, Eithne gasped, the sharply inhaled air remaining momentarily caught in her lungs. Believing she was about to unfairly be in trouble, Eithne started in on a furious protest that she had done no such thing when Irial began to laugh.

"She isn't much of a student in the kitchen," Irial said. "If Eithne had made you dumplings, you wouldn't have been able to describe them with the word 'delicious'."

Eithne flushed red and stomped out of the room, the expression of malice and disdain all too real this time.

"That has to be the tenth time today she has done that," Edryd reported, exaggerating only a little. "At least she is angry with you this time instead of me."

"Eithne has become very invested in getting you better, and takes watching over you very seriously," Irial said. "You probably shouldn't tease her like that."

Edryd's smile faded as guilt began to rise slowly to the surface. "I expect that I have been a real burden, and I must seem ungrateful," he said with remorse.

"I won't say it was no trouble," Irial admitted. "But your survival is a matter of no small consequence... important to many others to be sure, but not least of all to me either."

Edryd knew he was taking it the wrong way, but his heart ran faster at hearing Irial say he was important to her. He remembered Eithne had mentioned that Irial needed him. Rather than follow his awkward interest in pursuing clarity in the matter, he changed the topic to a related subject.

"If you know the answer," Edryd began cautiously, "can you tell me what it is that Seoras wants with me?"

Irial paused before responding. "Do you remember I told you that he trains enslaved men to be soldiers?" she asked.

Edryd nodded. He did remember, but he wasn't sure how it related to him.

"To say that he trains soldiers doesn't really suffice. When he finishes, they are more than just ordinary soldiers, they are special," she continued.

"I'm sorry," Edryd scoffed, unconsciously adopting an officious and condescending tone, "but from what I have seen there is very little that is special about his soldiers. Hagan and Cecht were poorly trained, ill-mannered, and lacked any discernable discipline." In truth, both had been surprisingly fast and resilient, but Edryd didn't feel like either could do anything other than cheapen the very concept of what a professional soldier should be. Had Edryd been responsible in any way for their oversight or training, he would have been quick to avoid accepting credit for the results.

"Those two are examples of his failures," Irial corrected. "His more accomplished students have been dealt a more horrible fate than simply remaining in service to Seoras here in An Innis. Those that show proficiency and learn to shape darkness are made into thralls to undead spirit creatures that serve Aed Seoras's master."

"You're talking of the draugar," Edryd said with a shudder that came despite his best efforts to remain calm. He didn't know what was meant by 'shaping darkness' but his own experiences with being followed and pursued relentlessly by a draugr pushed all other thoughts from his mind.

"Yes, that is one name for them," Irial confirmed.

Skipping the more obvious question as to who was Aed Seoras's master, Edryd focused on his more immediate predicament. "He means to make me one of these thralls then?"

"I don't think so," Irial disagreed. "He seems to see you as something else."

"Meaning what?"

"I think he believes you could become his equal, or even more than that," Irial explained. "I think he is looking for an ally and partner."

"An ally against whom or a partner in what?" Edryd questioned.

"I am sure I do not know," Irial answered truthfully but unhelpfully.

Edryd began to understand just how difficult his position was, and wondered if it might have been better if he had simply not survived his illness. He had narrowly slipped a draugr who seemed to have a personal mission to unrelentingly follow him across the breadth of the known world, only to end up mixed up with a man who paired unwilling captives and slaves to those very same deathly creatures. He could hardly have found a less safe place to escape to.

"I have no right to ask more of you, but when we met you told me you could help me leave An Innis," Edryd reminded her, holding onto the small hope that this gave him.

"I am afraid it is too late for that," Irial responded. "I should not have spoken about that, not without better understanding the situation. I was lacking some important information, or I would never have suggested it."

Edryd assumed this to mean that Seoras's interest in him was much stronger than she had imagined, and he didn't push the matter any further. He would have to face the realities of the situation without complaint. Seeing the look of sudden resignation on his face, Irial made an effort to reassure him. "No reason to worry for the moment, you are nowhere near well enough to leave here. I can buy you time to figure things out before you will need to resume training with Seoras."

"I really am grateful for your help," Edryd said sincerely. "Tell me what I can do for you in return. I am sure there is something."

Appearing uncertain, Irial looked Edryd over intently, considering what she should say. "We will talk of it when you are better," she finally offered, explaining nothing at all.

Irial closed the conversation by asking after anything he might need. Insisting that he didn't need anything, Edryd was then left alone in the room, sitting on the edge of the bed. Immediately, he regretted not having asked about a change of clothes.

It was no more than a few minutes later when Eithne intruded upon his solitude. "If you were wondering," she began slowly and seriously, "Irial was just being mean when she said that I was bad at cooking." Eithne seemed to be very worried on this point.

"I'm sure she was," Edryd replied.

"I don't know how to make chicken dumplings," she admitted. "But I watch over the goats and chickens, and I work in the garden. I help harvest vegetables, I tend the fire, and I help clean everything."

Edryd smiled as he listened to the unending list of things that Eithne did to contribute.

"If I don't know how to cook, it is because she doesn't either," she continued, rationalizing any perceived shortcomings she might have. "I've seen how she does it though. If she would let me, I could cook what she does," Eithne insisted. She didn't seem to realize that she was contradicting her earlier claim that Irial couldn't cook at all.

"You have left something important out," Edryd objected.

Eithne tensed, expecting Edryd to challenge the glowing review she had just given herself.

"You know how to nurse a poor sick stranger back to health," Edryd said. "I understand I have you to thank for watching over me and getting me better."

Eithne blushed happily at the compliment. Suddenly self-conscious of her reaction, her mood shifted and she tried to feign indifference.

"Maybe you can give me a tour now that I am well enough," Edryd suggested.

Eithne's eyes narrowed into a familiar expression. "You are not well enough," she said. "And what makes you think I want to show you around my house?" she argued as an added measure.

Trying to demonstrate that he was strong enough, Edryd stood up and began walking towards the door, ignoring the aches felt in just about every muscle in his body.

"Well come on then," Eithne said with an exaggerated sigh, realizing that he was determined. Without further argument, and in truth quite pleased to be relied upon as the source of privileged information, she led him out the door.

On the other side of the doorway Edryd found himself in a short, confined hallway, open on either end with archways that led into the main living area. This space served solely as a screen to the entrances to the bedrooms. It was an interesting but apparently unnecessary feature that struck Edryd as an unfortunate misuse of space. A stone fireplace and a kitchen area could be seen through the archway to his right. Eithne headed in the opposite direction into an open doorway a few feet away that led to the other bedroom.

"This... is my room," she declared proudly. It was the same size as Irial's room, but crowded with two beds, a trunk, a dressing table, and a small shelf full of books, there was scarcely any space left in which to move around.

The realization that his presence had meant that Irial was now sharing a room with Eithne, mortified him in no small measure. "I'm sorry that you had to give up part of your room," Edryd began to apologize.

Eithne interrupted him before he could say more. "It's only temporary," she said. Her eyes brightening in anticipation, she suddenly blurted out, "let's go to your room!"

She had not meant the room he had been staying in. Edryd followed after her as she bounced excitedly out of the room and hurried through the nearest archway into the large double-bayed open hall that made up the main living area in the cottage. Stout oak timbers rose up at regular intervals along the low stone plinth walls, curving as they ascended. Joined tightly at the top with mirrored timbers from the opposite side, they supported a steeply sloped thatch roof. A fire pit, lacking coals or ash or any other signs of recent use, dominated the center of the room. Thatch, blackened by smoke all around a small opening in the center of the hall, suggested that the fire pit had at times been used extensively in the past.

Two tables filled the far side of the room, one a large oak slab bordered by long low benches and the other a smaller roughly squared surface covered by a linen cloth and edged with mismatched chairs neatly arranged on each side. Irial sat beside the fireplace in the corner next to the bedrooms, comfortably relaxing in a chair while tending to the contents of a large iron pot heated by hot coals and a low flame in the fireplace. Closed doors along the wall opposite his current position suggested rooms on the other side of the living area. They lacked the screening hallway, but he anticipated that they would otherwise be largely identical to those he had just seen.

Eithne headed directly toward the door nearest the back of the cottage, pushed it inward, and disappeared inside. Pausing to acknowledge a curious look from Irial, Edryd followed after the enthusiastic guide. The room shared the same dimensions as the others he had seen, but had fewer furnishings. Seeing a modest bed against the back wall, Edryd took the opportunity to both test the bed and rest his tiring body by taking a seat on the wool stuffed mattress.

It seemed obvious that the room had been prepared for him, even though he had not been put in it. He wondered why with so much space he had been using Irial's room and she had doubled up with Eithne. Then he began to notice how much colder this room was. Irial's room shared a wall with the kitchen fireplace and would probably have been the warmest place in the cottage. The arrangement had been out of necessity, and wouldn't continue. Edryd's attention was then caught by the solid wood bar supports fastened to either side of the door frame. An oak beam matching the width of the supports stood upright in the corner. He tried to remember if this had been a feature in the other rooms as well but couldn't recall. Certainly, housing a strange man in the room next door, he wouldn't be surprised if they barred their bedroom door each night.

Eithne looked at Edryd expectantly, gauging his reactions and seeking approval. "It's a nice clean room," Edryd remarked. "I'll bet you helped get it ready specifically for me," he added.

"She did," Irial said from the doorway. "You are only just beginning to recover though, and you are not well enough yet to move into a drafty room like this one."

Overcoming his surprise at her sudden appearance, Edryd met her concerned stare directly. "I would be far more comfortable in here, and there are plenty of blankets. I'll be fine," he insisted.

Irial looked doubtful and clearly had her misgivings, but she didn't argue.

"Your things are already here," Eithne said, looking pleased and pointing to a trunk along the outside wall. His dark oiled coat hung on a peg in the corner and his shoes and belt rested atop the trunk Eithne had identified, which he assumed must have held his clothing. He was too tired to do much more in the way of moving around, so there wasn't much point in getting dressed, but it was a relief to know where his belongings were. Eithne appeared dissatisfied when he didn't open and inspect the trunk.

"We will try it for the night," Irial said, "but if your condition worsens in any way, you'll be moving back to a warmer room."

Irial had Eithne bring him another bowl of warm broth, and she watched as he finished it. Afterwards she wouldn't leave until he agreed to get some rest. Feeling rather foolish and uncomfortable at being mothered like a young child, Edryd allowed her to help him into bed, and without protest, he also allowed her to also tuck the sheets in tightly around him. Sleep refused to come at first, but when it did he settled into a deep uninterrupted slumber.

Chapter 9

King of the Ascomanni

The next morning, Edryd woke to find that he was alone in the cottage. Feeling determined not to waste another day lying in bed, Edryd dressed slowly while making plans to explore the rest of the building. He was still weak, but he had more energy and his body no longer ached so much with each exertion. It felt good to move around and he felt light on his feet. This wasn't just in his head he realized; he was in fact much lighter than he had been.

Eithne had shown him nearly everything there was to see the night before. There was one last room which remained unexplored, but it was barred shut from the inside. Curiously, there was also pair of sliding wooden bolts attached to this side of the door that allowed the room to be secured from the outside as well. He could think of only one purpose for this: it could be used to lock someone inside. He was glad that this was not the room that had been prepared for him. Feeling chilled by a current of cold air as he stood beside the door, Edryd decided to return to his room, where he retrieved his coat from where it had been hung on a peg in the corner.

Satisfied with his explorations within, Edryd wrapped himself in the dark coat before turning back around, going through the open hall, and then out the front entrance into the bright morning sunlight in front of the cottage. His canvas coat was not especially warm, but it was of a good quality and provided protection both from the damp and from the wind. It was loose and comfortable, and he had to overlap the open ends a good four to six inches before it went tight around his body. Choosing not to think about this in terms of how thin and weak he had become, Edryd instead admired the cut of the coat, feeling not quite like the person he had once been, and welcoming the idea that he could become someone different.

Eithne was tending to a group of goats penned inside a fenced yard a short distance to the south of the cottage. Settling down on a large stump beside the wood pile that was stacked just in front of the house, Edryd watched as Eithne separated two milking goats and led them to a feeding trough. She glanced in his direction only once, and then proceeded to collect milk from first one and then the other, partially filling a wooden pail in the process. When she finished, Eithne transferred the contents into a hardened clay jug, and with one hand on each handle, she began lugging it up the gentle slope that led up towards the entrance of the cottage. Edryd instinctively wanted to help, but he decided against it. Better to be thought of as weak and enfeebled, than to publicly demonstrate it.

Eithne paid him no heed, either distracted by her burden, or more probably making a deliberate effort to ignore him as she disappeared inside without any comment, leaving Edryd to believe that she was annoyed with his failure to offer help. Alone once more, and feeling the uninhibited freedom that came with such solitude, Edryd stood up and went through a series of unhurried motions. It was a type of mock combat exercise, designed to develop efficient transitions between attack and defense. In this instance he was not training, for he needed no practice in these skills. His intent was to test the extent of his recovering energy reserves and to measure what strength remained in his body. His movements and his timing were good, but he could feel that his strength and his stamina were compromised. Even so, Edryd found himself wishing that he had a good solid sword. He couldn't truly test his conditioning without the heavy weight of a finely balanced weapon in his hands.

Edryd spotted a long-handled axe resting head down against the wood pile. It was no suitable stand-in for an actual sword, but it would test his strength and start the process of reconditioning his disused muscles. A considerable supply of fuel had been piled up, ready to be cut into smaller pieces. It was work begging to be done. Edryd was discouraged to discover that he could not raise the axe head without difficulty, and worried that this would tire him out before he could accomplish much, but he worked out a technique quickly enough. Lifting the axe above his head, he let the weight of the tool do much of the work, bringing the force stored in his muscles to bear on the task only after the axe wedge began to descend.

It was only a short while before he had to stop and rest, tired and drenched in sweat, but he had managed to produce a reasonable pile of split logs. His exposed hands ached both from gripping the axe and from the cold air. He stuck them inside his coat for warmth before standing up straight to take a look around in an effort to get his bearings. The roadway he had travelled on that first night in An Innis was just north of the cottage. He was far enough away that he could not see the town, but the palace atop the peak was plainly visible. It was an isolated location, near enough to but also a healthy distance away from the settlement at the western edge of the island.

Realization struck Edryd in a moment of clarity. Fumbling through a pocket in his coat, he confirmed that it was still there. The coin Logaeir had left behind with his message glimmered in the morning light. The piercing in the coin matched the location of this cottage perfectly. Irial's home was an Ascomanni safe house. Random pieces of information were now connecting together. Irial and Logaeir had been exchanging information from the beginning. She knew exactly who he was. He had any number of immediate questions, but there was no one there to answer them. Eithne wouldn't know much—and he didn't like the idea of trying to make her to reveal what little she might—but lacking another means to learn anything useful, Edryd collected an armful of wood and headed back inside the cottage.

Inside, Eithne was busy trying to appear as if she had not noticed his entrance. A small crack of an opening between the shutters and a dent in a cushion on the bench beneath the window near the front door, exposed Eithne's demeanor for what it was, a transparent attempt to conceal that she had spent the last half hour watching him.

"Should I put these beside the fire?" Edryd asked, tilting his head towards the bundle of firewood cradled in his arm.

Eithne's eyes tightened in the way that they did when she wanted him to believe she was angry with him.

"What have I done?" he asked as he deposited the wood atop a dwindling pile beside the fire. When she didn't respond, Edryd walked over to the small table and dropped eagerly into one of the chairs. "I'm sorry I didn't help with the goats," he apologized, guessing at the source of her irritation.

"I wouldn't have let you," Eithne declared firmly. "And who told you to cut wood for the fire?"

"I just thought..." Edryd began.

"If you get sick again, I will be blamed for it," she said, cutting his defense short. Pouring Edryd a cup full of milk, she brought it over and planted it on the table. "Irial says you need to drink more milk. It's what will help you the most."

Edryd gladly accepted the cup and consumed its contents without complaint. Eithne refilled the cup and he drained that quickly too. The milk tasted better this time. It was fresher and he was also becoming more accustomed to it. Eithne seemed to relax upon seeing Edryd demonstrate an improved appetite.

"I promise not to do any more work without permission," he said, easing Eithne's demeanor even further. Sensing an opportunity, Edryd took the coin out of his coat pocket and placed it on the tablecloth. "Have you ever seen one of these?" he asked.

"That's from Uncle Logaeir!" she said excitedly.

"Uncle Logaeir?"

"Well he isn't my Uncle," Eithne clarified. "I don't think he is anyone's Uncle really, that's just what I call him."

"How do you and Irial know him?" Edryd asked.

"He is one of the Ash Men!" she boasted conspiratorially.

Despite his desire to get Eithne to provide more information, Edryd cautioned her against it. "Are you sure you should be telling me this?" he asked.

A look of fear and panic spread across Eithne's young face. "But, you have his token, and Irial said that you know him," she said with startled worry.

"Its fine," Edryd said, trying to calm her down, "the two of us are old friends."

Color returned to her face as she began to breathe normally again. "That was mean," Eithne sniffed, "you made me think I did something wrong."

"I didn't mean to," Edryd apologized, "I just didn't think that the two of you knew him."

"Irial and Logaeir are friends too," Eithne explained. "They knew each other when they were kids. He left An Innis when he wasn't very old, but he came back."

Eithne might have thought she was explaining all there was to know, and the intelligence that she had provided did suggest a reason for Logaeir's obsession with conquering An Innis, but it did not fully explain how he knew Irial or how they were connected to each other. For some reason, Edryd wasn't quite sure whether he wanted a more detailed account. "I'm sure Logaeir and I will have the chance to catch up with each other later," he said, trying to reassure her again that she hadn't said too much.

"He'll be here tonight," Eithne volunteered. "He is coming to talk with you and Irial."

Still amazed at how forthcoming Eithne was, Edryd pressed for more. "To talk about what?" he wondered.

"Something about the Red Prince," Eithne answered.

Apparently Eithne knew pieces, perhaps just things she had overheard and not fully understood. Edryd had no desire to let her know that he was the man they were calling the Red Prince, and he very much preferred it if she never did. She already knew more than was safe.

"What would you know about the Red Prince?" he asked innocently.

"He joined the Ascomanni. They are all following him now, and he is going to help Uncle Logaeir take back An Innis."

This was surprising news to Edryd of course, but he couldn't very well explain to Eithne why it was also all very impossible.

"You're sure?" he asked with a bit of an edge to his voice, unable to completely disguise the surge of anger he felt at hearing that he had supposedly become the leader of the Ascomanni.

Ignoring his tone, or perhaps simply failing to notice it, Eithne nodded her head in confirmation. She was quite certain. "Everyone in town knows he is here," she insisted. "He has a ship with red sails, and the Ascomanni have been attacking ships under the banner of the Red Prince for weeks now."

"And you say the Red Prince is going to attack An Innis?"

"Well, I heard Uncle Logaeir say that he had to use the Red Prince in order to make it all work," Eithne explained. "Irial got mad, but he said there wasn't any other way."

"She isn't the only one that's angry," Edryd responded before he could catch himself. Seeing a nervous uncertain look on Eithne's face, he quickly gave a vague explanation for his comment, "Logaeir is playing a very dangerous game. I am worried he won't like some of the consequences."

He had meant to soften his tone and sound concerned for Logaeir, but what had come out was a thinly veiled and none too subtle threat directed at the Ascomanni strategist. Eithne didn't seem to notice. "Don't worry about Uncle Logaeir, he will have thought everything through already," she said with complete confidence. "He is always five steps ahead of everyone, you'll see," she added, obviously repeating something she had heard others say.

"Maybe," Edryd said, managing to bring his anger under better control. If Logaeir was really going to be here tonight, it was going to make for an interesting evening. For a second time this morning, Edryd keenly felt the absence of a good sharpened blade. It made him feel... incomplete. He wondered if there might be something stored somewhere on the property, but he couldn't bring himself to ask Eithne. He also knew he was not strong enough yet to be thinking about such things.

Edryd thought about Eithne's observation that Irial had been angry with Logaeir. It was comforting to learn that she was actively against whatever strategy Logaeir had settled on and was not participating in it, but he would need to determine exactly what her relationship was with this scheming and duplicitous would-be conqueror of An Innis. Irial had provided him with useful information about Aed Seoras. Hopefully she would be prepared do the same with respect to Logaeir.

As the day progressed, Eithne spent most of afternoon outside. She had demanded that he remain indoors, as she was only too willing to fully enforce Irial's orders that he should be resting. There really were an unending number of things that needed to be done about the property on a daily basis, and Eithne was staying well on top of them. While she worked, Edryd passed the time by going through all of the books he could find in the house. One was an extensive collection of information on medicinal herbs. It seemed to have been used a great deal by Irial. Another gave instructions on animal husbandry.

He found others that were more along his lines of interest, including a philosophical treatise on the nature of reality. He liked to consider himself reasonably educated, and by Nar Edor standards, where he was from, he would most certainly have qualified as extremely well-read. But distracted as he was by Logaeir's misappropriation and misuse of his name, Edryd didn't have the concentration needed to properly absorb and interpret the concepts described by the author, who argued that all existence was a malleable manifestation of our imperfect perception of a deeper and simpler underlying frame. Edryd seemed to be able to tease any meaning he wanted out of that asseveration, which as he thought about it, was perhaps a small part of the point that was being made.

Several frustrating and unproductive hours later, which had been spent entirely on reading through this baffling text, Edryd realized that the entire day had passed him by, becoming aware of the late hour only after he noticed that it had become too dark to read. Eithne brought more milk and a lantern, and reminded him that Irial wanted him to drink as much as he could.

"I like that one," Eithne said. She peered across the table at the open book with interest while he finished his milk.

Edryd, irritated by his inability to digest the material, wasn't about to believe that Eithne could possibly have read the book, let alone understood it. "Don't go and spoil the ending," he said.

Eithne's eyes narrowed in her signature and peculiar way, in what was at this point a much overused expression of disapproval. "It isn't a story book," she lectured. "It doesn't have an ending."

"A book... with no ending?" Edryd teased, pretending to be simple.

"It says that nothing is real," she explained, ignoring his remark and summarizing the books contents as simply as she could for Edryd's benefit.

"I understood that much," Edryd said. Apparently Eithne did know something about the book.

"I don't think that's right though," she continued. "I know I'm real. The table is real. I'm pretty sure you're real too."

"I'm glad I'm not some figment of your imagination," Edryd said with mock relief, "but I can't say that I know how I should feel about ranking as possibly being less real than the table." Whatever her understanding of the book, it was without any real depth. He was impressed nonetheless that she understood it at all.

"Well I have known this table for as long as I can remember," Eithne laughed, "I've only known you for about a month."

If there had been any reason to doubt it, it was becoming ever more evident that Eithne was unusually smart. Perhaps she did understand the book better than he did. He found himself laughing at her joke. Doing so lifted him out of the disgruntled mood he had been in, and made Eithne beam happily with confident satisfaction.

The moment was interrupted by a sound coming from the locked room. Edryd was startled, but Eithne ran to the door without the least hint of concern. Before Edryd could react or recover from his surprise, the door to the room swung inward, and out walked Logaeir with a foolish grin on his face. Eithne held out her arms expectantly and Logaeir grabbed her up in a big bear hug.

"You are getting too big and fat to be picked up like that," he said as he dropped her back to the ground, pretending he had hurt his back.

Eithne kicked him as hard as she could in the shin, which wasn't very hard, and he collapsed backward onto a bench, grabbing his leg in exaggerated distress. "That was mean and it wasn't funny," she said with a smile that suggested that she had thought it was at least a little bit funny. If nothing else, she had enjoyed the opportunity it had given her to kick him.

Edryd would have laughed at this spectacle, if he hadn't wanted at that moment to kick Logaeir a good deal harder than Eithne had just done.

"Were you in there all along?" Edryd asked in amazement.

Logaeir looked around, confused by the question. "What... in the room?" he said, requesting clarification. "No, not in the room, no," he said answering his own question, realizing that to Edryd it must have seemed like he had miraculously appeared from nowhere at all.

"Then how?" Edryd asked. "I thought that was some sort of makeshift prison."

"Wouldn't make much of a prison," Logaeir laughed. "Lock someone in there and it would barely be five minutes before he found the escape hatch in the floor and was out the other end of the tunnel."

"Why is there a tunnel?" Edryd asked, still a little confused.

"Wouldn't be so good for the girls if they were seen letting an Ascomanni in the front door," Logaeir responded. "When I visit, I take care to keep it a secret."

The bolts on this side of the door made more sense now.

"You look good for a dead man," Logaeir said. "Wasn't sure it was true when I heard you had rejoined the living."

Edryd's face curled into a scowl, but he didn't say anything. He couldn't figure out where to begin.

"Back from the brink like that, you have more of a claim to the title of Ash Man than any of the rest of us," Logaeir said, more to himself than to Edryd.

"I am not one of your Ash Men," Edryd said, "even if you have thought it your privilege to make me one."

Feeling the anger behind Edryd's words, Logaeir turned his attention for a moment to Eithne, who stood a few feet away unobtrusively taking in every word exchanged by the two men. "Could you go up to the road and wait for Irial, she should be on her way soon," he said to Eithne. "I need to talk privately with Master Edryd for a little while."

Edryd thought she would protest being sent off, but Eithne obediently left without complaint. He could not help noticing the marked contrast between the judgmental disregard he was typically subjected to, and the unreserved respect she was showing to Logaeir. He wasn't in a competition to impress anyone, but the disparity did not make him like Logaeir any better.

"You linked my name to a group of murderous thieves," Edryd said to Logaeir, laying out the accusation only once Eithne was well away from the cottage.

"And what name is that?" Logaeir asked rhetorically. "Aisen? When we last met you did not answer to it. You were anxious to be rid of the name. If you mean instead the title Blood Prince, I didn't think you liked that one either. I believe you insisted your name was Edryd."

Logaeir had a point, the accuracy of which was unassailable, but the observation was too clever by half. It justified none of what Logaeir had done, and in no sense, did it lessen the injury done to Edryd in consequence of falsely representing him as having a direct affiliation with the Ascomanni. Logaeir's response, with all of its sharp sardonic wit, had ratcheted the affront to a new level.

"I would be in the right if I were to beat you senseless for what you have done," Edryd warned, thinking that what he really wanted to do was to kill this cavalier little annoyance of a man.

"Do you think that you could?" Logaeir asked.

At first Edryd thought Logaeir was making fun of him. Logaeir though, was being serious.

"Were you in a better state, no doubt you could do it, but you were dead, or nearly so until only a day ago, and I am not so easy to catch as you might think," Logaeir continued, unaffected by the threat which had been directed towards him. "Are you capable of recovering from such a long and deep illness so quickly?" He asked, seeming to believe Edryd capable of magically healing himself.

Edryd, tired of being spoken of as if he had died, had to remind himself that it would serve no useful purpose to become more upset. Logaeir was an unusual man. Venting frustration at him was beyond pointless, and Edryd's attempt at a threat might as well have been an unconventional compliment for all of the discomfiture that it had provoked. Edryd suspected that Logaeir's behavior was all for effect, and was neither genuine nor random. It would be a mistake to become distracted by it.

"You are worse than Seoras," Edryd finally said.

"Worse than Seoras?" said Logaeir, protesting the comparison. "He all but put you in the ground. I haven't done anything that harmed you nearly so much as that."

"Perhaps, but Seoras, as dark as he might be, did have the decency to at least show some remorse."

"Well, he has always been flawed in that way," Logaeir commented.

Edryd hadn't thought he could think less of the man, but Logaeir did not seem to mind playing an indifferent villain. "You act as though you are innocent of having done anything wrong," he said, remonstrating against the other man for his refusal to accept any responsibility for what he had done.

"I never claimed such a thing," Logaeir said. "And let's be fair, we all thought you were going to die. If you had met that expectation, you wouldn't be here to experience any discomfort over the uses to which I have purposed your name and reputation. None of this would even matter."

It was an absurd but simple logic. Bait to draw Edryd into an even more meaningless argument. Edryd did, however, have something he needed to say.

"It may not matter to you, but there may soon be a war between the Sigil Corps and the King of Nar Edor. Whether or not it is the truth, whether or not I had died, news that the Blood Prince is now commanding an army of Ascomanni is sure to provoke a response that will accelerate the conflict."

"That will have to be your problem," Logaeir replied casually, but appearing a little uncomfortable for the first time. "If we succeed here, we can turn our attentions to Nar Edor," he rationalized. "We can overthrow your King."

"If I had wanted to fight the king, I would still be in Nar Edor!" Edryd shouted.

"If it helps at all, I am serious about putting you in charge. I have big plans for the Ascomanni. I intend to transform them into something more than a simple band of marauders and thieves, and that will only happen with your involvement."

It didn't help. It made things worse, and Edryd was now struggling to retain any semblance of composure. "And if as your leader I command you to disband?" Edryd asked pointedly, trying to expose the lie in Logaeir's words.

"I would disregard the order," Logaeir admitted. "The die is cast. It is too late to choose any other path. For better or worse, conflict is coming."

Edryd was not sure what he had expected, but he would have preferred something more than a vague, yet dramatic pronouncement. There was, however, no way to undo what Logaeir had done. Logaeir's actions had engendered in Edryd a deep resentment, but short of openly declaring his identity, there was very little Edryd could do about it.

"It seems I've done a great deal to advance your cause, though I didn't intend to," Edryd pointed out. "You could do me a service in return and find me a way off of this unpleasant little rock."

"That wouldn't be a good idea," Logaeir responded, rejecting the request.

"Why?" Edryd demanded. "If I remain here, you only risk having your lies exposed."

"There are at least two reasons," Logaeir replied. "Friends of yours appeared one week ago, looking for their captain."

"What do you mean?" Edryd demanded.

"Soldiers of the Sigil Corps, Oren and Ruach they said their names were, sailed out here knowing they would be captured by Ascomanni. They have demanded to see you, and I imagine that they want to take you back."

"I have no intention of returning to Nar Edor, if that is what you are worried about," Edryd said, perturbed by what Logaeir had just told him. These two men were ranked officers in his command. He did consider them friends, and they undoubtedly would expect him to return.

"No, that isn't it," Logaeir corrected, "I told them that you needed their help in training the Ascomanni for battle, but I don't imagine they will keep at it much longer if I don't bring them to see you."

"And what makes you think..." Edryd began to say before stopping himself. Logaeir had uses for him yet, and those uses included recruiting his friends into the Ascomanni. The inventive thief surely wouldn't pause before leveraging the two officers in his machinations to obtain cooperation from Edryd either. Eithne had said it earlier: the man planned several steps ahead. Edryd was going to need to think this through carefully if he wanted to extricate himself from the trap in which he was held.

At that moment the door swung open. Irial stood as straight as she could and used every bit of her diminutive height to appear commanding as she demanded an explanation. "I could hear the two of you shouting from the road. Have you no common sense?"

"It was only Edryd who was yelling," Logaeir disputed indignantly.

Irial rolled her eyes in response to the deliberately childish response. Edryd reddened a little, realizing he had in fact been the only one who had raised his voice.

"Why is it you went and detailed all of the many wrongs I committed while he was sick?" Logaeir demanded of Irial.

Irial cast a sidelong look back in the direction of the road. She knew better than to take Logaeir seriously, but she answered anyway. "I have not spoken to him about you," she replied.

"I told him," Eithne volunteered apologetically, coming into view behind Irial.

Logaeir smiled and said, "It's a small thing. I'm sure you told him nothing he couldn't have learned in less than five minutes from just about anyone in town."

"That's right," Eithne agreed, brightening considerably, and showing relief.

"And how would you know that?" Logaeir challenged. "You aren't allowed to go into town."

"But you just said," Eithne complained with frustration.

Irial interrupted her sister before she and Logaeir could devolve any further into one of his pointless arguments. "Ignore him, it is well past time you were asleep," she said to Eithne, as she firmly ushered her off to bed. Upon returning she pulled Logaeir aside. "You need to leave, now, and do it discreetly," she said in a hushed tone.

Logaeir raised an eyebrow.

"Seoras is anxious to see Edryd now that he is awake. He wanted to accompany me on my way back," she explained. "I convinced him that it was too soon, but he was barely persuaded. I am not certain that he won't change his mind and show up anyway."

Logaeir tried to appear unaffected, but all of the color had gone from his face. "Best I was on my way," he said. "Wouldn't help things any for you if he found me here now, would it?"

Without a farewell, other than an abbreviated and barely courteous nod in Edryd's general direction, Logaeir departed through the room from which he had first entered, closing the door behind him. Edryd could hear, but not see, Logaeir moving a floor panel in and out of place, and then everything was quiet.

Chapter 10

Into the Dark

Edryd arrived at his decision only after extended and unproductive struggles to ease himself to sleep. Though he had not come, as Irial had feared, images of Aed Seoras approaching the cottage, sitting in the open hall, or hovering over him as he lay in bed, assaulted Edryd's imagination each time he closed his eyes. He was putting Irial and Eithne at risk by staying, and yet he couldn't just leave either. If he could find a way off of this island, some way to leave safely, doing so now would have consequences, and he would be endangering Irial if he disappeared while under her care.

It was only after settling upon the necessary solution that Edryd relaxed enough to manage an uneasy peace during the few hours that remained before morning. He decided not to tell Irial of his late night determination as they ate a morning meal of porridge. After she left, he waited an hour before he too, took to the road above the house. He was going to speak with Aed Seoras. He would accept the offer to live and train at the estate, receiving instruction in whatever it was Seoras felt he could teach. This, he reasoned, would jeopardize no one but himself, and it would restore some of the respect for himself that he had lost in the process of running from all of his problems.

The cottage soon vanished behind a low hill, and he was no longer feeling as certain about his choice. Each step grew heavier than the one that preceded it. He didn't want to admit that this had more to do with his fear of Aed Seoras than it did with a reluctance to leave the cottage or the weakened condition into which he fallen. He was growing miserable the more he contemplated things. If he didn't include the time for which he could not consciously account, he hadn't been at Irial's cottage for even two full days, but in that time he had felt something close to happy while living in her home. He was sorry to be leaving.

A lone bright spot lay amidst the jumble of torment. Apprenticing under Aed Seoras was going to make Logaeir very unhappy. Encouraged by this thought, and enjoying the crisp morning air, Edryd came near to smiling as he continued along the road. Eithne had come along, alternating frequently between forging on ahead with seemingly unbounded energy, and then pausing to explore one distraction or another so that Edryd would pass her on his way and would get well ahead.

Back at the cottage, when it had become clear that he intended to leave, Eithne made an effort at denying him permission. Once she understood that he meant to make a trip into town though, she unreluctantly relented, making a rather unconvincing display of exasperation at his stubborn nature. She would come as well just to be safe, she had said, but only to the edge of town. It was as welcome an excuse as she could have hoped for to defy the prohibition against approaching the borders of the town, about which she was more than curious. As they walked, she had been making a pretense at being angry that he was forcing her to break one of Irial's rules, but Eithne couldn't seem to remember she was mad unless she knew Edryd was paying attention.

He was cheered by her distracted company during those brief moments when Eithne either caught back up, or he found her waiting for him after he had fallen behind. It barely mattered that she was refusing to speak to him. Rounding a corner, Edryd discovered Eithne cooling her feet in a small stream of water that bounced over scattered stones as it carved its way down a long tapering slope. A view of the town opened up beneath them. The rows of large slate roofed buildings, built along narrow streets contoured in curved shapes that were made necessary by the rolling terrain, appeared small in the distance. Edryd had come this way before, but that had been at night. Now the entire town could be seen in clear detail. The estate, towards which he was now travelling, was set up well above most of the town, and was much closer to where he now stood than to the piers where all of the ships were moored.

"I think this is far enough, you had better go back now," Edryd said.

Eithne looked up from where she was wading in the stream. "I'll wait here until you're done. We can go back together."

His mood dampened as he struggled to explain that he wouldn't be coming back. He would be trading her company for that of Aed Seoras. The built-up toll of fatigue from the distance he had travelled along the road hit him. Eithne had set upon the right idea. It would be much more pleasant to spend the afternoon here, wading in the cool water, exploring the stream for a while.

"I won't be back, not for a few days at least," he said. "Irial will explain it when you see her." It was not altogether a lie, just largely one. He wasn't sure why he hadn't just told the truth, and he didn't like the thought that he might be lying simply out of habit.

Eithne wrinkled her nose, shielding her eyes as she stared back at Edryd and into the sun. She accepted his explanation without an argument, which was unusual for her.

"When you get back, I will make you some chicken dumplings," she promised.

Edryd's mood, already low, sunk even further. Eithne's expression of determination, voicing a desire for his approval, was painful for Edryd, and he keenly felt in that moment that he did not want to be a source of disappointment to her. If she would even be disappointed that is. Eithne had made a consistent point of being mainly displeased with him at all times. He couldn't have a great distance to fall.

Too stubborn to change course, Edryd resolved to follow through with his plan. He parted ways with Eithne and left the road, heading across country in a direct route to the estate.

The first person he met was Giric Tolvanes. He was just inside the gate, coming out of the stables with a small crate that held an assortment of grain filled sacks.

Tolvanes stopped upon sighting him. "Master Edryd," he managed after collecting himself from the surprise, "it is good to see you are well."

"I'm sorry for showing up like this," Edryd said.

"No need to apologize. No need at all. You're looking...."

The pause made Edryd very aware of how thin he had become. Giric was probably thinking to himself that Edryd was still sick, and perhaps dangerous to those around him.

"You are looking well, Young Master," Tolvanes said, finishing his thought.

"By well, I suppose that you mean pale and not long returned from the grave."

"No, not that at all," Giric replied. "You are a good deal thinner, but that seems to suit you if you don't mind me saying so. You look more mobile if that makes any sense. Once you get yourself into a regimen, I think you are going to be faster and more agile than you were before."

Edryd wasn't enjoying these reassurances. It felt too much like Tolvanes was inspecting a horse and discussing its virtues. Except there were no horses on this property. Men, or more accurately, men with the potential for acts of guided violence, were the products that were developed here. It was no anomaly that Tolvanes should have such a practiced eye with which to evaluate the inventory.

"I was hoping to discuss something with Seoras," Edryd said, cutting short the unsolicited appraisal of his health that Tolvanes seemed ready to expand upon.

"He's in an outbuilding back behind the stables," said Tolvanes, who had begun to put down the crate, intending to lead Edryd to Seoras. Edryd waved him off.

"I can find it," Edryd said.

Looking uncertain, but not displeased, Tolvanes shifted the crate in his arms. "You will come and see me when you're done?" he asked.

"We should have time to talk," Edryd agreed.

Seoras was alone in the outbuilding. Eyes closed, with his face hardened in an image of deep concentration, Seoras sat with his legs folded on top of a collection stacked fieldstone, the relocated remnants of a wall that had been torn down somewhere on the property. Aed Seoras's eyes remained closed, with his focus unbroken by the sounds Edryd made as he entered. At a point not far past the threshold of the building, Edryd crossed some unseen boundary. Edryd's heart quickened and he felt fractionally lighter than he should have, even accounting for what he had lost during his illness. More than that, Edryd was undeniably aware of a subtle imbalance, and a sort of unnatural displacement in the area around Aed Seoras.

What Edryd hadn't noticed, was a single stone, resting unaided in the air above the ground in the center of the room. Edryd saw this impossible object, only after hearing a loud penetrating crack that warned him of the danger, and then only for the briefest of moments. This threatening sound was produced in correlation with the appearance of a sudden fracture in the stone block, which preceded a subsequent explosion in which the stone disappeared, disintegrating into a cloud of dust and chalk. Edryd had managed to turn and shield his eyes in time, but the exposed side of his face stung where it had been impacted by granules of stone, and he choked and coughed on bits of dust that had gotten inside his mouth. The odd sensation of displacement was gone, replaced for a moment by a rapidly diminishing tremor. Edryd perceived it as a tension breaking and then imperfectly seeking to return to a state of balance.

Before Edryd could react, before he could give a voice to the obvious questions racing through his head, Seoras spoke. "Did you feel it?" he asked as he brushed away a thin layer of chalk that had come to rest in his dark strands of hair.

"Feel? You must mean did I see! You... you were holding that stone up in the air, and then you shattered it into dust. What in the three realms did you do?"

"I'm not sure," Seoras admitted. "Lifting an object is fairly simple, but crushing it with such force, it isn't something I have done before nor is it something I could repeat again."

Edryd was not sure what he should find harder to believe: that lifting a stone through the air was trivial, or that the explosion had been a fluke. "You didn't crush it, you blew it apart," Edryd corrected.

"No, I crushed the stone, and when I let go it rebounded," Seoras explained. "I did not intend it, but that is what happened."

Edryd didn't understand the distinction. It also wasn't the first time Seoras had inflicted an injury, this time a minor one thankfully, and gone on to claim that it had been inadvertent. Edryd's knees buckled, and he came to rest, more falling than deliberately seating himself, down upon a wood crate across from the pile of fieldstone. Still very weak, and nowhere near recovered from his illness, he had lost the strength to keep himself standing.

"It confirms what I suspected," Seoras continued. "You are very much attuned to the æther."

"The what?"

"Sorcerers called it that. Sigil knights didn't speak of it, but if ever they did, they called it the dark. The Ancients, who first discovered it, and built the bridges between worlds, called it the barrier, or more properly the continuum."

Edryd had no idea what Seoras was talking about. He would have suspected that Seoras didn't really know either, but the smattering of powdered rock that blanketed every part of the room offered credible evidence to the contrary.

"Some men can shape it through force of will alone," Seoras continued. "Sigil knights devoted their lives to becoming spiritually attuned. Sorcerers experimented endlessly on it, devouring and hoarding whatever arcane knowledge they could pry loose in order to bend it to their will. The starting points and the ends differed, but at the core, the means were always the same."

"I don't understand any of this," Edryd said. And for the most part he didn't. He knew the story of the rise of the Sigil Order of old. They fought devastating wars to eradicate the immortal sorcerers who had dominated and defined the last great age. Those wars, the memory of which survived now more as myth and legend than actual history, belonged to another time. The rest of it, especially the parts about barriers and bridges, the æther or the dark, was mostly foreign to Edryd. The talk of starting and end points and methods or means seemed like nothing more than cryptic nonsense.

"You don't need to understand any of that, not at this stage of your training. What is important is that you understand your connection to the dark. All men, all physical things for that matter, are connected to it, and we displace it through the actions we take. Through it, everything that exists in this world, and in all others, interacts. When you entered, I was shaping. It intensified when you approached because you became a focus that amplified the strength of the distortion that I was already actively creating. That is what you felt when you came near."

Seoras was throwing a lot out at once and making too many assumptions. Edryd did not recall ever having said he had felt anything. He had not agreed to accept training either, or at least he had not verbally expressed that decision yet. Edryd stiffened. Could Seoras have known his thoughts? It sounded absurd, and Edryd was not willing to accept that such a thing was even possible, but he had just finished watching the man lift a rock in the air and completely destroy it, so he couldn't be quite so quick to dismiss the notion either.

"I never said I felt anything," Edryd said.

"You did feel something," Seoras insisted.

"I felt the shards of rock flying at my face, but apart from that, unless you are saying that you can read me, and know my thoughts, you cannot tell me what I did or did not feel."

"It is supposed to be possible, but no, that isn't something I know how to do," Seoras replied. "But, on a very good day, I can sometimes send a thought or an emotion, if the target is receptive enough."

Slowly, Edryd became aware of Seoras at a deeper level, and he could clearly sense a dominant emotion. It was an eager hope, akin to the experience of finding a wrapped item, which you believed to be a long sought after and much anticipated gift. There was something more; it was something seemingly unwarranted but there all the same. Seoras was regarding him with an undeniable sense of terrible awe. That feeling was reciprocal. Edryd could no longer doubt what was now evident. Seoras was an aberrant force in action, capable of manipulating unnatural powers.

And then the demonstration was cut off. Edryd thought it disappeared entirely, but after a moment he realized it wasn't gone. He felt instead an effort in the opposite direction, meant to dampen and conceal. It was a flawed technique. It greatly weakened the connection between them, but it actively drew Edryd's attention, and far from obscuring anything, the shield Seoras had raised was nearly transparent to Edryd.

"You felt something," Seoras said. It wasn't a question, but Edryd didn't acknowledge the statement. There was no reason to let Seoras know just how successful he had been, nor any reason to reveal that a window into the dark man's mind remained open. Better to keep those insights to himself.

"I don't know whether I felt anything," Edryd lied.

"You have potential, I am sure of it," said Seoras. "I can guide you, if you will let me."

"While I am getting my strength back," Edryd answered, "I don't think it would hurt anything to see if you can train me." He had done it timidly, but it was a relief to finally take the step he had been dreading that whole morning. There was no going back now.

"It will not happen overnight, but when you commit to it, I am certain you will become very strong."

"Would I be able to use my old room while I stay?" Edryd asked, interrupting his teacher's appraisal of his new student's prospects. He wasn't worried about imposing. Seoras was after all still holding a generous sum of money that he had refused to return, and he had no doubt that Seoras would want him to stay there anyway.

Seoras looked a little puzzled. "Are you not comfortable staying with Irial?" he wondered aloud.

"Of course I am," Edryd answered. He felt a little embarrassed for some reason. "Only, I feel I would be... I think that I would be a problem to her."

"Did she say so?"

"No, she didn't. It's just... I understand an impression has been formed regarding me in the town. Those who don't believe I am one of the Ash Men will surely think that I am at least a source of contagion." Edryd did not add that he was trying to avert the inevitable disaster for Irial that was sure to come if Seoras and Logaeir were both frequenting the cottage. Instead he merely said, "I would be doing her no favors if I allowed anyone to make an association between the two of us."

"I'm afraid it is much too late to do anything about that," Seoras said.

"People already know that I was there?" Edryd asked.

"No, but they will have assumed as much. Irial has what would in An Innis pass for a substantial amount of medical knowledge and training, but when people get sick they do not seek her out, not even if they are dying. You don't seek her help unless you are convinced you are afflicted by the contagion. You go there to be kept apart, and you go there because you believe she knows how to prevent you from living on in a half-death after you die."

"You can't be serious," Edryd said.

"I am perfectly serious. And your miraculous recovery isn't going to help things. People are going to say that you died, and that she didn't prevent you from returning. It isn't helping that she works for me either. People whisper that I am a necromancer, that I command draugar, and turn living men into the undead." This was all alarming to Edryd, even if it wasn't much different from what could have been expected. "Of course one of those things is completely untrue, and the other two are wrong in important ways." Seoras added with a laugh. "You see, you are putting her into a danger that was already there, and I can only see one useful thing for you to do about it."

"What is that?"

"You may not be adding to the problem, but that doesn't mean she is not in a position of some risk. She needs better protection. You can travel here in the mornings with her, serve as her guard if she needs to leave the estate, and return to the cottage with her at night."

"I will do all that I can to keep her safe," Edryd promised, agreeing much too quickly and without giving the situation any thought. He might have at least tried to first determine whether or not Irial would be bothered by the arrangement. Edryd knew that he ought to apologize to her, but Irial wasn't there to hear it.

"I will teach you as time allows. When you are here, you can use your old room to study and this building to practice," Seoras offered.

Edryd took in a breath of air, experiencing a rising elation that could not be stemmed. The dread that had been pressing upon him had lifted. He wasn't going to be condemned to remain trapped on this property. Seoras had been surprisingly open, and though Edryd knew that he was obviously not free of controls, Seoras was allowing a lot of room. It wasn't that Edryd felt grateful, but he couldn't deny that he felt excitement when he thought of what he had already witnessed this morning. He couldn't begin to understand any of it, but he wanted to. Edryd felt nagging doubts that he was overlooking something important, but this had gone far better than he expected.

"We get started now then," Seoras declared.

Edryd felt the change—the odd sensation that he was somehow lighter, or heavier, or both at the same time. Seoras had a stupid grin on his face that was both happy and full of expectation. A rock from the pile rose in the air and began to move smoothly towards the center of the room. Remembering what had happened to the last stone, Edryd began looking for a place to take cover.

"Don't worry, I was surprised by the symmetry when it broke last time, but I have a feel for it now," Seoras said. "You don't need to do anything. Just try to get an impression of the shape of the distortion as I make it."

Edryd wasn't sure what that meant, but he complied without argument. He could feel it, and he could make out the boundaries. There was an area that encompassed both Seoras and the stone where the displacement was more profound, and there was a range, measured from the center of the distortion, beyond which the effect decreased dramatically until it faded completely. A force was being exerted that countered the one that should have pulled the rock to the earth. Others were pushing in towards the stone from all directions to hold it in place.

"To do this, you create an upward lifting force that is equal to the weight of the stone. That is not all though," Seoras said, explaining the concept. "You push at it from all around, or it won't stay in one place. It will go in whatever stray direction imparted by the slightest nudge otherwise. If you stay calm and clear your mind, you should be able to begin to feel it. It will take time, but with practice, eventually you will form a picture of the distortion.

Edryd hid his reaction—eventually had already arrived. He could see what Seoras was describing, and he now knew what Seoras had meant before when he said that he had crushed the stone. The pressure Seoras had been exerting to hold the stone steady had pulverized it when the forces he was using suddenly intensified. These perceptions came to Edryd without any effort or practice. He wasn't sure, but he thought he might have a clearer picture of the displacement than Seoras did. Being able to detect it and being able to create it were different things though. Edryd didn't have even the hint of an idea on how to go about doing the latter.

"How is it done?" Edryd asked after Seoras had been silent for a couple of minutes.

"You need to be able to feel your connection to the dark before you can shape it," Seoras answered. "Don't worry, just focus on what you can feel. It will take some time."

Edryd gave Seoras another couple of minutes. He didn't want to seem impatient, but as amazing as it all was, he didn't seem to be advancing his understanding at all. "Why do you call it the dark?" he asked.

"Because it isn't something you can see. To the Sigil Order, they felt it as a type of darkness, incapable of holding or responding to the light. Those who called it æther, saw it as perfectly transparent, a medium through which all energy is transferred between physical objects. Both understandings are incomplete and wrong. Where these ideas venture close to the truth, it amounts to the same thing. No light will ever shine on it, it produces no sound, and it has no physical presence, though all of those things travel through it and could not exist without it.

"I'm sure you must realize that you haven't managed a very clear description," Edryd said. He was not trying to be rude, but this wasn't making sense.

"No one ever has," Seoras replied. "Trying to do so is missing the point. It is natural to want to impose some physical description to it, so that you can understand it and share it more easily, but that will always lead to a corrupted understanding."

Seoras altered the shape of the distortion, and continued to do so in irregular intervals over the next several hours. Sometimes it would make the stone rotate or move in one direction or another, and at other times it showed no visible effects. Edryd was supposed to focus and inform Seoras whenever he noticed any change. He obliged by making an outward show of strained concentration. In truth it required no effort and only a modest amount of attention. He identified most of the changes quickly, but some of the more subtle shifts he deliberately ignored. Seoras was measuring him, and it seemed a wise precaution to ensure there were some gaps in the information Seoras was collecting.

"That is a very good start," Seoras said, letting the displacement fall away, leaving behind subtle temporary reverberations in its place. "If there are not too many ill effects, we will take up something a little different tomorrow."

"What kind of ill effects?" Edryd asked. When Seoras paused and said nothing, Edryd became insistent. "You can't just say something like that without explaining what you mean."

"Let's just say you may get a very bad headache," Seoras said. "Forcing the mind to accept a new kind of perception can knock things around in unexpected ways," he explained. "You will be cursing my name this time tomorrow, but once you get over the first crisis, it won't happen that strongly again."

Edryd didn't know whether he should be worried or not, but he was. This seemed like information he should have known before Seoras started. "Did I pass your test?" he asked.

"I don't know if I would call it a test, but if it were one, I would say you performed well."

If this was a compliment, it wasn't an enthusiastic one. Edryd hadn't exactly been trying to impress, so that shouldn't have mattered, but he felt unsatisfied in the realization that he had become no more proficient than he had been to begin with. Everything he had experienced was entirely passive. He didn't have the vaguest sense of how to actively interact with what he was learning.

He could sense though, that Seoras was extraordinarily pleased. The transparent little window remained open, and Edryd could see that his teacher felt none of the same frustrations over what had been accomplished. From his perspective, all expectations had been exceeded. Edryd realized it was foolish to be so quick to discount the day's achievements. It was progress of a sort.

Sensing the discontentment in his pupil, Seoras offered some encouragement. "I think tomorrow will be more to your liking, you did well today."

His instructor had accurately read his feelings, either in a conventional way, or more worrying to Edryd, perhaps Seoras also had a little window into his mind as well. If so, he had been lied to. It was an apt reminder not to blindly trust the knowledge Seoras was offering.

Something else of specific import to Edryd had also been revealed. He was certain that he had experienced these kinds of distortions before he had ever met Seoras, before he had ever come to this island even. He had fought a shaper back in Nar Edor, though not one nearly so accomplished in the art as Seoras. Edryd understood that now.

There was no way that his brother and Seoras could ever have crossed paths. Someone else, someone in Nar Edor, had to have taught Beonen some of these skills. Seoras might be able to provide some insights on the subject, but only if Edryd dared to risk revealing who he was by asking some hazardous questions, and that, he instinctively knew, would be remarkably unwise.

"I promised Tolvanes that I would talk to him," Edryd said, trying to end the conversation and anxious for an excuse to get a little separation from this man who had become his teacher. He could not disclose to Seoras, any of the thoughts that were troubling him, not until he had had the chance to sort through them.

"He will be working on the noon meal," Seoras said, endorsing the implied request. "If he hasn't finished, he might be able to use a little help if you can convince him to accept it."

Edryd found Giric Tolvanes in the kitchen of the barracks common room, in the middle of preparing a porridge made from the cereal grains he had been carrying earlier. He was already getting help. Irial was placing round flat sections of dark fresh dough into an oven.

Tolvanes, who had been expecting him, barely looked up, but Irial stopped in surprise.

"What are you doing here?" she asked.

"He came to see Master Seoras," Tolvanes answered on Edryd's behalf.

"Did you now?" Irial said. It was plain that she was not pleased.

The kitchen grew quiet. They both wanted to talk with Edryd, but neither of them wanted to do so in the other's company.

"Won't be ready for another half hour, but you are welcome to share the meal," said Tolvanes, interrupting the silence.

Irial bricked up the oven and walked over to Edryd. Without warning, she began to brush away the layers of dust that had settled on his coat. Bits of white chalk clouded the air as she hammered away at him. "How did you manage to collect a year of neglect in less than a day?" she complained.

"Seoras said it was an accident, but I'm not so sure."

Irial gave him a disapproving stare. Now he knew where Eithne had learned her craft. Irial didn't demand any further explanation, but she clearly would have liked a more complete account of his visit with the master of the estate.

"I will prepare your old room," she said, abruptly taking her leave.

With Irial gone, Tolvanes took a break from preparing the food and looked to Edryd in expectation. Edryd remembered what the older man had asked of him when last they spoke on that first day at the estate. Edryd was no more willing now to commit himself to that request than he had been before, and in truth he was certain that he had moved much closer to ruling it out, but he did not need to tell Tolvanes that.

"I have agreed to let him train me, and he seems convinced I will be a quick study," Edryd said.

"That's good... that's very good," Tolvanes approved. "What did happen though? You look like you took a nap in a pile of chalk." Irial was not the only one who was curious about Edryd's appearance.

Edryd thought back to what Irial had said before leaving and realized that she had made a point of telling him where she was going. She had also chosen a task that would create a natural opportunity for them to speak alone.

"The less I say about that, the better for everyone," Edryd evaded. "I need just a minute to settle a few things, but I'll be back to eat and we can talk more then."

Tolvanes opened his mouth in an aborted protest. He seemed a little flustered as he accepted that he was going to have to wait to discuss what he felt were pressing matters. "I suppose it isn't the best time or place," he acknowledged, giving Edryd permission to leave.

It was a short trip across the courtyard to the room he had stayed in before. Irial was seated in a chair that was near the window at the back of the room. Her face was full of color and her hands were balled up, tensely gripping the ends of the arms on the chair. She stood stiffly as he entered.

"What are you doing, I told you I would buy you time didn't I?" she demanded.

"I'm sorry," Edryd began to apologize.

"No you're not. What I was doing, it wasn't without cost. Don't you understand the risk I am taking to protect you?"

"I do understand, and I appreciate all of it, but I don't want you or anyone else taking those kinds of risks," Edryd replied. He really hoped she would understand.

"He is a danger to you," Irial responded.

"I understand that, but..."

"No, you understand he is dangerous, but you don't know everything you should. He is dangerous to you in particular. If you accept his training, it will darken you. You will change, and not for the better."

Edryd didn't know what to say to that, or why it should matter so much to Irial. Seoras was an unlikeable person, and clearly dangerous, but he wasn't exactly the embodiment of evil that she was portraying. Edryd reasoned that Irial must know more about the man than he did though, and he had already decided to trust her.

"I don't see a way around it," Edryd said. "Last night, you told Logaeir that you were worried Seoras might decide it was a good time to visit. If I don't do this, Seoras will only come and seek me out, and I don't think you or Eithne need him as a house guest."

Irial fidgeted with an ornament attached to a silver chain around her neck. She was thinking, and clearly unsettled.

"If he is as bad you say, I am not the only one who needs to be protected," Edryd pointed out. "We can protect each other."

"And how do you propose we do that," she replied. She obviously thought him very naive.

"Seoras feels that you need a guard when travelling in town, and I have agreed to be that guard," said Edryd. Irial's eyes widened. "I will continue to stay at the cottage, and I will make sure you are safe whenever travelling to or from the estate."

Edryd was not sure what he expected, but he worried that Irial would find the idea insulting and reject it. Irial's face contorted into an unusual expression. Edryd tried to interpret the reaction but he couldn't tell if it was relief or annoyance, and ultimately decided that it was probably both.

"If you are going to follow me around, don't think I won't put you to work," she said.

Chapter 11

Irial Rohvarin

Edryd had at first questioned the sincerity of Irial's threat to make her new protector earn his keep, but those doubts had been dispelled over the past several weeks. He had been thoroughly disabused of any notion that he was in any way in control of his own time. Irial put him to work often, and had demonstrated no undue concern as to whether he was sufficiently recovered.

If there was a burden to carry, an errand to run, or any other sort of work which could be aided through the use of his menial physical exertions, she showed no reluctance to task him with it. For his part, Edryd was grateful. Every humble undertaking he finished pleased him more than the last, and with his strength recovering at a reassuring pace, Edryd felt full of unexpected energy.

Training sessions with Seoras were the low points each day, and as low points go, these were deep. It was terrible to confront failure each time he tried what Seoras called 'shaping the dark'. Edryd had hidden from his teacher the clarity with which he could sense the displacements that occurred when Seoras warped the forces that gave power to his techniques, but Edryd had no need to hide his own skill at shaping the dark. He had no skill. If he was frustrated, so was his teacher. Seoras remained stoic and said little, but the window that looked in on his teacher's mind remained open. Edryd could clearly see the confusion and disappointment.

He was acquiring a detailed inventory of his teacher's capabilities, which was valuable in itself, but other than that the training was unproductive. Seoras demonstrated, and then left Edryd alone for hours at a time with instructions to reproduce what he had been shown.

Over the course of a few weeks, Edryd had witnessed amazing things. He had watched Seoras gather tension within the dark and impart that energy into a moving weapon, increasing its momentum.

He had seen Seoras absorb, store, and release energy from violent impacts, seize and manipulate objects from a distance, and use subtly patterned displacements to project sounds, and alternately, to dampen them.

In what he said was key to developing a strong connection to the dark, Seoras had instructed Edryd on concentrating through a focus—a sword with a particularly pure and consistent alloy was ideal—to become more attuned. Edryd had watched Seoras do this for the better part of an afternoon, but apart from producing a particularly strong field of displacement, this attunement had no observable effects. Edryd had made sincere attempts at all of these things and shown aptitude for none of them. All except for the last of these abilities, with which he believed he had once had some success, only that had been before An Innis, with a true sigil blade, and it was still a very painful memory.

Today, Edryd was learning something Seoras said would be crucial in order to advance his combat training. Remembering the sword Seoras had shattered in his hands, Edryd well understood why it would be an essential ability, but it was also one for which he had no hope that he could master.

Laid out on the most central of the marble benches at the edge of the courtyard were a collection of thin glass cylinders. In the way that iron or steel ingots were worked into tools by a blacksmith, these delicate lengths of glass were the most basic refined material used in glassblowing. There were no such craftsmen in An Innis, and for that matter, there were none in Nar Edor. To Edryd these were expensive treasures, known to him only in books, produced in lands that lay beyond the extent of his very limited experience. How Seoras came by them, Edryd could not guess, but it was reasonable to assume that their history included one or more acts of theft as part of stolen cargos, only to end up forgotten for some number of years in a warehouse belonging to one of the harbormasters.

Edryd was meant to strengthen a length of glass until he could swing one against the marble bench without breaking it. He had seen Seoras prove it was possible. It looked like nothing more than an entertainer's trick, but the clear pattern of displacement Seoras summoned to life around the thin glass rod had been enough that Edryd did not dismiss it so lightly. He had been working at it now for several hours. All of the lengths of glass that Edryd had been supplied with remained safe and unbroken. It was going to stay that way too. Edryd had complete confidence that any attempt he made would only result in a scattering of broken shards of glass across the ground. He wondered what Seoras would make out of his reluctance to even make an attempt.

Edryd knew he was not doing it right—and at this point he couldn't even imagine doing it right. He could sense the dark, and even his place within it, but he felt no connection. Seoras insisted this was wrong. Everyone and everything was linked. The bonds were at times strong in some, and in in others they were weak, but it was always present. You could only become attuned by grasping and understanding your relationship with the expanse of dark that underpinned all of creation. If you could perceive the dark, you could shape it. There were no exceptions. Edryd hated to be the embodiment of an argument that contradicted this theory, but it wasn't something he could change. None of this was ever going to work, and there was no need to destroy these fragile things just to further prove the futility of what it was he was trying to achieve.

He had more time, but Edryd had given up a while ago. Carefully gathering the glass together into a bundle, Edryd headed for the stables and settled the glass back into the crate they had been pulled from. Forcing all thoughts of this most recent failure into the furthest recesses of his mind, Edryd concentrated instead on something more pleasant as he made his way to a wooden building not far from the bathhouse. The pleasant scent of lavender and orris root filled the damp air of the laundry. Edryd loved this smell, strongly associating this simple mixture of scents, with Irial. It was infused into her hair and skin from the weekly washing of the estate's linens and clothing.

"If you're here, you are going to help," she ordered.

Familiar with the process, Edryd gathered armloads of damp sheets and carried them outside, where with an efficiency born from practice, he began hanging them on a suspended line to dry in the sun. If he finished quickly, he and Irial could spend more time together on the trip back. By midafternoon everything was dry, folded, and neatly stacked, and Edryd helped distribute the finished laundry to all the appropriate places. Finished, they met in the barracks common room and shared a late lunch.

"I'm ready to leave if you are," Edryd said, as he finished off a biscuit drizzled in honey. He was always happy to leave the estate. When she was working at the property, Irial tended to be formal and even a little highhanded. In her home, to a degree, she seemed a little cautious. Outside of those environments though, what Edryd chose to see as her natural personality would surface, and he would feel more like a respected friend and less like a subordinate or a houseguest.

"I do need to make a visit in town," Irial replied, satisfied that everything that needed doing had been done. As she stood, Irial arranged a short pale white cloak over her shoulders, slung the strap of a leather bag over her head and across her chest, and hung a woven reed basket in the crook of her arm. "It will be out of the way, but we have time." Irial looked overburdened, and Edryd felt awkward not carrying anything at all. At least this meant his hands would be free in the unlikely event he needed to respond to some unexpected danger while they travelled through the streets.

Edryd followed Irial out the gates and took up a protective position beside her as they headed through the periphery of the town. People were growing accustomed to seeing them together. Not so long ago, the streets emptied before them when they passed. People still shied away and kept a healthy distance, but there was no longer as much urgency in their efforts to avoid contact. Edryd's ego suffered no small amount of damage when Irial explained that these reactions had more to do with her reputation than it did with the menacing guard she travelled with. The townspeople, who were convinced that Irial practiced forbidden rites and commanded evil powers, believed that associating with her was a sure way to risk inevitable harm of an unnatural variety. The natural conclusion then was that Edryd was bound to her, taken by the darkness that created the Ash Men and returned from the dead with a sworn obedience to Irial that had been forged through a dark contract.

The negative attention did not seem to bother Irial. It did, however, deeply amuse her. She laughed quietly when a self-important looking tradesman stopped upon seeing her, turned around as though he had forgotten something, crossed the street, and then ultimately turned back in the direction he had originally been headed. The sight of otherwise confident and self-assured men and women feeling intimidated by Irial, whose height did not reach far past most of their shoulders, was entertaining when you were not yourself one of the people terrorized by the experience.

"I didn't think I would, but I am beginning to appreciate the benefits of having my own personal guard," Irial said. "I never realized how often I was sending Tolvanes out for things, instead of going myself. I certainly wouldn't ever have braved these streets when they were this crowded."

"You could have had Hagan or Cecht accompany you," Edryd suggested.

"That would have felt less safe than going out alone," Irial said. "Hagan maybe—if he could be persuaded to bathe—but I wouldn't go anywhere with Cecht." Irial's shoulders tightened, becoming tense even thinking about Cecht. Edryd held neither of these two in any high regard, but Irial had known both of them much longer, and her low opinions of both Hagan and Cecht, strongly bolstered his own reasons for retaining a grudge.

"You are more tolerable in most respects, but only marginally so," Irial remarked, watching Edryd for a reaction.

"Tolerable?" Edryd responded as he widened his eyes and smiled. "I could not have guessed that I held a place so high in your esteem, or that my reputation had undergone such an improvement so quickly."

"Well I doubt everyone would agree with me," she laughed.

"More than a few wouldn't," Edryd agreed, thinking that the citizens of An Innis would hardly tolerate him if they knew him to be the nominal leader of the Ascomanni, and the living scourge of this dreadful island and all who lived upon it.

Irial had grown comfortable talking with him on these trips, but she never spoke of her past. Edryd didn't pry. He assumed that Irial would share only what she was comfortable with and only in her own time. She afforded him the same courtesy. It wasn't altogether fair though. Rumors regarding the important recent events in his life were not what could be called secrets, having been broadly shared, and dispersed as fast as that information could travel, carried by ships sailing across the oceans.

Edryd shook his head. It continued to be an unaccountably strange experience whenever he heard descriptions, some invented and others real, retelling the murderous exploits of the Blood Prince. Much to his relief, though Irial knew him to be the subject of those stories, and also knew that there was a great deal of truth in most of them, she seemed little interested in it. She let him be the unremarkable contracted protector he was more than content to be.

"Uleth?" Edryd asked, recognizing the route they were taking. Uleth was an elderly friend of Irial's who shared her interest in all things botanical. She had sought out his expertise, Edryd had learned, for assistance in his treatment.

"I need to return a book," she explained, confirming Edryd's guess. Though left unsaid, it could be assumed that she also intended to borrow something new from Uleth's library, to take the place of the book she was returning.

Unimpeded throughout the remainder of their trip, Irial and Edryd soon arrived at Uleth's home. The stone walls of the building were in need of repair, but it was remarkably clean in comparison to its neighbors. A low walled enclosure protected a carefully tended garden in which there were prominent plantings of flowering herbs, including yarrow, black horehound, anise, rosemary, mint, and sage. Edryd was sure that if he asked, Irial could have identified dozens of other plants that were represented in various parts of the garden and detailed their medicinal uses.

An irregular chunk of iron, affixed to the entrance with a knotted rope, was apparently intended as the appropriate means by which to announce their presence. Edryd used it to knock twice on a thick, dark monstrosity of segmented oak that served as the front door, and together he and Irial waited awkwardly for a good long while. Edryd knocked again, more forcefully this time, and as he did so the door cautiously swung open, seemingly under its own power, as Uleth invited them inside.

"I brought a couple of loaves of bread," Irial said, extending the basket from her arms.

"Set them in the Kitchen," Uleth instructed.

"And I'm also returning a book," Irial said, handing the basket of bread to Edryd, and pulling a smallish book from her bag. The book's pages were protected by wooden covers wrapped in green fabric which were in turn protected by metal pieces that adorned the corners. The center of the book was embellished with a silver medallion fitted with colored pieces of glass. The arrangement left no room for doubt; this was an object of value.

"Theredan's *Study of Affliction*," Uleth said aloud.

It was a very suspicious sounding title, not inconsistent at all Edryd thought, with a book of spells and hexes.

"It's a medical book," Irial explained, noticing Edryd's sudden intense interest.

"I know," Edryd responded. "It just looks and sounds like the kind of thing that would lend credibility towards the prevailing notions people have about your assumed dealings in the arcane."

Flashing a look that let him know she was not amused, Irial tucked the book under her arm. "I consulted it while keeping you from succumbing to your illness," she said. "I suppose you would rather I hadn't?"

"I don't know. Did anything in it help?"

"No," Irial admitted. She turned away without saying more and headed for the library. The unsubtle show of disapproval reminded Edryd of her sister. Irial and Eithne did not share much if anything in the way of a physical resemblance, but they were similar in other ways.

"The kitchen is this way," Uleth said, breaking Edryd's attention away from Irial.

"Of course," Edryd replied. He had forgotten about the basket that Irial had handed off to him.

Edryd followed Uleth down a hallway that led to a small kitchen in a back corner of the house and removed the loaves of bread, setting them on a small table in the middle of the room, before placing the basket down beside the doorway. Uleth continued to stand when Edryd took a seat. Edryd was a little uncomfortable. He wasn't sure what he would have to talk about with the man.

"I remember when she was a little girl," Uleth reminisced. "Her family was a prominent one, and her father was an assemblyman. That was twenty years ago, before the Concursion of course."

Edryd was immediately interested. This was a rare opportunity to learn a little more about Irial. If that information came bound up somehow with the history of An Innis, he didn't mind.

"By the Concursion, are you are talking about Beodred and the collapse of his alliance?" Edryd guessed. He didn't know what concursion meant.

"Not directly, no," Uleth said, "but if you mean what happened in the battle's aftermath, then yes. Of those who had fought with

Beodred, and surrendered after his defeat, some several hundred were summarily deposited on our shores courtesy of the Ossian League. Added to that were the thousands of Rendish men and women who were later expelled from Nar Edor. The results were predictable."

"What do you mean?" Edryd asked.

"What do you think happens when a settlement of less than four hundred suddenly expands to between three and four thousand in a matter of months? People began to starve, to kill each other, and to die from exposure."

Edryd was subdued by shame in that moment, listening quietly to Uleth's recounting of the events of the Concursion. Edryd's own father had set every one of these events in motion. Aedan Elduryn had killed Beodred in combat, destroying the alliance of raiders who had attacked Nar Edor twenty years ago. In the years that followed, on the orders of his grandfather, Edryd's father had also overseen the expulsion of Rendish foreigners, all of whom were forced from Nar Edor and transported here.

"The Ossians, they sent in aid, but by then things had already broken down," Uleth continued. "Strongmen, remnants of Beodred's forces mainly, took control of the food and provisions. They used it to empower themselves. By the time the Ossians understood the mistake they had made, the league did not have the will to commission a force capable of restoring order, so they stopped trying to help and walked away. The shame of Ossia, it has come to be called."

"That is how the harbormasters took control An Innis," Edryd said, beginning to understand the history of this place.

"Yes, but they were not calling themselves harbormasters, not back then. And there were about forty of them, not the four we have in power now."

"I don't think I would estimate that An Innis supports more than a thousand people now," Edryd pointed out. "That would suggest that in twenty years your population has declined by something close to three thousand."

"Some," Uleth said, "those not entirely deprived of means, were able to leave by ships that could take them back to a homeland that would accept them." Uleth paused for a moment, collecting his thoughts, recalling dark memories from the past. "The rest were stuck here, with too little food, inadequate shelter, and no means of escape. Plagues and diseases took the lives of hundreds of them."

Fresh shame confronted Edryd. He had felt sorry for himself from the moment he had arrived in An Innis, but these few months of troubles were nothing in comparison to what others had been subjected to.

"I understand the reasons behind the fear of contagion now," Edryd said, his voice solemn and tired.

"It wasn't any one disease," Uleth continued. "There were at least three or four different afflictions spreading through the settlement. I made it my work to save as many as I could. You could say I did what Irial does now, only most people have forgotten it."

"Irial learned from you," Edryd said, realizing it for the first time.

"She did," Uleth confirmed. "I did what I could for the people, including her family, but Irial was the only one of the Rohvarin line who survived. In the end all I could do was to see that she was cared for after they were gone."

"What about her sister?" Edryd asked.

"You mean Eithne?" Uleth asked. When Edryd nodded in confirmation, Uleth continued. "Eithne is not Irial's sister. None of Irial's family lived through the events of the Concursion. Irial had no surviving siblings."

This had happened nearly twenty years ago, long before Eithne would have been born. That all seemed obvious enough now, Edryd just hadn't connected the information together.

"She isn't her mother either," Edryd concluded, trying to determine how the two were related. Edryd understood now why the two sisters had such little familial resemblance.

"No, Eithne is an orphan," Uleth replied. "Irial took care of her after Eithne's mother died. By that time she was already on her own out there at the cottage."

Edryd wondered who Eithne's mother might have been, but realized Uleth might not know and decided it didn't matter. Eithne probably didn't know she was not Irial's sister.

"So it's you and Irial who keep the supernatural contagion at bay," Edryd commented.

"There is no supernatural element to any of it," Uleth declaimed, a little anger in his voice. "There was none of this Ash Men nonsense until Seoras returned."

Edryd wanted to know more. How could he not? But Uleth was no longer so willing. He had become angry and reluctant to go on, and a moment later, Irial's return ended Edryd's chance to pry more information from him.

"Why are you both so quiet?" Irial asked, noticing the silence her appearance had seemingly prompted. Concerned that Uleth had been sharing embarrassing stories from her past, she sought to see if her fears were correct. "What did he say about me?" she asked.

"I didn't know that Uleth was your childhood patron," Edryd answered. That comment seemed to confirm for Irial that something had passed between the two of them, and she looked even more uncomfortable.

"It isn't a secret," Irial replied. "Why else do you think he trusts me with his books? He gives his pupil the run of the library."

Irial produced one of the two books she had carried in, and held it up for inspection.

"*On Matters of Interest Regarding the Ossian Oligarchs*," she said, reading the title aloud. "I picked that one out for you Edryd, if it's all right with Uleth." Uleth assured her with a simple smile that it was. Privately, Edryd thought that the title of the tome suggested a very heavy and labored accounting of dated political theories for which he had little use.

"And the other one?" Edryd asked, trying to get a look at the second book which was largely hidden behind the skirts of Irial's dress. He could see only the corners on one end of the white cloth-covered boards that protected the bound pages.

"That one is for me," she said, declining to give any description of the work she had selected for herself.

Irial grabbed the empty bread basket, and they both thanked Uleth for the books as they left. The sun was behind their backs and already beginning its slow sinking approach with the open sea as the two of them began the trip home.

The streets were active at this hour, but in the diminishing light fewer people recognized them. It made travelling on the streets more comfortable, if a little more crowded. Edryd watched Irial exhale in relief once they passed through the outer edges of the town. He had never heard her complain, but he knew An Innis was an unpleasant place for Irial.

As they travelled along the roadway, Irial glanced once or twice at the hillsides to the north.

"I wish there was more daylight left," she said.

Edryd knew what she was thinking. As was her frequent habit on their way home, she wanted to harvest some useful part of a plant of one kind or another growing wild in the overgrowth that clung to the rising slopes.

"Wild blackberries are ready to be picked, and we have an empty basked to collect them in," Irial lamented. "A shame it's too late to pick them without risking our necks tripping on the undergrowth while trying to get at them in the dark."

"It is a shame," Edryd agreed.

"They will still be there tomorrow," she sighed, "we will just need to make sure we get away early enough."

There would have been time if not for the trip to see Uleth, Edryd thought to himself, but he didn't regret that diversion. He was glad that the visit had been a revealing one. He had learned more about Irial's past today than he had in all the rest of the time that he had known her, but he still knew very little.

"What was the book you borrowed for yourself?" he asked, hoping both to satisfy a nagging bit of curiosity, and to see if he could ease his way into the subject of her connection to Uleth.

"Just something with instructions on food preparation," Irial answered, as her face flushed with embarrassment. "It isn't that I need it myself, but I want to show Eithne. She's wrong when she complains that I don't know how to cook."

Edryd laughed without meaning to, causing Irial more embarrassment. "I wonder if there will be more dumplings tonight," Edryd wondered aloud, trying to make it seem like he had been laughing at Eithne rather than Irial.

"Oh, I hope not," Irial said, in complete sympathy with her protector's own feelings on the subject. Edryd's joke the day he first met Eithne had produced a long lasting consequence. Every alternate day, Eithne insisted on preparing one of two varieties of dumplings that she had learned to make. It wasn't that they hadn't been appetizing in the beginning, but both Edryd and Irial were beginning to give up hope that Eithne would ever lose her enthusiasm for making them.

"I'm sure the book will have something useful in it. Whatever you find, when you prepare it, I will be sure to give it some excessive praise. If we motivate Eithne to master something new, perhaps it will be dumplings only every third day. I might even begin to enjoy them again."

Irial laughed. "That should work. She doesn't like to be outdone."

"You knew Uleth while you were growing up?" Edryd said, ungracefully steering the direction of the conversation. They were nearing the cottage and he wanted to learn what he could in the little time that remained.

"He did it, didn't he? He told you about...."

"Told me about what?" Edryd asked when she stopped.

"This isn't fair," she complained, "I wish I knew someone who could tell me embarrassing stories about you when you were growing up."

They were at that moment just a dozen yards away from the cottage and Edryd stopped dead in his tracks. Irial stopped as well. Beside the door on the large tree stump that served as a chopping block, sat a tall man in a grey coat. Not young, and not yet old, the man had a handsome face and light rust colored hair that seemed brightly burnished in the faint moonlight.

"Ruach!" Edryd exclaimed softly, at a loss for any other response. The man was a friend of more than fifteen years, appearing before them almost as if in response to the summons of Irial's wish.

"Captain Aisen," Ruach called out, with unsuppressed joy in his greeting.

The man stood and eagerly rushed to his captain, spontaneously wrapping him in a brief hug that was quickly retracted.

"I can't believe it's you," Ruach said, grabbing Edryd's shoulders as if to reassure himself that he really had found his friend. "You look different. You're thinner, and I think more intimidating than what I remember."

"What are you doing here?" Edryd demanded. It wasn't that it did not feel good to see a trusted friend, but Edryd feared what Ruach's arrival meant, and what it was he would ask. Perhaps he shouldn't have been surprised, Logaeir had told him about Oren and Ruach nearly a month ago, but it was still a shock to see him. Irial, he noticed, had only briefly reacted. She was now behaving as if this had all been expected.

"I would have come sooner, but no one would tell us where you were," Ruach apologized. "Then, this morning, one of the men from Krin's crew tells me you are at this safe house on the island, and he offers to smuggle me over."

"I'm not going back to Nar Edor," Edryd declared.

"Oren will be happy to hear that," Ruach responded. "He has bought into Logaeir's grand vision of things."

Edryd was surprised. It was a strange thing to hear that his friends had been willingly cooperating with Logaeir, but it confused him even more to learn that they were not trying to immediately return him to Nar Edor to face off against the king's armies.

"I'm not of the same mind myself of course," Ruach clarified. "I want you to return. But it isn't my place to give orders to a captain. I am here to receive your instructions. Tell me what you need us to do."

Edryd was about to tell Ruach that he was not a captain in the Sigil Corps, not any longer, when someone else spoke up. "Can you tell Oren that his captain has instructed you both to stop providing aid to the Ascomanni?" Irial asked.

Both Edryd and Ruach turned to Irial in surprise. Realizing she had overstepped, Irial looked down at her feet instead of meeting their stares.

"If you are in agreement of course," she clarified to Edryd.

"That will cause some problems I think," cautioned Ruach.

"I think that is the whole point," Edryd explained, beginning to understand a little of what Irial intended.

"Logaeir will know that I came here and met with you if I tell him that I am acting on your orders," Ruach argued.

"You don't need to tell him how you received the orders, only that they came from me and that you have been instructed to stop assisting the Ascomanni," Edryd reasoned.

Ruach smiled. "This is going to give you some serious leverage," he said, recognizing the strategy behind his orders, but not their ultimate purpose. Ruach didn't know what Edryd's plans were, but he didn't need to. He was enthusiastic about doing anything that would aid his captain.

For that matter, Edryd had no idea what his plans were either, since he had none. Doubtless, Irial knew a few things, and possibly she had arranged this whole thing. At some point, he was going to need her to share with him what it was he was trying to do here, assuming she did have some plan.

"You had better get back before you are missed," Edryd suggested. Ruach pointed out that his absence had almost certainly already been noted, but on the chance he could get back to the Ascomanni encampments on the mainland before morning, he agreed and reluctantly took his leave.

"We will meet again soon," Edryd said, reassuring his officer as they parted. He didn't know if that would be true, but he suspected it would be.

As Ruach's long form faded into the darkness, Edryd turned to face Irial. "You sent for him," he accused.

"You remember that there was something I needed you to do for me?" she reminded him.

"Time you told me what that was," Edryd said. He was beginning to feel uneasy. She was broaching the subject so carefully.

"I need you to send a message to the Ossian First Fleet Navarch," she explained. Seeing a blank stare from Edryd, she expanded her explanation. "His name is Aelsian. He pulled you off of that burning ship and helped you get here. He commands an entire fleet of ships, and as a friend of your father, he is the Steward of House Elduryn."

These were more revelations than Edryd could properly absorb all at once. He had Aelsian's image fixed in his mind. He could remember the noble man's aging features, with hair graying around the edges. Edryd had not known the man well, had known nothing of Aelsian's connection with Aedan Elduryn, and had not thought of him as anything more important than the captain of the *Interdiction*. Edryd was about to say that he had no way to send such a message when he made the connection. There was a reason why Logaeir had known who he was—someone had told him. Logaeir and Aelsian were allies. Edryd had no means to contact Aelsian, but Logaeir would.

"More than you may have realized, you have some powerful friends," Irial said. Edryd was not sure he really agreed, but the way Irial said it, she made it seem like she had understated the obvious.

"What will be in this message?" Edryd asked.

"Just that you need to meet with him as soon as he can get here," she said, getting right to the point but going no further.

"There is more to this," Edryd said, urging her to elaborate on what it was she really wanted.

"Nothing I could safely entrust to a messenger and nothing that you need to know about just yet either," she replied. The promise was there that he would learn soon enough, but that she had no intention of saying anything more right now.

He was deeply dissatisfied with the situation. He trusted Irial, and wanted to help her, but it was troubling to be used in this way while being kept in the dark. He almost began to press for a more complete explanation, but he was afraid of what she would think of him if he did. Instead, Edryd contented himself with the knowledge that he would soon be getting a visit from Logaeir. From that man, he would happily demand all of the answers he wanted.

Chapter 12

Focus of the Dark

Eithne sat with her bare feet planted on the floor and her back against her door, barricading her room against anyone who might try to enter. It seemed like so much had suddenly changed. Why had they both kept something so important from her? Mostly, it hurt to know that neither of them saw her as old enough or strong enough to trust with their secrets.

Feeling the unfairness of the world, and her total lack of a prominent place in it, Eithne ignored Irial when she knocked on the door to ask whether she was alright. Later, Eithne similarly remained silent when Edryd tried to speak to her through the door. She didn't know how to explain how she felt, and didn't believe anyone would understand, and so she had decided that she wouldn't try. They could go on keeping their secrets, she told herself bitterly.

Eventually, Irial's patience with her sister's behavior was exhausted, and she ordered Eithne to come out and eat. Eithne complied, but she made certain that they could both feel just how unhappy she was, even if she wasn't about to tell anyone why.

In response to specifically directed questions, Irial compelled an occasional nod or grunt out of Eithne, but nothing more than that, and they all shared the evening under a miserable pallor. Eithne was so consumed with her own hurt feelings, that she barely noticed the unease between the two adults. Her sister's conversations with Edryd had grown awkward.

In other circumstances, Edryd might have tried to gently tease Eithne, in an effort to liven the mood. Provoking her had a way of infusing careless fun into a moment like this one, but with Eithne pouting like she was doing now, working so hard to punish him for some offense he couldn't quite divine, Edryd could do little more than sit and mull Irial's refusal to share the plans in which she had involved him. Long before he was tired, Edryd went to his room feeling deeply discontented, unable to solve even the simplest of his more immediate problems.

In the morning, as he sat finishing his breakfast, and while Irial was still in her room getting ready to leave, Eithne finally deigned to let him know what it was that he had done.

"You didn't tell me you were the Blood Prince," she said. There was an angry blue fire behind her eyes, and Eithne was filled with a little awe, a measure of disbelief, and a great deal of hurt and betrayal, as she made this accusatory declaration.

"You heard us talking," Edryd guessed.

"No, I heard him before you came back. He said that he was looking for Captain Aisen. When I didn't let him in, he kept pounding on the door, asking for Lord Aisen of House Edorin." The last part she accented to show what she thought of 'Lord Aisen of House Edorin' and of the man who had come looking for him.

"That doesn't mean..."

"Yes it does. He was looking for the Blood Prince. He was looking for you." There was fresh hurt in her eyes and she began to cry. He was still, even now, trying to continue to conceal who he was from her.

"I didn't want you to know," Edryd said. He wanted make this better for Eithne, but he did not know how to help her understand.

"Why?" she pled.

"Irial once told you that I was dangerous," Edryd explained. "She was right."

"You've killed people," Eithne said, starting to understand.

"And hurt many others," he agreed. "I didn't want you to know that."

Despite the serious nature of the discussion, the conversation was making Eithne feel better.

"The people you hurt were trying to hurt you," Eithne said, trying to reassure him.

"One of the people I hurt and killed was my younger brother," Edryd said, trying hard to keep his emotions in check, and immediately regretting what he had just revealed. Painful memories were surfacing, and thinking that it wouldn't help if he began crying too, he said no more for a while. In the quiet that followed, Edryd recognized how misguided it had been to share the grief and the guilt that he felt over his brother's death, with such a young child. Berating himself, he changed the subject.

"I promise I won't ever lie to you again," he said.

"You are not a bad person," Eithne insisted. Her tears were now dry, but she looked worried about Edryd. "I know you didn't do it on purpose." She could not have known whether her profession of faith in his good nature was true, but Edryd was comforted in the depths of his heart to hear her express it. The sentiment would have sounded so self-serving and feeble had he made the same protest on his own behalf.

As Edryd walked beside Irial on the road that morning, the memory of Eithne's confident assurances regarding her unshaken belief in him softened his suffering, but it had still been a poor start to the day. He could have used time to himself and was in no mood to talk. Irial seemed equally content to walk in silence, fearful that he would be demanding answers to the questions that she knew he must have. As they continued, Irial became increasingly tense, feeling pressure from anticipating the questions that never came, and attributing Edryd's dark mood to frustration borne over her failure to be open with him.

"I will tell you what I can," she suddenly blurted out.

Edryd looked up in surprise and met her serious and worried gaze.

"I need help from both you and Aelsian," she said. She seemed frustrated, realizing how little she was prepared to reveal. "I need you to accompany Eithne, and get her away from An Innis," Irial continued. She had no choice but to take into her confidence, the man in whom she had decided to entrust her sister's safety. The disclosure was met with silence.

"I think you will agree that An Innis is no place for her," Irial pointed out. Edryd did agree. He couldn't agree more. He just didn't see how this connected to him.

"Why didn't you have Logaeir get her out a long time ago?" Edryd asked.

"I don't trust Logaeir," she said, "and neither should you." She didn't have to tell Edryd why he shouldn't trust Logaeir. It was also unnecessary to include in that statement that she didn't trust Seoras, Esivh Rhol, the harbormasters, or anyone else in An Innis who could possibly arrange a means for Eithne to leave. Also implicit was the fact that she did trust Edryd.

Edryd was confronted by a set of opposing emotions. He would do it. Of course he would. But it had at first been lost on him, that her proposal also included his escape from An Innis as well. Perhaps it had not occurred to him because at some point, he couldn't say with precision when, he had stopped wanting to leave the island. As Edryd thought about this, he desperately wanted Irial to modify her plans.

"You have to leave with us," he insisted.

"I can't," was all she said.

Infuriatingly, now that he had agreed to her request, she was no longer willing to bargain away anything else, and she gave no explanation for why she would have to remain behind. Gentle but earnest efforts to question Irial further led nowhere, and Edryd could not get her to say much more. Irial had given him answers, not to all his questions but to most of them, and he was made miserable by what he had learned.

There was time yet. It would take weeks for a message to reach Aelsian once it was sent, and weeks more for the navarch to travel to An Innis. He would have to persuade Irial before then that there was no need for her to stay behind, and argue that Eithne would never leave without her.

Edryd was looking down, distracted by his troubles as he walked beyond the gates of the estate after passing through them. Irial was no longer beside him, having taken a path behind the stables that led up to a side entrance of the manor as Edryd had continued towards the practice yard. He would have been caught unaware had he not felt the shifting flows of the displacement when it formed.

He recoiled from the boundaries of the distortion as they passed over his body. It felt to Edryd like a sudden change of pressure in the air, preceded by a sense of the ground falling away from underneath his feet. The odd but familiar experience was accompanied by waves of anger emanating from the man who stood in front of him, effortlessly shaping the dark to his will.

Jumping back, as if he had stumbled into the menacing path of a rabid animal, Edryd drew his sword on instinct. He kept moving back until he was out of the range of the displacement that surrounded Seoras. His teacher's sword was drawn as well, held low, and ready to strike at any moment.

"I warned you," Seoras said. "I told you what would happen if you held anything back from me."

Edryd was confused. He couldn't think what had triggered Seoras like this.

"You did not break any of the glass," Seoras continued. "I am left to suppose then, that you are already a master of the technique. If not, then this will be a short and painful lesson."

Edryd could not comprehend the motivations that were driving this dark and unbalanced behavior, but he did have insights gained from a month of peering in through an unnatural window into the man's emotional state. There was more behind this than just unbroken glass.

The displacement in the dark around Seoras shrank as it intensified, and then momentarily wavered as he exploded forward, attempting to close the distance between them in an instant. Edryd anticipated, reading his attacker's intent, and reacting to the charge before it was ever executed. He was safely away and beyond the boundaries of the distortion that was now reforming around his attacker. Edryd could not allow the gap to be closed or he would be out of options.

The anger in Seoras rose even further, coupled with frustration, but he did not charge again. He settled into place and began to concentrate. An area of distortion began forming at Edryd's feet. His first impulse was to push the displacement away, to shred it into oblivion, but like always, he had no purchase on it. Edryd understood what was happening though. Seoras was binding him to the ground, keeping him in one place so that he would be unable to escape.

The task of shaping became increasingly difficult with greater distances, or so Seoras had said on more than one occasion. Moving something large in near proximity might be done with little effort, but when extending the range of the object you intended to affect by even a modest increment, a small stone could begin to feel to the shaper as though it had the weight of an enormous boulder. Seoras was trying to disguise what he was doing, but at this range it had been overly ambitious, and Edryd could sense the strain behind the effort. Edryd calmly stepped away before the patterns could be properly formed, and the displacement collapsed. As powerful as Seoras was, his capabilities had limits.

Seoras appeared to have become fatigued from the exertion, and he was clearly surprised that Edryd had evaded his trap, but he seemed to almost calm down as he took a moment to recover. Seoras was no less angry, but the frustration he had been feeling was gone. In its place there was deep satisfaction, a definite sense of having accomplished something.

"Your senses would not be this sharp were you not deeply and intimately attuned to the dark," Seoras declared. "You can no longer deceive me. I have measured your strength, and now I am going to make you show it to me."

Seoras didn't give Edryd a chance to try and comprehend anything. He exploded forward again. Edryd could not concentrate on anything but evading the charge. He had to think ahead, and choose efficient movements in order to keep the distance from closing. Illness had robbed him of strength, but his recovered body was lighter, quicker, and had increased stamina. These latter qualities were better tools in this exchange.

The anger from his opponent continued undiminished as Seoras charged relentlessly, surging forward over and over again. More than once Edryd barely slipped beneath the lightning quick arc of his opponent's weapon, avoiding fatal injury in the process. Following each momentum-aided rush, it took Seoras a fraction of a second to restore the gathered tension. This delay was enough to make it possible to continue to dodge the attacks, but it left no margin.

Were they not in an open and unconfined space, or had his opponent been calm enough to better calculate and manipulate his movements, Edryd would have been quickly trapped in a corner. As it was, Edryd could not survive this much longer. He had to hope that it would be over soon. Such hopes were not entirely unfounded. Seoras was rapidly growing tired, recklessly giving no moment for either one of them to rest.

As the tactical exchange played out, Edryd felt something entirely unexpected in Seoras. It was deep pain born out of humiliation. His teacher had declared that he would force his student to use his abilities, and the student was making a joke of it, evading the attacks without resorting to anything other than skillful timing and fluid movements. It was an unforgivable slight—a dismissive insult that had to be answered. Frustration once again dominated the shaper's emotions, and with it had come an unmistakable desire to kill. It frightened Edryd to realize that up until this point, Seoras had not been trying to kill him.

After a single misstep by Edryd, a miscalculation in the placement of his feet, Seoras was able to reduce the separation between them, and a sharp line of pain flared in Edryd's right leg as Seoras scored a shallow cut across his thigh. It wasn't serious but it made Edryd freeze for just a moment. It was more than Seoras needed. The shaper closed the remaining distance and a decapitating blow came slicing through the air.

Edryd felt the sharp steel of the blade penetrate his neck. It took him a long surreal moment to realize that he wasn't dead. Edryd reached up with his hand and pulled the sword away without stopping to wonder why he was able to do so without encountering any resistance. He felt heat as he traced the wound on his neck. When he pulled his hand away, it was covered with warm blood.

The sword had stopped at the exact moment it had come into contact with his skin. It didn't seem possible, but he had to accept that Seoras was capable of a good many things that no one should be able to do. Edryd looked toward Seoras for the first time. The man's dark blue eyes were dim and devoid of awareness, appearing as fixed empty points in a hollow tormented expression. Seoras's mind was a blank.

It seemed to Edryd, quite convincingly, as if time had stopped. But it hadn't. It was only Seoras that seemed to be frozen. That illusion fell away too as the tall man's legs collapsed and he crumpled to the ground. Edryd couldn't see whether Seoras was breathing, but he felt certain that the shaper wasn't dead, at least not yet. There was an emotionless and incoherent chaos stirring within the man's unconscious mind. It was an opportunity, one that would not come again, to kill Seoras. Edryd would have had a host of points of solid justification for doing so if he chose to act. Self-preservation was high on that list.

Edryd rushed off yelling for Irial, and was still running up to the manor when he saw her running towards him in the opposite direction.

"What did you do?" she asked.

"I didn't do anything…" Edryd began defensively, failing to realize that her question wasn't meant as an accusation. She just needed to know what had happened. Irial didn't wait for him to figure it out; she started hurrying down the path again.

"He attacked me," Edryd explained as he ran along behind her, trying again to make it clear that he deserved no blame for what had happened. "He tried to kill me, and then he stopped."

Irial glanced back at Edryd, thinking that he wasn't making much sense, and doubting that he had given an accurate description of events.

Edryd could see the suspicion on her face, but he couldn't blame her, not when he didn't understand what had happened himself. It only stood to reason, that once she saw Seoras lying on the ground, she would have to then think him guilty of having struck Seoras hard enough to knock him out.

Had he done something though? His memory of that moment felt indefinite and unreal. He had believed that he was going to die. Might that have broken something loose? It wasn't without precedent. Something not altogether dissimilar had happened when he had fought and killed his brother Beonen. No, this time had been different; he no longer even had the sigil blade. Whatever had happened in that moment when Seoras's sword had begun slicing into his neck, Edryd was certain that he had played no part in it other than the innocent object of the unprovoked attack.

Edryd began to consider whether Seoras had done something to himself, waiting too late to stop the momentum from a shaped swing. Seoras could have created a force in opposition to the one imparted into the original attack. Nothing else could have stopped the strike so suddenly. Edryd thought of the stone Seoras had been holding in the air, pushed at by opposing forces, before it exploded inside of the outbuilding behind the stables. Seoras had grasped it so tightly that it had been crushed. Had the mental equivalent happened within Seoras? It was a horrible and unpleasant thought.

Arriving in the practice yard, Edryd stood beside Irial as she knelt over Seoras. He braced for the accusations that were sure to come, but Irial was too focused on Seoras to notice him. She loosened the injured man's shirt and listened for his breathing. Putting the side of her head to his heart, she listened intently for a short while before pulling away.

"Apart from being entirely insensible, he is perfectly fine," she said. "He is worn out, but not injured."

Irial began to check for signs of any bruising on his head.

"I didn't hit him," Edryd insisted. "He fell, but he was already unconscious before that."

Irial turned to Edryd and noticed the long cut across the side of his neck as well as the gash in his leg. The bleeding had stopped on Edryd's neck, but blood was still soaking into the cloth on his leg, drawn from the wound on his thigh. Forgetting about Seoras for the moment, Irial focused on attending to Edryd's injuries.

Tolvanes came into the square holding strips of cloth and a bucket of water, which Irial used to carefully clean and then bandage Edryd's injuries. When she was done she asked Edryd again what had happened.

"I didn't kill him," Edryd said.

"No, but you would have been within your rights if you had," she said, looking at his injuries.

Irial turned her attention back to Seoras. She seemed to be going through the same debate he had only moments before. It was an opportunity to end the man. An unnecessary one, Edryd thought, remembering again the stone he had seen shattered into thousands of pieces.

Tolvanes, who had quietly moved closer to Edryd, leaned in close. "Why didn't you kill him," he hissed.

Edryd was a little taken aback, until he remembered what Tolvanes had once asked of him.

"If you want him dead," Edryd said, "do it yourself."

Tolvanes regarded Edryd warily, his gaze travelling to the short sword resting in its sheath at Edryd's side. Edryd could not tell whether Tolvanes was eyeing it as an implement with which to carry out his ambition to kill Seoras, or whether he was just worried about what Edryd might do to intervene.

"We need to carry him to a bed," Irial said. Whatever Tolvanes had been contemplating, this pulled him out of it.

"Of course Mistress Rohvarin," Tolvanes obliged, positioning himself near the feet of the still unconscious Aed Seoras.

Edryd moved into place opposite Giric Tolvanes and together they prepared to lift Aed Seoras from the ground. As he knelt and took hold of Seoras, placing his arms under the injured man's shoulders, Edryd felt Seoras begin to stir.

"Get back!" Edryd ordered, jumping to his feet and shielding Irial.

The displacement emanating from Seoras was unfocused and without form, but it was powerful, encircling all of them and extending past the edges of the courtyard. Irial and Tolvanes had not noticed anything, apart from Edryd's strange behavior, but Edryd felt successive waves of pulsing distortions that left him feeling disoriented and unsteady. Loose gravel began to vibrate around the still prone figure of Aed Seoras, and seeing this, Irial and Tolvanes backed away cautiously. Edryd couldn't move. He was fixed in place within a smaller circle of gravel that was resonating around his own feet. Some of the small stones began to rise in the air, and then they fell abruptly to the ground as Seoras woke and stabilized the distortion.

Seoras rose to his feet, untroubled by, or perhaps just unaware of, the several vacant minutes he had spent laying on the ground. The distortion he was shaping and maintaining with ease was more powerful than ever. It stretched far beyond the range he had formerly been capable of, and the window through which Edryd could observe his teachers mind was clearer than it had ever been. Seoras was admiring the strength he was now wielding with a look of wonder and awe. He turned to Edryd and stared in amazement.

"You really can't shape," Seoras said. "I can see that now, I just don't understand why. If you could touch the dark, you would be something this world has not seen in hundreds of years."

Seoras allowed the displacement he was shaping to dissipate. It continued to shrink until its boundaries passed over Edryd, at which point it collapsed to nothing and vanished. Seoras ceased his hold on the dark reluctantly, feeling the loss of the raw power that had been at his command.

"You may not be able to pattern the dark, but you see it clearly. Far better and much further than I could have imagined. We will work with that. There is a way forward, but we have to approach everything differently."

Seoras said nothing more for a moment, formulating new possibilities as he integrated the fragmented discoveries he had just exposed. "I need to think on this," Seoras said, and then turned away, looking confused.

Edryd wanted to tell him to take all the time he needed. He did not understand any of what had just happened. He ought to have demanded answers, but he felt too frightened to try to follow Seoras, who was now heading up to the manor. Edryd felt weak, and realized he was shaking. Seoras was nothing less than an absolute monster. No person should be able to control so much power.

He felt Irial place her hand on his arm. "Let's go home. You don't need to be here today," she said, her face tight with worry.

Edryd didn't argue. His head hurt fiercely and his body ached. It seemed to Edryd as if his soul had fought against the confines of its vessel, exceeding what should have been withstood, leaving him worn and unstable. There was a residual effect in the courtyard left over from what had just happened, undermining the reality of the place where they still stood, and Edryd wanted nothing more than to get as far away as he could.

He began to feel better almost immediately after they left the estate, but one lasting aftereffect remained. It lessened but did not disappear. Edryd felt like something trapped within him was trying to force a way out. The concept terrified him, and he did what he could to put it out of his mind.

After rounding a corner that blocked the town from view, they travelled another half mile before leaving the path and climbing a short distance to a field of grass that lay beside a cold clear stream. It was the same stream that met the path further down the mountain, following alongside it until reaching the town where it flowed through a channel that fed into a pond on the southern edge of the settlement.

Edryd gathered water in cupped hands and drank deeply, before dipping his hands back in again and bringing up more water to wash over his head and across his neck and face. The water was neither deep nor wide here, or he might have been tempted to submerge his head in it.

Irial unwound a scarf from around her shoulders. Edryd supposed that she planned to gather some of the blackberries that they had spied yesterday, and maybe collect assortments of herbs growing in the wild. He normally would have offered to help. It wasn't often needed, nor was he often much use when he did help, but he usually learned something from assisting her.

"You should rest for a little while," Irial said, concerned about the injuries that she could see, and even more worried over those that he hid from her. She couldn't experience changes in the shape and pattern of the dark the way Edryd did, and so would not have been able to directly understand the magnitude of what had taken place that morning, but she could see that it had shaken him.

"I'll just take a nap then until you get back," Edryd agreed. He smiled, trying to reassure her that he was fine.

"I will be quick," she promised.

"Not too quick," he said, still smiling, "or it won't be much of a nap."

Edryd watched for a little while as Irial picked berries from the branches of a nearby bush. Lying down in the low grass, he closed his eyes for a moment. She was gone when he opened them again.

Closing his eyes once more, he tried to calm the thoughts and worries racing through his head, but failed. He tried again to shut everything out, the fragrance of the fresh grass, the sound of the wind filtering through the leaves of the forest, and the warmth of the sun washing over him. Achieving no measure of success, he settled on the opposite approach and opened himself to everything at once. He was aware of pain from the cuts in his skin, the damp ground beneath him, currents of air carrying bits of pollen and the aromatic fragrance of juniper trees, and the sound of water splashing over the stubborn stones that impeded the stream's descending route down the mountain. Each additional sensory contribution weakened distinctions between all of the others until they bled together into a meaningless union.

His physical awareness receded, his mind disregarding signals to which it could no longer assign meaning or importance. Conversely, his comprehension of the dark, and through it his connection to everything else, deepened. Everything, living things in particular, distorted the shape of the dark into subtle but complex patterns. He could intuit information about the objects that created these patterns, and in doing so construct an understanding of the world around him.

It felt unexpected yet familiar, as if discovering a depth that had always been there in the periphery of his experience. It wasn't new. He had been discerning patterns in the dark for a long time now, but by subduing his other senses his mind was able to see the world in a new way. It afforded a unique and fluid perspective.

As if from an external viewpoint, Edryd could see himself, and he saw that he was warping the shape of the dark in all directions, a constant unchanging passive effect fixed tightly around him as its source. From within the limited range across which this envelopment extended, Edryd's mind accounted for the effect and subtracted it out. From beyond its circumference, it disappeared as if neither he nor the displacement were even there. Edryd could infer its existence, only while shifting perspective near the edge of the effect. He tried to alter the shape, believing that something might have changed, but was rewarded with confirmation that nothing was any different. He might as well have been trying to form a piece of pottery out of flowing water.

The new mode of experience was taking a toll. It felt ungrounded, and it was disorienting to feel so disconnected from physical perception. Concerned that he could become lost, Edryd discovered that he did not know how to exit this altered state. In a panic he tried to tear free. As had happened earlier that morning, he became aware of something inside. Some shaped piece of the dark nestled in his mind, resisting his every effort. Terror sparked a cascade that collapsed everything. Edryd was assaulted by blinding light and roaring sounds, and the pain from his injuries was overwhelming. Then everything returned to normal. Edryd blinked. The world was again a place of physical sights and sounds.

Irial was no longer there. He judged that less than half an hour had passed. He was nervous, but he had to try again. He closed his eyes and tried to repeat the process, but it wouldn't work. The experience had unsettled him too much. He wanted to talk with someone. The fear and excitement that he felt were too much to be held in. Edryd stood up, shook his coat to loosen bits of grass and debris that clung to his back, and began looking east. He wondered for a moment why he felt so certain about the direction. He wasn't sure, but he suspected he had recognized her in the patterns left in the dark. He almost felt like he still could. Edryd sat back down and decided to wait, trying to see if he could get a sense of Irial's location in the woods, and perhaps fooling himself that he could.

She returned with a pile of blackberries loaded into her scarf, covered by mint leaves layered above them. She also had a piece of honeycomb wrapped in some leaves and a bundle of hedge cleaver plants collected from the edges of the meadow. Sitting down beside him, she began mashing the hedge cleaver in the hollow of a stone until it became a moist paste. She mixed this with honey and spread it over Edryd's cuts.

"Does Seoras know who I am?" Edryd asked.

"I don't know," she answered. "You think he might?"

"If he does, he hasn't said anything. But he was already in a rage when I showed up. He attacked me only moments after I came through the gate. Something was different."

"I didn't hear anything," Irial objected. "I couldn't have been very far away when it started."

"Swords were drawn," Edryd explained, "but they never crossed."

Irial popped a blackberry in her mouth. "You are going to have to explain that to me," she said.

"He was out of control. I didn't dare block his strikes, and there was no way to fight back. All I could do was run and dodge the attacks."

"Dodge some of the attacks," she corrected, looking critically at his injuries.

"He was trying to kill me," Edryd said. He had no doubt this was the truth. "He stopped just short of doing so."

Irial placed a couple of fingers on his neck, tracing over the paste-smeared line of the cut. "Maybe you did fight back," she said. "Sigil knights were said to be able to create spiritual armor. Maybe something like that stopped Seoras, and saved you."

Edryd thought of what he had discovered only moments before, the warping of the dark that surrounded him, but that was more a cloak of concealment than it was a form of physical protection.

"I am no sigil knight," he said. She hadn't mentioned anything like this before. Seoras had spoken of Edryd being something that had not been seen in hundreds of years. That reference seemed clear now. It was an unpleasant and suspicious coincidence that Seoras and Irial had both reached and expressed similar conclusions mere hours apart.

"But you were a captain in the Sigil Order," Irial protested.

"There are no sigil knights in the Sigil Order in Nar Edor," Edryd insisted. "It is made up of men. I wouldn't call them ordinary men, but there are among them no masters of spiritual energy, nor any shapers of the dark—just ordinary soldiers."

Irial was unconvinced. "If what I have heard can be trusted at all, you awakened a sword—your father's sigil sword."

Edryd did not like this topic, and he particularly did not like discussing it with Irial. "What happened that day... it left my brother dead. It had never happened before and has not happened since. I have tried for a month now to grasp hold of the dark, and I am no more capable than I was when I started. Seoras is stronger than ever, but I am exactly the same as I was before I got here."

Irial did not give up. "It isn't supposed to work that way," she said. "An apprentice in the Sigil Order drew the strength to manipulate spiritual energy from his master. The relationship did not strengthen the teacher."

A warning tone crept into Edryd's reply, an unconscious reaction to his presumption that Irial had failed to appreciate the degree to which this topic troubled him. "This isn't the Sigil Order, and that distempered wolf, Seoras, is no source of strength. Not to me or to anyone else." Irial began to respond, but Edryd wasn't done. "How is it that you suddenly think yourself an expert on all these things?" he demanded.

Edryd was surprised at how harsh his complaint had sounded, but it engendered an unexpected reaction. Irial seemed to be embarrassed, as if she did not want to answer that question. Edryd let it drop and Irial dodged the subject by moving to another topic. "How would you feel about rearranging some of Logaeir's schemes for you and the Ascomanni?" she asked.

The spontaneous smile on her protector's face gave her all the answer that she could have needed as Edryd listened carefully while she explained the details of her plan.

Chapter 13

A Captain of the Sigil Corp

Currents of smoke drifted in the air above the cottage, drawn not through the stone chimney vent, but through the hole in the center of the thatched roof of the cottage. Edryd was alarmed. He had never known the fire pit to have been put to use, and he couldn't imagine Eithne would have built up a fire in it while they were gone. Irial was untroubled, for she knew what it meant.

"He's here already," Irial said.

"Who?" Edryd asked.

"Logaeir. He will be inside waiting, and he will have brought others too."

Edryd did not think there would have been enough time from when Ruach had left last night for him to have made it back to the Ascomanni camp and return with Logaeir, but Edryd had no clear idea as to precisely where the encampment was, so his assumptions could have been wrong. The encampment would have to be closer to the island than he had thought. Even assuming that it was, Edryd wasn't sure how Irial knew that Logaeir was inside.

"Whenever he comes with a group, he makes use of the fire pit," Irial explained, answering Edryd's unspoken question.

Feeling protective towards Irial as he thought about Logaeir, Edryd moved a hand into position near the hilt of the sword at his side. He had made the movement without fully appreciating the depth of the feelings that motivated his response, and in truth, had not noticed that he had even done it. Irial noticed, and was annoyed, thinking that Edryd's overtly vigilant reaction was disproportionate to any actual threat, but she did not say anything.

"Remember, you have leverage," she reminded Edryd as they approached the cottage together. "He will have no choice but to agree."

Entering through the door, they were greeted by the smell of cooked meat. A wild pig, its skin blackened and charred by the heat from the coals of the fire, was roasting in its own fat on a spit in the center of the room. Edryd had walked in full of caution, but he was made eager by the food. Other than fish caught in the ocean waters near An Innis, meat was difficult to procure here, and Edryd had not had the chance to enjoy a feast like this one since before he had first arrived.

Oren and Ruach looked on from the back of the open hall as Edryd stepped forward. Logaeir, seated beside Captain Krin at the end of the table next to the fire pit, was going through a collection of pages which were bound up between white cloth-covered wooden panels. Eithne sat opposite, silently staring with obvious interest at the book in Logaeir's hands.

"*A Compendium of the History of the Sigil Order*, by Ludin Kar," Logaeir said without looking up.

Though he had not known its title, Edryd recognized the book, along with the much larger book about the 'Ossian Oligarchs' that sat unopened on the table alongside it. A leather bag that had once held both of the books lay discarded on the floor beside Logaeir's feet. Surprised, Edryd turned to Irial with an unspoken question, wondering why she had lied. She had told him it had been a book on food preparation. He now understood the source of her sudden expertise on the Sigil Order.

"To think I studied under this fool," Logaeir laughed.

"That's unkind of you to say so, Logaeir, considering you would still be nothing more than the backwards and ignorant little boy of no consequence that you once were, if you had not met him," Irial chided.

"Logaeir might be the size of a little a boy, but I'm not sure I believe that this devil ever was one," Krin laughed. "And he remains a man of no consequence, though he would have us all believe otherwise."

The deliberately cavalier attitude that Logaeir had cultivated with so much care fell away for a moment, as he took umbrage at the insults. "I am not ungrateful to him, but this nonsense isn't scholarship, it's a work of fiction," he said, stabbing a finger at the pages of the book.

"A quorum of sigil knights, assembled together, could defeat even the darkness of the night, summoning the light of day to illuminate a battlefield," Logaeir said, reading from the book. "First of all, is it likely that a pitched battle would be fought in the middle of the night?"

"I can think of several reasons why one might be," Edryd said.

"It wouldn't be likely," Logaeir said, ignoring Edryd's answer to his question, "but if it were, and the Sigil Knights could summon light, why would they want to? A spiritual warrior who can fight with his eyes closed would have an advantage in the dark. Even if you let that pass, doesn't it strike anyone else as so much mythical absurdity?"

Oren and Ruach took on serious expressions, looking to Edryd, expecting him to put Logaeir in his place. Edryd, who would have been of a similar opinion as Logaeir not so long ago, didn't bother to object, even though he had recently seen for himself some of what Logaeir had just now dismissed as 'mythical absurdity'.

"We have ourselves three sigil knights gathered right here," Logaeir mocked, "shouldn't you be glowing? Or are there not enough of you for a quorum?"

Oren started to stand with a fierce look in his bright eyes, intending to confront Logaeir, but he was held back by Ruach, who stretched out an arm to restrain him. It was their captain's place to choose how to handle this affront and respond to the disrespect that Logaeir had directed towards them. Edryd's response was calm and even.

"There are no longer any sigil knights, but Oren and Ruach are trained officers of the Sigil Corps. You have lied to them, and misused my name in persuading them to give you their service. Give any more provocation, and I will not prevent them from seeking retribution against your deceptions. They will not need the aid of spiritual powers to settle things with you."

The room had gown tense, with everyone watching Logaeir's reaction to the force of the condemnation so flatly expressed in Edryd's threat. Everyone except Logaeir, who looked at Edryd approvingly, with no care at all for what anyone else thought of him. Logaeir had sought this reaction, making calculated taunts and verbal attacks, all in order to overcome the other man's passive predisposition in the hope that it would provoke Edryd to action.

"I have no doubts about your ability to carry that threat through," Logaeir said. "Either of your officers could take on any five of my men, and do so without wasting much effort. I have seen what they can do firsthand, and as for you... well, I have heard slightly less credible things, secondhand. If even half of it is true..." Logaeir said, letting his words trail off, not bothering to finish the thought. He allowed the others to complete the idea with whatever stood in each person's imagination.

"Considerably less than half of it is true," Edryd clarified. He could see that Logaeir appeared to be pleased, and that was reason enough for concern and caution, and a cause for irritation.

"You don't need to convince me," said Logaeir. "You are nothing like the stories that are told. It isn't you that I need, just your reputation. Well, that and your two officers," Logaeir said, looking towards Oren and Ruach. "They have stopped helping. It's unacceptable."

Edryd reminded himself that it would do no good to get angry, but it was a feat of restraint for him to speak calmly. "Against my will, you have made me a leader within the Ascomanni," Edryd began.

"He has made you a captain," Krin said, interrupting Edryd in what appeared to be an effort to be helpful. Logaeir gave his friend an angry look. This had not been information that he had wanted Krin to share. Undeterred, and with a mischievous look in his eye that betrayed his motives, which were above anything else focused upon his own immediate amusement, Krin then sought to inspire even more conflict between Edryd and Logaeir. "You are the Captain to be more precise," he continued. "Logaeir is first under your command. Quite a few of our men are eager to follow the Blood Prince, and some of them are stupid enough to believe that Logaeir represents you. He is commanding a ship under your banners. He calls it the *Retribution*. Several times now, Logaeir has gone so far as to pretend to be the Blood Prince."

The last part, Krin had said in disbelief, expressing his inability to comprehend anyone accepting Logaeir as a convincing stand in for the Blood Prince. "I have a passing resemblance," Logaeir said, giving Krin a punishing look. Krin laughed, enjoying his friend's discomfort.

"I need your officers to help me," Logaeir said quietly when Krin's laughter died down. It wasn't a demand. For once it seemed he was being respectful, having been forced to do so out of necessity, with no choice but to beg for what he needed. In that moment, Logaeir seemed to Edryd more like the man he had first met and talked with alone at the bottom of the cliffside trail. It was a reminder that Logaeir could, in his better moments, be contemplative, polite, and softly persuasive. Not at all like the parody of an unscrupulous man that he played whenever there was an audience.

"As their captain," Edryd said, "Oren and Ruach follow only my orders."

"Yes, but what would it take to formalize a temporary arrangement where they will also follow mine?" Logaeir asked. He looked like he was swallowing a bitter potion, but he was clearly ready to negotiate.

"There is nothing to discuss," Edryd said, rejecting the suggestion out of hand. "I told you they are officers in the Sigil Corps. I cannot ask them to follow the orders of some frivolous criminal with petty dreams of conquering small islands."

Oren and Ruach straightened their backs in pride. Logaeir's face darkened, his demeanor approaching the verge of an apoplectic fit. Edryd had never seen the man at a loss for words and was pleased to have affected him so, if only for a short moment. Krin seemed to be enjoying the moment as well, engaged as he was in loud expressions of uncontrolled mirth.

"Well said," interjected Krin, once he managed to stop laughing. "But they don't need to take orders from Logaeir. We only need them to provide training for our men, and they can do that under your orders if you prefer. That much at least should be open for negotiation."

Edryd gained an immediate appreciation for Krin's unsubtle diplomatic skills. Logaeir frowned openly at his partner. This was not what he wanted, but it might be as much as they could hope to achieve.

"Provided we understood that these are my men, no one else's, I will consider it," Edryd said, "but if I am to be a captain in the Ascomanni, I think it is time I had my own crew."

"No one is giving you a ship," Logaeir said defiantly. He thought he understood Edryd's intentions, and he was not going to provide him with the means to flee An Innis. "There are none to spare."

Krin gave Logaeir a hard look. "Forgetting the *Retribution*, which you have told the rest of the Ascomanni is already his, we have at least a dozen unmanned ships, anchored in inlets near the encampment," he said, contradicting Logaeir. "I'll give him one of mine if that is what it takes."

"And will you give him some of your men as well to sail the ship?" Logaeir challenged.

Krin looked uncertain as he considered that prospect. "That is going to be a problem," Krin admitted. "Plenty would be willing to follow the Blood Prince, but it isn't going to sit well with the other captains if he siphons away the best of their men."

"I don't need a ship, and I don't need any of the Ascomanni," Edryd said, dodging the entire issue.

The conversation stopped as the participants reacted with confusion, everyone except for Edryd and Irial who had carefully planned this ahead of time.

"Are you going to call up a phantom crew to operate a phantom ship?" Logaeir demanded, tired of waiting for an explanation.

"I was thinking more along the line of fresh recruits," Edryd said. "I will need you to transport Oren and Ruach back to Nar Edor."

"You don't just sail into the Citadel Harbor," said Logaeir dismissing the request. "It is closed to everything but approved Ossian merchant vessels."

"Once there," Edryd continued, ignoring Logaeir completely, "they will choose a dozen or so volunteers from amongst the soldiers of the Sigil Corps. Under my command, those men will aid the Ascomanni."

"It wouldn't take but a couple of days," said Oren, completely transparent in his enthusiasm.

"I know of eight who would go immediately," Ruach agreed, thinking of the remaining men under Edryd's old command.

"They will be my crew," Edryd finished.

Logaeir looked like he was choking on something.

"We could get an escort from Aelsian's fleet," Krin said, countering Logaeir's earlier argument regarding the impossibility of entering the Citadel Harbor. "It won't be any trouble getting into the port."

Logaeir was once again speechless. He didn't seem to be breathing and his face was turning a darkened shade of red. With the flat of his broad fully-spread palm, Krin gave Logaeir a short powerful thump on the back, forcing out a gasp of held air from the smaller man's lungs.

"Barely different from what you spoke of when you convinced me to go and recruit the Blood Prince in the first place," Krin pointed out. "Are you going to tell me this isn't exactly what you wanted?"

"When someone, who doesn't hold you in any high regard, grants all of your wishes, leveraging them upon you as though they were demanded concessions, you get suspicious," Logaeir explained.

Edryd understood the hesitation, and he knew that the Ascomanni strategist's concerns went deeper than mere suspicion. Logaeir was getting more than he had dared to ask for, but imagining Edryd as a captain in the Ascomanni with a company of Sigil Corps solders under his command, gave him reasons to fear that this might all come at the cost of his control over the Ascomanni. Beyond this, he had to also be wondering what had motivated Edryd's sudden willingness to cooperate.

"Agreed," Logaeir said after some thought, making new plans even as the words escaped his lips. "But understand, you are committing your men to help us as needed when we take the island."

"Your men will get equal shares afterwards," Krin added. "As a captain, you will get four."

"We won't need them," Edryd declined. Everyone but Irial reacted with surprise. "I will, however, take Esivh Rhol's palace and everything in it. When this is over, it belongs to the Sigil Corps."

"Agreed," Logaeir said quickly, much too quickly.

Krin thought it was a little too hasty as well. "We need to talk about this," he complained.

"Aisen will be the ruler of An Innis, of course the palace is going to be his," Logaeir said.

It was Edryd's turn to feel uncomfortable about getting something he had asked for: the palace, offered to him now along with an unwanted encumbrance. Edryd did not intend to allow anyone to install him as the ruler of this horrible island. He didn't need to refuse though. If Irial's plan worked, he and Eithne would be away on one of Aelsian's ships before that attack happened, and if Edryd could manage it, Irial would also come with them.

"You can't decide that," Krin continued to protest. Esivh Rhol's palace was too big a prize to just give away.

"The others will agree," Logaeir insisted. "The bulk of the wealth on the island is in the hands of the harbormasters. Once the captains understand that we are getting Sigil Warrior reinforcements, with no reduction of their shares, it will be easy to convince them."

"One other thing," Edryd interrupted. "Oren and Ruach are my representatives with the Ascomanni, not you."

"No," Logaeir refused.

"They command my men, they come and go as they please, and they take orders only from me. If you need help from any of my men, you run it through Oren and Ruach."

"Of course he will," Krin said, "those are the rules as they apply with any of the captains."

"No," Logaeir said again, even more firmly.

Logaeir had already positioned himself as the Blood Prince's second in command. Denying him that was a step too far, it would deprive him of every last shred of his credibility.

"I don't care what you tell the rest of the Ascomanni, as long as you understand that my men do not answer to you," Edryd said, offering a compromise.

"I will want to arrange introductions with the captains," Logaeir said, modifying Edryd's offer. "When I do, you will back up what I have told them, and you will endeavor to impress them."

"Shouldn't be a problem," Edryd assented.

"Now that is where I will have to disagree," Krin said. "After the stories people have been telling, you need to understand that meeting you for the first time can be a disappointment. It isn't going to impress anyone."

Edryd laughed at the disparaging comment. The insult had been friendly and warm, instead of filled with the condescension and disrespect that came so naturally to Logaeir, and it made Edryd feel like at least one person didn't expect impossible things out of him. Krin was especially honest and direct for someone in his profession, and was in many ways, Logaeir's complete opposite.

Having brokered an understanding, tension faded from the room, under the realization of that rare circumstance where those who had participated had all gotten what they wanted. If everyone was also a little unhappy about it, then that only meant it must have been a fair exchange. There was, however, one person who was entirely unconflicted, holding no misgivings about the outcome. For Irial, the results could not have been better. Irial had been silent throughout, but Edryd had taken her advice and accomplished everything she had asked of him.

Sensing that everything had been decided, and without waiting on anyone else, Krin carved out a choice section of the roasted pig. Others followed, and soon most of them were busily engaged with their food, bringing a welcome silence to a room that had moments ago been filled with loud arguments.

Edryd noticed Eithne, still sitting in the same seat across from Logaeir. She had quietly listened to everything, and had now gotten a hold of the white cloth-covered book that she had been admiring. It took him a moment to accept the idea that they had just plotted the overthrow of An Innis in the presence of an eleven year old girl. No one else seemed to be bothered by it, but it made the whole scenario seem completely unreal to Edryd. He took a seat beside Eithne, more than a little curious himself about the contents of the book.

"So what do you think of it?" he asked her. He meant her opinion of the book about the Sigil Order, but she took it to be a question about the agreements that had been reached over the course of the evening.

"You gave Uncle Logaeir what he wanted, but I don't know what you got in return," she replied.

Logaeir had turned away towards Krin, but it didn't escape Edryd's notice he was paying close attention to this conversation with Eithne.

"That's a good sign," Edryd replied. "If you haven't figured it out, then it will be much too hard a puzzle for him."

Logaeir's face tightened, unable to stifle his reaction.

"He thinks he is very smart, you know," Eithne laughed. "He would be angry if he heard us." Eithne knew very well that Logaeir was listening, and was having some fun of her own.

The evening wore on, and soon everyone was well fed with the roasted meat and helpings of vegetables that had been harvested from Irial's garden. Edryd chose that moment to pull Ruach aside, and leaving everyone else behind, the two men took a walk out in the night air. Something was bothering Edryd, but there was little time to work with, and so he ignored his misgivings.

"Ruach," Edryd said as they stood in the cold beneath a starlit sky, well away from the cottage, where no one inside could possibly overhear, "I need you to get a message to the Ossian First Fleet Navarch,"

"Who?" Ruach asked. There wasn't any surprise in the question, just the need to clarify who it was Edryd was speaking of. Ruach knew little to nothing about Ossia or the officers in its fleet.

"His name is Aelsian," Edryd replied. "His ships secure the trade between Ossia and Nar Edor."

"I'm not sure I understand," Ruach said.

"You don't need to. On your way back to Nar Edor, the Ascomanni are going to have to meet up with one of Aelsian's ships. When that happens, arrange a private meeting with the captain of the ship."

"And give him what message?"

"Have him get word to Aelsian that Edryd needs to see him."

"Edryd?—or Lord Aisen?" Ruach questioned.

"No, don't use my real name. Don't mention the Blood Prince or anything else of the sort. Aelsian will already know who I am, no one else needs to."

"I understand. I assume we should keep this all a secret from the Ascomanni as well," he said.

"Tell Oren if you get a chance, but no one else," Edryd confirmed.

Edryd looked around and saw nothing, but remained troubled by something he couldn't quite place. Whatever it was that was bothering him, it was somewhere nearby, hidden by the dark. "You had better get back. I will be along in a minute," he said to Ruach.

Edryd watched Ruach leave, watched the light scatter out from the cottage when he opened the door, and watched it disappear again as Ruach stepped inside, shutting the door tight behind him. Edryd had now pinpointed the position of the irritant that had been disturbing his thoughts. There was someone there, close enough to have overheard the entire conversation. Edryd turned, but all he could see was darkness. It was clouded and obscured, but the hidden person had a mind with an open window through which Edryd could look.

"Aed Seoras," Edryd called out.

"Well met, Lord Aisen," Seoras said, shedding fragmented distortions as he emerged from out of the night. To Edryd's eyes it looked as if Seoras was taking form directly from shifting flows of the dark. As the shaping ceased, the window became clear and Edryd sensed that Seoras was wracked with worry.

"You knew all along," Edryd said.

"No," Seoras admitted. "At first I had no idea. More recently I have had my suspicions, and this morning I thought that I was certain, but until I overheard you and Ruach, I can't say that I knew for sure."

"What are you going to do?"

"Nothing," Seoras answered, as though he were surprised that Edryd would ask.

"Then why are you here?" Edryd had picked up on Seoras's fears, but they were not so deep as his own in that moment. Seoras was a threat that he could not ignore.

"I made a discovery this morning," Seoras began. He spoke now as though his discovery had not come about when he had tried to kill Edryd and as if this were some ordinary conversation between friends. "Through the dark, there is hint of a deeper level to the world. You may have felt it yourself. In a fight it often manifests as a sort of intuition. If someone begins to shape the dark, it creates an echo that travels. I can detect an attuned individual from a great distance away, just by the ripples they leave in their wake."

"That is why you thought I could shape."

"It was why I was willing to believe you when you said you could not," Seoras corrected. "In subtle ways, we all shape as we interact with the world. Some of us do have a greater affinity for it than others, but with you, I can see nothing. It is as though you don't exist. You appear to have no connection to the dark."

"But that shouldn't be possible."

"No it shouldn't," Seoras agreed. "And there is an even bigger mystery. Do you remember I showed you how a sword can be used as a focus for the dark? Well a focus doesn't need to be a sword. In particular, a well attuned person naturally aligns the currents that flow through the dark in a way that amplifies the effects of shaping. Anyone who does this should be a beacon to anyone who can comprehend the dark."

Edryd felt an awful sensation in the pit of his stomach. The implication was clear. Powerless on his own, he was an awful tool in the hands of someone like Seoras, whose power multiplied in his presence. He had even more reason now to be fearful of the man's intentions.

"You do have a connection to the dark, and you do alter its pattern, you just happen to be doing it in a very specific way. You bend and reshape the dark in a way that conceals. It makes you invisible to someone like me."

Edryd might have failed to grasp this concept, if not for what he had discovered that afternoon. He had observed what Seoras was describing. He hadn't understood its function then, but it was clear now.

"I spent all of this afternoon trying to replicate the effect. Unfortunately you were not there for comparison, but what you are doing defies study and observation, so maybe it wouldn't have helped. I managed a crude and flawed version, but you saw through that a moment ago. What you are doing is incredibly stable and far more complex."

Edryd didn't want to tell Seoras how effective his crude and flawed attempt had really been, but Seoras was right, it hadn't been the same thing.

"How can I do something like that when I can't actually shape?"

"It is proof that you are shaping all the time, even in your sleep," Seoras suggested confidently. "There is something profound at work here, some knowledge that was lost even before the Sigil Order was destroyed. You and I can rediscover it."

The worry was gone from his teacher's mind. He had become so excited that he had forgotten whatever it was that had been troubling him. Seoras didn't care who Edryd was, he only cared who it was he might become. The shaper had a singular obsession, and that was uncovering the secrets that had once been mastered in an earlier age by the Knights of the Sigil Order, and he saw Edryd as the means by which he could achieve that goal. This conversation was forcing Edryd to make alterations to the plans that were even now in the process of unfolding, and he was going to need to be ready to make some rapid adjustments.

"This isn't what you came here to tell me," Edryd said, trying to sound unimpressed. He knew that Seoras was here about something even more important.

"That discovery, this skill of yours, it is no minor thing," Seoras replied. He was surprised by Edryd's even reaction, and he was further impressed by his students having somehow divined that he was here for another purpose. "I did also come with a warning," he said. Fear was encroaching once more upon the shaper's mind. "You need to leave the island."

This was not amongst any of the things that Edryd could have imagined Seoras might say, and he was unable to form a response.

"I know you think I have tried to keep you here, but you have made false assumptions on that subject. Logaeir wants to keep you here, and so does Esivh Rhol. I have an interest in you as well of course, but I have only been trying to keep you safe in a very dangerous place."

Edryd could not accept this as the truth. The only person Edryd needed protection from was Seoras. Ignoring Esivh Rhol, it was troubling that Seoras knew Logaeir by name. Rather than confirm a connection to Logaeir, Edryd focused on the other man.

"What does Esivh Rhol want with me?" Edryd asked.

"He's interested in you because I'm interested in you. When he learned of what you had done to Hagan and Cecht, he decided right then that he wanted you working for him."

"I have had no dealings with the Ard Ri at all," Edryd said, reacting with disbelief.

"Rhol has Vannin tracking your movements, and he made the harbormasters deny you any other means of employment. They all also have instructions to refuse you passage off of the island."

Edryd didn't know what to believe. He had assumed that Vannin worked for Seoras. He would have to see what Irial could tell him, because he wasn't ready to believe Seoras.

"And this Logaeir, he is one of the Ascomanni?" Edryd asked. He didn't know how much Seoras knew, but he had to at least pretend to be ignorant.

Seoras fixed his eyes on Edryd in long penetrating stare. "The soldier friend you were speaking to just now obviously came here on an Ascomanni ship, and will be leaving on one as well. Don't tell me you don't know who Logaeir is. He's probably in the cottage right now."

"Why would he be here?"

"He will be expecting you to help when the Ascomanni attack An Innis," Seoras suggested. "Probably hopes that you can keep me away from the battle when it happens."

His guesses were all hitting the mark, if they were guesses at all. Denying any of it would amount to much the same thing as proving the suspicions. Whatever Seoras thought he knew, there was nothing to be gained by confirming it for him.

"If you really haven't met him yet, you will be interested to know that he is the one who is attacking ships around An Innis claiming to be the Blood Prince," Seoras clarified. "None of this matters though. It isn't Esivh Rhol or Logaeir that I came to warn you about."

"No," Edryd laughed, "why would the interests of the ruler of An Innis, or the leader of a company of pillaging warriors pose a threat that would merit a warning?"

"There are worse things that frequent this island, I can assure you," Seoras said. "I am about to have some unpleasant houseguests. They may be here as soon as tomorrow."

"Draugar," Edryd guessed.

"Not a correct name for them," Seoras confirmed, "but yes."

Edryd recalled a conversation he had once had with Irial, and this felt eerily like an echo of that earlier discussion of these creatures. She worked for the man, and so must have picked up on how he spoke of them. Still, it bothered Edryd how closely Seoras's reaction to the term draugar had mirrored Irial's. "Reason enough to be away when they arrive I suppose," Edryd concluded.

"They are following rumors of the Blood Prince and at least one of them knows you on sight," Seoras replied, clearly thinking that Edryd was not taking the news seriously enough. "These creatures cannot be killed and they are more dangerous than you know. Logaeir did you no favors by making use of your name."

"No, he didn't," Edryd agreed. "He will realize that he has done himself some harm too when he ends up face to face with an angry immortal creature wanting to know why he isn't me."

"That might be funny to see, if he had any chance of surviving the experience," Seoras said, laughing as he imagined it. "He is about to get his first up-close look at a true Ash Man."

"I will be glad that I am not him then," Edryd joked.

"If he tells them where you are, you will wish you weren't you," Seoras warned.

"I will stay away until they have gone. I'm only too happy to take a few days off while you catch up with these friends of yours."

Seoras reacted with a look of concern. He couldn't tell if Edryd was being serious or not. "That isn't good enough," he said. "These creatures won't kill you Edryd. They will bind you and deliver you to my master. You will be forced to serve him unless you leave the island tonight."

It wasn't that Edryd needed convincing. He just didn't know where he would go or how he would get there. The Ascomanni encampment wouldn't be safe; the draugar would be hoping to find him there. A better option would be too flee by ship. Logaeir would have plenty of incentive to leave with him.

As if anticipating Edryd's concerns, Seoras offered a solution that was more of an order than it was a suggestion. "You leave the same way you came, across the causeway. They don't like being near anything deeper than a few feet of water. If one of them should pick up your trail, it might be hesitant to follow it across."

Edryd did not much enjoy the idea of spending time with Logaeir as a travelling companion, but getting away in his fastest ship still seemed like a better idea. It wasn't an alternative he wanted to share with Seoras though.

"A few miles inland, there are some old ruins," Seoras suggested.

"These would be the same ruins that haunt the dreams of the inhabitants of Ann Innis?"

"They are not dangerous," assured Seoras. "At least not in the way that people think they are. But they are old—predating the last age. You in particular should find them interesting."

"All right," Edryd agreed. "I can forage for a while. While I was on the mainland on my way in, I noticed plenty of wildlife."

"I will come when it is safe to return," Seoras promised.

"I need to know one thing," Edryd said. "Who is this master of yours?"

Seoras paused, considering the question. "I think that is something I'm not prepared to explain just yet," he answered. "It is enough that as yet he has no hold on you. Just know that it would be a bad result for both of us if that ever changes."

Edryd could see that Seoras was not going to explain any more than he had.

"I can't stay any longer," Seoras said. "There are preparations I need to make before morning."

"Don't let me stop you, I will be off of the island before the night is over," Edryd promised.

Edryd watched Seoras fade into the distance before making his way back to the cottage. Logaeir better still be there, he thought to himself. Surely his patron amongst the Ascomanni would be able to appreciate the wisdom of getting far away, and doing so as quickly as possible.

When Edryd returned to the cottage, Logaeir was still there. He was standing alongside Irial and Krin, all crowding the entrance as Edryd opened the door.

"What was he doing here?" Logaeir demanded. "Why were you talking to him? What were you talking about?"

"He came to warn... " Edryd began to explain.

"He knows who you are," Logaeir said, anticipating that Edryd would surely confirm his fears.

"He overheard me talking with Ruach. That did give it away," Edryd admitted. From the other end of the room, Ruach and Oren looked on in confusion. They did not know who it was everyone was talking about, or why they were all so concerned.

"He came to warn you about something?" Irial asked, bringing things into focus.

"Draugar will be in An Innis, possibly as soon as tomorrow morning. They have come looking for me."

There was a collection of audible gasps as nearly everyone in the room reacted. Oren and Ruach took the information evenly, probably convinced that there were no such things in the world, but Krin, Logaeir and Irial were all well aware of the truth. Eithne was there as well behind everyone else, looking appropriately worried.

"This isn't uncommon," Irial said, trying to build the argument against overreacting to the news. "They come regularly, several times a year. It doesn't mean that they know you are here or that they are looking for you."

"They don't know that I'm here," Edryd agreed. "But they do know that an idiot, who has been boldly flying the banners of the Blood Prince, has been capturing ships and cargo in and around An Innis."

Logaeir's face went white. He didn't even notice the insult, he was too aware of the danger he had put himself in.

Krin seized the opportunity to put forward a plan. "The two of you need to get on my ship, and we need to sail as far away from here as fast as we can," he concluded. Edryd was glad to learn someone was thinking along the exact same lines that he was.

"No," Logaeir said. "They are looking for Aisen, but when they start tracing the source of these rumors, it will lead back to me. If they don't find someone, they won't stop looking and we will have to keep running. I can't afford that, it will ruin everything."

"If they find and kill you, might that not even more thoroughly ruin your damned plans?" Krin argued. "I'm not saying that would trouble me much, but I wouldn't expect you to stay and face down one of those things."

"I'm not an important part of my plans," Logaeir countered somewhat oddly, seemingly lost in thought, unaware that he was sharing those thoughts with everyone. "Aisen is, and so are the Ascomanni, but—"

"When are you going to learn that that name is dangerous?" Edryd shouted, tired of hearing Logaeir utter the name which he had so often and so unwisely put to ill-use. "Throwing it around, especially right now, is going to end up getting someone killed."

Edryd's anger shocked Logaeir back into a more coherent state. "You are right of course," he agreed, surprising Edryd. "This is my fault," he admitted, "so I think we can all agree that it is appropriate that I take the necessary risks to fix it."

"Risk your own life, not everyone else's," Edryd responded. "You may not want to take Krin's offer, but I will be getting on his ship and leaving tonight."

"Hold on," said Krin, "let's hear what he would do instead."

"What did Seoras say?" Logaeir asked.

"He wants me to cross the causeway and hide in the forests on the mainland," Edryd said without any trace of enthusiasm.

"I think that's the right thing to do," Logaeir said, sounding uncertain.

"Seoras will be so pleased to hear that you agree with him," Edryd said with an exaggerated sharpness which bespoke his low opinion of the idea.

Undeterred, Logaeir continued to explain. "It is important to remember that they don't actually know you are here. If we run, it will signal that we knew they were coming. They would reason out that Seoras warned you. But if they learn that I am an imposter, they will leave once they have confirmed it. I will make them see what they are probably already expecting. It will even make them dismiss any future news that places you here as just more false rumors."

Edryd had to admit the reasoning was sound. Logaeir seemed reckless and frivolous, but only if you were not paying close attention. He had a mind for strategy that had to be respected.

"I would still rather go with Krin," Edryd said to Logaeir. "If you don't want to come along, that's up to you."

"Let's try Logaeir's plan first," Krin said. "It will be his skin in the fire. If it goes wrong, we will still be able to get you out of here."

Things were not going well. Logaeir had persuaded the only person here with a ship. Irial stepped close to Edryd. "I need you to give this a chance," she whispered. "We have plans that will come to nothing if you leave now."

Edryd was embarrassed. He had given no thought to what he had promised Irial. In a room that included his subordinates, a woman and a young girl, and two criminals, he was distinguishing himself as the biggest of cowards. None of them are being hunted by draugar, he thought to himself, and then felt even worse, reflecting with shame on his selfish reaction, knowing that these people were all taking dangerous risks on his behalf.

"All right," Edryd said, "we go with Seoras's plan." He wasn't going to call it Logaeir's plan; he was feeling too spiteful for that. Either way, Irial's endorsement had set Edryd's path. He had no choice but to see where it led.

Chapter 14

The Construct Chamber

Dark shapes were silhouetted in the midmorning sunlight, revealed now as arched walls which loomed above the bed of pine needles that Edryd had slept in. He had spent the night shivering in the cold after having made his way to the edge of the ruins and finding it too dark to either build or locate better shelter.

The oversized stonework structures made Edryd feel small, but they were dominated by another even more impressive feature of the landscape, massive towering trees which cast everything in perpetual shadows. Edryd could not get a sense for the scale of the place. There were no forests like this in Nar Edor, and while he had seen even larger stone constructions, including the Port Citadel, none of those could be compared to the sophistication of the buildings in this ruined city. The structures were pitted with age, but it only added to the beauty of the intricately shaped blocks that created complex spans and rising columns throughout the diverse architecture.

Seoras had said it predated the last age, which would put the civilization that built all of this more than a thousand years in the past. Edryd could easily believe that the ruined city was at least that old. Looking like something grown out of the rocks of the forest, the city had lost much of what once would have marked it as a place of human habitation.

Compelled by an overpowering desire to explore, the appeasement of which became his most immediate concern, Edryd passed on beyond the crumbling walls, drawn in toward what he imagined to be the still pulsing heart of the city. Guided by skeletal remains of buildings long since reclaimed by the forest, Edryd wandered into the depths of the place and lost all track of the passage of time. The morning was all but spent when Edryd reached an opening where five evenly spaced towers, positioned in a circle, anchored the center of the city in place.

Four of the towers, seemingly unaffected by time, stood proudly still, each of them pristine and perfectly smooth in appearance, as though formed from uniform and unbroken dark grey granite pillars. The fifth tower lay collapsed in a circular mounding of broken rubble piled to more than double Edryd's height. In the midst of these spires, at the center of a slightly inclined hill, a set of wide spiraling stairs led down into the earth.

Edryd hesitated when he came to the steps. He had no means to light the way. Curiosity won out over the pounding in his veins that warned him to stop, and it continued to force him forward when after a single turn of the stairwell, the light began to disappear. Edryd kept a hand on the outer wall for stability, and was greatly startled when it abruptly fell away. The stairway, now supported solely by a thick central pillar, extended just one more turn before the passage emptied onto a landing at the bottom, but Edryd did not know this yet. He conquered the remaining descent only by fighting against a growing terror that intensified with each downward step that he took into the darkness.

Once he reached the floor, Edryd did not dare leave the foot of the stairs. Echoes from his footfalls on the stairwell had made hollow sounds which suggested his enclosure within a vast open expanse. He felt that if he were to move from where he was, he would never find the landing again. The darkness was complete. Not even a bare hint of light made it this far from the opening in the ceiling. He wondered if he might get a little illumination at the height of the afternoon when the sun was directly overhead, but Edryd didn't intend to remain in this place as long as that.

The air felt heavy around him and a strange pressure was building inside his head. Edryd tried to ignore his physical senses. In the darkness there was no need to shut his eyes, and if he remained still there were no sounds, but he could not rid himself of the damp on his skin or the cold smell of stone that saturated the air.

Edryd failed to fully achieve what he had only once accomplished before, but he did succeed to a degree, and his efforts were not wasted. His awareness was now dominated by the five immense towers, their footings sunk in the earth to a depth that exceeded their height above the ground. The towers and the chamber operated together as a mechanism of sorts, broken and out of balance due to the collapsed tower. They no longer functioned for their original purposes, but the towers continued to be repositories for, and conduits of, immense energies.

His head aching fiercely now, Edryd made the decision to leave. He stumbled up the stairs, impaired by a clinging thickness to the air that resisted his efforts to climb. The darkness that he felt in this place had nothing to do with an absence of light. Edryd emerged into the open from out of the chamber, feeling as if he were taking his first desperate breaths of air after having been held submerged at the bottom of a pool of water, and realized that he had in fact been holding his breath.

Moving as quickly as he could manage, Edryd ran and did not stop until he fell, collapsing on the ground well past the borders of the ancient ruins. He crawled to a tree, and resting his back against its base, positioned himself so that the massive tree would shield him from the darkness in the city. For a time in that chamber, he had felt immense. His physical body had felt so frail and feeble that he wondered how it could withstand all that it held within it.

Had Seoras known? Had he intended for this to happen? Seoras had said only that the ruins were not dangerous in the way people believed. He had not said that there was no danger. Perhaps Seoras had given a warning of sorts, but that warning had been incomplete and despairingly inadequate. It was as though while crossing a stream, Seoras had given assurances to Edryd that he needn't worry about the depth of the water, while keeping silent about the swift currents that would grab hold and wash him away. Edryd had been caught in that current and plunged into the depths at the bottom of a steep fall. He had not taken physical harm, but Edryd knew that he would never be free of the memory of the place, or the idea of a damp clinging residue that defiled his skin with filth and corruption.

***

It had been a while since Irial had made the trip into town without Edryd beside her, and it felt strange now to walk unprotected in the near darkness of the morning. It was a revelation for Irial to see how strongly she now felt the absence of something that she had so unexpectedly grown accustomed to. Edryd's company and friendship had given her a sense of security that Irial had, until this moment, never fully appreciated. And with thoughts of what she knew would be in residence at the estate when she arrived, Irial had other reasons for feeling especially nervous and vulnerable today.

Irial knew of at least two specific variations among the ashen creatures that came to see Seoras, but she had only ever seen the least dangerous of these—dry desiccated personages whose dull grey skin smelled strongly of balsam resin mixed with fragrant spices. The sweet odor came from the application of a preservative mixture that was carefully attended to by their thralls. With limited success, it sealed the scent of disease and decay that would have otherwise been overpowering.

Irial knew far less about the others, who were of an ethereal nature and entirely devoid of lasting physical form. That she had never seen them was not a sign that Irial had never been near one, it only meant they had never had a reason to reveal to her their presence, for which circumstance she knew that she should consider herself blessed. They gave off a less intense but otherwise identical smell of death and decay, but it lacked the sweet perfumed odor of their counterparts. Irial knew these smells from experience, and she was conditioned as all people naturally are, to fear its source.

These monsters had come and gone regularly over the past ten years, beginning from when Seoras had first returned to the island. They came to take possession of the men trained by Seoras to serve as their thralls, and they were the original source of all the legends in An Innis about the Ash Men. Logaeir had capitalized on their reputations, creatures mistakenly regarded as plague victims returned from death, by having his men cover their faces with a thick grey pigment made of ashes mixed with animal fat, appropriating the term 'Ascomanni' with the same bold and reckless disregard that had led him to impersonate the Blood Prince—having done both for many of the same purposes.

When she arrived at the property, Irial learned from Tolvanes that there were two new occupants in rooms within the westernmost of the barracks buildings. Two Thralls meant at least one of the creatures, but possibly two, staying in prepared quarters up at the manor.

"One of them is Thovin," Tolvanes said. "I didn't recognize the other, but they change so much it can be hard to tell them apart after a while. He looks as if he travelled to the next realm and returned to this one lacking a certain something that he first departed with."

Irial experienced an involuntary shudder, having understood quite perfectly what Tolvanes had meant. She would have known both of these men and attended to them during the time they had spent training under Seoras. After a short time in service to a draugr, if ever she saw them again, these thralls returned as dangerous husks, soulless versions of the men they once were, often unrecognizable and showing no signs that they remembered much of their past lives. That they no longer remembered her, Irial could feel grateful for. Sharing recollections would only have been painful for them and difficult for her. Despite this, Irial was determined to talk with Thovin, believing that a short conversation could yield important information.

She entered Thovin's room carrying a pitcher of warm water and some towels. Thovin, without looking up, and showing no more awareness of Irial's presence than was essential, allowed her a clear path to the basin which rested on a table against the back wall. When, after setting them down, Irial in turn allowed some space in which to make use of the items she had brought, Thovin moved forward and began to wash his face as though she were not there. Either Irial was beneath his notice, or he was deliberately ignoring her. Irial suspected the latter and saw it as confirmation that he remembered who she was.

"If there is anything else you need, Thovin?" Irial said.

"No," he replied, answering the question quickly to discourage further conversation.

Undaunted, Irial pressed further. "Is it just you and..."

"Hilek," Thovin finished for her, sticking to his pattern of minimalist responses.

Irial remembered Hilek. After completing his training with Seoras he had been taken as a thrall four years ago. Thovin had been gone only six months.

"And you are both bound to the same..."

Thovin frowned, carefully considering his response. "You don't want to be too curious, Irial," he warned.

Irial drew back. She was being clumsy and far too obvious.

Thovin's serious expression changed, remorseful over having frightened her, and he tried to explain. "Being bound to Herja isn't just a tether. She has a connection with my mind, and through her I have a connection to Hilek. Trust me—you don't want the attentions of either one of them. We shouldn't talk again."

"I'm sorry," Irial apologized. "I'm really sorry," she said again as she backed out of the room and Thovin closed the door.

Irial was sorry. She wished that she could somehow help Thovin, but also understood that it was much too late. She could give him no comfort, and had caused him pain instead. In the process, Irial had also frightened herself half to death. However, balanced against the impairment of these regrets, the conversation with Thovin had still been a successful one. Irial could now confirm that there was only one of the creatures here, and more than that, she had discovered its name. As unprecedented a piece of knowledge as that was, she had been even more surprised to discover that Herja was female. Irial couldn't recall ever seeing a draugr whose figure showed even a hint of feminine qualities, and if she had ever thought of any of these monsters in terms gender, she had imagined that they were all male.

Curiosity overwhelmed caution and all good sense. Without stopping to give it the careful thought it deserved, she made her way up to the manor. Irial wanted to know what Herja looked like. She had nearly finished the trip up the hillside before it occurred to her that the entire premise might be flawed. If Herja was of the ethereal variety, there wouldn't be anything to see. Maybe all the females were of this kind. It would explain why Irial had never seen one.

Entering the manor through a servant's entrance, Irial began looking for Seoras, heading towards the small study just off of the library where the Shaper spent most of his time. Irial smelled a distinctive balsam fragrance as she approached, and so she knew to prepare herself for what she would see as she entered the room. Nothing would have ever prepared her. A thin grey-skinned woman turned her head as Irial entered.

She wasn't a woman exactly—she wasn't even human for that matter—but apart from skin color, the differences were subtle. Herja was tall, almost as tall as Seoras, and so slender that she appeared fragile. Her arms were bare but her chest was covered by a loose black tunic that was held in place by dark plates of metal armor at the shoulders and across her waist. Dark pleats of folded crimson cloth encircled her hips. Narrow golden bands circled both of her wrists and she wore a golden pendant around her neck. Herja's pale clouded eyes were housed in an expressionless face, and dark black hair which fell over her shoulders terminated in a series of loose braids midway down her back.

Herja had a regal bearing, and if she could have better disguised the fact that she was essentially a skeleton covered in dry cracked pieces of dead flesh, she might have been beautiful. Irial had seen these creatures more than once, but those she had seen had always taken great care to remain completely cloaked and shrouded, and none had ever so completely terrified her before.

"Now I understand," Herja said. "You were the one talking with Thovin. He thinks very fondly of you. I suppose maybe you already knew that."

Herja's halting guttural voice had an unsettling quality, and it made her description of Thovin's affections even more terrifying than the confirmation of how intimately she was linked to her thrall's mind. Irial was too frightened to do anything but remain where she was, frozen in place.

"If you have satisfied your curiosity," said Herja, becoming annoyed with Irial's frightened stare, "you are not needed."

"I'm sorry," Irial apologized. "I was curious. I wanted to see you because I have never seen a female of your kind." It was the truth, or at least as much of the truth as Irial could safely disclose. "You are very beautiful," Irial added. That was a lie, but it was a polite one.

"You are kind," Herja said accepting the compliment and reacting with pleasure. "You are a beautiful woman in your own right, for a human. I can see why Thovin admires you."

"It is time you excused yourself," Seoras interrupted, giving Irial a look filled with irritation.

"Don't be so inconsiderate, Lord Seoras," Herja protested. "She can bring some refreshment."

Seoras gave Herja a quizzical look which prompted the draugr to respond. "Well of course I won't be having any, but you could eat, and I might enjoy watching your woman eat too. It would help me remember what it was like."

Irial excused herself and tried to walk calmly as she left the room. Once clear, she hurried away as fast as she could go without breaking into a full run. *This has to be the dumbest thing I have ever done in all my life* she thought as she fled.

After preparing some tea and a plate of buttered bread, Irial took a moment to calm down so that she could begin building up her courage as she made her way back to the study. Again, her preparations did not suffice. When Irial entered the room for the second time, it was every bit as shocking to see Herja as it had been the first.

"He is less than a nuisance," Seoras said, growing irritated with Herja. "I can think of nothing that would make me want to spare the effort."

"To you perhaps, he might not matter," Herja disagreed, "but do you think our master will be pleased if you allow this man to overthrow the rulers of An Innis?"

"Our master does not care, so long as whoever holds power is under our control," Seoras countered.

"But would this Logaeir be amenable to taking orders from us?"

"No," Seoras admitted. "But that isn't the present problem."

"The problem is that he claims to be the Blood Prince."

"But he isn't," Seoras pointed out. "He is an opportunist, taking advantage of Aisen's disappearance, nothing more."

"I believe you," Herja replied, "but what if he knows something about the Blood Prince? Aisen might be our only hope against Irminsul. We must follow every lead we have. Even if I find that he knows nothing, and can offer nothing, I am not inclined to allow this Logaeir to be left alone."

Seoras paused, trying to formulate a new approach. "I am hopeful that we can gain control of the Ascomanni," he began. "Without Logaeir, the Ascomanni will fragment into a useless band of criminals."

"And would that not make Esivh Rhol beholden to you?" Herja pointed out.

"The only thing that makes Esivh Rhol listen is his fear that the Ascomanni will someday kill him," Seoras disagreed. "Remove that threat by collapsing the Ascomanni, and the Ard Ri will grow bold once more. This needs more time. I don't want Logaeir killed, not yet at least."

"Esivh Rhol should be made to fear us, not these Ascomanni," Herja complained. "But I can see your point. If we control these raiders, we also control Esivh Rhol and all of An Innis."

Irial set the tray down on the table between the two of them. Herja indicated with a gesture that she should take a seat beside her, and Irial did, almost falling into it as her legs lost their strength and gave out. Irial could not believe what she was hearing. Seoras was trying to save Logaeir's life. She could understand that Seoras didn't feel threatened by Logaeir, but that did not explain why he was trying to persuade Herja to spare him. Perhaps Seoras really did want to take control of the Ascomanni.

Much to Irial's relief, Herja did not follow through on her threat to vicariously enjoy the food that Irial ate. The grey skinned woman ignored Irial altogether, focusing instead on Seoras, who was discussing a way to arrange a meeting with the man who was posing as the Blood Prince. Irial listened closely to everything, knowing that Logaeir and his Ascomanni allies would need to know as much as possible. A simple mistake here could guarantee that any meeting would end in certain disaster.

***

Logaeir waited in the cabin of his ship, anchored off an inlet south of Ann Innis. The Red sails of the *Retribution* were raised part of the way, meant as an aid to identification, openly broadcasting the presence of the Blood Prince, but also in preparation to leave in a hurry if need arose. Logaeir's misgivings about this plan grew as he continued to wait, but he did not dare back out now.

A second ship had sailed from An Innis a few hours ago and was now anchored less than half a mile away. That ship, Logaeir knew, carried Herja, the draugr woman who sought this audience. The arrangements had been proposed under the pretense of a request for an alliance. It was supposed to be a meeting with an envoy for Kedwyn Saivelle, but he could trust that Irial's information was surely correct, and so he knew it for the lie that it was. Having spent the past two nights worrying about this dangerous encounter, Logaeir was anxious to get past it.

Rowing ashore with a small party of four others as night fell, Logaeir hoped that he and his men would live to see the sun rise again in the morning. Together they walked down the rock covered coastline towards two shadowed figures from the other ship. The first was tall and completely shrouded in a cloak. The other stood back a few feet with a hand near the sword hung at his side, staring with an unbalanced look in his eyes at something no one else could see out in the sea. This had to be Herja and one of her Thralls.

The shrouded figure spoke.

"Lord Seoras demands your obedience."

It was a man's voice. This wasn't Herja. It was one, or maybe both of her thralls, but she was not present. Logaeir scanned the tree line. She might not be present, but that didn't mean she wasn't somewhere close.

"In what way could I possibly help the great shaper of the dark?" Logaeir asked, feeling confused and lapsing into sarcasm.

"Lord Seoras means to move against Esivh Rhol and the four harbormasters," the voice explained.

"If Lord Seoras wished to, I have no doubt he could kill them on his own," Logaeir said. His mind was scrambling to try to understand what was happening. This was not what Irial had told him to expect. Plans must have changed, and changed recently.

"Lord Seoras doesn't need help removing Esivh Rhol," the shrouded figure agreed. "He is in need of Lord Aisen to take Esivh Rhol's place, and he wants the Ascomanni kept under control."

"The Ascomanni are under control, and I will be taking down Esivh Rhol soon enough," Logaeir replied. "If Seoras is smart, he stays out of the way. Tell him the Blood Prince says that if he wants to negotiate his place in things to come that he must come speak with me himself."

Logaeir might have been overselling things, but he didn't mean for it to hold up, and he was performing for an audience that he wasn't sure had shown up.

The shrouded figure lowered the hood of his cloak, revealing short dark hair and a carefully trimmed beard. He matched the description Irial had given for Thovin. That meant the man still staring out at the sea would be Herja's other Thrall, Hilek.

"Is that really what you want me to tell him?" Thovin said.

Logaeir stumbled a little. None of this had been any part of any plan.

"Tell him that so long as he does not interfere, I will leave him alone," Logaeir said with finality.

Hilek laughed in a disturbed way that inspired a chill in Logaeir's veins. The man's sanity appeared fragile at best, and he was no doubt all the more dangerous because of it. "Time to go," Hilek said to Thovin.

Thovin took a few steps forward so that he was right next to Logaeir. "This opportunity will not come again if you pass it by, Logaeir," he whispered.

That Thovin had known who it was he was speaking to was no surprise, that had been a given from the outset. But the man was earnestly trying to persuade him, and seemed to being doing so out of honest sympathy, and this gave Logaeir reason for pause before he responded. "You can tell him that so long as our goals coincide, I am sure we can work something out," Logaeir whispered back.

Hilek was still laughing softly to himself as they parted company. Logaeir couldn't imagine what was so amusing, but he knew he wasn't going to like whatever it was. His head was spinning as they made their way back aboard the *Retribution*, failing in all his efforts to understand what had happened. He was supposed to pretend to be Lord Aisen the Blood Prince, convince Herja that he was nothing more than a simple criminal with vain ambitions, and hope that she didn't decide to kill him.

Instead he had made some sort of tentative bargain with Seoras and had not seen Herja at all. He might have taken it as a positive outcome, after all he didn't want to go anywhere near Herja, but Logaeir knew that this couldn't be over, and as such he felt no relief. There was something else at work here and he needed to understand it before he could move forward.

He was puzzling over these concerns when he closed the door to his cabin and noticed a strong sweet smell. It was the balsam resin that protected Herja's skin. Now he had some understanding of what it was Hilek had been looking at when he was staring out towards the ocean, but Logaeir couldn't guess how Herja had gotten onto the ship and then entered his cabin without ever being noticed by any of his men.

"You are not him," she declared from where she stood in a dark corner of the cabin. Her deep voice sputtered as if obstructed by fluid in her throat.

"Not… who?" Logaeir fumbled unnecessarily, caught completely off guard. He flattened his back against the door and began reaching for the handle. How is that going to go? he wondered silently to himself. Images of Herja chasing him down as he tried to flee his own ship convinced him that it would be a bad idea.

"You are not Aisen," she clarified. "Maybe the same height, but your build is wrong and your eyes are the wrong color. He doesn't carry himself like a mouse hiding from a snake either."

Logaeir expected he probably did look something like a trembling mouse just at the moment, and Herja seemed to detest him for it. Herja could certainly play the part of the snake in the analogy that she had given, and Logaeir found it illuminating that she saw herself that way. Invoking what composure he could manage, Logaeir stepped forward towards a table that was bolted to the floor in the center of the room. Logaeir surreptitiously drew his knife while taking a seat, keeping it hidden from view beneath the table, gripped firmly in his hand and ready for use.

Herja left the corner and took a seat as well, her chair protesting under the weight as she settled in beside Logaeir. The sheen from the coating on her dark grey skin glistened under the light of the oil lamp that hung from the ceiling.

"Now there's a brave man," she said with approval. "What did you think of Thovin and Hilek?"

"Hilek, he was the short one, had an unbalanced look in his eyes?" Logaeir asked. "He wasn't what I would consider the best of company."

"Nearing the end of his usefulness I fear," Herja admitted. "But you don't throw a thing away just because it's broken and can't be fixed. Not until you can replace it." Suddenly her face brightened. "How would you like to be bound?" she asked.

It was an impossible thing to do, but as best he could, Logaeir tried to contain the revulsion he felt at this vague proposition. "I don't think it agreed with Hilek all that well," he said, "and I'm not sure I would like it much either."

"No, you probably wouldn't," she said, almost rueful as she reluctantly rejected the idea as well. "But that doesn't leave me with a reason to let you live."

Logaeir decided to employ his contingency plan, which even after all the time he'd had in which to consider it, still struck him as pure stupidity. In one quick motion Logaeir drove the dagger he had been hiding into Herja's midsection, just above the armor around her waist. It stopped, striking something hard less than an inch beneath her skin. Logaeir pulled the weapon free. There was no blood, but the knife was sticky with resin, and the point of the blade was chipped from the impact.

"Why!" she demanded. "Why in the three realms would you do something so stupid? Just because I can't be killed doesn't mean I enjoy having my stomach cut open."

Herja was angry and annoyed, but she had made no move to respond. Logaeir knew that if she decided to kill him, there would nothing he could do. He had been assured that he could not hurt her and told to expect this exact sort of reaction, which in the context of the circumstances was unbelievably muted, but as he watched Herja, Logaeir still wasn't convinced that he was going to survive.

"I thought your skin was armored. I didn't think it would do any damage."

"So you just decided that you were going to test it out!" She cried. Herja remained angry, but she was also looking at Logaeir with respect that had not been there before. "The armor thing is usually true," she said, calming down a little. "Just not in my case," she added with a hint of embarrassment.

Herja began to examine the cut in her tunic where the blade had gone in.

"I hope I didn't do any serious harm," Logaeir said, still worried that she might yet decide to retaliate.

"One of the first things you do when you find out you are dead," Herja said, "is to get rid of most of your internal organs." She apparently didn't understand how this sounded to someone else. Logaeir tried not to react.

If he had possessed enough courage, Logaeir would have liked to have asked what it was that he had hit with his knife that had prevented it from going deeper. Logaeir was sure that it was not bone. He suspected it was hardened metal.

"There isn't really anything you could have damaged," she continued. "My shirt though, it isn't the sort of thing I can replace. And you wouldn't believe how terrible Thovin is at mending. Hilek is surprising' good at it though."

Logaeir shook his head as he listened to her talk at length as if these were all very ordinary things. "You are rather grounded for an immortal being," Logaeir said, expressing in an understated way, the discordant wonder which he felt so strongly each time Herja spoke. She did defy every expectation he would have presupposed of an undying corpse. Logaeir didn't dare say it out loud, but once you got past the more menacing aspects of her appearance and behavior, she had something resembling a sense of humor and was companionable in her own fashion. Or at least she might have been were it not absolutely imperative that she be persuaded to leave the island as soon as possible.

"Seoras was right about you," she said. Her pleased expression projected what Logaeir was certain must be a draugr's approximation of happy. "You and your Ascomanni could be very useful."

Chapter 15

Commander Ledrin

Ruach's efforts to carry out his captain's orders had been repeatedly frustrated. They had met up with an Ossian ship named the *Wave Splitter*, but there had been no opportunity to speak with the ship's captain. He and Oren had been kept on Krin's ship, the *Black Strand*, and were at this moment sailing into the Citadel Harbor under escort.

Two short stints at sea had been enough for Ruach to know that he was never going to enjoy the constant rolling motion of a ship, and he looked forward to setting his feet upon the earth once more. Krin had watched them for the entire three days at sea, and he followed them even now as they disembarked the Ascomanni vessel.

A solemn face greeted both Oren and Ruach. Patiently waiting on the weathered planks of the waterfront dock, stood Commander Ledrin. News of their return had obviously preceded their arrival, or the foremost among the eight commanders who shared in the leadership of the Sigil Corps wouldn't have been here. Ledrin looked both anxious and displeased as he waited for his men to approach.

"I don't see him," Ledrin said, stating the obvious. "I hope you at least managed to locate him."

"We found Aisen," Oren said, eager to share the news, "but he isn't with us."

Oren was about to continue but Ruach interrupted, directing a casual momentary sideways glance in Krin's direction. "It would be best if we spoke somewhere else."

"Have your little meeting of Sigil Order initiates," Krin joked. "I can see that I'm not invited. I'll stay on my ship, and have a secret meeting of my own."

"This is Captain Sarel Krin," Oren said, belatedly introducing their companion. "He is a leader among the Ascomanni."

"You will be coming too, Captain Krin," Ledrin ordered. "I have questions that you will answer once I have spoken with Oren and Ruach and our 'little' meeting is over."

The Ascomanni strongman cracked a smile at the remark, which he had taken for an attempt at humor, but Ledrin just continued to frown.

"I'll not complain," Krin said, looking up at the tall walls of the white fortress that overlooked the harbor, "if I get a tour of that place."

"I can do better than that. I can arrange a room for you," Ledrin said.

There was an unused dungeon in the fortress, and Ruach wondered whether things were going so poorly that this was what the commander was making reference to. Deciding not to share that particular speculation with Krin, Ruach made an attempt to make it clear that the Ascomanni captain was here as an ally.

"Captain Krin is here at our behest, with an offer of support," Ruach said.

"And he is welcome to stay," Ledrin replied. Almost as an afterthought he added a qualification to the offer. "If you are willing to accept an escort that is—neither you nor your crewmen are permitted to enter the city or leave the dockside areas unless you are accompanied by one of my officers."

Ledrin began to walk, followed closely by the two officers. Krin hoped they would be going to the fortress, but Ledrin was taking them to a group of garrison buildings, advantageously positioned between the bustling harbor and the sprawling town built up beneath the protective shadows of the Port Citadel.

The soldiers who policed this area, as well as many of the tradesmen and a few of the laborers, were of apparent Edoric descent, but the waterfront was otherwise dominated by men from different Rendish nations, primarily Ossians, moving merchandise to and from the ships that were tied up in the harbor. Goods moved between the docks and the city via checkpoints, manned by uniformed soldiers from the garrison, and tariffs were collected with each exchange.

Krin knew that on the Edoric side of these checkpoints, there would be no corresponding mix of cultures. Foreigners were banned from traveling within the borders of Nar Edor, except as Ledrin had said, under a protective escort provided by the Sigil Corps. It wasn't quite clear who was being protected from whom under this arrangement, but he understood the reasons for the animosity and distrust. Given a history of attacks by Rendish raiding parties in the past, it was remarkable that a ship belonging to a man of Krin's reputation had been allowed into the harbor.

After reaching the garrison, Ledrin soon ushered Oren and Ruach into his private offices and was about to leave Krin in the company of a couple of soldiers who were standing guard beside the door. Neither of them stood out to Krin as particularly intimidating men, and they were nowhere close to the Ascomanni captain in terms of size or strength. However, Krin had received enough training from Oren and Ruach while they had been at the Ascomanni encampment to understand just how capable these soldiers would be.

"We are not to be disturbed for any reason," Ledrin said to the waiting guards. Before closing the door, Ledrin gave the guards one more instruction. "See to Captain Krin. I am sure he is expecting our hospitality and could use a little refreshment."

"Neysim Ells," said one of the soldiers once the door had been shut, addressing his towering guest while extending his hand in greeting.

"Sarel Krin," the Ascomanni captain replied. He accepted Neysim's hand and gave it a firm shake, testing the strength of the other man in the process.

"The common room is this direction," Neysim said, pointing the way as he began to lead Krin out from the anteroom of Commander Ledrin's office.

"If it means food and drink, I'll follow where you lead."

The other solider remained posted outside Ledrin's quarters as they headed down the corridor and travelled towards the center of the garrison.

"It's a shame your friend isn't coming," Krin said.

"Egran? He isn't exactly a friend, and he would be abandoning his post if he left, though I don't think he would even want to come. He isn't over-fond of Ossians."

"I'm not an Ossian," Krin responded. "I'm a citizen of An Innis, by way of Seridor."

Neysim blanched at the revelation that Krin was from Seridor.

"Last I saw of Nar Edor, was from the deck of a ship, twenty years ago."

"You came with Beodred's men." Neysim concluded.

"And left a prisoner to the Ossians," Krin answered. "I may have come here with him, but as to actually being one of Beodred's men, I wouldn't make that claim, not as such, or at least not willingly so. I was maybe fourteen and wasn't part of the fighting in the city. All the same, I did get to enjoy several months in a makeshift prison camp overseen by none-too-friendly Edoric soldiers when everything was done."

"You were a conscript?" Neysim asked.

"That would be one way to put it. I was a barely grown young man forced to join the Alliance, little different from so many others who made up the bulk of Bedored's forces," Krin confirmed. "Most of us were only too ready to turn on Beodred given an opportunity, and ultimately, that is what we did. We murdered the men who had been left in command of our ship, but we were captured by the Ossians when we tried to get past their blockade."

As they arrived at the common room, Krin's recounting of these events was interrupted by the bustle of sounds which on a daily basis could always be heard in consequence of the garrison's soldiers gathering for the afternoon meal. Several dozen of these soldiers were at this moment eagerly consuming dark bread and large quantities of pork taken from butchered hogs that had been roasted on spits in the center of the room.

"Joining the Sigil Corps doesn't pay much, in fact it doesn't pay at all, but we do eat well," Neysim said as he cut open two loaves and filled them with portions of meat carved from one of the animals.

Neysim found an empty spot for them at one of the tables and deposited the food there before leaving to grab a couple of drinks. Krin had barely had time to sit down before his host reappeared holding two large cups.

"Are you really an Ascomanni captain?" Neysim asked as they ate.

"There are a few now, but I was one of the first," Krin bragged. Krin might have argued that he was the very first; however, it sounded like an exaggeration even to Krin, despite knowing it to be the truth.

"I've heard that Aisen is raising an army of Ascomanni to besiege the capital," Neysim said, hoping that his guest could confirm the rumor.

"I wouldn't say that there are enough of us Ascomanni to amount to what you would consider an army," Krin said.

"I shouldn't be asking," Neysim apologized, "not here, and not before Ledrin has had the chance to meet with you. It's hard to not be curious though, not with the way things stand."

Krin didn't ask how things stood. He was caught on something his host had said a little earlier.

"You really don't receive pay?"

"Even a first year initiate has access to disbursements. You can obtain Order funds when needed, but no one receives wages, and you don't own anything but your sword, and that only once you have earned it. Not even the commanders own anything."

"My men get an equal share of all that we capture," Krin said. "I'm surprised the local lords don't hire away your best men."

"It can happen, but never our best," Neysim said. "In the first place, most of the nobility distrust the Sigil Corps so strongly that they would never allow one of us into their employ."

"I thought that Edoric lords sent their children for ten years of service to be trained by the Order," Krin said. He really was confused by this. It was commonly repeated outside Nar Edor that service in the Sigil Corps was in some way compulsory for younger sons among the elite of that insular land. It was strange to hear that nearly the opposite was in fact closer to the truth, and that the nobility did not trust this re-founding of the Sigil Order.

"It isn't common, but there are some that do," Neysim acknowledged. "And there are others that are willing to recruit from the ranks of the Sigil Corps, but they understand they may be adding men with divided loyalties. You swear only one oath when you join the Sigil Corps, and that is that you will swear no oaths."

"So a former soldier of the Sigil Corps is always either an unsworn man, or an oath breaker. No wonder the nobility doesn't approve."

"It's more than that. Time in the Order changes a man. We are bound to principles that guide our actions in ways that often conflict with the interests and unchecked ambitions of powerful men."

"There is nothing wrong with ambition, and nothing keeps loyalty like coin," Krin argued. "I'll wager I could buy yours."

"You couldn't," Neysim disagreed. "I have already finished my ten year service. The wealthiest and most powerful merchants in Nar Edor all arose from out of the ranks of former Sigil Corps trained soldiers.

The connections you make while in the Order are a guarantee of well-paid employment once you leave service."

"That is how you maintain loyalty then," Krin concluded.

Neysim nodded his head in agreement. "A man motivated by money or power will hardly purchase it at the expenditure of his freedom, swearing service to a Lord and landowner who would never share with his men what the Order does."

"But did not Aedan Elduryn swear his loyalty to Kyreth Edorin?"

"He did," Neysim agreed, "but that was before the re-founding of the Order, and it is said that he later rescinded that oath."

This was all intensely interesting to Krin. Most of what he had heard of the Sigil Corps and of Aedan Elduryn had not come from someone so close to the source, and what he was learning now differed from most of what was widely believed beyond the borders of Nar Edor.

"If a man leaves the Corps before finishing his service, I suppose he isn't much use then to anyone," Krin said.

"We would let even the worst failures enlist again if they desired it," Neysim said, "but they start a new ten year term if they do."

Krin was starting to see the appeal of a group like the Sigil Corps. It went beyond the romantic notion of the near mythical order of Sigil Warriors of old that this group was trying to emulate. Recruiting even a few of these men into the Ascomanni would be invaluable, but it was going to be a difficult bargain to sell.

Oren and Ruach arrived a moment later, abruptly interrupting Krin's efforts to progress the conversation further. Egran followed along a short distance behind, but he continued on past the group without bothering to acknowledge any of them.

"Ledrin wants to speak with you," Ruach said.

Krin stuffed pieces of meat and bread into his mouth, hurriedly finishing what was left of his food as he casually complied with the summons. Neysim started to rise as well but Ruach stopped him.

"Oren and I will take your post for a while," Ruach said to Neysim. "Finish your meal and head back when you are ready."

"Lead on," Krin said, his voice muffled by a mouthful of food that he had yet to swallow.

Oren and Ruach exchanged a few looks as the three of them travelled back down the corridors on the way to Ledrin's quarters.

"Is he even going to get the message through?" Oren asked his companion.

"He has channels, and I think we can trust that he will use them," said Ruach.

"I don't suppose anyone would like to tell me what we are talking about?" Krin asked, only to be rewarded with an uncomfortable silence. "Someone, please say something," he demanded with increased volume when it became clear that no explanation was coming.

"Ledrin has reassigned us," Oren said unhappily, diverting the topic by not actually answering Krin's question, but making it appear that he had. "We will be reporting to a new command."

"You are released from Aisen then?" Krin asked.

"Not until the transfer takes effect three days from now," Ruach said.

"There is more, isn't there," Krin said, prying away at them for more information.

"He won't be sending help to Aisen, says that he can't," Oren siad, showing intense disappointment, the tone of which bordered on being insubordinate.

"He has his reasons," Ruach said, feeling compelled to defend the commander. "We are stretched thin already. The other commanders aren't going to allow him to allocate scarce resources for an expedition to retrieve a man who doesn't want to come back."

"I can't believe you are saying that. We can't afford to do nothing. It is well worth the risk if we can return with an army of allies," Oren countered. There was a heat behind his words, and Oren was clearly ready to defend the stance which he had taken.

"The Ascomanni don't really constitute what I would call an army," Ruach disagreed.

Krin had made much the same point to Neysim only a few minutes ago, but he wasn't about to help settle anything by coming into this on Ruach's side, with which he did not agree.

"Can we just say that you both have positions with merit?" Krin laughed. He was taking pleasure in watching the two men argue.

"You have no say in this," Ruach said. Oren seemed to agree, as neither appreciated Krin's deliberately unhelpful interference.

"We are no army, but it isn't our numbers that would be valuable," Krin pointed out, taking the situation more seriously. "It's our mobility that would be of benefit. With our ships, you could threaten anywhere along the coastlines."

Oren quickly jumped in to support the argument. "It would persuade houses to stay close to home, protecting their own holdings instead taking risks by joining the king's effort to strip House Edorin of its lands."

"All good in theory," Ruach said, "but we are a long way from achieving anything of the kind."

"With even a small complement of Sigil Warriors backing us up we would make quick work of An Innis," Krin disagreed. "We could be here with a fleet of ships in less than a month."

The notion put fire behind Oren's eyes, but he had been sold on all of this long ago. Ruach however, was dubious of Krin's claims, and he wasn't going to get behind this plan, not without support from his superiors.

The Ascomanni captain was ushered into Ledrin's office before they could discuss the matter any further, and Sarel Krin now stood alone facing the Sigil Corps commander. Ledrin was perhaps twenty years older than Krin, but he was still a solidly imposing figure. It wasn't a sensation that Krin experienced very often, but he felt intimidated under the stare of this man.

"How is Aisen doing?" Ledrin asked.

"Well enough, but despite his many efforts, our young Blood Prince hasn't had much luck at running away from himself. He has attracted the attentions of every single faction currently competing for control of An Innis."

"These factions, who are they?" said Ledrin, interrupting Krin as if he were conducting an interrogation.

"The Ascomanni captains of course. That absurd Ard Ri for another. The one person of real consequence though is a far more dangerous man, a dark sorcerer named Aed Seoras. All have tried to make use of Aisen in one way or another."

"He won't like that," Ledrin said. "There was a misunderstanding between us, and Aisen no longer trusts me. He thinks that I tried to use him."

"I don't think that was a misunderstanding," Krin said with a wry laugh. "I have no doubt you did use him, and would be doing so now if you could get your hands on him."

Ignoring the accusation, Ledrin continued with another question. "He left under some interesting circumstances, and he would have had a sword with him, the family sword of House Edorin."

"That would be a big weapon that casts bright white light when he wields it? Never seen it."

Ledrin appeared unconvinced.

"I don't know if he knows where the sword is, but he does not have it," Krin insisted. "He had no weapons when he arrived, and he carries nothing more than a simple short sword now."

"What are the Ascomanni intentions in regard to Aisen and with respect to Nar Edor?" Ledrin asked, moving the interview along.

"Logaeir plans to overthrow the Ard Ri, Esivh Rhol, and install Aisen in his place. He wants to make him the ruler of An Innis. Ultimately, I think he believes that Edryd, Aisen I mean, will be able to take firm control of the Ascomanni forces."

"Oren and Ruach have differing views regarding this Logaeir fellow. Tell me what kind of man he is. And tell me, why would he want Aisen put in control?"

"Logaeir was a young boy when the remnants of Beodred's forces took control of An Innis following their defeat here in Nar Edor. Logaeir witnessed what happened then, including the deaths of his friends, the exploitation of those that survived, and the violence that took place again each time power changed hands in successive upheavals. He doesn't want the Ascomanni to be one more example of the same. He thinks Aisen is his solution to all of that."

"And you agree?"

"I don't," Krin admitted. "Aisen on his own won't be able to control the Ascomanni when we take the island."

"Aisen alone could not control them, but Aisen backed up by a company of the finest soldiers of the Sigil Corps could," Ledrin said, completing the logical inference.

"He could. Logaeir doesn't want the Ascomanni to remain what they are right now. I think he dreams of something not unlike an extension of the Sigil Corps based in An Innis. Aisen could make that happen."

"And afterwards you intend to help us in our current conflict, and the Ascomanni don't want anything in return?"

"A few men to help Aisen now and a trade agreement once he is the ruler of An Innis," Krin answered. "There is great wealth trapped in An Innis. We won't need payment for helping in Nar Edor, just the means to convert our trade goods into coin."

Ledrin paused for a moment, ending his series of rapid questions. Krin knew the commander was considering his options and making a decision, but he could not read anything on Ledrin's face.

"You understand of course that I would never be able to convince the other commanders to accept what you are proposing," Ledrin said.

Krin started to argue but Ledrin cut him off. "You need to return to An Innis. I can give you three days. If you and your crew are not gone by then, you won't be leaving of your own accord, if at all."

"This is a mistake...." Krin started to argue.

"Three days, and no more," Ledrin said. He seemed to want Krin to read something into this.

Krin smiled. Ledrin had not offered to help, but he had not specifically rejected the request either. It was no coincidence that he had given three days for Oren and Ruach to report to their new captain, and that he was now giving Krin those very same three days to make his preparations to leave. Krin was more than willing to take this as his answer.

"Three days should be enough," he agreed.

* * *

Edryd's afternoon had been consumed by his efforts combing through the woods, hunting and looking for food. He was now enjoying the success of those efforts—a snared rabbit; skinned, gutted, and cooked over a fire beside his simple shelter, which he had built far away from the ruined structures of the ancient city.

He had been forced to travel closer to the coastline in order to find a place to hunt. The animals, he had discovered, were avoiding the forests and the Ruins in particular. The dominance of the towering trees prevented the development of undergrowth, leaving little cover and almost nothing for a large animal to forage on. Edryd suspected that the wild creatures of the forest also felt some of what he did whenever he approached too close to the orphic chamber and the enormity of the featureless enigmatic towers that channeled disrupted currents of arcane energy in that place.

What he experienced that first morning had been enough to convince him to keep his distance. Or at least it had for the rest of that first day. At the end of each subsequent day (this would now mark the fourth consecutive evening) Edryd returned to the center of the city, inexplicably drawn towards the source of the disrupted energies.

Feeling a pleasant contentment, which he attributed to having his belly full of the cooked rabbit, Edryd left his fire behind and started moving towards the ruins. He made occasional explorations as he travelled, so that it took a little longer than what would ordinarily have been needed to reach his destination. When he did arrive once more at the center of the ruined city, Edryd lowered himself onto the ground, sitting just inside the edge of the encirclement. As he sat there, he tried to reason out the purpose of the site. There were no displacements, a shaper was apparently required to activate the stone towers, but Edryd could sense the immense potential that could be harnessed within this location. He could discern only one thing; this place was broken, and it would break anyone who tried to avail themselves of its corrupted power.

His perceptions had grown no stronger despite days of practice, but he was getting better at recognizing the patterns for what they were when he felt them. Concentrating, as he was presently doing, brought a clarity which expanded the range at which he could sense the world through changes in the dark, and so he felt the approach at a great distance. Something, passing through the boundaries of the ruins, was moving in Edryd's direction. He recognized the pattern of displacement that had drawn his attention. It was Aed Seoras.

Edryd patiently waited as he tracked the shaper's progress, trusting that his own unique ability was preventing Seoras from doing the reverse. Seoras wouldn't know yet that Edryd was here, but it was obvious that he was searching for his student.

"I thought you would be here," Seoras said when he reached the encirclement of towers.

"What is this place?" Edryd asked. He had been puzzling over it for some time now, and his impatience had grown by the day.

His teacher's answer was a disappointment. "I don't know," he said. "I have studied it for years, and the only thing I can say with confidence, is that it is old."

"That's... incredibly underwhelming. You know more than that. You said before that this place predates the last age."

"It does, and by several thousand years at least."

Edryd had been thinking of it as a thousand years old and had been having trouble with that. Adding a few extra thousand years put it that much further beyond his comprehension.

"As near as I can tell," Seoras continued, "it was built at the dawn of the age of sorcery, created by a people who sought to imitate the achievements of the first men."

Edryd didn't want to admit that he lacked even a basic understanding of the subjects Seoras was discussing, and so comprehended very little of this, but Seoras could see it in the eyes of his student.

"Let's go inside, there are panels in the chamber that give an answer or two," he said.

Edryd hesitated. He had been down there once before, and felt then as if he had barely escaped the darkness in the chamber. The evening was already fading and he had no desire to go through this again, particularly not at night.

"I have a camp not far from here," Edryd hedged, "we should at least get something to light our way."

"No need for that," Seoras said. He extended his arms out in front of his chest and cupped his hands together. A blue white light leaked out of gaps between his fingers, and when Seoras removed his hands, he revealed a sphere from which emanated a light that had no apparent source. It rose a little higher in the air once it was thus freed from confinement, and as Edryd looked on, it remained in front of Seoras, suspended in place.

"A trick that I have been holding in reserve," he said, hoping that Edryd would be impressed. Seoras had shown far more powerful ways in which to shape the dark, but none of those shared the dramatic visual impact of this one, serving as a simple and unquestionable demonstration of a shaper's power.

Edryd wasn't so much impressed as he was startled. He had seen a variation of this kind of light once before. It had emanated from the

Sigil Sword of House Edorin, just before Edryd had used it to kill his brother. The recognition on Edryd's face must have read in a way that led Seoras to believe that he had in fact properly amazed his pupil, for he walked happily as he moved towards the descending stone steps, with the ball of light smoothly advancing ahead of him.

Seoras proceeded without the slightest hint of apprehension. Edryd couldn't understand that. If his teacher felt the pressures concentrated in this place, it should have unsettled him. Unwilling to show his own fear, Edryd followed behind Seoras, a few steps behind the dark-tempered shaper. The light from the sphere lit everything brightly, making this a much different experience from his original exploration, and Edryd made his way down the steps much faster this time.

When they reached the bottom, Edryd could see that the landing he had reached before was part of a raised dais, a flat circular area in the center of the chamber. On one edge, a broad shallow basin, its surface dark and discolored, was carved into the floor. Edryd took a wide path around it, choosing not to make any assumptions. Seoras was a good distance away now, having already stepped down from the dais, and afterwards continuing on straight across the uneven ground beyond the platform before eventually reaching the outer edge of this unnatural cavern. He was staring at a panel carved into the rock that seemed to confirm what Edryd had tried not to imagine.

Almost freshly carved in appearance, the panel displayed in beautifully detailed stonework an image of a wounded and dying man, whose blood was collecting in a pool within the basin.

"It was said that a Sigil Warrior was never any more powerful than he was when he faced his death," Seoras said, his voice taking on added depth as it broke the silence and echoed through the chamber. "When the soul transits to the next realm, it opens a gate. That gate develops conditions in the dark that allows it to be more easily shaped. Whoever built this, I think they tried to catalyze those conditions with a sacrifice."

"I think I know more now than I really care to," Edryd said. He could feel the pressure building and he wanted to leave. Unaffected, Seoras showed no concern for Edryd's discomfort.

"The next panels are interesting ones," Seoras said, looking at two more carvings that completed a grouping of three that had begun with the depiction of the dying man.

The two panels were interesting, if rather more obscure than the first. One of them showed another man, wreathed in flowing energies, standing over an opening in the floor of the upraised dais where the basin should have been. The last was an image depicting the circle of five towers, surrounded by runic inscriptions. Edryd couldn't discern any particular pattern to the placement of the runes, but they were not random. There was information in these symbols and in their positions if you could understand it, like locations on some kind of abstract map.

"I know what this is," Edryd said.

"By all means," Seoras said, inviting Edryd to share his theory, all the time looking at his pupil with a less than kind smile that suggested he thought Edryd was about to say something foolish.

"This was made by the first men. This is where they tried to build the bridge to the High Realms, and the gods destroyed them for it."

His teacher's face became very serious. "This was not made by the first men," he said. "But you might not be far off about the rest."

"We need to get out," Edryd insisted.

"This place was used for other things as well," Seoras said, "there are other panels."

"Can't you feel them pressing in on us?" Edryd asked. He believed this place had almost killed him once, and he was more convinced of that with each passing moment.

Seoras was confused. He was deaf to the danger of this chamber, Edryd could see that now. The window into Seoras revealed no fear. To him this place was dead. It posed no threat. But Seoras did keenly want to know what it was Edryd felt. He began to approach.

"Maybe together, there is something…"

Edryd stepped back. He didn't understand how it worked, but he knew that he increased the ease with which Seoras could shape. It was unclear what might happen if the dark man tried to use him as a focus in this place, but the two of them together could prove a very bad combination.

"Don't come closer, and don't try to shape the dark!" Edryd warned.

Seoras stopped, surprised at the urgency in Edryd's command. "I couldn't shape anything of substance if I wanted to," Seoras objected. "Something down here interferes and makes it difficult. I can barely maintain this," he said, looking at the glowing sphere casting its illumination throughout the chamber.

Looking at it now, Edryd could see that the light wavered ever so slightly. It might have been a deliberate effect, only it had not looked this way when Seoras had first conjured it outside. Edryd no longer cared whether he could convince Seoras of the danger or what it would look like when he ran; he left the chamber, hurrying up the spiraling steps without bothering to turn and see whether Seoras followed him. It had not been so frightening this time, but he had not been trying as he had before to open himself to whatever this place was, and as a consequence he hadn't felt the full force of the towers quite so strongly. Edryd took a position at the edge of the pile of rubble where the fifth tower had once stood. It seemed like the safest spot to sit and wait for Seoras.

He didn't expect that he would need to wait very long, but minutes continued to slowly pass until he had been sitting there long enough to start feeling sore. Stars were appearing in the sky overhead and he began to feel tired. Edryd might have thought Seoras was in trouble, if not for the light that leaked out of the opening where the steps descended into the earth. It didn't really matter though. Edryd was not going to go back in after Seoras for any reason.

Several times Edryd thought about returning to his camp at the edges of the ruins. In frustration Edryd stood up, determined to leave Seoras behind, but Seoras had not come out here to explore the chamber. He had something to tell his student, and Edryd did not yet know what it was. If he left now, Edryd could not expect that Seoras would find him in the dark, and he wouldn't learn whether it was safe to return to An Innis or not. His patience had completely eroded away, but there was nothing Edryd could do. He had no choice but to sit back down and continue to wait.

When Seoras did finally emerge, it was dark. Without the light Seoras was maintaining, it would have been very difficult to navigate a path out of the ruins. They did not speak as they walked. Seoras was angry, Edryd could feel that, but he didn't know why. Edryd did know why he was frustrated with Seoras though, so he was content to continue in silence.

They stopped to rest at Edryd's camp. When they did, Seoras finally said something.

"You are too afraid of your power."

Seoras didn't elaborate, and Edryd decided to ignore him. A good portion of the cooked rabbit remained on a spit above the cold fire pit. Seoras collected a pile of dead wood and threw it onto the remains of the spent fire, and after a brief moment the wood burst into flame.

"Those coals were not even warm," Edryd said in surprise. He had felt what Seoras had done, but he hadn't known such a thing was possible. "Another trick you hadn't shown me yet?"

As if in response, the light that had been hovering above and in front of Seoras disappeared in a short flicker as though it had never truly been there. "I was always especially good with fire," he explained. "It helps that the wood was dry and there were actually a few embers left."

Edryd added this to the list of things he had seen Seoras do that he had no hope of ever reproducing himself, another piece of the mounting evidence that demonstrated how dangerous the man was.

"I assume you came because it is safe to return," Edryd said.

"I wouldn't say safe exactly, but Herja is gone," Seoras confirmed.

Edryd did not know who Herja was, and he wasn't so sure he wanted to know, but he asked anyway. "Herja?"

"She is what you have been calling a draugr," Seoras explained. "She came to see the man who had been calling himself the Blood Prince. She left satisfied that he wasn't you. Trouble is, Logaeir overplayed his hand. She has taken an interest in him, and I worry she may be back again sooner than I would like."

"Everyone is fine?"

"Yes, nothing has changed."

The two men shared what was left of the rabbit. Before they left, Seoras began to shape and the fire died so suddenly it could not possibly have been natural.

"If you don't allow a fire to breath," said Seoras, "it dies quickly."

The same is true for a man Edryd thought to himself. It was becoming ever more apparent that if Seoras ever did get truly serious about killing him, there were a number of unusual but effective ways his teacher could choose from in order to accomplish his purpose. A healthy distance was the only defense that would afford Edryd any protection. He had a plan for that. Irial had worked it out. The unsolvable flaw in that plan continued to be Irial's refusal to leave with him.

Seoras conjured the spectral light again, and together they moved in the general direction of An Innis. They did not stop for another rest until they came out onto a rocky piece of ground, which held interspersed clusters of woody plants and low grasses, marking the end of the forest. A wide expanse of open land lay before them, extending all the way out to the causeway which split the sea and linked the coast to the island of An Innis. Seoras did not seem troubled that the unnatural light would have been visible from miles away.

Though Edryd had been through this area twice before, both of those times he had been travelling in the dark, and had carried no source of light. He had noted marked graves near the coast, but had seen little else. The illumination Seoras was creating revealed more of the landscape than he had been able to see on those previous occasions. There were a few raised areas, as well as two distinct depressions, that altered the otherwise flat landscape.

As they walked through this desolate area, Edryd noticed bits of rubble, discarded pieces of broken tools, and other signs that men had lived here once. It wasn't recent, and nothing still stood, but it wasn't very old either. Edryd guessed that it was some abandoned extension of the settlement on An Innis. He remembered Irial's friend Uleth having said there were at one time thousands of inhabitants. These were perhaps signs of that sudden expansion.

"Did people live here?" Edryd asked.

"People died here," Seoras corrected. "It was a dark chapter in the history of An Innis."

Seoras was not what could be considered an empathetic type. Edryd wondered what could move such a man to express even this modestly sad sentiment.

"I didn't see much of this, as I left before it happened, but not long after the island became the new home for Beodred's men, along with all of the people who were expelled from Nar Edor, things went very wrong. Starvation threatened the people of An Innis."

"So some left the island and tried to make a go of it here," Edryd surmised. He had heard parts of this before from Uleth, but he didn't know anything about this settlement on the mainland.

"They did, but it did not go well," Seoras confirmed. "Their arrival in large numbers pushed the deer herds away and they quickly depleted the rest of the remaining animal life in the area as well. They just as quickly consumed most of the fish in the rivers. Those who pushed further into the woods seldom returned, and of those that did, some returned incoherent and addled, ruined by things they had seen but could not explain."

Edryd had been in those woods and had some idea now why it was a place to be avoided. He was happy to move off the topic and didn't press for details as Seoras continued.

"The bulk of those who remained tried hard to survive, but nature conspired against them. As the weather grew cold they faced predation by packs of starving wolves and the threat of death from exposure. What they fought most though were the diseases that had come across with them, which only grew worse when those still on the island began burying their dead on this side of the causeway and forcibly expelling anyone who showed signs of illness, consigning them to die in this impoverished community."

"Didn't anyone go back?" Edryd wondered.

"Once you were here, you could not return. The causeway was guarded night and day by armed men to prevent anyone trying to get back across."

"They can't have all just stayed here and died," Edryd protested.

"Of those that lived here, a quarter were dead before the end of the first year. Those that remained were offered a salvation of sorts by the strongest of Beodred's men, who had by then taken control of An Innis."

Edryd had guessed what was coming next, but he allowed Seoras to continue uninterrupted.

"The starving survivors agreed to be transported by ship to other lands and sold as laborers. This was the beginning of An Innis as an exporter of slaves to markets throughout the world."

It was clear now how the population had regressed back closer to the number of original settlers. Those who hadn't left or died of disease had been enslaved and sold.

"It didn't stop there of course. The whole thing was far too lucrative and it was a trade these men already knew well. End up on the wrong side of a power struggle and you found yourself a fresh supply in the chain of human merchandise moving through An Innis."

"I hadn't known," Edryd said. "I knew An Innis was a market for exporting slaves, with raiders capturing ever more from ships and from unprotected villages on return trips. But I didn't know it had all begun by enslaving their own."

"This island has made an outsized impact on the world, but that is all part of the past," Seoras said. "The Ossians forged the agreement banning the practice of buying slaves, as much to stop the spread of diseases which accompanied the trade as for any other reason. They also sent Aelsian to protect the trade routes for merchant ships sailing to and from Nar Edor, and they began secretly backing the Ascomanni. An Innis is dying, and not many will miss it when it is gone."

It was clear that the master shaper of the dark was among the many that would not miss An Innis. He didn't need a one way link to see that Seoras hated this place. Edryd understood now. Seoras too had been entangled with and trapped upon the island of An Innis. There was some hope of escape for Edryd, but for Seoras, it seemed like there was none.

Chapter 16

Ældisir

Thirteen men, twelve if you counted only the men of the Sigil Corps without including Sarel Krin, gathered on the docks. Seven of the most recent to arrive were from Aisen's command who, when added together with Oren and Ruach, made it nine out of the original ten whose service to their captain had been assumed. With the addition of two eager volunteers recruited beside them, as well as Neysim Ells, there were now a dozen soldiers represented in the group. Once Krin had convinced Oren and Ruach that their efforts had Ledrin's unofficial approval, it had taken not even two full days to organize these select few, all of whom could be said to possess an excess of courage in proportions nearly equal to their total lack of prudence.

"Where is Alef?" Ruach asked Oren.

"He won't be coming, he's sick," the other officer explained.

Ruach, certain of the loyalty of the men who had served under Aisen's command, had anticipated they would bring the entire unit, but assembling all but one of them was still as a very good result. These were not just any soldiers pulled from the ranks of the Sigil Corps. They were all of them among the very elite in the Order.

"We could have had more," said Oren. "A lot more, but we were careful to keep this quiet."

"I'll be hard pressed to find space enough for all of you as it is," said Krin. "Everything has been prepared. We leave when you and your men are aboard. Better sooner than later, and best if we leave now, without any delay."

It was now the evening of the second day, and not yet the end of the full three that they had been given, but there was no reason to stay and every reason to be gone before morning.

"We really should go," Neysim agreed. "Egran suspects... something. I saw him heading in the direction of Commander Ohdran's offices as I was leaving the garrison."

If there was any reluctance among those in the party, no one showed it. There would be no return to Nar Edor if they did not succeed in their mission, but this did not discourage them, and a sense of excitement was shared by the men as they boarded Krin's ship. Their light armor had been stored below decks in advance and they now removed and folded the white overcoats that made up the most recognizable part of their uniforms. Unless someone were to look closely, and notice how lost they appeared on the deck, the soldiers would have appeared little different from the rest of the crew as Krin's ship, the *Black Strand*, set sail.

Ruach and Oren watched the other soldiers, all of whom took pains to hide their unease over what was surely their first voyage out on the sea.

"A brave group," Oren said.

"I'm sure they think they have a handle on this, but wait until we get underway beyond the harbor," Ruach said.

"Which one loses his dinner over the railing first?" Oren asked, joining in on the joke.

Ruach wished Oren had not made that last comment; it conjured unpleasant memories of his own experiences. The first voyage was still fresh in his mind, and the trip back to Nar Edor had been only marginally better. "I hope it isn't me," Ruach said.

Some of the men in Krin's crew were smiling. They were anticipating the same thing Ruach and Oren were. The sight of these allegedly invincible warriors emptying their stomachs over the side of the ship was not going to enhance the credibility with which the Ascomanni viewed the soldiers of the Sigil Corps.

***

Though she had been woken in the middle of the night, there was relief on Irial's face as she opened the door to admit Edryd. Eithne was awake too, bleary eyed confused. Irial ordered her sister back into bed, and waited for her to leave before she began to talk with Edryd. She told him what she knew about Herja, and filled Edryd in on the events of the past few days.

Edryd told Irial some of what had happened in the ruins on the mainland, but he said nothing of the underground chamber, and he did not speak of the fear that had been planted within him by those experiences. They didn't stay up long; they were much too tired for that. Irial left first once they were both done talking. Edryd headed in the opposite direction, glad for the shelter of his drafty room and grateful for the comfort and warmth of his bed after nearly a week of sleeping out on the ground.

The next morning, Irial encouraged Edryd to remain behind. Herja and her thralls had been gone only since yesterday afternoon, and it made sense to remain cautious. He could not be persuaded though, for Edryd was determined to resume his role as Irial's protector.

It was a mild and pleasant day, of a kind which one might keenly feel should not be wasted, and as they travelled on the familiar road towards the settled parts of An Innis, Edryd made a direct plea aimed at convincing Irial to modify her plans for Eithne.

"When Aelsian comes, you will need to go with Eithne. With who knows how many draugar out there searching for me, I might be the single worst imaginable travelling companion."

"There are at least ten of them," Irial said, "but no more than twice that number."

"Even if there were only one," Edryd emphasized, certain that Irial was missing the point, "I would be powerless to stop it. Eithne would not be safe."

"Your mother was of the Edorin line, descended from the last of the ancient Sigil Order, and your father was the founder of a new Sigil Order," Irial said. The subject of his family was not comfortable for Edryd. His few memories of his mother before her death were vague and unclear, and his father had abandoned him when Edryd was no older than Eithne was now. "Your father wielded the Edorin Sigil Blade," Irial continued. "Some speak of him as if he were a sigil knight— the first in hundreds of years. Seoras believes you to be even more powerful than your father, and I do as well."

"How would Seoras know how to compare me to my father," Edryd said, pointing out what he was sure was a flaw in her logic.

Irial did not answer, and Edryd remained quiet for a while after this as they walked. Finally Irial continued. "Even I see that you have powers that were only ever known to exist in the greatest of the sigil knights. The Sigil Order defeated the kingdoms of the sorcerers. You can manage a handful of these creatures and their thralls," she said.

Edryd thought about the book Irial had borrowed from Uleth. It must be filled with a great deal of nonsense to have moved her imagination to create such an unrealistic estimation of her protector.

"Irial, I have no power. It is true that my father could do things. He may have even been something like a sigil knight, but I have no power of my own."

"You can't know that," Irial said. She was not ready to believe him.

"The day before he left Nar Edor, my father took my head in his hands and held me," Edryd said. He felt the need to convince her, and so he began sharing a story that he had never told to anyone. "He was testing me, taking a measure of the composition of my soul, looking for any hint of unrealized potential. I could feel his spirit plying its way through mine. I was just a child, but I got a glimpse at that moment of the power my father wielded, of what he could do."

"With children of sigil knights, spiritual power passed down along family lines," Irial said, interrupting. "Surely his strength passed on to his son."

"Not in my case," Edryd said. "My father wanted to find a kernel of ability buried inside of me, but it was not there. He kept trying and trying. In the end, when he finished, he was exhausted. He had found nothing. He looked so sad it scared me. I knew then that he was ashamed of his son. He wouldn't even look me in the eyes anymore, and in the morning, he was gone."

Edryd didn't know to this day why his father had left, but the experience had filled him with a pain and resentment that he continued to struggle with. In response to his having shared with her this memory which he so closely kept, Irial began to develop a resonant empathy towards Edryd, and she was at the conclusion of the story, visibly flushed with emotion.

"He was wrong about you," she insisted.

Her declaration carried the weight of certain knowledge, not mere belief. Edryd could see he was not going to convince her. He had, he realized, also not been entirely truthful in his efforts to persuade her. There was something he possessed, but it seemed like the opposite of power, only giving added strength to his most dangerous enemies. If she knew this, maybe then she might understand, but he didn't feel like sharing his fears.

"It still seems like..." he began to say, intending to argue once more that Irial needed to be the one to protect her sister.

"It has to be you," Irial cut him off. "No one else can do this."

Recognizing this was not the right moment to demand an explanation, Edryd let it pass. He needed to get a look at this book she had been reading. It was reinforcing the strange notions Irial seemed to have about him.

When they reached the estate they both headed towards the manor. Edryd had never actually visited this place where Seoras lived alone, but he needed to see him and had already traced the shaper's distinct pattern and determined his location on the lower floor of the building. As Edryd drew closer, he began to get a picture his teacher's emotions. Seoras was excited about something, something he was bursting to share.

Upon entering the building, it was obvious that no effort was being made to make use of, or to in any way maintain the upper levels. Everything on the main floor was kept clean, but the wooden stairs and railings that led up a level were covered in dust. Edryd located Seoras in the study near the back of the building next to the library, sorting his way through a pile of freshly made drawings. Depicted on some of these were renderings of the panels from the orphic chamber in the ruins.

"I've figured something out," Seoras boasted, as he turned his head to greet Edryd. Seoras, Edryd realized, was in his true environment. Half of the library's books were scattered about this room, a dozen of them cracked open on the table. Scrolls of loose parchment lay everywhere he looked. Edryd would never have imagined that this harsh manipulator of men, this shaper of the dark and master of steel, would have had so much passion for research and knowledge.

"The towers," he began, "all five of them, or just four now I suppose, are massive constructs."

Edryd did not understand the excitement. He expected more was coming, but Seoras seemed to be waiting for the importance of what he had said to sink in.

"Of course they were massive, seems you would have noticed that straight away," Edryd said dryly. "And it isn't a great discovery to point out that they were constructed, without knowing how or why."

Seoras shook his head. "Constructs are, or were, tools created by sorcerers," Seoras explained, "shaped pieces of the dark, torn loose from the barrier, and confined in a vessel."

"I don't understand."

"You must have heard stories of creatures of stone and earth, magical weapons, sorcerer's staffs, and spirit familiars that protected their masters?" Seoras asked. "Those things were all constructs. Anyone could be a sorcerer. Sorcerers did not need to be able to shape, or to attune their connections to the dark. All they needed was knowledge, and they used that knowledge to create constructs through which they could wield more power, stave off death, and unlock even greater secrets. Those towers were built as vessels to house constructs of incredible strength and power,"

Edryd still did not truly understand, but he did make the connection that this is what he must have been picking up on when he was in the ruins.

"Why could you not feel them?" Edryd wondered.

"It isn't so much that I can't," Seoras said, "it's more like they couldn't see me."

"You are not explaining this very well," Edryd said. "Try something less cryptic, if you can manage it."

"Their attentions were all directed at you. That is what you felt. While you were in there, as far as the constructs were concerned, I didn't register as being worth notice."

"You make it sound like the towers are alive," Edryd said.

"Not the towers, but rather the constructs contained within them," Seoras corrected. "Not exactly alive either, but over time, they can develop something close to a will of their own, even personalities. I have been in that chamber many times. Always, I felt a hint of animus focused on me, but just a hint so small that I dismissed it as a nervous reaction."

"What I felt was not a hint or a nervous reaction. When I entered that chamber alone I was submerged beneath forces that overwhelmed me."

"Whatever you may lack in talent for shaping," Seoras said, the words coming out slow as if being pulled loose with effort, "your perceptions are far beyond my own."

It was a startling admission. Edryd had a healthy respect for the powers Seoras controlled so easily. That Seoras should see in him something which surpassed his own mastery over the dark, filled Edryd with a profound fear. He remembered then something that Seoras had said to him only the night before. He had accused Edryd of being afraid of his own power. Those words had made no sense to Edryd then, but he began to understand them now. It suggested another possibility as well. Seoras was learning far more from Edryd than he was giving back in return.

It wasn't that Seoras wasn't eager to teach, Edryd just hadn't proved to be a very capable student. Edryd took a renewed interest in the papers spread out on the table.

"This morning I realized something else," Seoras said, taking a hold of one of the drawings he had made from memory, "the runic symbols from this panel, are a map of sorts."

Edryd took a moment to himself to feel superior. He had noticed this the moment he had seen the panel. Seoras however, had gone considerably further with this line of reasoning.

"The chamber wasn't a failed bridge to the High Realms, but it might have been a portal to similar chambers in other cities. This one here, it corresponds with Alseam, and this one could be Orlon."

"You can read these symbols?" Edryd asked. The names were not familiar to Edryd, but he got the idea; Seoras was listing off the names of ancient cities, some of which now survived only in the form of rumors of a lost age.

"No, no one can anymore," Seoras said, "but if I am right, this could be a key to deciphering them. And if this is a map, it gives the locations of cities whose names are no longer even whispered, having long ago been lost to the ravages of time. We could find them again, and the knowledge hidden within them."

Seoras was barely restraining his excitement now, and he was taking it for granted that Edryd would be at his side travelling the world, uncovering the hidden remains of sleeping construct chambers. Edryd silently wondered how best to tell this dangerous man, of whom he felt terrified, thanks but no, and wish him the best of luck. Edryd was curious about the runic inscriptions though, so instead of explaining that he had no wish to go and see any of these places, he began to help

Seoras puzzle out what could be learned of the meanings behind the symbols.

Edryd learned that Seoras had an entire collection of transcriptions taken from various surviving sources written in these ancient symbols, and he had compiled a collection of notes drawn from years of study. This was not some recent fleeting pursuit meant to help pass moments of boredom. Seoras had already invested a great deal into this project. His discoveries to this point had been modest. He could interpret the system used for numbering and for giving dates, the names of two significant sorcerers, and a symbolic representation for 'construct', but that was the extent of what he knew for certain. The speculated names of known cities on the panel, believed to represent a crude sort of map, had the potential to significantly expand what was known.

It soon struck Edryd as quite impossible. These were not arcane coded symbols that had evolved into more modern equivalents, they were messages written in an unknown language that was long lost to history. The futility of the task drained his level of interest, and Edryd soon found himself distracted by something else. A small leather bound book lay on the table, with its pages open to a description of the funereal practices of ancient mythical beings, alternately known either as the Huldra or the Ældisir.

Edryd paged through the book, scanning its contents. The title had worn away, but what the pages described was a race of beings from another realm, trapped in this world after the bridges built by the first men collapsed. Of particular interest was a description of their physical appearance: tall beautiful men and women with ashen skin that resembled the surface of roughly polished stone. These were the true Ascomanni.

"I was looking for a way to destroy them," Seoras said from over Edryd's shoulder, causing Edryd to look up from the book. "But it wasn't much use. They are no longer much like what they were when they were alive."

"This book is about the draugar?" Edryd asked. It was a reflexive question, seeking unnecessary confirmation of the obvious.

"No, the book describes what they once were, not what they are now," he repeated. "The few Huldra and Ældisir that survive are all changed into what you are calling draugar, which isn't an altogether inaccurate description for what some of them have become."

"You sound as if you feel sorry for them," Edryd said.

"I do," Seoras agreed. "They are anchored to a world that is not theirs, witnesses to the destruction of all their kind, and denied the possibility of release through death."

"But you want to destroy them?"

"I possess no power that can help or harm them," Seoras said, straightening his back as he spoke, "but you might."

Edryd could feel a pressure behind those words, an accusation of sorts—a suggestion that he had hidden away something important.

"Where is the Edorin Sigil Blade?" Seoras demanded.

Aed Seoras began to shape. Edryd tried to move but he couldn't. He was held down as if by coils of rope securing him to his chair.

"I'm not trying to take it from you, but I must know if you have it," he said loudly, reacting to Edryd's attempts to break free.

Seoras's demeanor was not much different from any of the several times the shaper's cultivated calm had been obliterated in a fit of anger. But what Edryd saw in his teacher's mind now was not anger; it was something more frightening. It was an intense desperate thirst, borne out of a hope that the weapon could somehow save him from bondage and damnation.

"Let me go, or I will refuse to help you," Edryd insisted.

The forces holding Edryd in place weakened reluctantly. Edryd stood up slowly with an attitude of indifferent composure, which he in no way truly felt, and backed away from his teacher.

"I dropped it into the middle of the ocean," Edryd said.

The lie had a visible effect on Seoras, whose shoulders fell as he exhaled all of the air in his lungs. The shaper stumbled over to the other side of the table and slumped despondently into a chair.

"You can't imagine what you have done," Seoras lamented.

"There was something in that sword," Edryd explained, "an evil that I couldn't control."

"Those weapons were forged by the Sigil Order specifically to destroy constructs, and you may have discarded the last working example," Seoras said, admonishing his student. "I cannot imagine a more stupid act."

"I had no use for such a thing," Edryd said. The rebuke from Seoras had set him on edge even more than having been confined in the chair.

He hadn't truly discarded the weapon, but he had seriously considered doing so, dissuaded only by Aelsian's promise to hide it away.

"You should realize nothing has only one use. That weapon could have been used to defeat Huldra and Ældisir. They will come for you again, and you will wish then that you had such a weapon."

Deciding it was time to put space between himself and the dark, unpredictable shaper, Edryd left. He had unanswered questions, but he hoped that many of them would be answered by the small leather bound book he had tucked inside his coat.

Edryd sought Irial without success, and ended up in the little used room that had been made up for him in the barracks. Suspecting that she was probably still up at the manor, where he didn't intend to return for fear of running into Seoras, Edryd settled into a chair and began to read from the book he had stolen. She was certain to find him here if he waited.

The book was an account summarizing the history and culture of the Huldra and Ældisir, whose long story traced back to a time when the first men had bridged this world and theirs, driving a period of trade, with shared exchanges of knowledge and materials that were previously foreign to the respective worlds. The Huldra and the Ældisir were descended from ancestors who were trapped on this side when the bridge collapsed. Many men were also trapped at that time by this collapse in numerous other realms, including theirs, Huldasvárri.

The Huldra were a warrior caste, predominantly male and often exceptionally strong. The Ældisir were the exclusively female practitioners of a unique deistic form of sorcery called Seiðr, with which they performed an essential role for their people. Denied admittance to the High Realms of men, when one of the Huldra died in this realm, displaced so far from the paths that led to their own afterworld, they were at risk of being condemned to wander, forever lost in the æther. The Ældisir were living guides, travelers of the æther who helped the dead find the paths which would enable them to make their journey to the afterlife.

Edryd continued to read, but he had to agree, the people described in this book were alive, vulnerable to death, and not much like the monsters he had either encountered himself or heard descriptions of from others. Nothing in the book hinted at what might have transformed them so cruelly.

He had been reading for a few hours and was half way through the text when Irial arrived.

"What is that?" she asked.

"A book borrowed from the library of our good Lord Seoras," Edryd said to Irial, who gave him a critical look upon hearing this description.

"Alright, stolen from Lord Seoras then," he said, admitting to the act of theft.

"I'm not sure what he would even do, but it would be best if you don't let him know you have taken it," Irial cautioned.

"Have you seen the state his study is in? If he misses it at all, he will think it is buried under a pile somewhere."

"Maybe," Irial allowed, without expressing any real confidence in Edryd's logic, "but what was so interesting about it that you would even take the risk?"

In answer, Edryd turned the pages of the book to a detailed drawing. Reversing his hold on the book he raised it in the air so that Irial could see the image.

"That looks like Herja!" Irial gasped.

Edryd closed the book and tucked it back into his coat. Irial clearly would have liked to take a closer look, and Edryd did want her opinion, but this was leverage with which he could pry information from her first.

"How did Seoras become connected with the draugar?" Edryd asked.

Irial glanced around nervously, reacting with a conditioned alarm caused by recent memories of Herja and her thralls in residence at the estate.

"Do you not think that conversation would be better suited for another time, and any place but here?" she asked.

"It definitely would be," Edryd agreed. "I'm ready to go if you are."

Edryd was pleasantly surprised to learn that Irial was ready to leave, as he had not realized that a good part of the day had already passed while he was reading. As they left together and headed for the gates, Edryd was troubled by the idea that he would be stopped by Seoras, but he did his best to conceal the anxiety.

Once they were well away from the edges of the settlement, Irial and Edryd stopped to rest and talk on a grassy slope overlooking the city. The air was still and quiet, with occasional currents that transported the fresh lavender scent from Irial's hair and her simple dark woolen dress. Edryd was suddenly aware of the fact that he had not done anything to clean himself up since his time out in the forests. He wore fresh clothing, but his black canvas coat had become worn and dirty, and he didn't want to consider what a week spent in the woods must smell like.

"Seoras came here with Beodred's men," Irial began, answering the question Edryd had posed about Seoras while back at the estate. "He had been one of Beodred's personal guards, and as such had some status. He could have vied for control, but he was only here for a few months, leaving at the first opportunity."

"He would have fought in the battles in Nar Edor then," Edryd said, realizing as he said it how little he knew of Seoras prior to when he had met him.

"He did. He surrendered directly to your father in fact."

"He knew my father?" Edryd asked, clearly astounded by that information.

"I would not say that he knew your father," Irial disagreed. "It's more like he worshipped him; but, what their relationship was, if anything at all, I don't know. When I picture Seoras, sometimes I can see a little boy who desperately wanted to grow up to be a sigil knight."

Irial smiled as she spoke. It was a pleasant way for her to imagine the dark shaper. Edryd found it an impossible thing to reconcile with his own conception of the short tempered man who had been instructing him.

"That childish part is still there. It has driven him to make a series of bad decisions, compromises made at great cost in pursuit of his goal. He is a dark man now, evil even, and very unhappy."

Edryd had not been expecting or asking for her opinion of Seoras as a person. What she was describing though, was consistent with what Edryd knew in a very direct way from the link he shared with Seoras.

"He isn't intentionally malicious though, or needlessly cruel," she said, softening the appraisal of the man she worked for. "If he seems frustrated, it is because he doesn't like who he is, or the things he has done. It isn't that he ever feels guilt or remorse, he doesn't, but he measures himself a failure, and is a man filled by regret. I think he would find another way if he believed that he could."

Edryd didn't know what she meant by this, and Irial probably didn't know either. It was just a generalized impression that conveyed a sense of who she thought Seoras was.

"And his connection to the draugar?" asked Edryd, trying to move the conversation back to his original question.

"He returned to An Innis a little more than a decade after he left. The draugar began to show up in the months that followed. They were ragged and befouled creatures back then and they didn't have any thralls."

By all accounts, draugar were still fairly horrific in appearance. Edryd could only wonder how bad they must have been for Irial to think they were less ragged and foul now.

"Why did Seoras help them?" Edryd asked. He couldn't reason out what held the shaper here.

"People think he is a necromancer, able to command the returned. It is very much the other way around. The draugar come to him with instructions, always demanding new thralls. Bound by some agreement he made with their master, he remains here, doing whatever they require, which mainly involves training more thralls."

"Why do they even need human servants?" Edryd wondered.

"The thralls help in conventional ways, such as carrying burdens and applying treatments that preserve and augment the bodies of the draugar. They also serve as human agents to do everything from hiring ships and negotiating deals to carrying out missions of their own. Basically, they do whatever their masters wish, and they do so with complete obedience. This makes it possible for the draugar to remain mostly hidden from the world."

"They don't want anyone to know about them," Edryd concluded, realizing just how crucial the thralls were to the draugar.

"No, and to that end they travel mostly at night, avoiding contact with living things. But travelling to and from An Innis so frequently, occasionally they were seen. People began to associate them with plague victims. A few swore they recognized them as men and women that they had known in life, the specters of family members returned from death."

"But why would anyone recognize them? They were not anyone's family members."

"Some of the creatures no longer have bodies, but they can be seen when they want to," Irial explained. "They don't appear as themselves. They can't. They play tricks with the mind, and you see someone you can remember from your past. It can be someone still living, but usually they choose someone who is already dead."

Edryd was stunned. He had experienced what Irial was describing. Until this moment, he had not understood. Irial caught the expression on his face.

"You have seen them before," she said.

"I was followed when I left Nar Edor," Edryd confirmed. "I ended up in the hands of smugglers who I had fallen in with as a means to travel from Nar Edor without being known. They thought I was just a hired sword. A day out of Nar Edor, they decided they didn't need my help defending their cargo, and that they would do better by selling me. I ended up bound and imprisoned in the hold of their ship."

"Hard to imagine how they managed that," Irial said. "I would think that would have cost them dearly."

"I was drunk," Edryd said reluctantly, "perhaps drugged as well, and feeling very sick on my first experience on a boat out on the ocean."

"They regretted it in the end," Irial said. She knew some of what he was about to tell her, having made the connection to things she had learned from Logaeir, and tales spread by the survivors of the ship that had taken him captive.

"They did," Edryd agreed. "What they didn't know, and what I was only vaguely aware of, was that there was a draugr on the ship with us. It had been following me for weeks and had boarded the vessel when I did. Late at night, I woke up as she was cutting my ropes."

"She?"

"I saw a woman," Edryd explained. "I barely remember my mother, but I am sure for a moment that I saw her face leaning over me. I thought it was delirium from the wine or the drugs, but someone cut my ropes."

Irial shifted, growing tense and anxiously waiting to learn more.

"I killed two of my captors, and then I burnt the ship down around the heads of the rest of them."

"You burnt the ship down while you were still on it?" Irial asked with skepticism, even though she knew it for the truth. "You must have really wanted them all dead."

"I killed only four of them in the end. The rest escaped in a smaller boat that they had been towing."

Irial thought that she knew the rest of this story. "And you remained alone on the burnt out ship until you were rescued by Aelsian."

"Not alone no, the creature, I guess it must be one of the Ældisir, was there, though I could not see her. I think she must have been terrified that the ship would sink, but it held up long enough. Aelsian somehow knew that she was following me. He drew her away so that I could escape, and I ended up here."

"That was a dumb thing to do," Irial complained.

Edryd thought that she meant that Aelsian was stupid to draw the attention of the creature, but that wasn't it.

"You don't go to An Innis to avoid draugar," she said.

"Not for any other reason either," Edryd agreed. "It would be a dangerous place even without Seoras and the likes of Herja. I don't understand his reasons for staying here."

"I don't either but I have heard Seoras complain that his fate is not so different from that of the men he trains. Maybe he has no choice."

"If he is something like a thrall, then he isn't a very good one. He seems to have chosen to protect me from his master."

"No doubt he does so for reasons of his own," Irial said. "Perhaps it is that part of him that wanted to be a sigil knight. He might believe that you can somehow help him out of all of this."

"You could be right," Edryd agreed. "Today, he told me of a way to defeat them."

"The draugar?" asked Irial.

"He said that a sigil sword could be used to destroy them," Edryd explained, "but I told him that it was at the bottom of the ocean between here and Nar Edor."

Irial's eyes lit up at the mention of the sword. "That could be used to destroy a construct," she said excitedly. "Please tell me you didn't really throw it into the sea."

It struck Edryd yet again that he needed to read this book she had borrowed from Uleth. Irial seemed to know more about the ancient

Sigil Order than he did. Even if it was full of nonsense, a lot of people seemed to be operating under the assumptions that it held the truth.

"Aelsian has the sword," Edryd said, feeling troubled at revealing where it was.

"He will surely have the good sense to bring it when he comes," she replied.

I won't know what to do with it if he does, Edryd thought, worried that Aelsian would bring the weapon. Edryd wanted nothing more to do with that aberrantly willful artifact of power.

Chapter 17

Feyd Gerlin

Aelsian stood beside his desk studying three scraps of paper, two of which were scrolled pieces of text carried by feathered messengers to a roost on the roof of his home on the Elduryn estate. One of those, penned by Commander Ledrin, had arrived this morning. Devoid of useful context, it read: need to meet – Edryd. The other, sent by the Ascomanni, had arrived two days ago with the message timeline accelerated three weeks – Logaeir.

Preparations had been underway to return to the waters near An Innis before either of the messages had come, but there was an increased urgency now. Logaeir's message he had understood. The Ascomanni attack on An Innis would now be taking place before the end of the month. The fleet navarch would not be involved in the attack, but his forces needed to be nearby as a contingency. The ships were already in place, but Aelsian needed to leave soon if he meant to be there himself.

Edryd's message communicated almost nothing, but it did reveal that Ledrin must now know what had happened to the heir of House Edorin as well as Aelsian's role in it. He wasn't certain, but Aelsian didn't imagine that it meant that Edryd was back in Nar Edor. Edryd was most likely still on An Innis, or the message should have said otherwise.

It was reasonable to assume that some single factor had motivated both messages. Ludin Kar's prediction had come true. Logaeir was making use of the situation and had placed the Edorin heir in a position of terrible risk. Feeling a personal obligation, and fully appreciating his responsibility for having put Edryd under Logaeir's influence to begin with, Aelsian could not quiet his own unease, and he resolved to leave as soon as he could.

This made it an especially inopportune time to have received the summons from Feyd Gerlin, the Sovereign of Ossia. As outlined on the third, larger sheet of paper, delivered moments ago by hand and now crumpled into a misshapen lump near the edge of the desk, Aelsian had been commanded to leave immediately to attend a council of the Ossian Fleet. The council was comprised of Aelsian, commanding the famed Ossian First Fleet, Morven Tevair commanding the much larger Second Fleet, and Feyd Gerlin along with whichever of his advisors were currently in favor at the moment. He could expect that they would want an update on the Ascomanni.

The timing was suspect. Aelsian wondered whether Feyd Gerlin might have a source either on the island of An Innis or in the Ascomanni encampment. A more direct explanation might be that a member of Aelsian's staff, or one of the officers under his charge, was spying for the sovereign.

In any case, this was not a message that Aelsian could ignore. He left his office and hurried down the hall to his simple living quarters, where he proceeded to change into a crisp cerulean formal uniform. He had dispatched Ludin Kar this morning with instructions for the crew of the *Interdiction*, ordering that it should be made ready to leave immediately.

Aelsian had one remaining problem. He was debating what to do with the sigil blade. He had to take it back to Edryd, but he hadn't been comfortable entrusting that responsibility to anyone else, except for Ludin Kar, who had refused it. As a result, the ancient weapon was stowed discreetly away in a pine crate under Aelsian's bed, where it had continued to trouble his sleep on a nightly basis. If Aelsian left it behind, he would have to return to the estate before he could leave.

Deciding that he needed the flexibility to go directly to his ship after the council concluded, Aelsian retrieved the sword from its place beneath his bed and belted it on at his side. Aelsian did not have a suitable sheath, so the weapon hung at an angle, blade exposed, through a banded metal throat piece that he had scavenged from a scabbard meant for a shorter sword. Having completed all preparations, Aelsian made his way towards the front of the Elduryn family estate.

Availing himself of a carriage sent by the sovereign, Aelsian had time to anticipate numerous questions that he thought he might be asked regarding the Ascomanni, for which he prepared a series of noncommittal responses. However, as he did not know specifically why he had been summoned, he was not confident that this would do him any good.

On his way to the sovereign's palace, Aelsian struggled with doubts over his decision to wear the sword. It was plain and unadorned, but the unusual length and simple metallic beauty of the weapon drew attention, and he dreaded the possibility that it might inspire curious questions. Unnervingly, Aelsian felt like the weapon was pleased to be out from beneath his bed, excited at the prospect of being carried. It wants to return to Edryd, Aelsian reminded himself, thinking that he would be relieved to be rid of it.

He was the last to arrive in the carpeted council chambers adjoining the common audience hall of Feyd Gerlin's palace. Feyd, seated in a comfortable chair, was flanked by a silent advisor who cautiously appraised everyone in the room. Tevair, navarch for Ossia's Second Fleet, gave Aelsian an unfriendly stare, glancing only briefly at the weapon belted at the First Fleet Navarch's side, apparently angry at having been made to wait on the arrival of his more accomplished counterpart.

"I hear that you have plans to travel," Feyd began. "But I am sure you didn't mean to go before advising on your progress."

Aelsian hadn't made a secret of his plans to leave, but he hadn't been advertising them either. It confirmed what he could reasonably have expected. He was being carefully watched by enemies and friends alike.

"I received a message from our agent," Aelsian confirmed. "The schedule is being moved up by three weeks."

"Why I wonder?" Feyd puzzled with disguised interest, speaking to no one in particular. Though the question had not been specifically directed at him, Aelsian knew that it was expected that he provide the sovereign with an accurate explanation.

"Our agent did not say," Aelsian answered. "I assume, though, that he judges the Ascomanni forces are sufficiently prepared. If we delay too long, there is a risk that disunity among the Ascomanni leadership could develop, which would then make the entire project impossible."

"No other reason than that?" Tevair interrupted.

"You are free to offer your own speculations, Tevair," Aelsian said. "If you think you know more than I, you should enlighten us."

"I have heard rumors that Aisen has taken command of the Ascomanni," the Second Fleet Navarch said.

Aelsian needed to be careful how he answered this question. It would be dangerous to lie to the sovereign, but it would not be safe to tell the truth either, not that he knew with any precision what that was.

"Our agent within Ascomanni has made use of Lord Aisen's disappearance. Posing as the Blood Prince, he has given the Ascomanni a central figure to lead the attack and better control the aftermath once they have taken the city. It may be a contributing factor in the sudden acceleration to the timeline."

"Did you approve this?" Feyd asked.

"No, I was never even informed until after it had already been done," Aelsian said.

"You need to reign in your man," Tevair suggested. "We can't have him acting of his own accord."

"I agree," said Feyd. "This is a risk. If Aisen should reappear, proving your man a liar..."

Feyd's suggestion hung in the air for a while before Aelsian responded.

"That won't happen."

"How can you possibly be sure," Tevair argued.

Aelsian cursed his own stupidity. He had managed to talk himself into a corner. A direct lie would eventually be exposed, putting him in a precarious position when the truth ultimately did come out. He could not keep this from Feyd Gerlin, but Aelsian was not about to share it with anyone else.

"I have information that you need to know Feyd," Aelsian said, "but it is for your ears only."

Aelsian looked around the room, waiting for the others to leave.

"You can trust Ambassador Seym," Feyd said, meaning the advisor by his side who had so far said nothing during the meeting.

"I am sure that I can," Aelsian agreed, striving to sound diplomatic, "but I would like you to hear the information first before you decide whether it should be shared with Seym or Tevair. They must leave."

"I have the right to be here, and you have no authority to give me orders," Tevair said to Aelsian, furious over being dismissed by his rival.

"No, but I do," Feyd said, his voice a command. "A certain amount of deference has always been afforded by the Second Fleet to the navarch of the First. It is a weakness, Tevair, that you cannot manage even the pretense of courtesy. You are excused with my permission. We will conclude the meeting without you."

"I apologize," Tevair said quickly, his tone anything but apologetic. "But I will hear what it is that Aelsian has hidden from us."

"I can share this with you alone, Feyd," Aelsian said with a firmness that made it clear he would not change his mind.

"Both of you out," Feyd ordered.

The sovereign looked uneasy as his advisor, followed by the still fuming Tevair, left the room. Aelsian couldn't blame him. History had shown that the ruler of this country had good reasons to be careful of his navarchs. Feyd had just angered one of his, and had agreed to an unwitnessed audience with the other.

The sovereign knew though, that the best way to avoid joining Ossia's infamous list of deposed or murdered rulers, which Feyd Gerlin had successfully managed to do now for more than two decades, was to maintain a balanced rivalry between the two powerful men who commanded Ossia's naval forces. Measured by that goal, Feyd Gerlin had just made some considerable progress.

"You know where the son of Aedan Elduryn is," Feyd said once the doors had closed, not giving Aelsian the opportunity to control the conversation.

The navarch was not altogether surprised. He had already suspected the sovereign had been getting information from somewhere. This wasn't an example of the Feyd being perceptive.

"He must not be allowed to ever set foot on Ossia," Feyd ordered.

This reaction too was of no particular surprise to Aelsian. Wealth and influence were the instruments of power in many places, but nowhere more so than in Ossia. The Elduryn family had consolidated enough of both to be a serious threat to Feyd.

"For your sake as well as mine," Feyd elaborated. "If Aisen were to take control of his properties here, you would be relegated to nothing more than his servant."

Aelsian understood this reminder of his subordinate role in service to the Elduryn family, as an attempt—none too subtle in its purpose—to identify where his loyalties might lie. Feyd respected Aelsian, but he did not trust that their interests were well aligned.

Choosing his words carefully, Aelsian responded. "I can assure you that Aisen has no desire to claim the legacy Aedan left for him."

Feyd nodded at Aelsian, prodding him to continue. Aelsian knew that he needed to be careful. He did not know how much Feyd Gerlin already knew.

"He was a lone survivor on the burnt out wreckage of a ship when I found him. I have no idea how he came to be there, and he did not divulge his identity. He was calling himself Edryd, but of course I knew him, even if my crew did not. You should not fear him. He is a coward in flight from his responsibilities and his identity. He will keep running. He has no interest in becoming enmeshed into the world of Ossian politics."

"That is all very reassuring," Feyd interrupted, "and I'm glad you had the sense not to bring him here, but where is he now?"

"He was fleeing from more than just himself when I last saw him," Aelsian continued. "He was being pursued by a draugr. I am no longer sure where he is."

"Where did you last see Lord Aisen," Feyd said, growing impatient.

Aelsian thought Aisen beyond the sovereign's reach, and doubted Feyd would do anything at all so long as he stayed away from Ossia. Regrettably, Aelsian failed to note that Feyd had shown almost no reaction to his inclusion of a draugr into the account, or he might have thought through the situation differently.

"He was put ashore near An Innis. He could still be there, either somewhere on the island or in the hands of the Ascomanni."

"Are you certain?" Feyd asked after a momentary pause.

"No. He could easily be back in Nar Edor by now, or somewhere else entirely. I can make inquiries and confirm," Aelsian replied.

"Do that, and return as soon as you learn anything," the sovereign commanded. "We should meet again tomorrow," he added as an afterthought.

Aelsian watched Feyd rise from his chair, and he remained standing at attention while the man exited the room. The Ossian Sovereign, flanked by two armored guards who had been waiting outside the doors, continued across the large audience hall to which the council room was adjacent, and disappeared down a hallway on the other side. The meeting had ended too abruptly, and Aelsian noticed something else that was wrong. He would have missed it if months of paranoia had not trained him to continually look for such subtle signs. A thick piece of carpeting, which extended a few feet through either side of the entrance, bore several marks. These included outlined shapes of rounded boots, some of which, freshly left by Feyd as he exited the room, had been partially obliterated by a smaller and heavier set of impressions where an unseen creature had followed.

Aelsian had only one thought. It did not involve concern for the safety of the sovereign, who, upon further reflection, seemed to be directly acquiring information from the draugar or their servants. Aelsian understood at once that he had committed a grave error; he had revealed to these undead creatures the location of their prey.

Following the deep narrow impressions, Aelsian was soon on the other side of the door, but where the carpet ended, the trail disappeared too. Aelsian looked around the audience chamber. Feyd had already left, and Tevair was nowhere to be seen. He spotted Seym near the entrance. Already a tense bundle of heightened awareness, what Aelsian saw then, or rather did not see, caused him to freeze entirely. Seym, dressed darkly in expensive silk, was nodding his head as if he was having a strange conversation with some figure that only he could see. That was of course precisely what he was doing.

Aelsian waited for Seym to leave the audience chamber before he too headed in the direction of the entrance to the palace. He could see where Seym was, but he had no idea where the draugr might be if it was still there at all. At a distance, Aelsian continued to follow the advisor, whose dark expensive clothing stood out amidst the whitewashed buildings and the brightly colored crowds of ordinary people. Aelsian's worries continued to grow as he tracked Seym down a seemingly endless series of streets that wound through the Ossian capital.

Eventually, as they were approaching the harbor, Seym entered a tavern called the Water's Edge. Aelsian kept his distance and waited patiently for Seym to re-emerge. It didn't take long. Seym was joined by two rough looking men who wore plain clothing, blank expressions, and knives belted at their sides. After exchanging a few words, and a few coins, the two men parted ways with Seym, who headed back the way he had come, his coin purse now heavier than it had previously been. Making a quick decision, Aelsian ignored Seym, under the assumption that Feyd Gerlin's advisor would simply be returning to the palace.

The two men hired passage on a small boat. By now Aelsian knew what to look for. After the two men boarded, but before the boat could push away from where it was moored, the vessel swayed a little and rode even deeper in the water as a substantial weight settled into place. The boat's owners showed a little surprise, but they didn't understand what had just happened and gave it little thought as they began to row, propelling the craft out into the harbor under more effort that they might have expected.

Aelsian watched as they ferried the two men, as well the third passenger of which they clearly were not aware, towards a cedar planked galleon with a worn marque that he couldn't quite make out. As the passengers boarded the larger vessel it immediately pulled anchor, and raising the sails on its three masts, it began moving swiftly out to sea.

Aelsian was now in a race, one that he had to win. With all the energy his aging body could manage, Aelsian sped his way towards the berth where the *Interdiction* was tied up. As he pounded up the boarding ramp he began shouting instructions. He had a fleet of ships at his command, but only a few were here in Ossia, and none of them were any faster than the *Interdiction*. The entire fleet would do him little good now if he allowed that ship to sail out of view.

***

Ruach was pleased to find that his third journey at sea had gone better than either of the previous two. The short interval between the second and third trips could be credited for that, making it unnecessary to become re-accustomed to the rolling of the ship.

Three days at sea had, however, taken a toll on the other soldiers during their time aboard the *Black Strand*. A few of them were actually kissing the ground of the isthmus where they had come ashore. From where they stood just beyond the encampment, An Innis could be seen to the north, a tiny speck rising out of the waters which separated it from the forested lands on the coast. Ruach counted two dozen longboats sheltering in a pool created by a bend in the river that split this flat strip of land on which the raiding base had been established. A handful of larger warships and captured merchant vessels were anchored offshore.

Near the mooring points for the longboats were numerous fires, several of which were heating large iron cooking pots. Above a few others were butchered segments of deer roasting above warm coals. An entire area of the camp was dominated by racks of fish curing in the air. Logaeir was in amidst the crowd that greeted them as they approached a small collection of temporary shelters erected with little evidence of planning beside a newly built fire pit.

"Welcome to Darkpool," Logaeir said to the band of Sigil Corps soldiers.

Logaeir led them to the tents that had been prepared and encouraged the soldiers to enjoy the food and drink that was soon brought in to them. Most of the men accepted with gratitude, but a couple of them, still queasy and unable to eat, retired to the tents to sleep off the lingering nausea that had been induced by the trip.

Oren and Ruach, joined by Neysim Ells, sought out Logaeir, who was observing the arrivals with interest from just beyond the fire in the midst of the soldier's tents.

"If you will divide your men, we can start training them in the morning," Oren offered.

"In the time we have, I am not sure how much that will accomplish," Logaeir replied. "I think you will be of more use as a unit, rather than dispersed out and mixed in among our forces during the attack."

Ruach was surprised, but he reasoned it out quickly enough. Logaeir was concerned that in the process of training his men, the Sigil Corps soldiers might begin to dominate the ranks of the Ascomanni, wresting control from Logaeir and shifting it to the real Blood Prince.

"I assume one or both of you would like to meet up with Aisen," Logaeir said, referring to Oren and Ruach. "I need to see him myself. We can leave as soon as you are ready."

"Oren is going to stay here with our men," Ruach said, "but Neysim and I will go with you."

"I will meet you in an hour at the moorings," Logaeir said. "We will try to arrive on the island just before dark."

Logaeir ambled off leaving the three officers of the Sigil Corps alone.

"Why am I being left behind?" Oren wanted to know.

"Because someone needs to be left in command," Neysim said.

That was all the explanation Oren needed, his bolstered egotism banishing any sense of having been left out.

"Since it seems he does not want his men to practice with us any longer, you will have to make sure the men train as a group on their own in the morning," Ruach said. "Make sure you choose a spot where everyone will see. Give the Ascomanni a show."

Oren smiled. "I think I can manage that."

The three officers joined their men, and after finishing their food, Neysim and Ruach separated from the group to meet up with Logaeir.

They found him conversing with Sarel Krin and a handful of his crew.

Krin looked pale as he listened to Logaeir.

"You are a liar, Logaeir," Krin said, disbelief plain on his face. "I'll not believe you attacked one of those things. If you had, you'd not still be alive now to speak of it."

Logaeir produced for everyone's examination, proof of his attack against Herja. "I looked her straight in the face, and stabbed her with this," he said, holding out a thin metal knife with a broken point. "It stopped not even an inch inside. Didn't draw blood, but it did leave some sort of tincture on the end of the knife."

Krin accepted the knife from Logaeir and inspected it closely. "What is this, tree sap?"

"I think so, it looks and smells like pitch from a blister on a fir tree blended together with some kind of oil," Logaeir said as he took the knife back from Krin.

"Why would you even try something like that?" Krin asked.

"I was following advice from Aed Seoras passed on through Irial."

"That doesn't make it better," Krin complained. "I'd sooner have faced one of those creatures alone and on my own terms than listen to anything that sorcerer told me."

"Those weren't my choices," Logaeir pointed out. "I was going to be confronted by Herja either way, and I had to trust that maybe Seoras does know a little bit about them. I was assured that I wouldn't hurt her, and that she would barely care."

"Who's Herja?" Neysim asked, inserting his question into the middle of the conversation without taking the trouble of introducing himself.

"A very strange, very dead, draugr woman," Logaeir replied.

Neysim, taken aback by this answer, looked towards Ruach, searching for an indication from his friend that the Ascomanni strategist was putting one over on him. If he was, Ruach's reaction betrayed nothing.

"Is she still here?" Ruach asked.

"What was it doing here in the first place? And aren't they supposed to be ghosts with armored skin?" Neysim asked before anyone could answer Ruach's question. "You shouldn't have been able to stab one."

"Herja and her two thralls left several days ago," Logaeir said, answering Ruach first. "And no, draugar are not ghosts with armored skin. Some are ghostly apparitions, and some have armored skin, but not both at once. Others, well Herja anyway, seem to have their armor on the inside."

Neysim couldn't tell if he was being taken seriously or not. "Forgive my ignorance," he said with no sincerity.

"I would forgive the ignorance, if you could offer any sort of suitable excuse," Logaeir criticized, the fullest extent of his winning personality on brazen display. "Why would a spirit creature even need armored skin?"

"You meet your first draugr, and suddenly you are an expert," Krin said to Logaeir, mocking his friend's tendency towards exaggerated pretensions. In a moment of unexpected genius, and looking very pleased with himself, Krin then treated Logaeir to the same sort of elaborate condescension that the strategist had so often dispensed to others. "If anyone demonstrated unforgivable stupidity, it is the brave little man who, rendering questionable the intelligence on which he has built his reputation, stabbed an immortal warrior on advice from an enemy."

"Aed Seoras isn't an enemy," protested Logaeir. "He's... well I don't know what he is exactly."

"A good deal more dangerous than any of your actual enemies, that's what he is," Krin said helpfully.

"My point is, that while this might have been the first I ever met in person, I have seen draugar often enough. They are in and around An Innis more often than anyone should find comfortable, and I would say I am more expert than most on the subject."

"We have had encounters with them on Nar Edor as well," said Neysim, "so do not think I am as ignorant as you might suspect. Their servants have been making inquiries in the cities, seeking out news of Lord Aisen. The draugar themselves, the ones you can't see, still have weight and they take up space. I don't see why they couldn't be invisible and armored."

"A fair point," Logaeir agreed. "If you ever encounter one, take a swing at it and let me know what happens."

"Let's not argue this to death," Krin said cutting off further debate. "We are not seeking a conflict with apparitions or immortal returned. Our enemies are flesh and blood."

There were nods of general agreement from all of Krin's men. Nobody, with the exception of Logaeir, seemed at all comfortable discussing the draugar.

"Let's go," Krin said, waving everyone on towards a waiting boat.

"Who exactly is this guy, and what is his problem?" Neysim asked Ruach as they were getting into the boat, referring to the Ascomanni strategist.

"Logaeir is the architect of the push to conquer An Innis. We tweaked his plans and he is holding a grudge. He wanted our help, just not under the terms Captain Aisen extracted from him."

Neysim and Ruach helped man the oars as they pushed out into the river and followed the currents that would deliver them to the sea. After several hours of hard rowing they arrived under darkness on the banks of a small inlet on the southern shores of An Innis. Together with Krin and Logaeir, the two officers made their way up a steep embankment, leaving Krin's crew behind with the longboat. It was not long before they could see the cottage in the moonlight.

Instead of heading directly for the building, they worked slightly eastward as they approached. Neysim discovered why they had diverted when they came upon a hidden crevice, well concealed by the branches of bushes that grew around the sides. One by one they entered the opening, and walking by the light of an oil lamp carried by Krin, they proceeded down the length of a crooked tunnel.

Eventually they reached a ladder. Neysim, climbing up last, found himself crowded into a small room together with the other men. Logaeir took the lamp from Krin, who set about replacing the section of wooden planks that covered the hole in the floor behind them. When he was done, Logaeir doused the flame, leaving the group in darkness. Light from a fire leaked in through the gap between the door and the floor beneath it.

Neysim wasn't sure why the feeling was so acute, but Ledrin had entrusted him with messages for a man who would be waiting on the other side of this door, and he felt nervous waiting in the dark for someone to open it. The voices of a man and a young girl could be heard arguing on the other side. Logaeir gave a firm series of knocks signaling their arrival, and pulled the door inward, flooding the darkened room with light from the main hall.

"Make sure you call him Edryd and not Aisen," Ruach whispered in Neysim's ear.

A thin man in a black coat, who Neysim barely recognized as Captain Aisen, turned to face them as they entered. A young girl with dark black hair ran around the table and began pelting Logaeir with a series of unusual questions. "Did you really see Herja?" followed by "is she a Huldra?" and "what did she smell like?"

Logaeir was momentarily staggered by the onslaught of rapid demands, but his confusion progressed to bemusement and he grinned as he begged the girl to slow down. "One question at a time, Eithne," he said.

"Edryd says that there are two kinds, Huldra and Ældisir," Eithne said, "and Herja sounds exactly like a Huldra."

"And what would Edryd know about it," Logaeir said.

"He has a book," Eithne explained, "but he won't let me have it."

"Well I don't know what a Huldra is or what's in this book, but I've seen Herja and she definitely isn't whatever it is Edryd said she was."

Eithne wrinkled her nose in frustration. "Edryd met an Ældisir once," she said, "and Irial has seen lots of Huldra."

Edryd smiled as if he had won something. "You are losing credibility, Logaeir," he said.

"Seems I didn't have any to begin with," Logaeir complained. "People have been calling me a liar and arguing with me all day." This last part he said with a mock injured look directed at both Krin and Neysim. "But I know something that I'll bet isn't in Edryd's book. I know how to destroy them."

This caught everyone's attention, drawing in Irial as well from where she had been experimenting on some complicated mixture in a wooden bowl. Logaeir took a seat beside Edryd and placed the broken knife in the center of the table. Everyone else huddled around.

"Herja's skin was covered in a resin. I managed to collect some of that coating on this knife."

Eithne pulled herself up and leaned over the table, inhaling the sweet balsam scented air through her nose. She looked back at Irial and said, "It smells just like you described it."

Logaeir waited a moment, hoping someone would ask him how he had collected the sample on his knife. He liked telling that story. When no one did, he sighed with disappointment and proceeded to explain what he had discovered.

"This stuff has at least one interesting property," he said as he took a candle from the table, and ignoring a shout from Irial telling him to stop, he held the lighted end beneath the tip of the broken knife, immediately producing a bright orange flame.

Logaeir looked around the room gauging the reactions. Irial's posture slumped, staring hopelessly at the still burning end of the knife. He had the attention of the others, but they all showed only moderate interest.

"This is your plan to kill a draugr?" Edryd laughed. "I want to be there to see it—Herja wreathed in flames and chasing you down like some angry living torch."

The comment must have caused Logaeir to picture the image as well, for he shrank reflexively for a moment, and a shiver traversed his spine.

"I'm not suggesting it would kill her," Logaeir clarified. "But she has some kind of metal infused inside her body. With enough heat, it would melt, and then she would only be wishing that it could kill her."

"That flame is barely even transferring heat to the knife," Neysim observed. "How is it going to melt a draugr?"

"We trap her in a room with plenty of fuel, and light it up like a furnace," Logaeir explained.

A moment passed while everyone mulled over the suggestion. Ruach decided now was a good time to add his input. "Doesn't it strike anyone how completely unworkable that sounds?"

"I'm not saying I have the details worked out," Logaeir admitted.

"An odd sort of discussion," Krin laughed, "us sitting around a table sorting out how to murder a woman."

"Maybe murder isn't the right word, seeing as this wouldn't actually kill her," said Edryd.

"More to the point, she's already dead," said Logaeir.

"She is no longer even on An Innis, probably wouldn't interfere if she were," Krin pointed out.

"Herja will be back though, and perhaps others as well," Logaeir said. "Even small things like knowing the properties of this resin could be useful to us then."

"Now that you have destroyed the only sample," Irial complained, her voice bitter over the lost opportunity, "we can learn nothing more of it. I have been trying for days to reproduce it with no success, and you have just ruined the little bit that you risked your life to acquire."

Logaeir pulled from a pocket in his coat, a thin splinter of wood tightly wrapped in a leaf, and offered it to Irial.

"Of course it wasn't the only sample. I had already removed and saved most of the resin."

Relief spread across Irial's face as she accepted the volatile substance. She began to unwrap it slowly, but quickly rolled it back up, too fearful to examine it near the light of a candle or a lamp. With unsought help from Eithne, who was quite interested in the project, Irial found a small clay jar in the kitchen, dropped the sample in, and sealed the lid tight with wax.

"Let's move on to our real purpose," Krin suggested to Logaeir.

"We will be attacking in force, ten days from today," said Logaeir to everyone. "When that happens, you need to make sure Aed Seoras remains on the sidelines," he added, looking at Edryd.

Irial looked worried, and Edryd thought he knew why. Aelsian might not get here before the attack. The mood turned serious in reaction to Logaeir's words, and everyone watched Edryd expectantly, waiting on his response.

"You think I can control Seoras?" Edryd laughed.

"I hear you spent some master and apprentice time over on the mainland," Logaeir said, carelessly mocking Edryd. "Plan out another forest excursion, challenge him to a fight, or pretend that you are escaping. I don't care how you do it; just keep him away from the fighting when it starts."

Edryd felt warmth rising in his chest. Logaeir had a skill for setting him on edge, and his taunts were becoming ever more childish.

"If Seoras wanted to impede any of this, he could have ended your plans long ago. What makes you think he would even want to interfere?" Edryd challenged.

"He may not want to, but if we do nothing, he will get drawn in. Esivh Rhol won't let Seoras remain unaligned once the fighting starts, and if he has to choose a side you can be sure it isn't going to be ours."

"He does not take his orders from Esivh Rhol," Edryd disagreed, feeling uncomfortable with the argument he was making. It sounded too much like he was defending Seoras, which did little to contradict the implication Logaeir had made a moment ago, suggesting that Seoras and Edryd had become friends.

"He may not listen to orders from Rhol," Irial said, mediating the disagreement between Edryd and Logaeir, "but he cannot ignore him either, and he will fight on their side, not ours. Until we have actually overthrown the Ard Ri we must consider Seoras to be a potential enemy."

"Oh I consider him an enemy all right," Edryd said, "but I also know that he does not care who rules An Innis. I don't see him standing in your way."

"This was a part of our bargain," Logaeir reminded.

"And I intend to keep it," Edryd promised. "Aed Seoras will be kept out of the fight."

Satisfied, Logaeir stood up. "We have to get back," he said. "There are preparations at the encampment that have to be made."

"I need to speak with Edryd before we go," Neysim objected, only just remembering not to call him Captain Aisen.

"Then you will have to remain here," said Logaeir. "We will be exchanging information daily now, so you won't be stuck for long."

"Give us a moment," Ruach insisted.

"A moment," Logaeir relented.

Neysim and Ruach both stood, and together they pulled Edryd aside in a corner of the room. Together, they relayed a condensed version of the situation at the Ascomanni encampment. Edryd voiced his support for the plans that they were already following, and after deciding that Neysim would remain here, as there was more that he wished to discuss with Edryd, Ruach left with Krin and Logaeir through the hidden passage under the floor in the adjoining room.

Edryd was pleased to hear that Logaeir had isolated his soldiers from the rest of the Ascomanni. They would appear even more impressive in a group, and remain less susceptible to Logaeir's manipulations. If that meant his men would have less personal influence with the Ascomanni crews, so be it. The Ascomanni were about to learn what a company of Sigil Corps soldiers were capable of on a battlefield, and Logaeir was not going to be able to keep his men from being drawn to it.

Chapter 18

The Purpose of Power

The room had grown quiet after Logaeir departed with Krin and Ruach. Edryd returned to the seat he had occupied earlier, and Neysim joined him across the table. Irial began dousing lamps until the room was cast in shadows by the light coming from the fire in the center of the room. Edryd's back was to the light, making it difficult to read his expressions in the darkness. Neysim wished he had chosen a different seat, one that would have forced Edryd to turn to the side.

"Commander Ledrin asked me to deliver a message," Neysim said.

"Tell me what he had to say," Edryd encouraged, his feelings towards his former commander exposed by a tension in his face that was hard to miss, even in the dark.

Neysim eyed the young girl who had quietly but unobtrusively taken a seat near them. Edryd had not even seemed to notice her.

"She will find a way to listen in, even if we send her away," Edryd said. "I'm not meant to keep any secrets from her either. She made me promise."

Neysim was still reluctant. He did not think that Edryd was serious.

"Eithne will be discreet, won't she," Edryd said with a careful stare in the young girl's direction. Turning back towards Neysim, he added for good measure, "I'm sure she won't repeat anything, and will keep everything we say in strict confidence."

Eithne stood, and with a grand show of silent annoyance, she crossed the room to join Irial who was pretending to repair a tear in her blue cloak. Eithne wouldn't be able to confuse Edryd with this routine, but Neysim might be easier to fool. Edryd could see from Eithne's posture that she had not given up on listening in on the pending conversation. She had a keenly honed talent for observation, and would certainly overhear the discussion and share with Irial anything that the woman might not catch herself. Neysim seemed satisfied though, and deciding that he did not care, Edryd let him begin.

"The situation is dangerous," Neysim said. "Fourteen thousand are encamped on the planes near the capital under King Eivendr's banner. Another eight thousand are quartered in the capital itself."

"And you have what, maybe four thousand if you raised the entire Corps?"

"About that many, yes," Neysim agreed. "Ledrin had his doubts, but your decision to entrust Lord Teveren with raising your liegemen has worked. He is in command of three thousand, with the expectation that those numbers will grow to five or six."

"I don't know if you can call them my liegemen, when their masters ran to Eivendr in fear of me and begged him for his protection," Edryd said. "And I didn't entrust Teveren with anything. He was the only one of our vassal lords who did not betray me. In fact he tried to warn me I was in danger. For that, I gave him the opportunity to choose a side, nothing more."

"It is well that you did," Neysim said. "If Teveren had opened his borders to the king's armies, it could have cut us off from our support in the south, and we would be drawing our battle lines much closer to home. Eivendr would have taken advantage and attacked weeks ago."

"Nothing says that couldn't still happen," Edryd pointed out, "Teveren could turn on us. He may have rediscovered his loyalty in a fit of conscience when he refused to take part in a plot against my life, but it doesn't alter the fact that it was Teveren who organized the efforts to replace me with my brother to begin with."

"We are keeping an eye on him, and he knows it," Neysim assured Edryd.

"This is sounding like a battle Ledrin would easily win," Edryd concluded. "The numbers are not on our side, but the quality of the soldiers in the Sigil Corps more than balances things out."

"King Eivendr seems to agree. He isn't moving yet. Ledrin does not believe we will face an attack until the king has raised a force of at least forty thousand. The numbers should ultimately reach as many as fifty thousand."

"That might be enough, if they can manage so many," Edryd thought out loud, imagining the way the battles might unfold. "I suppose Ledrin thinks I have a responsibility to return to Nar Edor and help him force the issue before Eivendr can finish raising his army?"

Neysim's answer surprised Edryd.

"Ledrin wants Eivendr to raise his fifty thousand," Neysim said. "It will take months, and it will bankrupt him in the process. If the king succeeds, he will have a force that is too large and too fragmented to control. Were we to face an attack right now, the outcome could be difficult to control, and there would be horrible bloodshed on all sides. But if we can continue to stall long enough, Ledrin believes that the king's armies will ultimately collapse without a battle. Either way, Eivendr will fall."

"Time is on your side then?"

"That is the current thinking, yes," Neysim agreed. "The last thing Ledrin needs is for you to return, or for a bunch of Ascomanni to enter into the conflict. Either would heighten the fears that are motivating the nobility and provoke a strong response, but both at once would completely enflame them."

"Eivendr isn't foolish." Edryd said, forgetting for a second that he was countering an argument that supported his intended refusal to return. "He won't wait. He will balance his resources and act when he is at his strongest."

"Not while his supporters are not certain of the outcome, and not with any urgency while the target of their war isn't even in the country. Your disappearance has worked strangely in our favor and kept things from escalating as quickly as they might have done otherwise."

Edryd felt a release upon hearing these words, inwardly reacting to the absolution of a guilty burden, a constant source of anxiety from which he had never felt completely free in the months since departing the shores of Nar Edor. Feeling misused at the time, Edryd had made the decision to leave, and had done so selfishly. He had tried to reconcile that choice by insisting that it was for the best if he removed himself from the middle of the conflict, trusting that it would help settle things down, but Edryd had not truly believed his own rationalization for abandoning his responsibilities.

Discovering that his absence from the country had in truth forestalled the onset of a bloody war soothed Edryd's conscience, even if it did reduce his personage to a nuisance that the country of Nar Edor could do without. Edryd felt better, but only until he saw the lie in Neysim's story.

Neysim surely believed that he had spoken the truth, but he was an instrument in another man's deception. Ledrin was not trying to forestall a war; he was trying to win one, and he had a strategy for doing so. The commander would not feel satisfied with a victory in a small battle that would only serve to provoke an even larger response from the nobility. He wanted to crush as large an army as could be raised against them, and take control of the country.

Ledrin might have sought his return, if he believed that he retained enough of his former influence over what had been a young and impressionable heir. But if Edryd were to return now to Nar Edor as the Blood Prince, bringing allies with him, Ledrin would no longer be in complete command. He would lose the pretext under which he now carried out his own plans, while pretending that he was acting solely in defense of House Edorin and in the interests of its dispute with the King of Nar Edor.

"If he wants me to stay away, why has he sent me help?" Edryd wondered. "I would have been quite content had he refused."

"Officially, he didn't send us," Neysim explained. "And it isn't that he doesn't want you to return. He does, just not until after we have Eivendr over a barrel so to speak. We want him prepared to negotiate."

This did make things more clear. Ledrin did not need his help, not with the fighting or with planning the future of the country, but he would need the heir of House Edorin to legitimize his actions once he had taken power.

"Ledrin needs to understand. I am never going to be his puppet," Edryd said. He was angry, but he made this declaration calmly. "I don't intend to ever return."

Neysim looked troubled. "We are all hostages," Neysim said, "whether of rich and powerful men, superior officers, the gods, or simple men and women whom by choice we have promised to protect. It doesn't matter which of these we serve. We are all at the mercy of our masters."

"You may be at peace with your place in the world, Neysim," Edryd said, a sad calmness making his voice quiet, "but I have not found my own. Nar Edor is no longer a home to me. I will not willingly give it, or men like Ledrin or Eivendr, my trust. Doing so cost me more than I could spare."

Neysim understood the depth of meaning behind Edryd's words. The heir to House Edorin had lost every one of his living relatives. Ledrin, who had once held his trust, had used him for his own purposes, and in the process destroyed his deep faith in the Sigil Corps. Even the common people, to whose interests Neysim might have appealed, saw this man as a foreigner, most of them wanting the head of the Blood Prince displayed on the end of a spike every bit as much as the king did.

Neysim was all the more troubled for understanding these things, and he sympathized with, but could not admire, this broken man who had cast aside his very name. The finality with which Edryd had spoken, confirmed now to Neysim, that he had witnessed the end of the Edorin line.

"Ledrin told me you felt this way," Neysim said.

"But yet you still have something to ask of me," Edryd discerned. Neysim was older than Edryd, but he looked like the younger of the two of them. Harsh events in his young life had awakened Edryd to realities that had aged him, and he looked at Neysim now as though he wished to share wisdom which he knew the other man was not yet ready to understand.

"You will no longer follow Ledrin or serve Nar Edor or its king," Neysim said. "I understand that now, but I hope that I may yet appeal to the ideals that you share with your brothers."

"What would you want of me?"

"The Sigil Order needs a navy," Neysim said.

The request was clear, and plainly expressed. Ledrin did not want Edryd back in Nar Edor. He wanted Edryd to remain in An Innis with these men, starting the first stages of the expansion of the Sigil Order, beginning with the integration of the Ascomanni. Though Edryd didn't expect to remain on the island long enough to see such a plan through to completion, and he had little desire to do anything to help Ledrin, Edryd did not reject the idea. He talked with Neysim about it throughout the night, focusing on working out ways to build a chapter of the Sigil Corps here in An Innis. Esivh Rhol's palace, which had been promised to Edryd once the Ascomanni seized control, would be an excellent base for the organization. Edryd was more than a little surprised by how much the idea excited him.

Neysim slept on a blanket spread over the cold stone floor in Edryd's room. It wasn't comfortable, but it was an improvement over the cramped arrangements he had endured the three previous nights aboard Captain Sarel Krin's ship. He woke in the morning knowing that he would be spending the day here, unable to leave until they received another visit from the Ascomanni. After sharing a morning meal, he watched as Edryd and Irial stepped outside, ready for the daily trip in to the settlement. Edryd automatically took up a protective posture beside Irial, regarding her with fond respect.

"She doesn't like him," Eithne said, loud enough so that Neysim would overhear her frustration, but not so loud that it risked being heard by anyone else. Her face was wrinkled up in a way that made it easy to see that she was upset. "Not the way that he wants her to," she elaborated.

"I dare say she shouldn't," Neysim said.

Eithne turned to look at Neysim. She hadn't expected him to respond to the comment.

"If it were my sister, I would feel like she could do much better," he said, making it clear that he sympathized.

Eithne leapt to Edryd's defense. "Edryd is a prince," she reminded Neysim. "And not just the ordinary kind either, he's going to become a sigil knight."

Neysim doubted that. Some in the Sigil Corps had watched Aisen closely, hoping he might show potential for developing some of the abilities his father had been rumored to wield, but to his knowledge, Aedan's son had not been anything more than an accomplished solider.

"There are no sigil knights anymore," Neysim said, wishing it was not the truth.

"That isn't even the point," Eithne continued. "She is too old for him."

Neysim was starting to understand now.

"You're probably right. A good thing then that she doesn't like him back even a little bit," he said, gently teasing Eithne.

Eithne was quick to pick up on the possibility that Neysim was more perceptive than she had thought to give him credit for.

"I don't like him either," she said a little too strongly. "I don't like anybody," she added with more control.

"You don't need to," Neysim said. "I've only just met him and I wasn't impressed. In fairness, he may not have an especially high opinion of either one of us either."

"Edryd thinks of me like a little sister," Eithne said with a sigh of resignation. She could not hide or disguise how disconsolate she felt in confessing this. "I know it. I always know exactly what he feels."

"If you are his little sister, and he is a prince, wouldn't that make you a …?" Neysim asked, hoping to cheer her up.

Eithne rolled her eyes. She knew she was being humored, and she didn't appreciate it.

"You don't have to treat me like a little girl," she said. "Besides, that wouldn't make me just any princess. It would make me the Blood Princess." Looking like she had just bit into a bad piece of fruit, it was clear what Eithne thought of that.

Neysim began to laugh. Not the kind of laugh which signaled a failure to take Eithne seriously, but one that showed an appreciation for her sense of humor. Eithne remained mad for a little while longer, but soon she was laughing too. She had known from the start that Edryd was a good person, or so she told herself. Eithne decided that she could trust Neysim as well.

***

The air was cold and dry and the sky was clear. It was the perfect weather in which to be outside in the practice yard training. The combat was proving more enjoyable than usual. Edryd had not been asked to try and shape or to absorb any instructions. Instead, pledging to remain completely on defense, Seoras had tasked Edryd with breaking through.

Given the state of his clothing, dampened now with perspiration, the sharpness of the chill in the air could have been a cause for concern, but it did not trouble Edryd. Directed light from the bright sun, which constantly worked upon his exposed skin, made Edryd feel as if he were standing too close to an overfed fire, and the surfeit of heat and warmth building up throughout his body in consequence of his exertions was more than enough to counter the cold. Under these conditions the temperature had a pleasant quality, with a reviving effect that made Edryd feel like he could continue indefinitely. Relentlessly pressuring his teacher, Edryd was, with regular consistency, scoring successful hits during the lengthy exchanges.

These successes did not come easily. Edryd's sword would at times be deflected by a wall of air just when he thought he was about to connect through an exposed weakness in the shaper's defenses. More often, he found his target gone when Aed Seoras evaded with impossibly quick movements. Seoras also employed several strategies that involved shaping the dark to disguise his positioning and obscure his presence. These efforts to confuse his pupil had all failed. If anything, to Edryd, it made his teacher's movements unfailingly easy to measure. The shaper was using every evasive and defensive trick in his arsenal, but Edryd was proving that he could overcome them with accurate predictions and expert skill.

Edryd felt the satisfaction of resistance as he struck Aed Seoras on his right shoulder with the flat of his blade. He allowed his teacher to back away and re-enter a fighting stance. In a real fight, that strike could have inflicted a crippling injury to his opponent. Then again, in a real fight with Seoras, there wouldn't have been any long exchanges like the one that had been necessary to score that hit. At this range, his teacher would have ended it all very quickly with lethal and unblockable attacks of his own.

Edryd drove forward, initiating a complex series of slashing strikes that were intended to lure his opponent into a predictable rhythm of alternating high and low blocks. It was an especially strong technique against someone with more skill and training than actual experience, and Edryd held out little hope that it would ever work on Seoras. Defying Edryd's expectations, Seoras was fooled by the faint near the end of the combination, and Edryd's sword thrust at the end of the maneuver made it through cleanly, ending with the tip of his blade firmly pressed against the center of the shaper's chest.

There was surprise on both men's faces. Edryd could feel his teacher's shock disperse in a transfer of emotional energy that was soon consumed by building anger, but Seoras forced the reaction down, holding it in with effort. There was a real danger to Seoras in these exchanges, and he was placing extreme trust in Edryd's abilities.

"If you had stepped through, that would have killed me," Seoras said. "I'll count it as confirmation of your skill, and your restraint, that it did not."

Edryd lowered his sword. "A compliment?" he asked. The question was a necessary one. The remark on its surface had sounded like praise, but it had been delivered with a hint of disapproval.

"An observation," Seoras disagreed. "Take it how you will."

"I should have pushed the blade through your chest?" Edryd asked, trying to understand but certain that he did not.

"As a rule, I don't tell anyone what he should do," Seoras said.

"Only what he must do, and what he is threatened with if he refuses," Edryd said.

If Edryd thought he had scored a point here, Seoras did not seem to notice. His reinterpretation of his teacher's comment had not produced the disparaging effect Edryd had intended. Instead, Seoras took it as an opening to make a point of his own.

"You have devoted your life to training in its uses, but you don't seem to understand what a sword is for. It is unlike other weapons. It is not a bow or an axe or a knife, all of which serve equally well at, and are more frequently used for, ordinary things such hunting, chopping wood, and cutting food. The weapon which you have chosen to carry is used by one man to kill another. It is designed for no other purpose."

"A sword is more than that," Edryd insisted. "It does not have to be used to maim or kill. It can be a weapon of defense. It can protect. It can deter violence without ever being drawn."

"That last part is wrong," Seoras disagreed. "A sword deters violence by threatening to inflict the same in return. A purely defensive weapon would have no need of a point or an edge. They make such things you know, but that is not the kind of tool you have trained yourself to use. A sword serves its true purpose only when it is held by a man who is prepared to put it to a violent use."

This particular philosophy was well supported by what had just taken place. Without the threat of a counter attack, Seoras had not been able to stop Edryd from getting through. Without its ability to cut and pierce your enemy, a sword was severely impaired as a means of defense.

Unable to come up with a valid way in which to dispute the matter, Edryd conceded the point. "Granting all of that, having a sword does not give one the sanction to kill or injure others," he said.

"No, it gives you something else; it gives you the ability to take another man's life. Set aside the right or wrong of it, skill with a killing weapon is the power to take life."

"I am no killer," Edryd said. "I never wanted to kill anyone."

"If you believe that, you are lying to yourself on both counts," Seoras responded, amused by the ridiculous delusion embodied in his student's denial of what he had done. "You have ended more lives in these last three months than I have in the last six years."

Edryd could only wonder what had happened six years ago, and just how many lives the shaper had taken. He almost asked, but he wasn't quite sure that he really wanted to know.

"Mine is a more honest approach," Seoras continued. "I know who and what I am. And I know what I want."

"And what is it exactly that you seek?" Edryd said, insulted that Seoras saw himself as the more honest of the two of them. If he had stopped to think about it though, he would have had to concede that point as well.

"I want to experience the limits of my power," Seoras said. It was an honest answer, if perhaps an incomplete and simple one.

"Well I don't," said Edryd, not sure whether he meant his own power or that of his teacher.

"You may not desire power, Edryd, but you can't continue to pretend that you have none."

Seoras said nothing more for a moment, hoping the message would sink in.

"I'm not talking about using a sword," he continued. "The great powers in this world are pivoting on you right now. If you were more ambitious, Nar Edor could have already fallen under your rule. An Innis would be an afterthought, and Ossia would be very much in your grasp."

"I don't want any of that," Edryd insisted, cutting his teacher short.

"It does not matter what you want," Seoras said, brushing off Edryd's objections. "Your ability to perceive the patterns that shape the dark has surpassed my own. In time you will see much further."

"I don't understand," Edryd protested, speaking the truth. Despite his teacher's claims, Edryd knew that he could perceive very little, and understood even less.

"For better or worse, the choices you make, or don't make, are having profound consequences. The dark transforms around you everywhere you go. Your power can not be ignored."

"But it can be hidden," Edryd countered, referencing the strange ability which concealed him from people like his teacher.

"I'm not sure of that anymore," Seoras said. "In the ruins, I saw something. Your shroud was imperfect. It was distorted and broken in places, where what the Sigil Order would have called your aura, was leaking out. I don't know if it was created by disruptions in the barrier that emanate from the construct chamber, or if that place merely pried open cracks that were already there, but I could no longer detect them once we left."

"It's still working then," Edryd said, seeking confirmation and reassurance. He felt more frightened than he would have cared to admit.

"It is a hard thing, perhaps even an impossible thing to study if it were perfectly formed, but it is deteriorating even now and has begun to fray around the edges. That is what I was doing while we fought today, inspecting your shroud and trying to see if I could find the cracks."

The modest confidence that Edryd had gained from the morning training drained away, replaced by an informed acceptance of just how inferior he was. In addition to not fighting back, Seoras had been distracted during the entire encounter, focused on studying the unusual concealing effect that enveloped his student, instead of concentrating on defending against the relentless attacks.

"What's going to happen?" Edryd asked.

"I don't know. I think maybe you will be able to shape once it weakens enough, maybe not. One thing is certain. Once it fails, you will not be able to hide. When that time comes, you might then find yourself glad to be in command of a sizable army."

"I don't want this," Edryd said. He wanted to believe that Seoras was lying, but he couldn't think why his teacher would do so. "I don't have the right to use other men's lives to protect my own."

"But you do have the ability to do so," Seoras said, stressing a point that he thought he had made clear previously. "Though you may not like it, you are not some simple ordinary man. You are greater than other men. You are more important."

The dark and viscerally repellant words of his master, he realized now that this was what Seoras was to him, made Edryd convulse. He had known it before, but had not felt it so strongly as now, Aed Seoras had long ago been corrupted by something dangerous.

Seoras could see the revulsion on his pupil's face, and he thought he could understand why. "You may think me evil if you like," he said, "but I personally understand the position you are in better than you think. You need to accept what I am telling you. You may not want the power that you possess, but other men do, and they will make your choices for you if you do not act. If you do not seize control while you still can, you will never be able to escape them."

So much for not telling me what I should do, Edryd thought.

The unwanted advice was dark, carrying hints of his teacher's troubled past, but it was also insightful. In a fearful realization, Edryd also perfectly understood that his master's words contained nothing that was not the truth.

Edryd could see himself now the way that his master did, as a powerful game piece on a board that was controlled by a small number of practiced players. It didn't need to be said that Aed Seoras was one of those players; he was already using Edryd. Yet Seoras, seeing him as a potential ally, was also telling his student that he should choose to join the game. It was a rational solution, but a distasteful one. Edryd was determined to find some other way.

Aelsian woke just before dawn. For two days they had harnessed all of the speed they could manage out of the sails while maintaining the desired course, but the navarch could not be sure they were gaining any ground. Most of the time, the other ship could not be seen, having receded beyond their view. However, whenever the *Interdiction* rose on a swell, if the light was good, he could make out the object of their pursuit, a dark dot on the horizon. Had Aelsian not known the other ship's intended destination, they would have lost it long ago.

Even before leaving the *Interdiction*'s great cabin, which served as his living quarters, Aelsian knew something was wrong. Hurrying past the officer's berths and stepping out on the deck, Aelsian confirmed what he had suspected. The *Interdiction* was backing the sails on the main mast, effectively slowing progress to a standstill.

Aelsian scanned the deck, searching out Captain Hedrick, a small proud man with frail features. Hedrick was not The Captain, not with a fleet navarch aboard, but he had nonetheless taken it upon himself to slow the ship without consulting Aelsian. The insubordinate officer spotted him first and was already eyeing the navarch nervously when Aelsian located him on the foredeck.

Ignoring objections that it would take them away from the coast and deprive them of useful navigational aids, Aelsian gave orders to the officer of the watch to reset the sails and position the ship on a run, taking full advantage of the tail winds. He then returned his attentions to Captain Hedrick. He fixed his officer with an expressionless stare as he crossed the length of deck that separated them.

"Why did you slow the ship?" he demanded.

Captain Hedrick shrank, reflexively crossing his arms in a protective warding fashion. He began to mumble some nonsense about heaving to in order to wait out a contrary wind.

"You intentionally disrupted pursuit," he accused. "Why?"

Looking uncomfortable, Hedrick cast his gaze about as if looking for support, but there was none to be found.

"Some of the men..." Hedrick began to say, starting and stopping nervously. "There are rumors among the men that we are pursuing a ship that is carrying draugar," he finally answered, offering up his explanation in a hurried manner.

"And so you decided it would be a good thing if we couldn't manage to catch up," Aelsian said, finishing the line of reasoning being put forward by his subordinate. "What makes you think there are draugar aboard that ship?"

"Just a feeling sir," said Captain Hedrick. "That and the fact some of us have seen them."

"When?"

"You mean apart from the day you lured one away from the *Interdiction*?" Hedrick replied. "I seen one myself three days ago. Approached me directly, a dangerous looking fellow he was, all covered up in a foul smelling cloak, asking after you and saying things like did I know where the Lord of House Edorin might be."

Hedrick was clearly rattled, as evidenced by the regression in his speech patterns. The captain had worked hard to shed his local dialect in favor of a more formal accent while training to become an officer in

Ossia's naval fleets. Aelsian was also disturbed by the information which his officer had only just now seen fit to share with him.

"How did you answer?"

"I told 'em everything I knew, which was exactly nothing. I don't know no Lord Aisen of House Edorin or where he might be. I didn't know where Fleet Navarch Aelsian was nor what he was up to neither. Sir, I don't know how you got mixed up with these creatures, but I don't never want to see one again."

"When you said there was a rumor, you didn't tell me that you were its source," Aelsian said. As Hedrick's face flushed, covered with guilt and shame, Aelsian continued to question him, trying to see how widespread the damage might be. "Who have you spoken with about this?"

"None as really believed what I told 'em," Captain Hedrick admitted.

His officer had clearly been left terrified by his encounter with the returned, but Aelsian had no desire to waste any sympathy on the man. Worse, he did not have the luxury of appropriately disciplining Captain Hedrick, not if he wished to avoid drawing unwanted attention to the situation.

"We are not trying to catch that ship," Aelsian said to Captain Hedrick. "We are trying to outrun it."

This was pleasant news to Hedrick, who relaxed visibly, but his improved comfort lasted only a moment before it was broken when the fleet navarch pronounced his judgment.

"I will need names by this afternoon," Aelsian said, "of candidates I can promote in your place. If you speak further to anyone else about any of this, or if you fail to reach An Innis before the other vessel does, I will deprive you of rank and you will be held on charges until we return to Ossia—that is if I don't decide toss you over chained to a draugr who will feed upon your corpse."

Captain Hedrick's face went white. Aelsian's ridiculous threats were not entirely hollow, except for the last one, but in judging the effect they had produced in the captain, he was reasonably assured that there would be no more trouble. They had lost hours on the ship carrying the draugar, hours Aelsian could hardly hope to make up. He would need very favorable winds to blow if the *Interdiction* and its crew were to have any chance of reaching An Innis in time.

Chapter 19

The Rise of the Ascomanni

All attempts at limiting the influence of the Sigil Corps warriors had gone horribly wrong. Logaeir could not deny that. This had become clear from the moment he had returned to the encampment with Neysim and Krin not even two full days after the soldiers had first arrived. It was not possible to isolate them completely. They were already close with Krin and his crew, and interactions during meals when food was shared made developing friendships inevitable.

Then there were the daily practice sessions at the top of a rise in a hill that overlooked the encampment. Logaeir was sure that it was being done deliberately, in as conspicuous and spectacular a fashion as possible. The mock battles were almost theatre, violent entertainment that captivated the entire camp. The displays had also drawn interest from the residents of a sheltered community hidden in the woods near the encampment, comprised of the families of the Ascomanni people who had been displaced from An Innis over the years. They were beginning to come to watch in numbers that increased daily.

Two of Logaeir's men were dead of injuries sustained while participating in an attempt by a group of the Ascomanni to imitate what they had watched the day before. Logaeir wasn't about to put a stop to any of it. He would instead take full advantage.

Logaeir found Oren, and together they worked throughout the afternoon on staging a scenario that would simulate the planned attacks on the strongholds of the harbormasters. Oren was no less loyal to his captain than the others, but he was the most eager of them to work with the Ascomanni. A part of Logaeir regretted that things were not quite going the way he had planned them, but he was smart enough recognize that this was in reality far better than what was he had at first envisioned.

Taking and holding at least one of the piers was paramount. Realistically, he hoped to take both of them. Today's exercise would walk his men through this phase of the assault. Reserve forces, who would not directly participate in this initial part of the attack, were being prepared to play the role of the enemy. Woven mats had been laid out across a flat stretch of land west of the camp, accurately representing the rough dimensions of the two piers. Piles of loose stones marked out important structures, open mooring points, and significant ships that they would attempt to secure.

Logaeir could not be more pleased with the level of discipline and motivation that the men of the Sigil Corps had infused into his forces just by being among them in the camp. Swollen with confidence, he felt ever more certain of success. If preparations went well today and tomorrow, they would take a day to rest and the attack would proceed the following night.

"I still think we should disguise our true objectives by sending a diversionary force over land," Oren said. "We could attack one of the more poorly defended warehouses and then retreat as soon as we come under threat. That would pull the enemy away from the docks. All that matters is winning that first foothold. With their forces fractured the way that they are now, we can overwhelm them piece by piece, as long as we can secure our entry point."

"That would pose problems," Logaeir said, disagreeing with Oren. "We would win, but it would shift most of the heavy fighting into the city, where we would lose control of our own forces, pulled in ten different directions by different elements of no less than five disparate factions that will oppose us. It would turn into a blood bath where we are killing random men and women as we rampage through the town."

Oren accepted the wisdom of Logaeir's position. The Ascomanni were an imposing force, but they did not have the discipline of a professional army. There was a very real certainty that men would lose all purpose in the confusion that came with battle when communications broke down as they inevitably would.

"No, I want the fighting concentrated here," Logaeir said, pointing at a map of the stone structures that extended out from the island into the ocean. "We make them believe that they can repel us, and once we have concentrated enough of them together, we will slaughter them."

There was no emotion as Logaeir said any of this, just simple calculation.

"And you won't need my men to help with that?" Oren said, doubting the wisdom of holding his soldiers in reserve.

"Not at first. I need to be able to quickly move your soldiers where they are needed most, so I can't tie you up in the initial fighting. But don't worry—your men are going to carry more than their share. A counter offensive will come, and when it does, you will break it and lead the fighting as we enter the city."

Oren was pleased with that. He had never actually fought in what could be called a real battle before, but he had trained all his life for this and he had a solid grasp of what he and the other soldiers fighting with him were capable of. Soon everyone would know.

***

Edryd had persuaded Irial to return to the meadow by pointing out that there were still more ripe blackberries, but it hadn't actually required convincing. In the end it didn't even seem like it had been his idea. The days were getting warmer, with more stretches of clear weather, and Edryd wanted to use this opening to try something. He wanted to confirm for himself, whether he could see the cracks that Seoras had spoken of in the concealing shroud around him.

Irial sat down not far away, and removing a sandal, submerged her right foot in the fast moving water of the stream. It was running higher than it had just a couple of weeks ago. Picking the same spot as before, Edryd settled onto his back and closed his eyes as he tried to exclude everything else and focus only on his ability to sense the ways in which the world around him shaped the dark. It wasn't working. It didn't feel like the same place. The meadow had changed somehow. Or maybe he had.

The biggest difference, he realized, was the woman who sat only a few feet away. Irial had been there before, but she had been at the periphery of the meadow and in the woods beyond its edge. Now she distracted his attentions, no matter how hard he tried to divert his thoughts. His eyes were closed, but he could not banish the afterimage he could still see of this woman sitting beside the mountain stream. He heard her humming gently, but when he tried to concentrate on the sound it was gone, only to return whenever he gave up trying to make it out.

Abandoning any attempt at imposing control on the experience, he allowed himself to focus on Irial. He could see her after a fashion. Both of her feet were now taking comfort in the cold water. Edryd traced the water, travelling a winding path up to its source high in the hills above them. Losing his hold on the place, he washed back down the water's descending track and was deposited on its banks beside Irial who really was humming a tune now.

"This is nice," she said.

Edryd felt disoriented. He saw Irial, created from sensory images in his mind that were not fed to him through his eyes, but he continued to hear her in an ordinary fashion. He didn't yet have a good understanding of how to reconcile these two things at once without feeling confused. Irial was not a part of the dark, but she was something akin to it, nestled within its confines, and illuminating the things that she touched.

Edryd shifted his perspective, allowing a vantage from which to see himself as Irial would see him now if she were able to attune her mind to perceive the patterns in the dark. Where there should have been light, he saw darkness. He would have been impossible to distinguish from the ever present flows within the dark itself, but for the fissures in his shroud, where an angry red light fought to escape.

Edryd pulled even further away, trying to determine how noticeable he was from a distance. Without the concealment, he understood that he would indeed be a beacon to anyone nearby who could shape the dark. As it was, he was no longer invisible. Edryd expanded his perspective even further. He had no frame of reference from which to understand what he was doing, or just how much he was taking in, but it overwhelmed him. He couldn't resolve any of it. Returning his focus to Irial, everything faded, except for one unmistakable impression.

"Something is wrong," he said to Irial as he sat up and opened his eyes. He now perceived two images, each the same in many ways but different in others. One was the simple worried look on Irial's sunburnt face, and the other was a separate visual sense for the concern that his comment had inspired, contravened by Irial's desire to remain in the meadow with her feet in the water. The ideas were entirely compatible, but trying to consolidate the two into a unified perception was making him to feel lightheaded.

"I don't mean right here or right now," he clarified. Edryd's altered discernment was still influencing him, but it was balanced by the sights and sounds that were also competing for attention. "There is something out there gathering its focus on An Innis, and perhaps on me," Edryd continued, feeling more ridiculous and uncertain with each additional word that he spoke.

"That might have been expected I suppose," Irial sighed. "Something has been different about you since you came back from the mainland. I think you are about to awaken, and it hasn't gone unnoticed."

Edryd could tell the word awaken meant something specific to Irial. Something from that book of hers that she had gotten from Uleth. He didn't know where she had put it, but he had an idea of how to learn a little bit more about it when they got back to the cottage tonight.

"I don't know what that means," he said, "but we can't wait. Ruach and Neysim can steal a boat from the Ascomanni and we can sail up the coast. We will find a way to meet up with Aelsian later, but we need to be gone before the attack happens, and you need to go with us."

Irial looked frightened, but she did not disagree with him, not completely.

"We need to set this in in motion now," Edryd said, "or it will be too late."

"Do it," she agreed.

Edryd smiled with relief. This was what he wanted. He didn't know where they would go, but he was kept afloat by the hope that he was going to be able to keep Irial safe.

***

Pedrin Eksar was an unhappy man. He was the owner and captain of a first rate vessel of the very best construction and design, but he had no say over where that ship went. He had been forced to cede the great cabin, the only place of any space or comfort on the ship, to a pair of returned and their human thralls. This arrangement, which Pedrin swore had turned most of his hair grey, had persisted for more than three years now, and he had little hope that it would ever end.

It wasn't without benefits. Money was never in short supply, and his position as a captain on a ship frequented by draugar had earned him a dangerous reputation that he treasured. Pedrin Eksar ate well, having become modestly fat in fact, and the occasional trips to An Innis had its consolations as well. Esivh Rhol had an assortment of entertainments that appealed to Eksar. He just wished that he could also have the same freedoms that had once drawn him to this life on the open ocean.

"I'm pleased," spluttered a deep guttural voice from behind Pedrin. The voice belonged to, Áledhuir, a tall powerfully built monster, large even by draugr standards. Pedrin Eksar flinched. Even after three years, he cringed every time he heard these creatures speak.

"Yes, Pedrin," said another voice, this one clear and sweet, and disembodied. "We made good time." The words were in his head, he knew that much. She sounded to him like a girl from his youth, a former lover who he supposed was by now long dead, her voice appropriated by this ghostly woman that he had never once actually seen, who answered to the name Aodra. He would never get used to either of these masters of his, but Pedrin preferred the horrible burbling of the big ugly one to the morbid mental intrusions of the apparition.

They were approaching the island now. They had not seen any Ascomanni ships, but that was usually more of a problem on the way out of An Innis than it was on your way in. He almost hoped someone would try to stop them. Let them try to board his ship if they liked, they would regret it if they did.

They eased into an open berth near the end of one of the piers, in a section that was controlled by the Ard Ri. A group of Esivh Rhol's men were there to help secure the ship to its mooring points. They recognized the ship and its captain. The expressions on their faces told Eksar that some of them knew enough to associate this ship with the dangerous passengers it carried.

"You'll be wanting to visit the Ard Ri's palace," one of the men said, knowing of Pedrin Eksar's habits. "I'll send word to Aed Seoras and let him know you are here as well," he added.

"Seoras has been protecting him," said the woman's voice in Eksar's head. "He mustn't know we are here."

"It would be a favor to me if Seoras doesn't learn I am here," Pedrin said, tossing the man a coin. The worker's eyes were drawn for a moment towards Pedrin's coat, where it was weighted down in an interior pocket by the heavy bag from which the coin had been taken.

"My business is with the Ard Ri, and I don't want to involve anyone else," Pedrin emphasized to the distracted worker.

Esivh Rhol's man looked relieved. The poor fellow preferred to have as little to do with Aed Seoras as possible, something Pedrin could sympathize with. Aed Seoras was about the only thing that frightened Pedrin more than the draugar did.

"If he learns you are here, it won't be from us," the man readily agreed as he collected the coin.

Given the attention that the man had shown towards the money which Pedrin carried, he might have been concerned that the dockworker's greed had set some plans in motion, if he were not so absurdly well protected. Aodra was somewhere beside him, Pedrin guessed, while Áledhuir hung back in the shadows. The tall draugr had a way of not being seen when he wanted to avoid being noticed. Pedrin suspected that Aodra helped him with that. She could make you see what she wanted, or hide things from your senses, with all manner of illusory manipulations.

Three thralls also travelled with Pedrin as he made his way into the city and up the sloping streets. The thralls also seemed to slip from your awareness if you were not paying attention, as if they were beneath notice and not really there at all. They rarely spoke, except amongst themselves or to the draugar, and when they did it was as agents acting on behalf of their masters. Aed Seoras had trained these men, but they were weaker versions of their teacher. They seemed to wear down quickly in their service to the draugar, responding to the strain of supplying to their masters a reserve of strength and stability that was soon exhausted by the demands placed upon them.

Pedrin tried not to think about the thralls as they climbed higher. He had an unpleasant feeling of kinship with them, an association he did not care to make. He didn't want to understand even as much as he did about how these men were tethered to their masters. He too served the draugar, but in a lesser way that did not exact quite as heavy a toll.

As they came nearer to Esivh Rhol's palace, Pedrin began to distract himself with notions of how he would spend the money he had brought with him. It was a welcome diversion from thinking about the thralls and the draugar. He was still running these ideas through his head when they stopped at the heavy wooden gates set inside of the white outer walls of the palace. Guards let them through a passageway beside the gates, and they followed a finely dressed servant as he walked over white marble floors and past brightly washed stone colonnades.

The interior was warmed by a complex of heated baths, and the air was perfumed everywhere with pleasant scents. Pedrin welcomed all of it. He appreciated the perfumes in particular. They were a much needed contrast from the sickly sweet smell that came from the salve that the thralls regularly applied to Áledhuir in an effort to preserve his decaying skin.

"Not the same place it was when I last visited," Pedrin said to Esivh Rhol as they entered a large open room with couches and pillows arranged around three of the walls. "It seems a little... empty somehow."

Esivh Rhol also looked different than he had when Pedrin had last seen him. He was a less self-assured, and bore the look of a frustrated ruler facing the erosion of his declining sphere of influence and power. The Ard Ri had encountered draugar before. You could tell by the way he remained inwardly terrified, yet managed to hold himself together, straining to appear as if everything were normal.

"I have but six courtesans left, and only two young girls in training," Esivh Rhol said, acknowledging that his fortunes had undergone a few reversals.

Pedrin Eksar glanced quickly at a draped opening in the back of the room that led to the women's quarters. "Amongst many other pleasures, I'm sure," he said. He could have been referring to assortments of strong wines, stores of fine food, mind altering tonics, or a few of the other more hidden and less reputable indulgences this place had on offer. Pedrin had come prepared with a large sum of money and he was thinking about all but the last of these. Pedrin was no model of virtue, but he really didn't know what motivated some of Esivh Rhol's darker and more prurient obsessions.

"The son of Aedan Elduryn is here," Áledhuir pronounced loudly, interrupting and making everyone flinch in response to the deep broken resonances emanating from his throat.

Pedrin wished the draugr had let one of his thralls speak instead, as he usually would have done. The garbled and barely intelligible sounds had such a frightful dampening effect on the atmosphere.

"Lord Aisen? Here?" the Ard Ri declaimed, mistakenly believing that he was being accused of sheltering the man.

"Not, in this room, here," Pedrin clarified, hoping to forestall any attempt by Áledhuir to speak again. "But we have reason to believe he is here on An Innis."

"He is not on the island," Esivh Rhol said. "He is supposed to have taken over the Ascomanni, but I have it from a reliable source that the man calling himself the Blood Prince is a fake."

This was getting them nowhere. "The real one is also on this island," Pedrin said, "he is calling himself Edryd."

Recognition shone in Esivh Rhol's eyes. His lips parted as if to speak but nothing came out.

"Tell him to say something," Aodra prodded in a voice only Pedrin could hear.

"It's obvious you know something," Pedrin said, urging the Ard Ri to continue.

"He has been training with Aed Seoras. I thought he was going to be made into a thrall."

Pedrin could detect what only someone who had spent three years with the draugar could have both seen and understood. There was surprise in Áledhuir's expression.

Áledhuir exchanged a look with an empty part of the room. Aodra, Pedrin realized.

"Why would he train him," she wondered.

Pedrin almost answered, thinking no one else would have heard her, but he supposed that she had been speaking to the other draugr as well. The two draugar had suspected Aed Seoras of possible complicity in this to begin with, or they wouldn't have made the effort to keep him uninformed regarding their arrival, but they had not expected to learn that Seoras was actively training Aisen. Pedrin was imagining the violent confrontation that was about to happen between the draugar and Aed Seoras. He was going to want to be there to see it, albeit from as safe a distance as possible.

"He is with Seoras now then," Áledhuir concluded, already making plans to leave for the estate which the shaper kept as a place for visiting draugar and for training men to serve as their slaves.

"Yes," said Esivh Rhol. "I mean no," he added quickly after a confused pause.

Pedrin stifled the urge to ask 'which is it then?' It wouldn't have amused anyone but Pedrin.

"He is staying in some hovel halfway across the island," the Ard Ri explained, "with that evil spell casting woman who works for Seoras."

"Take me there now," Áledhuir ordered.

Esivh Rhol looked like he wanted to argue, or suggest some alternative, but he didn't dare show defiance. Pedrin understood the feeling all too well.

Esivh Rhol obediently stood and left the room one way, followed by the draugar and the three thralls, and Pedrin exited another, through the draped entryway in the back. He might have been expected to go with them, but no one said so, and he felt like things were getting much too complicated. He could well be missing something interesting, but half an island away sounded a good deal further than his aging body wanted to walk, and he did after all have money that needed to be spent.

***

The fleet navarch had learned the bad news only hours ago from one of the scout ships in his fleet. The ship he had been pursuing had slipped into An Innis just ahead of them. As he had promised to do, Aelsian had dealt with Captain Hedrick. He did not want that man in command for what was coming, and Aelsian could not stay aboard to remain in command at the moment either. Aelsian promoted the officer of the watch, and for good measure he moved Hedrick, now no longer holding the rank of a captain, to one of the other two Ossian ships that had joined them.

Nine more warships would be here tomorrow, and another half dozen support vessels soon after that. As Aelsian watched the *Retribution* pull alongside, he reflected upon what an inadvisably poor moment it was to be leaving his fleet, but hopefully he could accomplish the delivery of the item which he carried in good time, and be back soon enough.

Looking with derision through the darkness at the red sails on the Ascomanni ship, Aelsian allowed Logaeir to help him cross from the *Interdiction*, and then he helped Ludin Kar across in turn.

Ludin Kar gave Logaeir a judgmental appraisal. "Never one to trouble himself about the consequences of his actions," he said.

"I'm going to make this right," Logaeir said. "We are pushing the attack forward to tomorrow night."

It was refreshing to see Logaeir accepting responsibility for what was happening. So much so that Aelsian decided not to let him know that this wasn't his fault alone.

"I appreciate that, but tomorrow is going to be too late," Aelsian said.

"Ruach is on his way with a boat," Logaeir said. "He left before we got word, so he won't actually know the situation, but with any luck we still have some time."

"I need to see him," Aelsian said. "I have something he needs."

Logaeir eyed the cloth wrapped object in Aelsian's arms. It didn't take much imagination to see that it was a sword, and once you knew that, well the rest was obvious too.

"That's where we are going. I will get you there as quickly as we can."

***

Bringing a lamp to the table in the corner at the back wall of the cottage, Edryd settled into a chair and took out the small leather bound book. Having read it through multiple times already, he only pretended to be reading it now. Eithne had yet to read it once, and on more than one occasion she had shown that she was curious. Predictably, she ended up in a chair beside him. She had only glimpsed bits and pieces after a series of partially successful efforts to steal a look at the contents of its pages.

"Irial had a little white book a while ago," Edryd said, trying to sound as if he had only a minor passing interest. "Logaeir said he knew the man who wrote it. You wouldn't know what happened to it would you?"

"She hid it," Eithne said. Apparently it was a bit of a sore point.

"In her room?"

"No, I would have found it if it was in there."

"So you don't know where it is then."

"No, but I don't need to. I already read it," she bragged.

This was good news. Not as good as finding the book itself, but he had found a way to confirm what was inside.

"I don't imagine it was interesting," Edryd said, carefully watching for Eithne's reaction.

"Maybe not to some people," Eithne answered, and then said nothing more. Edryd had not hidden his interest as well as he might have thought. She was not about to tell him anything for free. He would have to buy what she knew with information of his own.

He opened the book to a page with a drawing and showed it to Eithne.

"That's what Herja looks like?" she asked.

"I haven't seen her myself," Edryd said, "but these are not draugar. These are what they were when they were alive, before they became what they are now. She probably would look something like this though."

"They almost look like people, except most people aren't so pretty as this."

If he hadn't picked up on it before, Eithne's interest in the book was now evident. He would have little trouble bargaining for what he wanted to know.

"They are different in other ways of course," Edryd said, sounding as if he were parceling out some exclusive collection of secrets. "You can't see it in the drawing, but the book says that they have varying shades of smooth grey skin."

"What color are their eyes?" Eithne wondered. She was more curious than ever now.

"All the different normal colors," Edryd said. "Usually green though, and once in a while, yellow or red." He had made all that up, the book had nothing to say on the subject, but for some reason, he did imagine that their eyes were green.

"Irial told me that Herja's eyes were white and cloudy," Eithne said, becoming a little suspicious.

"That's because she's dead," Edryd said without having any idea whether that was true or not. Eithne accepted the explanation as making perfect sense and moved on to demanding more.

"What else?"

"Tell me about Irial's book," Edryd said, "and then I might tell you a little more."

"Shouldn't you already know about it? You are in the Sigil Order aren't you?"

"Let's pretend I don't know any of the kinds of things I should," Edryd said. This suggestion brought a smile to Eithne's face. "What could you tell me then?"

"First," she began, "sigil knights always had a sigil sword. You don't have one, but if you did you would use it to kill sorcerers and destroy constructs."

"Everyone knows that."

"Everyone does not know that," Eithne protested. "People did, but some of them have forgotten."

"Maybe so," Edryd agreed, "but I would bet that there were more interesting things in there than just that."

"It said that the people in the Sigil Order were all men, monks who meditated in hidden places. When a monk showed abilities, he trained with an Archon. Just by being around the Archon, he would awaken, and he would become a sigil knight."

It was a simple and straightforward explanation, and it didn't resemble in any way the Sigil Corps in Nar Edor, not in Edryd's experience. "I hate to tell you, the Sigil Corps isn't like that," he said.

"That's because there are no more Archons anymore," Eithne said, displeased that he had contradicted her. "When they left, there was nobody to train more sigil knights."

That deserved a more thorough explanation, but Edryd didn't expect he would get one. Eithne seemed to have thought she had told him all there was to tell based on her estimation of what was and was not important to the subject.

"Did it say how this awakening happens?" he asked, hoping there was somehow something more to it.

"It said it was like a way stone."

"A what?"

"A magical rock," Eithne said. "It attracts iron, and it makes tools that help you navigate in a ship" she added as if that explained everything.

This seemed to be straying far from anything that might prove helpful.

"The Archon was like a powerful lodestone," Eithne continued, changing the name she was using for the rock, "and if the monk stayed near, he became powerful too. Over time, it awakened the monk to whatever potential he had."

This definitely was nothing like the Sigil Corps. It did neatly explain some of what had been happening when he trained with Seoras, only it was all backwards.

They continued to exchange this kind of information until well after it had gotten dark. Edryd learned all about the incredible things that he was meant to be able to do, and all the known deeds that the Knights of the Sigil Order had purportedly done in the last age. Eithne, unsatisfied with receiving the information she wanted about the Huldra and Ældisir filtered through Edryd, begged to read the book for herself, but Edryd made it clear that this would only happen if she could find Irial's book. Then she could trade for it.

Irial spent the evening a short distance away, pretending that she wasn't paying any attention, but she clearly was enjoying herself. She was the only one who could easily settle everything by producing the book, but she was not about to do so. In the end, long after it had gotten dark, Edryd tucked the book which he had stolen from Seoras into his coat, deciding that it had been enough for one night.

Alone in his room afterwards, Edryd struggled to get any sleep, troubled by something he couldn't place. It was the sort of feeling that you might generally have been well advised to try and ignore, and Edryd tried hard to do precisely that. Whatever it was though, the feeling steadily grew as he lay awake in bed. He focused on what it was that he could feel, but not see, and in trying to understand it, was able to get a sense of the direction of the thing that troubled his mind. Something was getting closer, travelling towards them down the road from the settlement.

Edryd got dressed in the dark, relying on memory and on his ability to perceive things through their influence on the dark in order to navigate his way through the cottage. The ability was coming to him more quickly now, but it wasn't of much use in detecting long dead objects like the leg of a chair, which produced what he felt was an unbearably loud noise against the near silence of the night as he crashed into it.

The sound woke Eithne up. She cautiously stepped out of her room and into the open hall to investigate. Edryd could see her clearly. What threw him was the reason that he could see her. Eithne was filtering the dark around her in a way that normal people did not. It was subtle and weak, but Eithne had an attuned ability to shape the dark. Eithne could see Edryd too, and knew it was him, even in the darkness.

"Wake Irial up," Edryd whispered. "Don't make a light and try not to make any noise."

He had frightened Eithne, and he regretted that, but he knew that there was a very good reason for her to be frightened, even if he didn't truly know why.

Edryd focused his attention on the roadway above the cottage with mixed success. He didn't know what was coming, but he suspected that they were most likely men from the city. Aed Seoras was not among them. Edryd was confident that his link to the shaper would have made Seoras easy to identify if he were part of the group. There were too many of them. That was the problem, perhaps a dozen or more in total, one person overlapping another, until he couldn't be sure of anything.

Something stood out though. Two at the front, were putting distance on those behind them, with three more between them and the main group. Edryd wondered why he could distinguish these more readily than the others. It wasn't just that they were closer. There was something familiar about the group in the lead, or perhaps it was just the one at the very front.

"Edryd," Irial said softly. "What is it?"

His concentration broken, Edryd lost his focus.

"I'm not really sure," he said.

Irial didn't press him for more. She went to her room, and hurriedly exchanged the robe which she wore over her shift for a warm woolen dress. Eithne too, following her older sister's cues, went to her own room to get dressed in preparation to leave.

Focusing again, Edryd located the two nearest enemies. They were leaving the road now, slowing down as they began heading toward the cottage. About a hundred yards from the cottage, they stopped and spread out, waiting for the others. Edryd felt confident that he could still help the girls escape down the tunnel. Whoever this was, they couldn't know it was there. Then something happened that changed his mind. The two hidden figures, first one and then the other, became intensely prominent, blinding him to everything else.

They were shapers. Edryd recognized what was happening. He had seen Seoras use a similar mixture of techniques to muffle lights and sounds, and disappear in the process. As had been the case with Seoras, Edryd only saw them more clearly for all their efforts to hide. One of them seemed even more familiar now, but he did not know who they could possibly be. He no longer felt certain that escaping out the tunnel would work.

Irial and Eithne were back, looking at him with well-placed fear. Whoever these people were, they were here for him. Far from protecting Irial and Eithne, they were in danger because of him.

He didn't have time to explain. "I am going to pull them away," he said.

Without waiting for anyone to object, Edryd stepped out the front door. He began walking toward the road, keeping a fix on the two shapers and trying but failing to stay calm. He stopped, and made an effort to look like he was admiring the stars and enjoying some fresh air. He felt very stupid. This was no kind of plan. The two shapers did not move.

Edryd continued walking and soon he was directly between them. They let him continue, planning to trap their prey between the two of them and the other men coming up the road. That suited Edryd's purposes for now. The unguent smell of balsam emollient, carried to him by the wind, gave Edryd a critical piece of information. These were not shapers; they were draugar.

He kept his own pace slow, waiting for the creatures to react. When the draugar finally began to move, Edryd did to, running for all he was worth in the direction of the road. He didn't stop when he reached the road, but he was forced to slow down as he crashed through the thick undergrowth that grew on its other side. Edryd turned east, away from the town and from the other men who were approaching.

Edryd knew the creatures were still pursuing him. They had demonstrated considerable speed out in the open, especially on the road, but the small trees and thick patches of low growing plants seemed to impede them. He had heard that draugar avoided contact with living things. Perhaps it was true. If so, he had made a good choice of terrain.

Edryd stopped for a moment, concentrating in order to locate the position of his pursuers. He had gained considerable distance on them, and they seemed to be confused. That is when he remembered the concealing effect of the shroud. He was hidden from them, and they had lost the trail. If the draugar couldn't find him, they might return to the cottage. One of them had returned to the road and was already doing so.

Edryd could not let that happen. He worked his way back to the road, and once there, he inspected his shroud. He couldn't see it, that was how it worked, but he could see its flaws. He tried to pry open one of the growing fissures, but he didn't have any idea what he was doing and the shroud tightened in response. Edryd relaxed and began to build a reserve for another attempt. Something began to happen as he did. He began to feel a pressure build up inside the shroud, something that agitated a piece of the dark buried deep within him, and his aura began to escape through widening gaps in the concealment.

The nearest of the two draugar reacted immediately. It made a direct line for him. The other draugr, the one that had gone back to the road, reacted a second later, moving with great speed towards him. Terrified, Edryd ran as fast as he could. He didn't want them to lose him again, for he still needed to pull them further away, but he certainly didn't want them to catch up either.

The first hints of the morning sun were beginning to brighten the outlines of the imposing mountain peaks that dominated the mainland across the causeway. Edryd realized that this was where he was running, to the causeway. Draugar hated the living world and the light of the sun, but there was something they feared even more, and that was the ocean. He wasn't sure it would stop them, but he might be safe if he could make it out onto the causeway. That is if it wasn't submerged in the tide. If it was, he would have to try to swim across.

Keeping his footing while running in almost total darkness required all of the attention Edryd could spare. He would have to slow down, probably stop altogether, if he was going to divert the focus he needed to accurately determine where the draugar were now, but overcoming his fear, he forced himself to do so. The creatures had both stopped at the spot where he had briefly forced open his shroud, and were now following the traces his boots had left upon the road. Knowing that they would soon determine his route, Edryd began to run again. These creatures were faster than he was, and he would need to be far ahead of them before they figured out where he was going.

As he ran he could feel them drawing close. They had sped up their pursuit. Edryd did not dare stop again. There was no longer any cover and he could not risk slowing down. He had to reach the causeway. His body was healthy, recovered fully now from the illness that had weakened him, but he was running too hard. His lungs were burning and his muscles were protesting the desperate strain that was being placed upon them. Fear pushed him on. His enemies were close now, and the causeway was several hundred yards away.

If he could shape, he could do something to impede them, or even fight them off. He tried, feeling closer to being able to touch and hold the dark than he ever had before, but it slipped away. That was something new to him. He had never before been able to touch it at all. The dark slipping from his grasp was an achievement, one he might have celebrated at another time. Right now it was perfectly useless. Speed was the only thing that could save him.

Seawater splashed up around him as he ran out onto the causeway. The shallow depth of water put even more strain on his already overworked legs as he continued to run. He knew that he had to keep going, and get farther from his pursuers. Edryd did stop running once he reached what he estimated was the middle of the causeway. Catching his breath, he looked back toward the island of An Innis, believing he was now in the safest place possible. In the growing light he could see a tall draugr menacing the shoreline, stopped at the water's edge. It had worked.

That is it turned out, it had worked in the way that ineffective half measures often do. Not all draugar had such an overpowering aversion to the sea. An Æ̃ldisir had followed him out onto the causeway, struggling not so much with the water, as she was with the wind. How he knew any of those things, Edryd wasn't sure. He couldn't physically see the ghostly creature at all, nor did he understand why he immediately thought of it as being female. He knew that she was very close to him now, and this left Edryd with a narrow set of options; he could give up, or he could run.

Chapter 20

Held in Darkness

Trying to catch up to the three thralls, Esivh Rhol transitioned his healthy young grey into a canter. In the process, he left behind a tired collection of guards struggling to keep pace on foot. His was the only horse on the island. It was an impractical thing in a confined and isolated place like An Innis. Esivh Rhol was on principle though, a fan of impractical things.

The Ard Ri was considerably less enthusiastic about the orders in response to which he had been forced to put the animal to use. The draugar had pressed him into service at this early hour as a guide. He had not been asked for help, it had been demanded of him, and this interfered with the illusion that he was something apart from and above everyone else.

The heir of both House Edorin in Nar Edor and the Elduryn fortune in Ossia, was however, an interesting individual, and Esivh Rhol saw the opportunities that lay before him. Capturing and controlling Aisen, the famous Blood Prince, would raise the prominence of and the respect with which the Ard Ri of An Innis was known throughout the world. That is provided the draugar did not immediately spirit Aisen off the island. It would also help if everyone ignored the part where such a famous rogue Sigil Corps captain had hidden himself here for three months, entirely unsuspected by Esivh Rhol.

When the Ard Ri caught up with the thralls, they were in the middle of a disagreement.

"What's happened?" he asked.

One of the three men turned to answer as the other two continued to argue.

"Something is wrong," he said to Esivh Rhol. "The Elduryn boy eluded them. He fled to the east, and our masters are pursuing."

"I don't see the problem, surely they will catch him."

The three thralls exchanged worried looks, still mired in indecision.

"Áledhuir won't be able to follow if Aisen makes it to the causeway," the shortest of the three thralls pointed out. "Aodra will continue the pursuit, but she won't be able to bring him back on her own. We need to provide support."

"He lost them once, he could do so again and double back," objected one of the other thralls, the one that had first spoken with Esivh Rhol when he approached. "We should wait and watch the road."

"You three," said the Ard Ri to the thralls. Ignorant of their names, and having no desire to learn them, this was the only way he could think of to address them. "Is that the woman's place?" he asked once he had their attention. There wasn't much light, but he thought he could make out the whitewashed infilling on the walls of the building. No one answered the question, it was the Ard Ri after all who was meant to be guiding all of them, but Esivh Rhol took their silence to mean that he was right. "I will tell you what we are going to do. We came out at this unseemly hour to see a hovel in the wilds. It wasn't my idea, but we are nearly there now and I mean to see it."

"But he isn't there," the small one argued. "There's no point anymore."

"There doesn't need to be one," Esivh Rhol replied. "We have to wait on your masters, whether they catch Lord Aisen or not. I would just a soon do said waiting indoors and out of the cold. We can decide what to do once we regroup together there."

He didn't wait for signs that he had any of their consent. He didn't care much whether any of them followed either. To the extent to which he did care, he favored scenarios that involved parting ways with the unsettling trio of owned men. They were slaves. Slaves trained by Seoras in the practice of dark powers, but slaves nonetheless. They could have at least shown him a little respect.

Eithne was crying. It wasn't something which the young girl did very often, but in this instance, Irial was having a hard time comforting her. For that matter, Irial could find very little to take comfort in herself. Cursing Edryd under her breath, Irial risked a quick look out the door. She saw nothing that could have been counted as the source of her protector's concerns. Edryd had explained almost nothing before going out alone, and while it was clear that there was some sort of danger, he had not said who or what that danger was. It occurred to Irial that this was most likely because Edryd didn't know himself, but she still resented that he had left her with no idea what to do.

"Is he going to be alright?" Eithne asked as Irial stepped back inside.

"Of course he will," Irial replied, trying to sound reassuring as she wiped fresh tears from Eithne's face.

Irial chose the best option she could think of. She barred the front door and decided to wait.

"Do you remember how to secure the doors to the bedrooms from the outside?" Irial asked.

Eithne nodded and scampered up a ladder to the loft above Irial's room. Irial closed the door and Eithne began inserting bolts that secured the doors from above into holes bored through the top of the door frame and deep into the thick door. They repeated this process for Eithne's room and then again for the room Edryd had been using.

"Grab your coat," Irial said to Eithne. Irial began putting stores of food into a bag as Eithne grabbed both her little cloak and Irial's warm shawl from where they hung near the door. Together they entered the room with the hidden tunnel entrance beneath the floor.

Irial and Eithne huddled in this last room, beneath a collection of drying plants which were strung over storage crates and pieces of unused furniture. They couldn't secure this door in the same way that they had the others, but there was no need. They simply barred the door from the inside. To anyone that came upon them now it would look like the cottage was empty. Even if someone were to force their way in, she and Eithne could hide in the tunnel. In the worst case scenario they could escape down that tunnel and run. If nothing happened and no one came, they would wait until morning or until Edryd returned.

Urging Eithne to remain still, Irial began to listen. She felt neither alarm nor relief when she could hear nothing, just unbearable tension from not understanding what the threat was. Irial had seen fear in Edryd's eyes, and if she was going to make a mistake it was not going to be a lack of caution. She was as prepared as she could be without knowing what was going to happen next. Had she known what was coming, she would have fled down the tunnel with Eithne right then and there.

***

Esivh Rhol was the first to arrive at the isolated hovel. Now that he was close enough to give it a close inspection, hovel wasn't really the right word. The home was clean and well maintained, as well as relatively large and spacious. He was going to stick with calling it a hovel though. Compared to the luxury in which he insisted upon surrounding himself, it was an all but uninhabitable dwelling.

He decided to wait before making his presence known to whomever might be waiting inside. In part, Esivh Rhol did so because he was accustomed to having a servant on hand to announce him. It didn't feel right doing it himself. If he had chosen to be honest with himself, which was something he never would have done, he would have admitted that he was also afraid of the woman who lived here. She had threatened him once and he had never forgotten it.

The thralls were all there a few moments later. Still, Esivh Rhol hesitated. He would have liked to wait for his men to catch up as well, but that was going to take several more minutes.

"Lord Esivh Rhol, Ard Ri of An Innis, demands the attentions of the inhabitants of this home," he said in a loud clear voice after he noticed that the thralls had been impatiently waiting on him. This declaration sounded pompous even to Esivh Rhol, but he attributed this to the fact that he really should have had a servant there to do this. But there was nothing to be done about it. The thralls were not about to perform this function for him.

One of the thralls, either the short one or the one he had first spoken with, or it might just as easily have been the third thrall since in truth Esivh Rhol couldn't really tell any of them apart, began to slowly work his way south around the perimeter of the home and disappeared around the corner. The thrall was reacting to something, but Esivh Rhol could not tell what. The other two thralls remained near him, off to one side of his horse.

"I demand that the owner of this blight of a hovel open up at once!" Esivh Rhol said in his most commanding voice. "If you refuse we shall force the door open." His demand, backed up by the threat, was met with silence.

"Can you get through the door?" Esivh Rhol asked one of the thralls.

The thrall smiled in response, apparently confident that he could. The draugar servant struck the center of the door with what Esivh Rhol took to be a gloved fist. It was actually bare skin stained with dirt and grime that adhered to the coating which was left on his hands from tending to Áledhuir. The impact produced a loud crack and a shower of wooden splinters. The thrall looked disappointed as he surveyed the damage. Esivh Rhol was disappointed to. All the thrall had managed to do was to gouge a small depression into the center of the door. It was going to take more than this to break through.

The thrall made another attempt. This time he chose a more effective spot, close to the left hand side of the door. He struck with the flat of his open hand this time, and with more force than before. The section of door frame that held the bar support disintegrated and the wooden door swung in on protesting hinges. They were in.

Elek had partially circled the building, in an effort to sort out an anomalous distraction. He had felt someone or something inside that house when they approached. That someone or something had since moved below the surface, retreating there when Esivh Rhol had loudly proclaimed their presence. Elek couldn't quite be sure what it was, as the feeling wasn't very specific. It was a bit like his ability to know exactly where Áledhuir was at all times, or his ability to feel the other thralls, only this was much weaker.

If it were just an ordinary person, he wouldn't have been able to notice, as he wasn't nearly that skilled. It was mobile, whatever it was, and moving in a southerly direction below ground. That meant it was either a shaper, or if not that then some less gifted person moving an object of power. Elek didn't imagine it would be Aisen. That would have required him to accept that the target of their pursuit had managed to completely fool his masters.

Making an estimate of the direction this person was taking, Elek tried to get ahead of them. In doing so, he stumbled across the hidden crevice that was the exit for the tunnel. It was still dark above the ground, but it was darker still inside the opening that led down into the earth.

Elek cupped his blackened hands together and summoned light after the fashion in which he had been taught by Aed Seoras. The blue white light produced in this manner, continually pulsed in an irregular rhythm and sparked violently in the air. Elek grinned. The constantly shifting shards of light looked intimidating and dangerous. Elek didn't care that this effect was due to the fact that he was too weak a shaper to maintain a controlled light. He felt that this was so much better than what Seoras had actually taught him to do.

Intending to intercept whatever or whoever was trying to escape them, Elek slipped through the narrow opening. Preceded by the unstable floating illumination he had summoned, Elek worked his way along the tunnel.

Eithne sensed it first, but Irial soon saw the unnatural blue light reflecting off the tunnel walls. It would have been impossible to miss. They could either confront whatever it was, or head back. It was an easy decision. In a panic, Irial and Eithne hurried away from the light, which was quickly growing stronger as it drew closer. They escaped the approaching threat by returning to the barricaded storeroom. Irial and Eithne pulled the ladder up behind them to prevent anyone from following.

They were now in no less danger than before, for behind the door only a few feet away, were Esivh Rhol and half a dozen other men making a fearful noise while trying to break into one of the other rooms. The first door, the one securing Irial's room, took them several minutes, refusing to give way even under the force of repeated shaped impacts delivered by the thrall. But it couldn't hold up forever, and when the door came apart, its secrets were revealed.

The next two rooms were breached without difficulty. Two of Esivh Rhol's men went to work on the next door over, one of them up searching in the loft and removing the bolts that secured Eithne's door, and the other making a rapid search of her room once he managed to gain entry. The thrall who had forced his way into the cottage, and also broken through the first room, headed across the open hall to Edryd's room. Esivh Rhol felt a little alarmed as he watched the bolts rise up into the air in the loft above the door as the draugar servant looked on with focused concentration.

The other thrall was trying to do the same to the last door, but without success. Failing to realize that there were no bolts inserted into this door, and hence the futility of trying to locate and extricate them, he became frustrated and confused. Unable to understand what was different about this one, he pushed against the solid wood, and found resistance that confirmed that it was secured with a bar across the width of the door. He began to shape the dark, trying to seize hold of the obstruction and lift it clear, but it was secured in place.

"Seldur," he called out to the other thrall, "could use your help over here. This one isn't secured the way the others were."

Seldur left Edryd's room, carrying the sword that had been left behind in haste. "Does this look like a prince's weapon to you, Hedryn?" he asked, doubting it belonged to anyone more important than an unskilled hireling.

"Never mind that, I have a door for you to bust through."

Hedryn, an Æeldisir's thrall, considered himself a more nuanced shaper than Seldur, less reliant on brute force and intimidation, and more adept with the use of intellect applied towards more subtle forms manipulation. Brute force, however, had its uses, and it could occasionally be the better tool.

It proved unnecessary in this instance. From inside the room, someone began to remove the bar. A moment later the door swung inward as she calmly stepped through to the open hall. "What possible cause could you have to destroy my property?" Irial demanded. She looked ready to set upon anyone who spoke, and when no one did, she focused her anger and attention on a single specific target, a nervous looking man who was standing in the center of the room, stone faced and quiet. "If this is your doing, Esivh Rhol, I will have you pay for the repairs or you will regret you ever crossed me."

"Keep her away," Esivh Rhol barked to his guards, showing no concerns that his fear of this small woman might appear embarrassing. His guards made no effort to respond to his call for protection. They were wary of this woman as well and in no hurry to get between her and the Ard Ri.

The two thralls seemed bemused by all of this. Her reputation as a practitioner of dark arcane secrets did not impress them. They knew none of it was true. They knew from their time training under Aed Seoras that Irial was just a servant woman, and a threat to no one.

Seldur took one step forward and confronted her. "You are hiding something, Irial. You know better than to do that." He stepped forward again, forcing Irial to backpedal through the doorway.

"Where is Lord Seoras?" Irial questioned.

Seldur stiffened, standing a little taller, as he reflexively reacted to the name of his former master. "I expect you know how these things go," he said, "it won't hurt Seoras, his being kept in the dark."

"It might not hurt him, but he will hurt you when he learns what you have done."

This gave the aggressive thrall a little pause. "If he is displeased, he can take it up with Áledhuir and Aodra. I'm sure you understand that my decisions are not my own."

"I don't see your masters here, thrall," Irial pointed out. "Are you telling me that they ordered you to break into my home and threaten me? I can't imagine your master gave any such command. Seems to me you are actually here under orders from someone else, some unconvincing excuse of man, a weak willed coward who has hired others to do what he would never dare to do himself."

She didn't have to look at Esivh Rhol, point him out, or say his name. It was understood from the context who she meant. Seldur constricted, his listless features even more pallid than usual, reacting to an accusation that bore some truth. Esivh Rhol, who had been used as the subject of this taunt, said nothing in response, but he was predictably livid. His face became at first pale, before turning an angry red.

"You will let us search the room won't you?" Hedryn suggested. "You seem to have known we were coming, and had time to make preparations before we arrived. It raises a suspicion that you are hiding something."

"No, I will not. And if I was hiding something, I was hiding myself, from a vicious band of thugs." Irial projected a firm countenance and continued put forward an aggressive offensive, preventing Hedryn from interrupting and continuing on at greater length as he had a tendency to do. "Look at my house! I had good reason to try and keep you out."

"If we find nothing, we will stop troubling you," Hedryn said, trying sound as if he were only trying to be reasonable.

Irial knew that for a lie and she was determined not to let anyone go into the room. "Whatever it is you are looking for—"

"Whoever," Seldur corrected.

"Whoever you are looking for, he isn't here."

"We know that already," admitted Hedryn. "He left just ahead of us, pursued by Áledhuir and Aodra. It is only a matter of time before they catch him."

"Then why are you here?" Irial asked, covering her concern for Edryd by expressing instead her genuine confusion.

"Because you're still hiding something, which begs a question that I'm sure we would all like answered, what exactly is it you are keeping in that room?" said Esivh Rhol, neatly summarizing the situation.

Emboldened by apparent support from Hedryn, and having become quite curious as well, Seldur began to move forward. Irial had no choice but to give ground. She retreated strategically, leading Seldur away from the corner where Eithne hid, silently huddled behind a collection of stacked crates. This was more of a desperate gesture than it was an actual strategy. It wouldn't buy more than a few seconds and would lead to the same ultimate end.

Esivh Rhol followed Seldur in. He had begun to imagine that Irial had hidden away something of value in the room. He was imagining things she could have taken from the many people who had died under her care. It could be a hoard of golden coins or collections of fine jewelry studded with gemstones; almost anything was possible. Reality proved disappointing for him as he entered the room, as it all too often was, but he didn't give up, for there were plenty of spaces where some treasure could be concealed. With Irial's attentions focused on Seldur, the Ard Ri was free to move around unchecked, and it took him only a moment to find Eithne hidden against a wall behind the crates.

"Look here, girl," he said gently. Eithne was already looking at him, a mixture of fear and contempt in her bright sapphire blue eyes.

Recognition struck the Ard Ri almost immediately. He had never seen this girl before, but the similarities were there.

"I think I knew your mother," Esivh Rhol said. As he looked at her dark hair and blue eyes he put something else together. "And your father as well." He realized immediately that this girl could be a useful piece of insurance.

Seldur and Irial were still on the other side of the room. They had not noticed he was there.

"I knew you had something in here that you were trying to keep from me," Esivh Rhol said to Irial with a triumphant self-satisfied smile.

He hadn't meant to imply what Irial had taken this to mean, what everyone in the room and the two guards in the doorway also thought he had meant. Irial rushed toward Esivh Rhol, trying to get between him and Eithne and ignoring his shouts to stay back. Reacting to the sudden protective fury of this woman whom he feared, the Ard Ri panicked.

His guards having failed to protect him, Esivh Rhol was left with only one weapon. It was a fine short bladed dagger with a hilt inlaid with gold, and a pommel decorated with emeralds. He buried the knife deep, through Irial's dark simple dress and into the flesh just below her ribs. The knife came away, the blade and the hand that had used it now covered in blood, and Irial fell backwards to the ground in front of Eithne.

Everything stopped for a moment. Esivh Rhol had killed many times before. This wasn't the first woman either. It just wasn't usually accomplished so directly with his own hands. The world inside the room began to move again at sounds from outside the cottage. Esivh Rhol's horse screamed as it broke free from the guards outside who had been holding it, and the sound of weapon strikes could be heard.

"He has come back," Eithne said. Her eyes red and her cheeks streaked where tears had washed through a layer of dust on her face. "The Blood Prince is going to kill every last one of you for hurting my sister."

The thralls and the guards all rushed towards the fighting, leaving Esivh Rhol behind with Eithne.

***

Ruach was alerted to Elek's presence near the crevice by what looked like sparks of lightning, which feverishly attacked the air in front of the thrall, before he disappeared. Ruach, still a good distance from the tunnel entrance, began to run. He did not know what he had seen, but he had no doubt that it meant his captain was in danger.

He covered the ground quickly and slipped into the tunnel, feeling that he had to move quickly if he hoped to be of any help. He could see that he was getting close to the source of the pulsing light, and as it grew stronger, he began to move with more care, stepping carefully so as to avoid alerting the man that he followed.

Easing around a final corner, Ruach shielded his eyes from the light with his arm. Before him stood a man dressed in a drab grey cloak worn over plain looking brown clothes. The man was staring up in the air at the bottom of a trap door.

Ruach had not thought far enough ahead. He should have drawn his sword long before he had gotten so near to the man, but he couldn't afford any indecision now. In one fluid motion he drew his weapon and aimed a fatal thrust at the man's back. He had no qualms about attacking the man from behind without warning. He had seen enough to know that this was a thrall, and Ruach knew his chances were poor at best if he were to try engaging the draugar servant in a fair fight.

Elek turned in surprise at the last possible moment. The thrust still hit Elek, but instead of piercing him through the chest as Ruach had intended, the sword caught Elek in the side, slicing through the muscle above the crook of Elek's right arm. Ruach felt the impact of his sword deflecting off of bone, heard Elek's muffled protest of pain, and saw everything go dark as the thrall's concentration broke and the ghostly light vanished.

The darkness might ordinarily have been an advantage for a shaper, but in this instance Elek needed the light far more than Ruach did. The sigil warrior did not hesitate. He struck immediately at where he judged his opponent to be, accurately tracking the movement he had seen as the light vanished. Ruach felt the point of his sword pierce completely through his enemy. He tried to pull the weapon free but it was held fast.

Ruach puzzled over this but the cause became clear a moment later when a dim red light began to cast sparse illumination, its source the red hot glow at the end of his blade where it was held in the grip of the thrall's black hands. Ruach protested in pain and let go of his grip on the hilt of his sword as the heat began to burn his fingers where they came into contact with the weapon's crossguard. The smell of burning flesh made Ruach retreat, flexing his hand several times to reassure himself that it was not his own injury that was producing the effluence of foul odor.

Elek eventually pulled the sword from his chest and it dropped to the hard rock surface of the tunnel with a muffled clatter. "You are a dead man," Elek spluttered, his speech sounding like a lesser weaker version of the voice that belonged to his Huldra master. "You are a dead man for what you have done," he repeated.

"You and I have something in common then," Ruach said as he stepped forward to retrieve his sword, guided by the faint red heat that still emanated from the deformed section of the blade where the thrall had held it. Ruach judged from the sound of the blood in the man's throat as he spoke, that his attack had pierced one of the thrall's lungs.

"Untended, that is going to kill you," Ruach said, "and no one is ever going to find you down here."

From his position on the ground where he had fallen, Elek spat a mouthful of fluid in response to Ruach's sober taunt. The blood and saliva broke into a misted spray that fell well short, as his efforts at showing his spite triggered a fit of coughing. Ruach left the man to choke on his own blood as he felt his way along the tunnel in the dark, travelling all the way back to the exterior entrance. Foolishly, he began thinking that these thralls were not quite as dangerous as he had been led to believe.

The sky was beginning to brighten as Ruach exited the tunnel, and he could just make out two simple looking guards standing outside the cottage. One of them held the reigns of a fine grey mare with an expensive looking saddle. He would have liked to take them out quietly, but they were a dozen feet apart and both of them were looking in the direction of the other. It just wasn't going to be possible. Relying on speed and surprise, he attacked the guard holding the horse first. He realized this had not been the optimal choice when the horse reacted with fright, alerting additional enemies who were inside the cottage. Ruach killed his opponent with a single piercing stroke, before the guard could ready a defense.

The second guard was strong, but he too was outmatched. Ruach blocked two attacks before finding an opening and delivering a crippling slash across the man's unprotected shoulder. The guard dropped to the ground, writhing in pain, and screaming for help. In that time, two new enemies had appeared. They were pallid looking men dressed in a similar fashion to the one that Ruach had fought in the tunnel. Four more guards also appeared just behind them, holding back for now, content to leave this fight to the thralls.

The most useful thing Ruach could have done then would have been to run. He largely understood this, but he also knew that he would not escape. Choosing to test himself against these men, Ruach decided he didn't want to leave without understanding what had happened here first.

***

Edryd could not see his pursuer, but he felt her constant presence. He was driven to run harder as she drew near. He gained some distance while on the causeway, and upon reaching the mainland, he maintained that advantage while being pursued across the flat deserted expanse that had once been the location of the satellite colony of An Innis settlers, but the margin was shrinking now.

Wrongly assuming that once he made it to the tree line he might be safe, Edryd relaxed and slowed his pace as he entered the cover provided by the forest. It was a mistake. The draugr was now moving even more quickly as she entered the forest behind him. The trees were spaced too far a part to give her any significant trouble, and unlike him, she did not seem to tire.

Running again now, Edryd started to bend north, thinking of turning toward the coast where he knew there were areas of thicker vegetation. He gave up on this when he perceived that the draugr was moving at an angle that would intercept him well before he could reach any cover. Edryd took a moment to reflect on the envelopment which shrouded him, seeking confirmation that it remained in place. He had dealt it some permanent damage at some point. The Ældisir had picked up on the exposed aura and was tracking it directly. Any hope of escape was gone. She would only close the distance that separated them faster, if he did anything other than run in a straight line.

Edryd no longer held any hope that he could hide, and recognized that eventually he would have no choice but to turn and fight. He could imagine fighting the other draugr, the Huldra. There was something physical there to contend with. The Ældisir though, was ephemeral and without form. In his haste he had not taken his sword, but a weapon such as that could not harm a creature such as this. In order to fight her, Edryd needed to be able to shape.

A realization came that there might be a benefit to the damage he had done to his concealment. If it had weakened, perhaps the limitations it imposed had weakened as well. Edryd tried to touch the dark, and like every other time he had ever tried, he failed.

The Ældisir was drawing close now, and Edryd heard a whistling sound as a hail of thin pointed projectiles flew toward him from several different directions in the trees ahead of him. They were not real. Edryd could perceive that they were illusions conjured to manipulate and distract him, all except for one, coming from the opposite direction. Reacting to the illusory needles in the way in which the Ældisir apparently intended would have positioned Edryd directly into the path of the real one. Edryd flinched in spite of himself as he allowed the insubstantial objects to pass, without any effect, through his body. The dart that posed true danger flew past Edryd on his left, embedding its sharp point in the trunk of a large tree.

Beginning to comprehend what he was facing, Edryd's desperation grew. The draugr might not have a physical form, but she carried and could manipulate physical objects. There was no way of knowing what poison that needle had been tipped with. Worse, Edryd could not trust his traditional senses. The Ældisir was manipulating some of what he saw and heard.

Edryd, under these difficulties, settled upon a dangerous solution. He would go to a place that he feared more than the creature pursuing him. It was the only plan in which he could envision any hope of success. Edryd took a path that led to the ruins deep in the forest.

Twice more he evaded the attempts to attack him with a combination of conjured illusions and actual steel projectiles. The foreboding presence of the construct towers worked at the edges of his mind, alternately pushing and pulling his focus in different directions, but there was a small comfort to be taken in the reactions he noticed in the Ældisir. She was troubled by the ruins and increasingly anxious to prevent her quarry from reaching them. She was no longer trying to distract Edryd. She was focused now only on reaching him as quickly as she could.

Accepting the absurdity of what it was he was trying to do, but feeling more confident that it was his only chance, Edryd summoned what little energy he had left to make the final frantic push for the borders of the long dead city. He wanted to collapse when he passed through the towering arches at the western edge of the ruins, but he forced himself to remain on his feet, walking in towards the center of the site.

The Ældisir hesitated at the edge of the ancient structures, before unleashing her abilities with an intensity that she had previously held back. Soldiers came charging out at Edryd from the shadowed entrances of the buildings nearest to him. Edryd ignored them and they faded away.

Confronted by the overwhelming presences of the constructs trapped within the towers at the heart of the city, and filled with a terror that was warning him to turn around and run, Edryd glanced over his shoulder. The Ældisir was somehow making these feelings stronger, and playing tricks with his mind.

Pushing through the fear, Edryd faced forward again. He found himself standing less than a foot away from a nearly seven foot tall creature. It was the Huldra warrior, the draugr who had chased him onto the causeway. He had fallen into a trap. Edryd fell to the ground and began to propel himself backwards. The draugr stepped forward, and Edryd tasted the decaying stench in the air that escaped through the masking odor of the salve that coated the creature's skin. Edryd felt the draugr's hatred, and experienced the depths of the pure animus under which it looked down now upon the only living son of a man who it hated far more deeply yet.

Edryd closed his eyes, emptying all of his senses except for his ability to perceive the dark, and looked at his enemy. There was something there, but it was not a draugr. It was an impotent shaped pattern that posed no physical threat. Edryd stood up. The illusory draugr remained a few feet in front of him. He could hear it rumbling in anger. When Edryd opened his eyes, the image of the creature was still there, but as he began to walk it retreated each time he advanced. As Edryd moved further from the Ældisir, the illusion began to seem less real. This was the art of Seiðr. He knew this from what he had read in the book that he had taken from Seoras. It was a form of shaping, and Edryd hoped that like shaping, it would be harder for her to maintain as the distance between them increased.

Edryd heard a chilling scream of frustration as the illusion disintegrated, a despairing noise that had seemed both real and audible, but he had to doubt his senses, given the specific brand of sorcery that this creature practiced. She was coming now, slowly, but she was coming. Edryd began to walk toward the towers in the middle of the city. He easily stayed ahead of the Ældisir, recovering some of his strength while moving forward at a comfortable pace.

Passing the ring of towers, Edryd walked to what he now knew was the center of the ceiling of the domed underground chamber. It was fully morning now, the sun having just cleared the mountainous peaks to the east. He took a seat on the top step of the stairs and waited. He was calm at first, until he realized that in this place, his perceptions were confused. He could still sense her approaching, but the harder he tried to accurately fix her location, the more disoriented he became. He had good reason to hope that this disrupting effect was even more of a problem for her.

The Ældisir stopped at the edge of the encircling monoliths, sensing that something was wrong here, and recognizing that she had been led to this spot. A turbulent wind began to churn in the air where the draugr stood, making the outlines of a female figure briefly visible amidst thickening clouds of dust. The wind died down more suddenly than it had begun and the fragments of dust and earth settled back to the ground revealing a woman. A woman Edryd recognize as his mother.

The wind had been real, a touch of showmanship by the draugr. The woman was not, she was an image awakened in his mind by means of Seiðr. Edryd understood now why she seemed familiar. It was more than the fact that she was appearing to him in the form of his mother. It was because she had done so before, when she had cut him free aboard the smugglers ship. This Ældisir had followed after him obsessively for years, observing his every move. Upon learning what she was, Edryd had escaped her unwanted warding only with Aelsian's help.

"I want to help you, Aisen," she said.

"I don't want your help," Edryd replied, looking away, unable to bear her presence.

"I am not here to hurt you," she said, sounding wounded and still speaking in his mother's voice. This was anything but comforting. She could hardly have chosen anything to say that would have unsettled him any worse or that he would have believed any less. This woman was death. Not merely some apparition, but death itself, walking among the living and corrupting and destroying all of the things that she touched.

She came no closer for the moment, either unable or unwilling to cross the boundary marked by the circle of towers. "Stay away from me," Edryd warned dumbly, having nothing with which to threaten her. The command seemed to provoke instead of deter. The Ældisir forced her way past the imaginary line between the two towers nearest to her, and as she did this the image in his mind disappeared. The Ældisir struggled to take form once again. When it did coalesce in a series of halting stages, Edryd could still recognize the face of his mother, but it was weaker, less substantial, and it more closely resembled the almost forgotten memory in his mind that the draugr was drawing from.

Edryd remembered the light that Seoras had summoned in the chamber. The image of his mother was like that. The Ældisir was having difficulties with her art, and Edryd could dare to hope, had become a little less dangerous. She advanced silently, and as she did she continued to become more solid, more vital and real. She might have been struggling, but she was not wholly weakened. He could not afford to let her get close. Edryd descended the stairs.

"Stop!" she commanded in the voice of his mother, affecting an expression of genuine concern for an endangered child. "What you are doing is dangerous."

Edryd ignored her warnings and the voice faded from his mind as he descended further down the steps into the darkness. He had opened himself to the dark, and guiding himself by the positions of the towers and the memory of previous trips into this orphic expanse, he made it to the bottom safely. Avoiding the pitted basin on his way to the far edge of the chamber, he settled in with his back against one of the carved panels on the wall and waited for the Ældisir. She came, descending each step slowly. She didn't seem to know where he was, and she could no longer make him see any illusions, but he could now see her with clarity. In the perfect darkness that existed in the depths of this place, she was somehow darker still, a female form whose edges were sharp and clearly defined.

Reaching the bottom of the stairs, the Ældisir turned and looked for him. He could see no features on her form, but he could discern dimension, and the outline of her shape, and so he knew that she was staring at him. Edryd didn't know what a being such as this, an immortal returned, had to fear, but he could easily discern that she was frightened. Edryd shifted his perspective, seeing himself now as if from a few feet away. This is why he had come here, in hopes that he could be freed from the confinement of the warping of the dark that enveloped him.

He had expected to see a widening in the cracks in his concealing shroud, disrupted by the influence of the construct towers. What he saw instead was nothing of the sort. There were no angry red fissures and there was no darkness—there was no shroud at all. In its place was a pure white aura, intensely agitated by flowing lines of energies directed at him from the four functioning towers. He understood now why the Ældisir appeared so dark. His aura was permeating everything and filled the air itself, but it could not touch the draugr. Its light flowed around her, incompatible with what she was. He could appreciate why she seemed so frightened, and now that he understood it as well, she was not half so terrified or frightened as he was himself.

On previous occasions, Edryd had felt an overwhelming pressure while in this place. This had been an internal effect, triggered by an interaction with the construct towers, which had been contained and held in check by the presence of the shroud. Without the shroud in place, there was no pressure. Making the supposition then that if he tried now, he would be able to shape, Edryd also recalled the premonition that if he were to try to do so in this place that it would destroy him. He had a sense that he stood now on a precipice risking unimaginable disaster. Edryd began to walk towards the Ældisir. She remained frozen where she stood, whether in fear, or stubbornly blocking his path, Edryd could not tell.

Eventually he could go no further without forcing his way past her. Edryd took another step, and that is when he saw the object she held between the fingers in her right hand. She raised her arm, preparing to push the dart into his flesh, but Edryd caught her wrist. The Ældisir screamed in pain and agony. What he had caught hold of was nothing with any true substance, and he was not holding onto it with his actual hand. He had broken through the darkened shell that held the soul of this creature, and it was his own aura that held her fast.

He would have let go then if he could. In something very much like the bond he had forged with Seoras, he could see into the Ælidisir's soul, and could feel her torment. He could feel the accumulated pain of years spent anchored to this world, trapped in a death that would allow her neither the simple joy of life nor the promise of transcending to the next existence. Most of all he could feel the pain of what she knew was about to happen.

Edryd tried to shut it out but he had already been pressed into a forced accord with the soul of this undead creature. He could find himself, with difficulty, but when he did he saw that the pure blackness which held her was now expanding to engulf him as well. This is what she feared most. It had happened before. It would crush the life out of whatever she touched, leaving tattered screaming traces behind imprisoned alongside her. It was easy now to understand why draugar avoided contact with living things. Edryd had gained insight into what it was that was happening, but there was nothing to be learned from the Ælidisir that suggested any means by which he could prevent it.

The constriction continued to progress. The pure dark extending from the draugr had engulfed his arm now, and was spreading up his neck and across his chest. He realized this was wrong, it was not enveloping his body; it was swallowing his aura. This malleable thing, whatever it was, it was not physical in nature. It was something in a sense akin to the shroud, in the same way that being wrapped in a warm blanket was like being stuffed into a cloth sack before being drowned in a river.

The Ælidisir knew that she was watching his death, and because she knew it, Edryd knew it too, through a bond that had been forged between them. He was having increasing trouble distinguishing his thoughts from hers. She was feeling pain and failure. He was struggling vainly to make it all stop and feeling the dread that came with knowing it was useless.

Edryd did not stop struggling, but he did try to calm his emotions. He needed to think clearly and use what time there was to study the draugr and find some weakness. Edryd could see her now in the way that she had once been, the way she tried now to still see herself. She was tall, at least as tall as he was, and young and beautiful. Worked through with intricate braids, her dark black hair fell past her shoulders. Her skin, a dark even shade of basaltic grey, had a warm vitality, and her eyes were an intense absolute green that evoked depths to which Edryd was bereft in all his limited experience of any adequate comparison. He knew that she was sorry for what was happening. Not just for him, but also for reasons of her own. Like so many others, she had wanted him to do something for her, something impossible.

Edryd saw that he was nearly enveloped now, and he abstractly realized that his body had gone still, having ceased its breathing. There was something he had not tried. He could make one last attempt to shape, but he still felt somehow that if he did the result might be far worse than what he was facing now. Edryd pushed the idea away as he continued to resist, prepared to endure for as long as he could. And then the balance to the struggle began to change. Edryd's aura expanded, straining against the piece of the dark that this demonic envelopment was composed of, and as Edryd exceeded its capacity to contain him, the unnatural confinement began to grow thin.

The Ældisir noticed too. An unthinkable hope ignited inside her and she began to assail the weakened walls of her cage. Edryd's aura continued to build. He discovered that he was only tenuously connected to his body which now lay unmoving on the ground, near to what would soon become a permanent and irretrievable death. This twisted shred of the dark that had imprisoned the Ældisir might prove to be a weapon strong enough to kill him, but it was nowhere near sufficient to contain his aura and hold his soul. Edryd felt powerful beyond comprehension.

And then the Ældisir broke through. He was still connected to her in that moment and he shared the unimaginable joy she felt at her freedom. The prison that held her had been unable to hold Edryd, and having lost her as well, it could not continue to hold itself together. It broke apart in a violent explosion, generating an unimaginable torrent within the currents in the dark that flowed through the chamber. The corrupted remnant of a construct that it had once been, dissolved into the barrier realm from which it had been formed, sending reverberations in all directions.

Chapter 21

The Sigil Blade

Edryd remembered some of what had happened, but none of it remained clear. He was unsure how to reconstruct the exact order of events which had left him lying on his back on the stone floor of the chamber. As he stood, Edryd saw a loose arrangement of objects scattered on the ground beside him. It was only then that he thought to wonder how it was that he could see anything at all. He followed the traces of illumination back to their sources, sconces carved out of the rock and recessed into the walls at even intervals along the edges of the chamber, sending cold blue light throughout the room. He couldn't guess what fueled these lights or what had caused them to ignite.

Abandoning this mystery, he looked once more at the objects on the ground, taking the time needed to categorize what he saw. The unusual items rested upon and were partially obscured within a strange low mounded pile of dust. Edryd sorted through the fine grains and retrieved one of the objects, a small metal needle. He dropped the item with far less care than he had picked it up, as if he were afraid it might burn him. He realized what it was. It was the weapon the Ældisir had attacked with during the struggle. These loose granules of material he had been sifting through were the creature's desiccated remains.

Ignoring his revulsion, along with the urge to frantically dislodge the thin layer of decomposition that adhered to him from head to toe, Edryd bent down and carefully cleared the pile of dust away. If there was any danger in touching the remains, surely he had already been completely exposed. Edryd found a scrap of leather with a series of sockets. It held one more needle, with spaces for four others. He rolled this up and placed it in a pocket inside his coat.

There were a few pieces of jewelry, one of which stood out. It was a golden band shaped tightly to the dimensions of what he supposed had been the Ældisir's arm. Edryd couldn't imagine how the bracelet could have been worn. It was too narrow to be pulled on or off, and it was perfectly smooth with no evidence anywhere of a break in the piece. It would have had to have either been forged in place, or placed on her arm as a child for her to grow into as an adult. Something about the object seemed hollow, as if it were an empty vessel with no openings. Believing it to be important, Edryd tucked the golden band away inside his coat beside the leather bundle.

At the bottom of the pile was an accessory that would have been worn by a woman over her clothing. It was a looping cord of golden braid that crossed in the front and was designed to be fitted around the shoulders. It was connected in the back to a pair of crossed sheaths, in which two thin knives were held firmly in place. It was designed so that the hilts were positioned down and to the sides so that the two knives could easily be drawn from concealment. This was the equipment of an assassin.

Edryd removed the weapons, the blades of which were perfectly transparent, each an identical match to the other. He marveled at their beauty as they picked up and filtered the blue light along gracefully curved edges. They were not made of glass, or crystal; they were entirely composed of something else, an otherworldly material more beautiful than either. The knife handles were decorated using thin golden threads, which wound through and around tiny faceted designs, providing for a firm grip. All of the other surfaces were smoothly polished and more clear and pure than the cleanest water.

The blades measured out to the length of Edryd's forearm. The two knives were impossibly light, and though they appeared delicate, they resisted any attempt at flexion when he tested them. Edryd ran his thumb across the cutting edge on one of the knives, and confirmed that it held as sharp an edge as any finely honed steel blade he had ever used. Feeling like he was committing sacrilege, Edryd cut through, unthreaded, and then discarded the golden braid that had held the sheaths.   With the blades returned to their housings, which he discovered could be detached from one another, Edryd hooked them, one on each side, between his hips and his belt. He would have preferred a sword, but at least he was no longer without a means of defense.

Satisfied that there was no purpose to remaining in the chamber any longer, and still as fearful of this place as he had ever been, Edryd ascended the spiraling stone stairway. As he neared the surface, the lights in the chamber died away. Edryd shivered, trying hard not to wonder what the extinguishing lights signified, feeling as though the chamber had chosen to accept him and was now going dormant while it awaited his return.

He was well away from the ruins before he even thought to try. He first confirmed that his aura was plainly visible. There was no longer any trace of the concealment that had once protected him. If as Edryd believed, the shroud had been blocking his attempts to shape, interfering with everything but his ability to passively observe changes in the patterns of the dark, it would no longer be an obstacle to him. Edryd tried to touch the dark, believing in his heart that he would be able to alter its shape. His aura intensified with his efforts, but he could no more grasp the shifting currents of the dark than he could hold onto the rising gusts of air that travelled up the forested slope which he was descending. The dark flowed around him as though he were a minor obstacle of little account, remaining unchanged by and oblivious to his vain attempt to bind it to his will.

The failure made Edryd desperate. He quickened his pace and did not slow until he reached the causeway, where he half expected to see the tall draugr still raging on the opposite shore. But there was no one on the other side. The water was deep now, reaching up to his waist in places as he made his way across. Upon reaching the other side he collapsed. He needed rest, if only just for a short while. He took the opportunity to try once more but the results were the same.

Edryd could see his own potential strength. It seemed incredible that he had proven so inept at putting this power to use. Nothing had been made better. He was no stronger than before, and now he was also exposed and would be unable to hide from his enemies. He didn't properly understand how, but he had destroyed one of the draugar. Perhaps there was hope that he could defeat the other as well. Seoras could be of some help, if he could be trusted. Edryd noticed then that his connection to Seoras was gone. However the link had formed, the confrontation with the Ældisir in the chamber had obliterated it.

Ominously, Edryd realized that there might be another reason why he could no longer feel his master. Aed Seoras might be dead. It didn't seem possible. Edryd knew that his teacher feared the draugar and did not have the means to overcome them, but he couldn't believe that Aed Seoras wouldn't be able to easily protect himself. Edryd began to hurry. He wanted to get back to Irial and Eithne at the cottage as quickly as he could. He could figure out what to do from there.

When Edryd arrived at the cottage, his strength exhausted and his concentration spent, he saw a man he had seen only once before, waiting beside the door. Aelsian stood, his movements showing the signs of a stiffness which betrayed his age. Edryd could also see a pair of bodies. They were lined up beside each other, well away from the entrance. Dark circles in the earth showed the places where they had died, only a few feet from where Aelsian now stood. A trail of blood led back inside the broken doorway to the cottage. Edryd was too afraid to ask the navarch what had happened.

"I thought for a moment that you might be Ruach," Edryd said, "but as I get closer, I can't see how I made that mistake."

Aelsian looked squarely in Edryd's eyes, his expression grave and severe.

"This does looks like some of his handiwork, unless I am to believe it is yours," Edryd said, looking at the bodies and trying to remain calm. "Can you tell me what happened?" asked Edryd, his body growing weak in anticipatory fear of the answer.

Aelsian said nothing. He could not think how to deliver the dark news he carried.

"Where are Irial and Eithne?" Edryd demanded. It was plain that something terrible had happened. Edryd silently prayed that they were simply missing, instead of come to some harm, but Aelsian's answer shattered that hope.

"She's gone Edryd; she's dead."

Edryd felt as if he had been struck by a weighted weapon, with the hammer of the impact felt all the more severely for his having anticipated the blow.

Aelsian had not said who it was he meant, but his phrasing indicated it was only one of the two girls, and not Irial and Eithne both together. Aelsian, having never met either of them before now, might not have known their names. Edryd dared to hope it was someone else, not the woman he had promised to protect or the young girl that she was caring for. He knew it was a false hope though.

"I will take you to her," Aelsian said, his eyes full of sympathy.

Edryd followed Aelsian and together they passed through the damaged entrance to the cottage. Edryd had expected scenes of a horrible slaughter in the large open hall, but apart from the damage to the broken doors, the building had barely been disturbed. Led by Aelsian, Edryd stepped into Irial's bedroom, steeling himself against the grief that he could not hold back as tears began to fall from his face.

Irial was laid out on the bed, her arms posed across her body so that they covered the wound that had ended her life. Her face was calm and peaceful, but utterly pale and drained of color. Edryd wanted to cry out, and he needed to find someone on whom to vent his anger, but he could do neither of these things. He had no words to give to his pain, and no target on which to exact any vengeance. And there was a more immediate concern in that moment than his need to express his sorrow or seek retribution.

"Where is Eithne?" Edryd asked, his fear for the young girl driving all other thoughts from his mind.

"Ruach said they took her."

"Is he alright?" Edryd asked, wondering why Ruach was not there. His officer apparently would have more answers than Aelsian did.

"He was out in front when Ludin Kar and I arrived," Aelsian explained. "He had tried to stop them and was nearly killed in the process. He is alive, but not by a wide margin."

Edryd recognized the name of the navarch's friend, but he couldn't remember from where. As to what had happened, Aelsian could tell him little more. The men who had done this had been gone well before he had arrived, so he had not seen himself, any of what had happened. Ruach possessed the only answers that could be had. At Edryd's insistence, they went to Edryd's room where Ruach was resting, carefully tended to by Ludin Kar.

"If you had been there with me," Ruach said, smiling weakly at Edryd as his captain took a seat beside the bed, "we would have killed the lot of them."

It was a perfectly horrible thing for Ruach to have said, and it filled Edryd with intense unbearable guilt. Ruach had not intended to suggest that any fault lay with Edryd for what had happened, but Edryd placed the blame where he knew it belonged. This had happened because of who he was, and it had happened because of the decisions and the mistakes that he had made.

Ruach, in trying to protect Irial and Eithne from the danger Edryd had brought to their door, had been severely hurt. The warrior bore dozens of superficial cuts. It was plain that these were not from combat. Ruach had been tortured. In addition to those lesser injuries, Ruach had been stabbed through once in the shoulder, deeply cut in several places on his sword arm, and twice pierced through by the end of a sword in each leg. It defied reason that he had survived so many injuries.

"They knew what they were about," Ruach said, shrugging painfully. "They were careful to keep me alive."

"But why," Edryd wondered.

"They had two types of questions, those which I refused to provide answers to, and a great many more for which I knew no answer."

Edryd did not doubt Ruach. The disciplined soldier would have told the enemies nothing. Edryd was worried that he might not be showing the appropriate amount of concern for his friend, but he wanted to know more, and he was far more interested in what Ruach could tell him about the men who had done this, than anything Ruach might have revealed under their interrogation.

"Who were they?"

"There were two groups," Ruach said. "One of them was led by Esivh Rhol. He was the one who killed Irial. I didn't see it happen but I'm sure that it was him."

"And what of Eithne?" said Edryd.

"It was Esivh Rhol who took her as well," Ruach replied. "I heard him tell the draugr that she was insurance." Ruach began to smile as he explained what had happened next. "Eithne must have told the Ard Ri at least a dozen times that the Blood Prince was going to find him and kill him, and he went a new shade of pale every time she said it."

The look on Edryd's face told everyone that he was going to go and do exactly what Eithne had predicted.

"A draugr?" said Ludin Kar, his voice laced with concern. Apparently Ruach had not yet told this part of the story.

"A great big fellow in a cloak showed up after everything had already happened. He said someone called Aodra was dead. A great shock that was to one of the thralls, but not to the other, Hedryn I think he was called. He seemed to have already known that she was gone, and if I am not wrong, quite relieved to know it."

Ruach seemed to be skipping important details, but Edryd needed just one more thing. "Do you know where they took Eithne?" he asked.

"Yes," Ruach said, "they left me alive for that very reason. You are supposed to go to them in town. The draugr told me to tell the son of Elduryn that he cannot run and that Lord Seoras can no longer hide or protect him."

Edryd had never quite felt as if he were being protected by Aed Seoras. Manipulated and outright directly endangered yes, but never anything that in any way made him feel supported or safe. It was possible, Edryd realized, when re-examined in light of all that had happened today, that he had failed to appreciate the extent of the dangers from which he had been shielded.

With his link to Seoras broken, Edryd had to rely only on his basic perceptions. Extending them as far as he could, Edryd searched for Seoras. Edryd was able to get a sense of his master, as well as the draugr and two others, all in the direction of the town, but he could be sure of very little at this distance. What he did know for certain, was that there was also a thrall who lay dying in the tunnel beneath the cottage.

Edryd told them then what it was he intended to do. It was completely foolish to go after Esivh Rhol, for there could be no real hope of saving Eithne, but Edryd didn't consider that there was any other choice. He had no powers with which to confront the thralls let alone face off against their immortal master, and someone should have tried to talk him out of it, but no one did.

Ruach had a word of caution. "Esivh Rhol and his men are not much to contend with. They are inferior really. But the thralls, you will need to be careful of them." Ruach's injuries were the only confirmation any one could have needed to affirm this. "There were three. I killed one, when I surprised him down in the tunnel. I fought two more outside, but either one would have been too much for me. They were fast. You wouldn't believe how fast."

Edryd did believe it. Seoras had shown him how fast an accomplished shaper could strike and how impossibly strong they could be. "Your friend in the tunnel," Edryd said, "he isn't dead. Probably best I do something about that."

Before anyone could stop him, Edryd was up and heading for the entrance hidden under the floor of the adjoining room. Aelsian trailed behind, grabbing a lamp as he went. Edryd pulled the entrance open, lowered the ladder, and began to climb down. Aelsian handed him the lamp before Edryd completely descended below the level of the floor.

"You are staying up there," he said to Aelsian when it became clear that the navarch intended to go with him. "I don't care what happens, no one else is to come down here," Edryd ordered. "He is still a danger to anyone who gets near him."

Edryd found Elek only a few feet away from the ladder, staring blankly into the air from where he sat with his back against the tunnel wall, his eyes blinded by Edryd's lamp. Edryd felt it as the thrall gathered in the dark and began to shape. He was trying to pull Edryd closer where he could really do some damage.

"I would stop now if I were you," Edryd warned, intensifying his aura as he did so. The bluff completely intimidated Elek into submission, and the shaper released his hold on the dark.

"You, you are the one who killed Aodra," Elek said, his eyes widening in comprehension. "If you could destroy Áledhuir as well, I would take it as a great favor. I would like to be freed from his tether before I die."

"They left you here. Why?"

"My master has no use for a dying servant. He has another thrall, and he will most likely manage to replace me with Hedryn as well, now that Aodra is dead."

Edryd didn't care about any of this. He needed to know where his enemies were, and what they had planned. Elek was more than willing to supply everything Edryd wanted. He explained that he could still feel the anger of his master. Áledhuir was somewhere in Esivh Rhol's palace. Elek also told Edryd of the ship that transported them to the island, and confirmed that they were here to capture Lord Aisen. Elek could not say why, other than that his master's master, for whom Elek either could not or would not give a name, took an interest in the politics of all the nations and in the men who ruled them. Elek provided another interesting detail. Áledhuir was more interested in killing Edryd than he was in capturing him. The draugr had been made wary though, afraid even, by what had happened to Aodra.

Edryd returned to the room where Ruach was resting under the care of Ludin Kar, who looked worried, both about Ruach and in fear of the shaper in the tunnel. "He won't live much longer, and he doesn't pose a risk to anyone as long as you stay far away from him," Edryd assured the scholar.

Aelsian entered the room a moment later carrying a long cloth wrapped bundle. Edryd knew it for what it was. This object was the locus of a sigil knight's power, a focus for spiritual strength, and a weapon against unnatural constructs born of the dark. Edryd was surprised to discover that he wanted to wield it once more, and he was unprepared for how desperately he felt he needed it.

Edryd unwound the sword from the cloth and used the edge of the blade to cut a long strip of the fabric. He secured the ends of the cloth in a knot around the short unsharpened ricasso at the base of the simple blade. Edryd removed his long dark coat and looped the improvised circle of cloth over his right shoulder, with the other end cradling the sigil sword on his other side. He would only need to draw the blade a few inches to cut through the knotted cloth. Edryd replaced his coat, and once he was satisfied that the sword was as reasonably concealed beneath it as could be managed, which was not very well, he bid a brief farewell to Ruach and Ludin Kar before leaving the cottage.

Aelsian followed him as far as the road. "The Ascomanni are attacking the island tonight," he said. "If you use the chaos to your advantage, it will give you a chance."

Edryd suspected that the reverse might prove true. If Esivh Rhol were to pull men back to the palace, having been made fearful of the threat of the Blood Prince, it was going to make it easier for Logaeir to take and hold the piers, but it would make it more difficult to fight through to get to the Ard Ri. It would be better if he hurried.

Aelsian turned south as they parted, heading for the boat that waited to return him to the *Interdiction*. He needed to get back to his fleet as he would need to be in command of his forces in the aftermath of the fighting. Edryd headed west by his usual daily route, feeling the pain of Irial's absence as he travelled the familiar path without her, drawing ever closer to the city of An Innis, the town which bore this island's name.

As Edryd continued to walk he began to feel calm. He did not understand it. He was as angry and hurt as he had ever been at any time in his life. The pain rivaled the loss of his mother, abandonment by his father, and even the death of his brother at his own hands, but it existed beside a subtle undercurrent of joy that was in no sense rooted within his own mind. Nothing that had happened to him today suggested a possible source that could explain this feeling, but it was there.

His awareness seemed to expand by the moment, and as it did the calm increased. His anger and his fear were still there, but they were felt as if from far away. The experience felt foreign and strange, and very wrong, but Edryd did not resist this broadening of his conscious boundaries, the source of which seemed probable enough. He glanced inside his coat, taking a look at the weapon. Edryd truly expected to see it glowing with a bright white light, or humming with spectral warmth, but the sigil blade remained in all appearances, a simple piece of well-crafted steel.

Edryd wished there were someone to guide him. That someone should have been his father. He could only hope that if he remained open to the sword's influence, something useful would come of that faith and bring clarity to his confusion. Past experiences offered no encouragement. It was difficult to place his trust in an object that Edryd believed had once impelled an action which had ended in the death of his own brother.

Even without a link to his master, Edryd recognized Aed Seoras's pattern and traced his presence long before he reached the estate. The property was shut tight, with the gates closed and securely fastened together. This was something Edryd could not recall ever having happened. Seoras stood before the entrance, waiting alongside another younger man with dark hair and a pale face, who looked completely inexperienced and out of his depth beside his former master. Edryd knew the man was a shaper. He was a former student of Aed Seoras and a thrall to the draugar. Edryd could no longer see his master's emotions with quite the same precision that he once had, but he did not need anything but the rapidly dwindling daylight to see that Seoras was troubled.

"Which one are you, Seldur or Hedryn?" Edryd asked of the man standing beside Seoras.

"He was Aodra's thrall, Hedryn," Seoras answered for his companion.

Edryd turned his attention to his master. "Why are the gates closed?" He asked Seoras. It could easily have been a trap, with men hidden in the courtyard, but Seoras would not have needed such help, and from what Edryd could tell, there was only one individual within the confines of the property.

"I won't be remaining in An Innis any longer," Seoras said. "I have returned control of the property to Master Tolvanes. He seems quite pleased, but he may miss our arrangement soon enough. It will be hard for him to hold onto it on his own."

"You are only here then, because you were waiting for me?"

"Better you had not come," said Seoras, his meaning plain despite offering no clue as to what side he had chosen.

"I have not come blindly or without the means to prevail," Edryd said, opening his coat to reveal the long blade that he carried.

Seoras didn't seem surprised, but judging from his demeanor, he was harboring a deep resentment. "You said that was at the bottom of the ocean."

"I'm sure you can understand why it wasn't my first impulse to tell the truth," Edryd answered. "Will you help me, or are you here to interfere?"

"I can take you to the palace. Those are my instructions actually, to find you and bring you to them, nothing more. I told them that it was unnecessary, and it seems I was right."

This was a frustrating answer, but Edryd should have expected it, given the company in which he had found Seoras.

"How can you possibly do this? After what Esivh Rhol did to Irial, I didn't think that you would side with them."

Seoras shifted his feet, discomforted at learning there was something he had apparently not been told yet. He looked expectantly at the man beside him.

"We never meant to harm her," the thrall insisted, his fear of Seoras evident. "She was kind to me when I was here. None of us would have ever hurt her." He seemed to think for a second and then said, "Well Seldur maybe, if he had a reason, but none of us had any reason."

"She's dead then?" Seoras asked, trying not to appear angry.

"Esivh Rhol gutted her," Hedryn admitted. "The idiot acted, and nobody was close enough to prevent it. It should not have happened."

"They will all wish it hadn't," Seoras said. He might have meant several people, but the comment most especially must have referred to Esivh Rhol. There was real anger in Seoras's eyes, but something was holding him in check, restraining the master shaper's desire to react. "I trust that you will see to that," he said to Edryd.

"I need your help, not your well wishes," Edryd said, feeling bitter. He had never once asked Seoras for anything, and he began to sense that needn't bother now, except as a means to extract a response to his request, the refusal of which he could then use to condemn his cold and unjust master.

"I don't know what happened in your battle with Aodra, but I am reeling from the echoes even now," Seoras said. "You announced your existence throughout this world to anyone and everyone that matters with the immensity of the strength that you displayed. With that kind of power, you do not need anyone's help."

"And if you're wrong?" Edryd asked. Edryd wasn't sure how to explain that he did not know what had happened, and Seoras did not look prepared to continue to believe that his pupil could not shape.

"I am not wrong, but if I were, my powers would not swing the balance in our favor. Áledhuir would kill us both. If you are unable to do this on your own, it will not benefit either of us to try it together."

"If he won't help you," said Hedryn, "I will."

This unsought offer caught Edryd unprepared. It seemed like an especially foolish thing to even consider, but Edryd wasn't sure he could turn down any kind of help right now. If Edryd had been surprised, Seoras was completely taken aback.

"He does not need your help," the master shaper said.

"But I do need his," said Hedryn. "I am a free man, or nearly so, for the first time that I can remember in my entire life. If he can destroy Áledhuir, there is a chance that I can remain free, and if Aisen should fail, I would rather die alongside him than end up tethered to that monster."

Seoras did not like this answer. His anger was on the surface now, but most of it was directed at Edryd. "If you come back from this, you and I are going to settle a debt," he said to Edryd, who had no idea what Seoras meant. By Edryd's reckoning, if Seoras thought he was owed something by his student, the two gold sovereigns the shaper had stolen more than covered it.

It was clear now that Seoras was not going to help, and so Edryd made the decision to leave. Every moment he wasted trying to persuade his teacher was adding to the risk of harm that Eithne would be exposed to under the care of the Ard Ri. Hedryn joined Edryd as he picked his way up a series of narrow streets that led to the palace. Edryd had not forgotten what this man had done. He had been there when Irial died, and he had fought with Ruach, and then tortured him close to death before leaving him behind to deliver a message.

"Were you the one who tortured Ruach?" Edryd asked him.

"No," protested Hedryn with a look of awe in his eyes, and pure horror in his voice. The thrall seemed to have no doubt that Edryd could destroy him at any moment. "I would never do something like that."

"But you wouldn't stop it from happening either," Edryd pointed out. "You were there, and you watched it."

"Do you honestly believe there was anything that I could have done?" Hedryn asked. "It was Seldur who hurt him, and he did it with his master's encouragement. If you knew anything of Áledhuir, you would know why I could do nothing to help your friend. I am doing everything I can now to make it right."

The young man appeared to be entirely genuine, and somewhere within Edryd's heart, something urgently persuaded him that he should trust this thrall. Hedryn had been given so few choices in this life, and the one he was making now, was to put that life in Edryd's hands.

Hedryn began to look at Edryd strangely. When Edryd caught him at it, the thrall stopped and apologized. "I'm sorry, but Seoras told me that you could hide yourself from shapers, and I was trying to see how it was done."

Edryd nearly told him not to bother, that the effect was gone, but upon checking, the shroud was firmly in place, perfect and without any flaw as if it had always been there. His heart sank with despair, feeling as if he had taken a great step backwards.

Edryd had to remind himself that he had all but confirmed that it was not the shroud that blocked his ability to shape, and given its sudden unsought return, it seemed clear now that his concealment must have been an ability that was granted by the sword. Reclaiming the blade had repaired the effect. He needed to believe that this could be a good thing, that it could have a purpose.

"I want to thank you for what you did for Aodra," Hedryn said, interrupting Edryd's reflections as they walked.

"Don't you mean to Aodra? Or maybe you mean what I did for you."

"All three I guess," said Hedryn. "It is a tricky business pairing a thrall with a draugr. If Seoras thought well of you, he would place you with a draugr that he also thought well of. The opposite was true too, and it can make a world of difference. In that regard I was fortunate."

"You're saying Aodra wasn't bad?"

"Compared to Áledhuir she was a blessing. She was kind to me. But being tethered to any of them takes a toll. I could always feel her, like there was a window through which I could see into her soul."

Edryd's blood froze. This description was too similar to ignore.

"That window went both ways. Being bound to a living mind seemed to stabilize her, but it did the opposite to me. You cannot hide anything, and you can't shut them out either. I felt her suffering every single day—and I felt her joy when you helped her break free."

Edryd shivered as he remembered what had happened that morning, and grew angry with the realization that Seoras had bound him not long after they met. The link, tether, or whatever you chose to call it, Edryd was grateful that it was gone.

"I had a sense of you in the link at the end. It works that way you know," said Hedryn. "Anyway, I'm glad you did what you did, and so was she."

Edryd didn't know how to respond, so he said nothing at all. He was feeling unusual. It had started before he had met up with Seoras and Hedryn, but it had only grown stronger since. Though he realized he might be marching to his own death, he felt an unshaken certainty that he was doing the right thing, and that he would have all the support he needed. He cared less and less that Seoras had chosen not to come, but accepting the fact that his master was not going to provide any help, had made Edryd no less curious about the reasons.

"Why do you think Seoras is standing aside?" Edryd asked of Hedryn. "It isn't like him to be so passive."

"They must be holding something over him to have backed him down like this," Hedryn agreed. "And Seoras is more powerful now than I remembered, certainly stronger than he was when I trained with him."

"He doesn't fear them then?"

"Collectively he might, but individually, I don't think he ever was especially afraid of any of the draugar even then. In truth, it might be the other way around."

"Áledhuir is afraid of Seoras?"

"When you can't die there are things that can happen to you that are worse than death, like being cut into pieces by an angry shaper and scattered across the landscape," Hedryn said.

"Or like being drowned at the bottom of an ocean," suggested Edryd. He also knew another theory for stopping these creatures, but he wasn't going to mention Logaeir's thoughts on melting one in a fire.

"Or like being drowned in the ocean," Hedryn agreed. "For you or me, the suffering would last only a few minutes. For Áledhuir, he would spend an eternity on the sea floor, cut off from all light with his body disintegrating around him."

Unless Esivh Rhol had an impossibly deep pool hidden somewhere in the palace, this was hardly any help to Edryd. "Any other weaknesses you can tell me about—any other way to kill one?" Edryd asked.

"I suppose you could say more on that subject than I can," Hedryn said, shaking his head.

Edryd chose not to tell Hedryn that he knew less and could do less than anyone seemed to believe. Edryd had only one hope. He had the sword. Seoras had been sure it could be used to defeat a draugr, though he had said nothing about how. More than just the sigil sword was needed, Edryd was sure of that much. What was needed was a sigil knight. It was reckless to think he could figure this out as he went, but deadly crisis had opened the floodgates and awakened the sword for him once before. Perhaps it would do so again, and this time he would just have to hope for a better result.

***

The sun had set over the ocean while they were departing, and everything was now dark as the Ascomanni fleet approached An Innis, led by warriors packed into grouped pairs of long boats. The stars were hidden behind thick clouds and the shrouded light of a new moon gave only scant illumination. Logaeir and his men need only remain as silent as possible as they rowed along the shoreline on their approach from the south, and the threat of detection would be minimal. Another group led by Krin was closing in from the north. The plan for simultaneous surprise attacks, causing as much confusion as possible while securing positions with open berths on both piers, was about to begin. Warships were following well behind the long boats, ready to disembark groups of reinforcements as soon as those larger vessels could be secured to the piers.

Logaeir focused only on his side. There was nothing he could do to help his allies until they won through to the shore and he could unite with them. The majority of the battle would take place later, but the greatest risks came now. If one or both of the initial incursions failed, and they could not secure their positions, it could become impossible to bring in support in sufficient numbers.

There was only one thing that gave Logaeir fear, and that was the pair of draugar that had come to the island the night before. He had prepared with an understanding that there was a real chance that these undead creatures could interfere, but he didn't have any good contingencies in place should it actually happen. He had ruled out setting one of them on fire. Edryd had been right about that. It would have been a horrible mistake. Tactically, he should have made the rather sound decision to delay the attack until he could confirm that they were gone, but there were now other considerations. It would have comforted Logaeir to learn that one of the two draugar had already fallen, and it would have comforted him more to know that the other one was holed up inside Esivh Rhol's palace.

As the boats settled in against the pier, Logaeir was the first to scale his way onto the stone surface. Some three dozen men, including eight from his boat, and the remaining men distributed amongst three others, followed him up. There were six key ships on this side that he intended to take, but first they would secure a landing for the *Retribution*.

He and his men began to set upon everyone they encountered. It was an uncomfortable business, but Logaeir was in his element. He had trained under various Ossian masters. Ludin Kar had been the first, giving him a broad formal education. Others had followed, training him in stealth and combat as an agent of their navy. Logaeir had no loyalty to any of them. They had been the means to an end, one that would be fulfilled tonight.

Logaeir did not need to remind himself that there were hardly any innocent men to be found in An Innis. If you worked on a ship's crew you were working with one of the harbormasters. You were a smuggler, a slave trader, a raider, or some combination of these three. In every case, you were almost certainly a murdering thug. He knew many of these villains personally, though they would not have recognized him now. He was no longer the reckless boy who had fought for his own survival in this dangerous city.

He had once been on a path where he might have eventually become one of the harbormasters himself. Back then, he believed he was going to be a different kind of leader, one that protected the citizens instead of exploiting them. He had led a band of thieves and he had secured the loyalties of the women who lived on the streets. That was until Esivh Rhol had forced him to flee, unwilling to face any competition in running the latter of those two trades. Logaeir felt grateful for what had happened. Had he remained, he surely would have been corrupted past redemption, becoming as evil as any of the men he was now trying to kill. Fifteen years had aged Logaeir, and few people here would ever know him for the boy who he had once been.

As Logaeir expertly killed unsuspecting men on the pier, he conveniently failed to include in his rationalizations that there were no small number of his own men among the Ascomanni who could be considered neither any worse nor any better than the men they were fighting.

The men guarding this pier, and those protecting the ships, had overcome their initial confusion, and the first group of four was charging his men now. As they rushed forward in haste, Logaeir deftly slipped between them, getting in behind and hacking at their calves, sending them to their knees. The Ascomanni fighters nearest to him finished the men off. They had not faced any serious opposition yet, and it was all working out almost too smoothly, but that would start to change when the enemies began to mass in larger numbers.

Logaeir began to hear cries across the water on the other pier as well. Men were dying. From the sounds he could make out, Logaeir had a pretty good understanding of how things were going. They were going extremely well, and his plan was unfolding flawlessly.

Chapter 22

Shaping the Dark

Edryd, accompanied by Hedryn, crossed the paths of troubled men and women as they travelled. They heard at first the whispers, and then later the shouts and cries, of frightened citizens circulating rumors of violence on the piers. Perhaps the fighting had drawn off some of the Ard Ri's men. Whatever the reason, the way was open and there were no guards to deny him entrance when Hedryn and Edryd reached Esivh Rhol's palace. Concluding this meant that he was being invited in, free to enter but perhaps not so free to leave, Edryd obliged. He could think of no good reason to trust the thrall, so Edryd was relieved when Hedryn readily agreed to remain behind, promising to keep the entrance clear. He shouldn't have been surprised. Hedryn was of course wise enough to be afraid of facing Áledhuir.

The place was to all appearances, deserted, and Edryd went unchallenged as he moved through the sprawling complex. Some of the Ard Ri's forces might have been away defending the piers, but the complete absence of resistance confirmed Edryd's suspicions. The way lay open, but he was only working his way further into a trap from which he was not meant to escape.

Edryd's anger had not lessened. The feeling of calm was at a peak, but it did not quiet an anger buried beneath the surface, demanding an opportunity to be expressed. His awareness was heightened beyond anything he had yet experienced, sharply enhanced by focusing his abilities through the sword. Aided by the calm and clarity that came with this coexistent affiliation, Edryd knew that a group of guards had taken up positions blocking the path by which he had come.

He could sense too that most of the building really was deserted, apart from two distinct concentrations of men and women. Edryd navigated his way down a hallway that took him towards the group that included the draugr Áledhuir and his servant Seldur. Esivh Rhol would surely be there as well. If the circumstances were less dire, Edryd might have stopped to wonder how he was seeing everything so clearly. Something had opened within, providing unexpected aid that augmented Edryd's mind and soul in a way that he did not understand.

He knew the positions of everyone in the room before he ever entered, and when he did step through to confront the waiting enemies, Edryd fixed his eyes on Esivh Rhol, who was seated in a large ornate chair at the end of a long wooden banquet table. Two men were hidden against the wall behind hanging tapestries at the opposite end of the room, nearest to where Edryd stood. Another guard left his position along the wall and moved to secure the doorway immediately to Edryd's left, and two more guards on the other side of the table stood nervously, with bolts loaded into the crossbows cradled across their chests.

There were also two guards with drawn swords casually held at their sides, flanking Esivh Rhol's chair. Áledhuir towered behind them in a corner, leaning on an enormous, heavy, two handed sword that was as long as anyone else in the room was tall. Áledhuir's thrall could be seen emerging from a room behind Esivh Rhol's chair, and taking up a position beside his master.

Esivh Rhol broke the silence. "Seoras said we need not send anyone for you. It seems he was right, you came of your own accord."

"He didn't share with you what I was going to do when I got here, or you wouldn't have let me come this far," Edryd said.

He didn't get to expand on this threat. At the sound of Edryd's voice, the guards hidden behind him left their concealment. They were rushing toward their target with thick wooden clubs upraised, ready to knock him down and pound him into submission. Edryd did not turn around. He drew both of Aodra's knives, and guided by the position of the patterns his attackers produced as they disturbed the flow of the dark, he struck hard. They fell, knocked back by the impact, crystalline weapons buried hilt deep in their chests.

The guard who had moved to cover the door backed through the archway, fumbling at the hilt of his sword, trying to draw the weapon from his belt. Edryd ignored him. It took the two arbalest wielding enemies a second to react, and when they finally did, they both fired wide. Edryd had been prepared to either evade or deflect the bolts, but there had been no need. The guards would not be able to fire again. It would take thirty seconds or more for either of them to reload, but only a couple to draw the small deadly axes belted at their sides. Edryd was not going to give them even that much time. He leapt onto the table, and in a move that none of the guards could even follow, he had his hand on the hilt of his sword and he cut through the knotted cloth that had held it in place beneath his coat. The wide arcing length of the sigil blade cut through the throat of the first guard and a second stroke cut deep into the neck of the second.

Half of his opponents were dead or out of the fight, but they were none of them amongst any of the enemies that really mattered. Esivh Rhol had retreated as far back as he could into his chair, paralyzed with fear. Neither Áledhuir nor his thrall had left their positions in the corner. The draugr had simply stood and watched with almost passive interest. He stepped forward now and raised his impossibly large weapon as high as he could—the ceilings were high but not tall enough to allow the draugr to raise the weapon all the way above his head—and in one sudden instant the towering monster brought his weapon down atop the table.

The entire near end of the table was obliterated by the impact. Edryd leapt clear before it collapsed, but the draugr, his thrall, and also Esivh Rhol and his two remaining guards, were all covered in shards of splintered wood. Áledhuir retreated backward into the corner. He did not intend to engage Edryd directly yet. He had just wanted to create some space in which the others could fight. He said something unintelligible in a low rumble that only his thrall understood. In response to his master's command, Seldur stepped into the middle of the room and waited for Edryd to advance. The two swordsmen protecting Esivh Rhol used this as an opportunity to skirt their way past Seldur and escape, following the lead of the first guard who had been covering the door, but was now long gone. No one made any effort to stop them.

Edryd moved forward to meet the thrall's challenge, and acting upon an insight that was not his own, he understood that he needed to take the initiative. For the first time in his life, Edryd consciously took hold of the dark and began to shape it into a pattern. His first swing was blindingly fast, carried enormous force, and was incredibly clumsy. Seldur managed to block but he should have evaded and used the opening that followed to counter. Instead he was driven back a step, staggered by the force behind the attack.

Edryd's second strike was better, more precise and delivered with improved control. His third and fourth efforts were better yet as Edryd incorporated the knowledge and experience gained from working with the speed and power of his own attacks. The thrall was unable to respond, stretching the limits of his skills just trying to ward himself and absorb the impacts. The uneven footing became a weapon for Edryd. Backpedaling precariously through large splintered boards that remained in the aftermath of Áledhuir's destruction of the table, Seldur could not retreat safely. The thrall stumbled, his heel catching awkwardly on the remnant of a broken table leg, compromising his balance and sending him to the ground. Seldur dropped his sword as he instinctively stretched out his arm to break his fall.

Edryd reacted instantly, but his finishing strike never landed. Áledhuir had intervened to protect his thrall. The sigil blade drove a notch an inch deep into the Huldra greatsword, and remained locked in place, bound up by some artifice of the towering draugr's making, shaping the dark with a skill and knowledge that Edryd could not counteract. The two of them struggled, pitting raw strength and raw power against one another.

Seldur broke the stalemate. Recovering quickly, he rose up beneath Edryd, striking upward with the palm of a bare blackened hand. Edryd recognized the technique. It had nearly killed him once. Remembering anew the painful bruising it had left behind and the long weeks it had taken him to recover, Edryd understood it perfectly for what it was now. He could see the components clearly. One part of the pattern protected Seldur's hand, and the rest was a buildup of raw compressed power that would be expended painfully into his chest once it made contact.

A flash of external insight transferred a crucial piece of knowledge into Edryd's mind. Seldur's attack, could with little difficulty, be turned against him. Edryd touched the dark, reshaping the pattern that protected Seldur's hand, shredding the thrall's simple warding in the process. It then took only the slightest of pressure against the compressed forces Seldur had bound together in order to release them. The result shattered every bone in Seldur's hand. The thrall screamed in agony, rolling on the ground clutching at his useless hand as it began to swell.

Áledhuir released the pattern that had been holding Edryd's sword locked to his own, and in a fit of disgust, drove his weapon through Seldur's head, pinning the thrall's lifeless body to the ground, and leaving the point of his great blade buried inches deep into the stone floor.

The opportunity was there, and Edryd did not waste it. He struck immediately, before there was any time for Áledhuir to free his weapon from the floor. Edryd swung the sigil sword at the corner of the creature's neck. The attack sliced through the bunched cloth where Áledhuir had lowered the hood of his cloak, but it glanced off of the draugr's hardened skin. The creature's armored exterior had proven stronger than even the sharpened metal of the sigil blade.

"You cannot kill me, Son of Elduryn," the draugr said. Pure hatred radiated from the creature as the words tumbled up his throat and through his decaying mouth.

Edryd struck once more, the sigil blade alive now with a profusion of intense white light. He smoothly pushed the weapon straight through Áledhuir's chest, right where Edryd supposed the creature's heart would have been. But this creature had no living heart. What had once been Áledhuir's heart had been transformed by arcane means into an object of solid metal. The same was true for the veins that had once carried blood throughout his body. He had no vital organs, only empty cavities where such things had once been. He was the morbid shell of what had once been a living breathing Huldra.

As he bound Edryd's sword to the metal inside his body, Áledhuir laughed. Or at least Edryd thought it might be a laugh, he couldn't tell. "You are as reckless as your father was," said Áledhuir. "His interference destroyed my people. You must content yourself in the next world with having achieved far less."

Áledhuir effortlessly freed his sword, extracting it from the stone floor and the ruinous divided remainder of Seldur's lifeless head. Áledhuir began to raise the weapon in preparation to strike, giving Edryd two obvious choices. He could abandon the sigil blade and retreat, or he could remain there and die. Edryd tried a third desperate option instead.

Reaching out for the dark, he began to shape. Edryd formed a simple pattern he had seen Seoras use before, a method for creating a flame. The technique produced heat, and nothing more. A flame came only if the heat could be made intense enough to ignite something. Edryd focused the pattern through the sigil blade, infusing energy directly through it into the veined metal structures that were embedded within Áledhuir's body.

The draugr did not immediately appreciate what was happening. His long dead body did not feel physical pain. He recognized the danger only when his flesh began to smoke, burning from the inside. Áledhuir tried to interrupt the energies flowing into him, and he tried to disrupt Edryd's shaping, but he lacked the strength to do either. He was not as strong as Edryd. It was too late anyway. Moments later the sigil sword came free as the creature's chest deteriorated into a red hot circular mass of molten metal and disintegrating flesh. Edryd, without taking any pause to wonder at what he had done, swung the sigil blade once more, cleanly passing through the weakened torso of the creature.

The draugr's riven body was split into two pieces. The creature's hips and legs remained upright, like some kind of monstrous statuary. Áledhuir's head, along with his arms which were still connected to what was left of his shoulders, fell to the ground. Disturbed, Edryd delivered a kick, pushing the set of legs over. There was no blood, just a spray of molten metal that rapidly cooled on the stone floor beside the ashen remains of burnt flesh.

"Finish what you started, Son of Elduryn!"

Edryd was startled at hearing his collapsed enemy speak. He couldn't think how Áledhuir produced these words without the help of lungs to compress any air. It soon came to him. Áledhuir had had no lungs to begin with. He spoke by means of subtle shaping, pushing currents of air through his throat. This creature, though horribly broken, was still dangerous.

"To what end?" Edryd said. "Do you think that I owe you such mercy, that I should choose to release you from your ruined body?"

"I will become as Aodra was," Áledhuir threatened. "I will haunt you to your death."

"I should leave you here then, as nothing more than two broken halves of one dead and useless body, sealed up forever where you can do no harm."

If Edryd doubted that the defeated creature was still a threat, that notion was dispelled when Áledhuir began to shape a powerful rage filled pattern. The creature was trying to replicate what Edryd had just done, continuing a process that had ceased before its ultimate completion. Edryd was unsure what would happen if Áledhuir succeeded, but he was reluctant to move close enough to do anything about it. He observed from where he stood, studying what he saw.

Edryd noticed then a golden band around one of the draugr's arms, exposed where the creature's cloak had burnt away. It was similar to the hollow bracelet he was carrying in his coat, only much larger. He thought he heard something for a moment, a kind of inaudible whisper telling him that the armband was Áledhuir's anchor.

The sigil blade surged with light once more and Edryd brought the weapon down, cutting through Áledhuir's arm and dividing the golden band cleanly into two pieces. His weapon did the rest. Without any participation from the exhausted man holding it, Edryd's sword finished the battle. In a struggle in which it was thoroughly overwhelmed, a shaped piece of the dark, a pair to the demonic thing that had been a prison to Aodra, faded from this existence, rejoining the æther where it was delivered into a prison of its own.

Áledhuir was truly dead now, leaving no one else between Edryd and Esivh Rhol.

***

Concealed within an empty storehouse, Oren and his men waited for a signal from Logaeir. They had been in place for several hours now following their arrival over land before the attack had even begun. The call to battle finally came, in the form of three low mournful blasts of an Ascomanni horn, which signaled that they were being called in to support Sarel Krin. The island's defenders had gathered their forces and were mounting an attack on the northern pier, trying to dislodge Krin and his men, who had by this point successfully taken many of the most important ships.

Oren, along with the nine other Sigil Warriors, each in light protective armor and clothed in simple white cloaks, closed in on the rearguard of the defending forces. Someone shouted in alarm as they approached, and several men turned to face them. Sword already in hand, Oren slashed through the exposed leg of the nearest enemy before turning to take another defender in the chest. The men of this island all had various weapons, but they had no practical sense for how to defend themselves. They were more familiar with the myriad ways in which these instruments of violence could be used against defenseless victims, than they were accustomed to engaging with armed opponents who were similarly equipped.

Oren did not forget that these now frightened opponents could still pose a lethal threat if he was careless, but that threat was growing less as he fought his way forward. The defenders were running from him now, wanting no part of the fighting with this group of professional soldiers. The overmatched men had witnessed a dozen of their friends fall in few short seconds of fighting and they had no wish to be next. Oren and his soldiers did not race off in pursuit. The enemies could only flee in one direction and could only run so far. There was no need to expend energy in a chase. This was going to be a long fight.

The panicked rearguard triggered a rush as they ran. Men coalesced into a frightened mass possessed with a combined will, most of them unaware of what it was they were escaping from. The crush of men put ever more pressure on Krin and his group of Ascomanni warriors, but they had prepared for this, and they knew what to do. They formed a phalanx in the middle of the pier. Enemies died, impaled on Ascomanni spears and cut down by Ascomanni swords, but even more fell into the sea on either side of Krin's formation, pushed by the crush of allies surging in behind them. Those that could swim would escape, but were unlikely to rejoin the fighting. Those who could not were fated to drown in the deep water where they had fallen.

Oren and his men were closing the distance and infusing urgency into the crowd of enemies struggling to flee. Not one man turned to face them. Oren had trained for battle since he was a young boy. This should have been the fulfillment of so many years of hard work. But this was not battle. He had never killed before, not until now, and he was not enjoying it. The screams of wounded men up ahead assaulted his ears, and the unheeded cries for help from men drowning in the water demoralized him further. This would be over soon, he promised himself. The fighting that would follow in the city would have to feel less distasteful than this one sided massacre, but if it did not, he was just going to have to withstand it.

Oren killed several more men, terrified men who were trying desperately to run, trapped between Krin's bloodthirsty raiders and the professional warriors over whom Oren had been given command. And then it was over. The surface of the stone pier was slick with blood, and crowded both with the dead and with the dying. Many of Krin's men were injured, and a good number of them were dead. Each and every one of them stared at Oren and the other soldiers with awe. None of the Sigil Corps soldiers had suffered even the slightest harm.

*   *   *

Edryd stood over the defeated draugr. He was reluctant to look away, fearing that Áledhuir might strike at him through the dark if he turned his back. The power that had flowed through Edryd dissipated, and the light from the sigil blade slowly faded away. The calm that he had been infused with faded as well, and Edryd's preternatural sensory perceptions collapsed along with it. He felt blind, and he was beyond the point of exhaustion. His anger had not lessened though, and it prompted him to turn and focus on the object of his ire.

Esivh Rhol was there, tightly gripping the arms of his chair, finding it impossible to respond to what he had seen. His breathing was rapid and his eyes darted around the room. There was no one left to help him. He lacked the will to confront Edryd, or even the resolve to rise and attempt to flee. His mind was working though, desperately trying to find a way to save himself from the Blood Prince. That is who this was—the man who the dark haired little girl had promised would be coming to kill him.

"I didn't hurt her," Esivh Rhol said, pleading fervently.

"Who didn't you hurt?" Edryd demanded.

Esivh Rhol didn't respond. He felt confused, and afraid to answer.

"I know that you killed Irial," Edryd said, helping Esivh Rhol along, "so who was it that you didn't hurt?"

"Eithne, I didn't hurt Eithne. I never touched her," Esivh Rhol said, stressing the point that he had never touched the girl. His reputation being what it was, it was important to be clear about that.

"You mean apart from leading a group of draugar and their thralls to Eithne's home, killing her sister, and subjecting her to the gods know what, you did not harm her," Edryd corrected. "Why did you take her? Was it all just to bring me to you? I hope you are pleased with the result."

"That isn't why..." Esivh Rhol began to explain, before stopping himself as he seized upon a small hope, a means by which he could negotiate his safety. "If you let me go, I will tell you where she is."

The Ard Ri's attempt to bargain with Eithne's life enraged Edryd. Without considering what he was doing, Edryd dropped the sigil sword and piled both of his arms into Esivh Rhol's chest. Grabbing a fistful of the man's expensive tunic in each hand, Edryd pulled the man up and slammed his back against the heavy oak chair. "I know where she is," Edryd said, "she's locked in the next room."

"There must be something," Esivh Rhol cried out hopelessly.

"Look around," Edryd said, gesturing towards the five dead men and what was left of the body of the draugr. "Those men are dead because I had to go through them to get to you. There are no bargains to be made here. Do you think that there could possibly be anything that would mean more to me than your death?"

Esivh Rhol tried to maneuver, reaching for the jeweled dagger belted at his waist. He managed to free it from its sheath, but Edryd easily wrested it from him before he could do anything with it. Edryd took a step back, examining the weapon, and saw the traces of blood that Esivh Rhol had not managed to clean out of the crevices between the hilt and the blade. Esivh Rhol had an unusual reaction to seeing Edryd holding the knife. The object was precious to Esivh Rhol, all the more so now for the memory of what he had done with it. He wanted it back.

Edryd saw the fire in the Ard Ri's eyes, and knew then for certain that this was the weapon Esivh Rhol had used to kill Irial. Esivh Rhol could in turn see what the Blood Prince intended to do now, and in reaction to that knowledge, he surprised both himself and Edryd by suddenly became defiant. "Give that back to me," he demanded. "Give that back, and then it will not be said that you were guilty of killing an unarmed man."

Edryd had become what could be called experienced in the discipline of inflicting death, but in every previous instance, when he had taken someone's life, he had never once debated in his mind how best to dispatch the opponent. The circumstances had dictated his actions, the immediacy of conflict recommending certain responses which were singularly appropriate in each situation. Edryd was now imagining a dozen different deaths for Esivh Rhol though, none of which would last long enough or cause enough pain.

Ultimately, he just wanted the life of this evil man to be ended, and it didn't matter how it was accomplished. Edryd drove the point of the blade upward beneath Esivh Rhol's jaw, pushing the point up through the middle of the man's skull. Edryd had thought this would kill the Ard Ri instantly, but it took a minute for the man to die. He felt very little satisfaction, but even less remorse.

Once he was sure that the Ard Ri was dead, Edryd inspected the door set in the back wall. Contrary to expectation, the door was not locked. He pushed it open and stepped inside. He was in an antechamber to a much larger space which was accessed through a broad open archway. Upon the end of a large canopied bed which dominated the center of Esivh Rhol's bedroom, lay a simple red dress made of fine silk cloth. It was sized to fit a young child. From where he stood, Edryd could hear her crying, but he could not see Eithne.

Moving through the archway, Edryd found her huddled in a ball, trying to hide in the corner. All of her clothing, everything but a short simple shift, had been taken. Upon seeing Edryd kneeling down and gently trying to reassure her that she was safe, Eithne's terror turned into teary eyed relief and she ran towards him. Throwing her arms around Edryd's neck, she locked them tightly as if her safety rested upon holding on.

"I knew you would come," she said. "I told them what would happen, but they didn't believe me." She stated this not as a confirmation of the faith she had held that he would come, but with the conviction that came from truly having known.

Edryd worked free from her grip, and looked her over to confirm that she had not been physically harmed. She had no injuries, and now that she felt safe again, she was probably handling the situation better than he was. Edryd removed his dark coat and wrapped her in it, the metal emblems pinned under his collar chiming as they made contact with each other. The coat was far too large for Eithne, and its length trailed behind her when she walked, but she needed something, and he was not about to use anything that might have belonged to the late Ard Ri.

Taking Edryd's hand, Eithne followed him into the anteroom and then to the door that led back to the banquet hall. Edryd sought out an alternate exit but he could find none. The remorse and shame hit him now. If he were given the chance to change what had just happened, he would not have done anything different, but Edryd did not feel prepared to enter that room again and confront the deaths that he had caused. More importantly, he could not bear for Eithne to know. She certainly could not be allowed to see any of it. Edryd remembered something now that filled him with even more shame. Irial had once told him that if he trained with Seoras, that it would darken him. He knew this now for the truth that it had been. He had ignored her warning, and the cost for having done so had been steep.

"You have to promise," Edryd said, "that you will not open your eyes. You have to keep them closed until I say it is okay to open them, no matter what."

Eithne obediently shut her eyes and Edryd took her by the hands and pulled her arms up and around his neck where she held on tightly. He could no longer see her face as he carried her, but he could tell that her eyes were still shut by the tension in her brow pressed up against the side of his head. Edryd opened the door and began to pick his way through the carnage.

He was in a hurry to leave the room, but Edryd took his time as he circled around the debris from the battle, carefully avoiding all of the fallen bodies. Everything was as it had been, except that reservoirs of blood had now expanded beneath some of the bodies of the men that he had killed. Esivh Rhol was still dead, and Áledhuir was still in two pieces, but something else seemed to be missing. As he neared the entrance that led out into the hallway, Edryd realized what it was that had changed. The first two men he had killed were still there, but he couldn't see the weapons that he had killed them with. It wasn't a trick of the light, the translucent blades disappearing when viewed at a certain angle, they were gone.

There was no evidence that anything else had been moved or taken, no other sign that anyone had been there, but it was enough to heighten the need Edryd felt to leave and find somewhere safe. He was down the hallway and had gone the length of another intersecting corridor before he told Eithne she could open her eyes. He realized he had not thought things through this far, and had no idea where it was he should go. There would be fighting in the city and no path leaving the palace was likely to be safe. Unhappily, he accepted that the best option for now would be to remain in the palace.

The confusing passageways, down which they travelled, often turned in unexpected ways and were frequently broken by archways that opened upon an unending series of small and large rooms. Among these were included the living quarters that housed staff, a few finely appointed rooms which were reserved for guests, multiple kitchens, and grand open spaces suited for large parties to gather for entertainment. Finding a small bedroom that could be secured from within and easily defended, Edryd let Eithne down.

"We will need to stay here for a while," Edryd said. "Your Uncle Logaeir is causing trouble in the city, but we can leave after it settles down."

Eithne, with an inclination of her head, indicated that she understood.

Edryd sat exhausted in the lone chair in the small room, and Eithne took a seat on the bed. She had not spoken since leaving Esivh Rhol's room. He was reluctant to speak himself.

"I'm sorry," he managed to say before his emotions robbed him of his ability to continue. "This, all of this, it was my fault," he said once he collected himself.

He could see from her reaction that this was not what she wanted to hear. She needed reassurance and words of comfort, not some weak apology for something she did not blame him for.

"I can't fix this," he admitted, "but I promise I will make it better if I can."

"Not just for me," she said. "You are going to make it better for everyone." She smiled when she saw that she had just taken away some of his sadness. A short while later she curled up on a corner of the bed, and using Edryd's coat as a blanket, she fell asleep.

***

The risks so far had been well within what could be managed under the constraints of Logaeir's plans. The heavy initial fighting had taken place on the other side, but once Oren and his men joined the battle in support of Sarel Krin's attack, it had turned into a decisive victory for the Ascomanni. Logaeir, while in the process of attacking the southern pier, had fared less well. He had not been reinforced quickly enough, and nearly all of his men were dead.

Logaeir had anticipated these difficulties, and knowing what he would face he had surrounded himself with the most violent and most dangerous of all the men the Ascomanni could boast to have in its ranks. These men had been ideal for the nature of the dangerous undisciplined fighting that had taken place on the southern pier. Their losses had been acceptable, perhaps necessary even. Paring down their number meant there would not be so many counted among these the least manageable and most bloodthirsty of the Ascomanni warriors, with which he would need to contend once the battle was over.

Their initial objectives taken, Logaeir ordered a pause to consolidate the positions that they now held and make the necessary preparations to organize the next stages of the attack. With the arrival of the *Retribution* and two other ships, Logaeir now had another one hundred twenty three fresh Ascomanni fighters to replace the thirty that had fallen beside him in the initial assault. Meeting up with Oren and Krin, their combined forces were about three hundred men. That number could swell to closer to four hundred Ascomanni if they needed to call in reserve forces that were remaining with the ships.

It was now time to turn their attentions to the scattered assets guarded by the four harbormasters, who were each jealously protecting their own properties. This predictable self-interested behavior, which had been an assumption in all of his strategies, effectively deprived the harbormasters of any chance to mount a credible resistance to the overwhelming forces that Logaeir would bring against each of them in succession.

The homes and properties of a man named Jedron Feld were the first to fall. In an entirely bloodless affair, Logaeir accepted the surrender of all his men. There had been inside help, including key men in Jedron Feld's employment induced by means of bribery and other persuasions to aid the Ascomanni cause.

Kedwyn Saivelle was the next target. In terms of raw numbers and enthusiasm for their employer, none of the other overlords could match Saivelle. Logaeir's men had long ago scouted the hidden positions of Saivelle's outermost guards. Oren and his men took to the rooftops and used that information, and their powerful Edoric longbows, to silently pick apart the deadly arbalest wielding snipers who occupied positions of advantage in and around their master's properties.

Logaeir then mounted assaults on the ground. The battle stalled at times, with the defenders using fortified positions to offset inferior numbers, but the men in white cloaks turned these fights into a route each time they joined the battle. In the end, terrified of Oren and his men, the last of Saivelle's forces threw their master out before them and begged for mercy. In this engagement, the Sigil Corps Soldiers had proven to be everything Logaeir expected, fulfilling their roles in ways that exceeded what Logaeir had actually planned.

Verden Dressore was next on Logaeir's list. Word of Saivelle's fate having reached him, Dressore gave up without a fight. He had always been weaker than the rest of the harbormasters, so this wasn't much different from what had been expected.

Sidrin Eildach was all that remained now. Being wiser than the rest of his counterparts, he understood this was a battle that he could not win, but he also knew that he had enough strength to give him a position from which to bargain, and he acted accordingly. He and his men barricaded their strongholds and refused to come out. A messenger was sent offering assurances to the Ascomanni that Eildach was willing to negotiate away his empire, giving it up without a fight, if he could secure a place for himself and his men in the new power structure that would be replacing the old one. Eildach could be practical like that. He had seen such radical shifts before and he had always survived them.

This suited Logaeir's needs perfectly. He had more than enough men to spare to besiege the last of the harbormasters indefinitely, and it was actually a matter of great advantage for Logaeir to occupy the Ascomanni forces with this final obstacle for as long as possible. Settling for something less than a complete outright victory was fine, if it deprived his men of the freedom to rampage through the town once there were no more enemies to defeat. Logaeir would have to start his negotiations for Eildach's surrender by sending the man a thank you note.

In all the fighting, Logaeir estimated that there had been eighty Ascomanni who had fallen. There were perhaps between three and four times that number dead among the defenders who had opposed them. He had asked Oren, who had refused to answer, how many the

Sigil Corps could take credit for. Logaeir's own count would have placed their contribution as at least a third of the enemy dead, and for all of that, Oren had not lost anyone. None of his men were even injured. The white cloaks of the Sigil Corps soldiers were stained crimson with blood, but it all belonged to their enemies. The men on every side of the fighting had begun to look upon them with awe.

The success was making Oren increasingly difficult to manage. Leading his group of ten sigil warriors, Oren was now acting on his own, and had become less willing to take any orders. The fighting had seemed to place him in a particularly foul mood. Logaeir, in the time that he had known Oren, had always imagined him as the type who enjoyed battle. The officer had certainly shown a passion for combat training. That he seemed so repelled by his own handiwork on the field of battle, was a surprise.

"We are leaving for the palace, Logaeir," Oren said, as they stood outside the gates of Sidrin Eildach's home.

"Not yet."

"You have this well in hand. It is time my men and I do what we came here for. We are taking our due."

Logaeir made his frustration abundantly clear in his response. "Don't expect me to rush in to help you if it goes wrong."

The bulk of Esivh Rhol's forces were already dead. They had fallen defending his fleet of ships and in the counter offensive trying to retake the northern pier from Krin, so it was not without reason that Oren felt that he and his men could take the palace on their own. So far though, no one had encountered the draugar or their thralls and it was becoming increasingly likely that they would find them at the palace. If they did, the small company of professional soldiers would not be enough to confront that threat. "There is too much unaccounted for," Logaeir cautioned. "Do no more than scout the area. I will have men ready to assist at first light."

"Take too long, and the fighting will be over before they make it," said Oren.

It would do no good to warn Oren about the draugar. Oren was already well aware. He understood the risks, and reminding him now would only make him more determined to rush to confront the danger. Believing that his captain would be in need of their help, nothing was going to stop or delay him. Logaeir watched the soldiers leave, and unable to do anything to stop their progress, he made all possible haste in putting together a complement of Ascomanni warriors to follow them.

***

Edryd, feeling grateful that Eithne was sleeping peacefully, left her alone in the room. He brought a chair with him into the hallway and positioned himself where he could see anyone approaching, and where it would not be obvious which door he was guarding. The clarity of vision with which he had been gifted earlier was gone. For a while it had seemed as though he had lost the ability to perceive the currents of the dark altogether, but he realized that this was wrong. He had simply been blinded by a bright light in the darkness. That light had illuminated everything for a time, but once its guidance faded, it took time to adjust to the loss. Even then, the world would forever seem a darker place for having had the experience of knowing what he had lost.

It was an altogether boring vigil. The palace was silent and almost completely empty. No sounds of the chaos in the city could be heard here, and the few people inside the palace, did not leave the shelter of their rooms. When someone finally did come, Edryd cursed his luck. It was Aed Seoras. Edryd was worried, as he had no idea what Seoras intended. Remaining seated, Edryd tried not to betray his anxiety, but his concern surged when he noticed that Seoras was carrying a long simple sword in his hand. He had the Edorin Sigil Blade. It made Edryd painfully aware that he no longer had a weapon of his own, but that concern was of almost no merit when compared to the more important problem. If the sword had enabled Edryd to manifest the powers which he had called upon during his battle with the draugr, just how impossibly strong might Seoras become when wielding it?

"Honestly," Seoras said, "leaving something like this lying about. How you manage to survive in this world I couldn't guess."

It seemed to Edryd that Seoras was impossibly blind to just how much his student was at the mercy of the master shaper's power right now. Seoras made an even less accurate judgment based upon Edryd's behavior, wondering how powerful Edryd must be that he could leave the sigil sword behind after a battle as though it were some trifling thing of only minor importance.

"I failed to see the truth all this time," Seoras said, shaking his head, "and in my arrogance presumed to be able to teach you." He held out the sigil sword, offering it to his pupil.

Edryd gingerly accepted the weapon, not quite wanting it, but grateful to get it away from his master. The sword seemed happy, somehow, to be back in his hand, but nothing happened as he took hold of the weapon. There was no expansion of his mind, no enhanced perceptions, and no external clarity.

"I said that if you lived through this, that we would have a debt to settle," said Seoras.

"You were angry," Edryd pointed out, "so I didn't take that to have meant that you owed anything to me."

"I was angry," Seoras acknowledged, "and I remain so, but it is clear to me now that I did, and still do, owe you a great debt." Seoras seemed relieved as he said this, as if at the release of some painful restraint. He was definitely pleased about something, but Edryd couldn't begin to guess what.

"I could have used your help today, had you been serious about balancing that debt," Edryd said.

The shaper's eyes hardened. He did not appreciate the criticism, or perhaps his reaction was covering some other emotion. "I was prevented," was all Seoras said.

"I cannot accept that," Edryd said. "If you cared about Irial or Eithne, nothing should have prevented you from protecting them."

Seoras became harder still. "No one said I cared anything for either of them," he said, glancing in the direction of Eithne's room. Despite Edryd's efforts to conceal it, Seoras knew exactly where she was.

Edryd pulled back. He didn't need to have an explanation, not right now at least, and the last thing he wanted to be doing was to make this man angry.

"I have questions about what happened," Seoras said, "and I have answers for you too, information that you need to know."

Edryd waited for Seoras to continue. He was certain he would not have the answers that Seoras sought, but he was willing to hear what the man had to say.

"There is no time to talk now," Seoras said, sensing that their time would be short before it would be interrupted by the arrival of Edryd's friends from the Sigil Corps. "We will need to talk where there is no chance it will be overheard. I want you to meet me tomorrow in the ruins on the coast," Seoras said, before leaving abruptly, eager not to be seen by anyone else.

Edryd's immediate inclination was to refuse this request, but Seoras had been assuming compliance, not asking for it. There would have been no point in expressing any objections to the proposed meeting. If Edryd decided tomorrow that it was unwise, he simply wouldn't go.

Chapter 23

The Broken Oath

Oren and his soldiers appeared almost before Seoras had left, but by an act of providence, or more likely as a result of the latter's desire to remain unseen and his skill in doing so, the soldiers had not crossed his path. There had been no fighting. Upon reaching the palace gates Oren had found Hedryn waiting, anxious to offer assistance, with the extent of his abilities to provide such service, evidenced by the corpses of a good half dozen of Esivh Rhol's men in the courtyard, among them Hagan and Cecht. This Hedryn had done in keeping with the task that Edryd had given him to keep the entrance to the palace clear. Those few remaining guards who had been in the palace but had not already fallen victim to the Blood Prince, were also dead. Seoras had seen to that, killing any man who hadn't had the good sense to flee.

Favored by these circumstances, all of which had proven contrary to the far more cautious expectations with which Oren and his men had begun their assault, the Sigil Corps had taken possession of the palace unopposed, and it was now being used as their base. By morning, it was also serving as one of several locations for treating men injured in the fighting. At Edryd's request, someone had been sent to bring Uleth, who was doing a thorough and competent job at directing the task of attending to the most seriously injured men.

Uleth still had some of Irial's old clothing, a dress and some shoes that she had once worn when she had been a child, and he had sent Neysim to go and collect them for Eithne, along with a number of medical texts. Near the end of the afternoon, when the city had settled down enough that it was safe to do so, Edryd left the palace along with Eithne and Uleth. Together they followed the familiar road that led east towards the cottage that Irial and Eithne had called home. Eithne held Edryd's hand tightly as they walked, trying to be strong, and remaining very quiet. Edryd understood her feelings. He wished they were going somewhere else and that he did not have to face this loss, or at the very least that Eithne should not have to bear it too.

Smoke rose in the air trailing off to the east. It was too far towards the south and east to be coming from the cottage, but it was still reason for concern. Eithne saw it too, and looked to Edryd for reassurances that he could not give her.

"We should gather flowers," Edryd said, as they came to the place where he and Irial had often left the roadway, seeking out a variety of wild plants which grew there.

"What kind?" Eiepilthne asked, very much in favor of the idea as she brought her hands up, letting go of Edryd's hand in the process. She was obviously eager to be off, needing only the least push of encouragement.

"Find some mountain iris," Edryd suggested, "and some of her other favorites as well."

Edryd thought that Eithne might run on ahead, but she remained with him, and together they walked towards the streamside meadow. He had formed such pleasant memories with Irial on those occasions when they had visited this place, and he could picture her now, enjoying the natural peace that could be found here. Edryd helped Eithne across the stream once they reached it, and she was soon roaming the boundaries of the meadow in search of beautiful flowers. Uleth arrived just behind them.

Choosing his customary spot, Edryd sat down upon the ground. Uleth remained standing, watching Eithne, who was carefully moving amongst and choosing out selections from the many flowers that grew here.

"Irial would have loved this place," Uleth said.

"She did love it," Edryd responded. He then fell silent for a moment, feeling something he did not know how to express. "I wish everyone could have seen her as I did. If they had, they would all mourn as I do."

Edryd looked to Uleth, who turned and answered, "She may have been feared and hated by those who remained in An Innis, accounting her a worker of evil spells, but years ago, Irial helped a great number of the disempowered victims of this island escape to the settlements." By this Uleth meant the people who now lived under the patronage of the Ascomanni encampment at Darkpool, former citizens of An Innis who had fled to escape enslavement under the rule of the harbormasters. "Those men and women owe Irial their lives, and they are among the many who will not soon forget her."

Uleth sat down a short distance from Edryd and proceeded to tell him more. The slave ships of An Innis had developed a reputation for being disease ridden nuisances, harming the prices the men of An Innis could expect to obtain in the markets. To combat this, they took to separating out sick slaves before departing. If the cause of illness was suspected to be one of the plagues that had ravaged An Innis in years past, those slaves would be killed. In desperation to escape their fates, even knowing it could mean death to do so, men and women began to feign illness to avoid being taken and sold.

Irial was known by then as a healer in An Innis. Uleth had trained her. She begged for permission to treat these men and women who had fallen sick, but their masters refused. They preferred not to assume the risk of the diseases spreading further.

By this time there were already rumors about the returned and whispers of cursed men and women walking the world as corpses after their deaths. Irial played upon these fears by telling the men who would one day become the harbormasters that this is what they were facing. She told them that only she could make certain that the dying would remain dead. If they did not allow her to do her work, she swore that when these men and women returned from death, they would seek out those who had wronged them and take their revenge.

"She hadn't planned anything beyond trying to frighten them," said Uleth, "and none of slave masters believed her."

"But then something happened to them. Something that changed their minds," said Edryd.

"Krin happened to them," Uleth said, confirming Edryd's guess. "All in the course of one night, he killed the slave masters of three different ships, stealing and escaping in the largest of them, a slave ship called the *Black Strand*."

"And that was the beginning of the Ascomanni?" Edryd asked.

"No, just the beginning of Captain Krin, the Ascomanni came later," said Uleth.

The old man went on to explain that Krin had not left any witnesses behind, only rumors. Those rumors became stories that were the fulfillment of Irial's warnings. Dead victims of these ships had returned, or so people believed, and they had killed the masters who had bound them in life. This became the accepted truth in An Innis, and so they all then heeded Irial's demands that she be allowed to calm the spirits of the sick, so that they would not return seeking revenge.

The cottage was just one of several buildings prepared as places away from the city, where Irial could help ease the suffering of the dying, and prevent their return once they succumbed to the final stages of their illness. For those who had become sick, she tried to heal them. For those who recovered, and those who had only pretended to be ill, Irial arranged in secret for their escape to a base Krin had set up to the south of An Innis. They made use of the tunnels hidden under the homes where she cared for them to avoid being seen. The people she cared for were all expected to die. No one would miss them when they escaped.

"Did no one wonder why everyone died?" Edryd wondered. "Were none of those who recovered ever seen by people in the town again in the years since?"

"But they were seen," answered Uleth. "That only reinforced the notions of the returned, making them ever more into things to be feared. They could not return to live in An Innis if they had wanted to, which they did not. Instead, by subterfuge, and with caution and care, we had their loved ones feign illness as well, marking them in places with dyes and paints to simulate disease. Irial rescued more than a hundred in this way."

Edryd understood now. Irial had through her kindness, created the Ascomanni. She was the benevolent patron to these men and women, who in a sense, had truly passed on from their former lives and yet lived on thanks to her intervention. It made sense now why she had been so connected to the Ascomanni, and it explained how she had developed the reputation which had made her an outcast.

"There are those that cared about her deeply," Uleth said. "I believe you will soon see how great her influence was felt." Edryd could feel that Uleth's grief was greater than his own. She was family to him. He had raised her as a daughter, and he missed her now as only a father could.

Their conversation was interrupted by Eithne's return. She held bundles of beardtongue, aster, and mountain iris, collected from across the meadow. The attractive purple and blue flowers were beautiful, bringing out the sapphire in Eithne's eyes. Edryd, seeking to confirm what he had seen the night before, envisioned Eithne through the effects she had on the currents of the dark. She manifested as a beautiful pure light, which interacted with the darkness in the way that only a shaper could.

Edryd understood now as well, why Irial had insisted that he must be the one to help Eithne. Irial had hoped that he would guide Eithne and protect her while she began to understand her potential. As he thought on this, Edryd was shaken by a fear as powerful as any he had ever experienced, feeling painfully unequal to the task with which Irial had entrusted him. He could not afford to fail Irial in this. He had promised her that much.

Turning towards Uleth, Edryd began to suggest that they should leave, but there was no one there. Edryd was still relying on his ability to perceive the dark. He should have been able to confirm Uleth's presence, even if he had moved somewhere else. As Edryd concentrated on finding the man, his attentions were taken eastward. Eventually he found himself focused on the ruins. No, not on the ruins, but on the forests which encircled and hid them, it made no sense.

Edryd tried to return to what he could physically see and hear. At first, although the meadow, Eithne, and everything else began to return into focus, Uleth was not there. Edryd was struggling to pick up on even a hint of the man's presence. Finally, concentrating fully on only what he could physically see, Uleth was there once more, having not moved from where he had been to begin with. Edryd wondered for a moment if Uleth could be shrouded. It didn't seem likely, but it was the only explanation he had right now.

There was another possibility. Edryd concentrated once more on seeing the man through the dark, and he found it, an insubstantial pattern that mimicked the presence of a person. Uleth was the mere image of a man. It could fool the senses, but it wasn't really there. Edryd immediately thought of the Ældisir and the false images she had made him see. Somewhere inside, he felt a confirmation that he was right to draw this connection.

"I thought maybe some lanceleaf too," Edryd said to Eithne, so that he could buy a moment to speak with the illusion that was Uleth. Eithne set the bundled flowers down and bounded away in search of the yellow flowers Edryd had named.

"You are not real," Edryd said. Thinking about it now, Edryd could not recall visibly seeing this man interact with anything. Uleth had unlocked the door to his home, but had not opened it. He had made Edryd carry the basket with the loaves of bread into the kitchen, instead of accepting them when they were offered. Edryd had seen Uleth tend to sick patients, but he had only examined them, directing others in the treatments.

"I would say that none of us are," Uleth answered. The conversation began to remind Edryd of the book he had read in Irial's cottage. The one Eithne had tried to explain to him. "I could not fool one who sees so clearly for long," Uleth said, sighing deeply, having understood that it had always been only a matter of time.

"You are a shaper," Edryd said.

"No, I do not shape," Uleth corrected, "or at least no more than other men. Less than any other man, I should say."

"Then by what power do you do this?" Edryd asked, believing that he was being lied to.

"Men shape the dark, but only as part of a greater design," Uleth explained. "We are all part of the shape. If you know the design, it can be made to suggest something else, all without ever touching it."

Edryd thought he almost understood some of that, but the idea seemed more of an illusion that even Uleth.

"A man is a pebble," Uleth continued, "sunk in the current of a stream if you will, that circles and flows around all of us. As pebbles go though, you are I think, a very important one. I tremble to speak with you like this, out of a fear that I might dislodge you from your place in the pattern."

"Who are you?" Edryd asked, having become timid with awe.

"One of the Ascetics," Uleth answered, "though, I do not know that I can call myself one any longer. I will have been the last, once I am gone. I had thought I might train Irial, so that she could carry some of my burden. I count it a kindness to her that I never did, and in any event, that opportunity has passed."

Edryd recognized the name Uleth spoke of. It belonged to a group of sorcerers who upheld an oath that forbade certain aspects of their arcane arts as a penance for wrongs committed by their ancestors. They had been destroyed over five hundred years ago by the dark sorcerer Ulensorl. Perhaps not all it appeared.

"Train Eithne," Edryd said. "She seems to have the mind for such things." Edryd did not know whether she really did, he just knew how smart she was. He had, he was ashamed to admit, suggested this idea because of how heavily he had begun to feel the responsibility that Irial had given to him. Surely Uleth was a more capable teacher.

"No," Uleth insisted firmly. "She is too much like you. She has a part to play, and I do not dare interfere with it. You will need to be the one to help her grow strong."

Irial clearly had been influenced by this man, Edryd realized. Her certainty about who and what he was, and insisting that he must help Eithne, all had a source. It had been Uleth.

"You speak as though you know what is to come?" Edryd said, not yet prepared to believe what he was himself suggesting.

"No," Uleth disagreed. "I am afraid I am giving you the wrong impression. I have no real wisdom or power, only a few weak tricks and bits of lost knowledge. I don't seek to see the future. It is, I think, unwise to try, for doing so would be to seek something that does not exist."

"But you know the fates of others."

"I see the world, and those of us who inhabit it, as they are, or I try to," Uleth said, trying vainly to explain himself to an uncomprehending Edryd. "I can see your place in the pattern, and the shapes you can take within it. I cannot predict what will come, but I can see that you bring change. That is all. I can tell you only this, when you act, you must try to see all ends before you decide."

Edryd had no immediate response for this. Uleth seemed to be speaking nonsense, but that nonsense was making Edryd feel uncomfortable, and he was beginning shake. "I have not often been faulted for having acted without thought," Edryd finally said, "only for failing to act, or for being too harsh or too selfish when I did."

"Then they have not understood you." Uleth's words were quiet and full of empathy, as though he could see Edryd's suffering. "You are not an ordinary man. You are burdened with an importance. Your choices will often be hard ones, and they will carry consequences."

These words recalled to Edryd's mind a similar admonishment Seoras had once given him. But where Seoras's words had been dark, urging Edryd to seek greater power, Uleth's words of caution were an expression of sympathy, and though Edryd took no comfort from them, he recognized the wisdom that they held. He could see Irial's kindness in this man, and he felt instinctively that he could trust Uleth.

"You should help me then," Edryd said.

"No," Uleth said, even more firmly than he had when Edryd had suggested that he teach Eithne.

"I need to understand my power. I have to learn how to shape."

"You have not been listening," Uleth replied. "I am a sorcerer, and an incompetent one at that. I do not shape."

"Shaping, is it something evil?" Edryd asked.

"No, it is neither good nor bad. But it is something I have no talent for, and it is an area in which you have been hobbled as well. Even if I were a shaper of great power, you would not have the ability to learn. There is a reason that Seoras failed to progress your awakening. There is nothing I can do."

Edryd was not convinced. Clearly there were things that Uleth could do, things that even Seoras could not. "I need guidance," Edryd pled.

"The things I could impart," Uleth said slowly, choosing his words carefully, "are things you should not learn from me. I would be a blind man teaching a child about a world filled with light and color. I would forever distort your perceptions, and it would prevent you from seeing truth."

Uleth went silent as Eithne returned. She smiled at Edryd and held out the samples of lanceleaf that he had sent her after. She had also harvested clusters of woodsage, and had picked several beautiful stream orchids. Edryd allowed his conversation with Uleth to end. Eithne and Edryd, dividing between them the flowers that Eithne had collected, made their way back to the road, followed by the image of Uleth, which of course carried nothing.

Falling back, so that he could inspect Uleth, Edryd noticed that the man's feet left tracks in the ground, but they did not stir any dust into the air as they should have done on the dry earth. As soon he noticed this, small clouds began to rise behind Uleth. It might have been Uleth, correcting a flaw, but Edryd suspected it was instead a product of being made to see, whatever it was that he expected he should see.

Edryd was able to confirm this suspicion, for he found that he could make Uleth's foot trail appear or disappear, by simply imagining that the earth of the roadway was either more hard, or more soft, than it truly was. There was a thrill in this discovery, but it left Edryd feeling unsettled. He had no idea who or what Uleth really was. These were not the questions Edryd should have been asking. Uleth was precisely who he showed himself to be. What Uleth hid, from everyone, was where he was.

The opportunity to explore the nature of the illusion did not last long, as they had not been far from the cottage. Arriving before the lonely structure, the scene of violence that had been in front of the building the day before was gone, with all traces of blood having been swept away. The bodies of the men that Ruach had killed had been moved a great distance away and burnt in a fire, accounting for the smoke that they had all seen earlier.

A crowd of men maneuvered massive stones off to the south of the cottage. They were constructing the cavity for a funeral barrow. Three women were not far away, weaving meadowsweet through the recesses of a funeral pyre that had been built up earlier out of stacks of dead wood. Neither Edryd nor Eithne knew these people, but those present had known Irial it seemed, and they had come to show her the honor and respect that she was owed.

Edryd felt numb as he entered the cottage. Krin was there, at the larger of the room's two tables. He was drunk, and it did not appear that he had slept. His left forearm had been heavily bandaged and he had an ugly red cut just beneath his left eye. Upon seeing Edryd and Eithne he moved from his seat, and Edryd was caught unprepared as the large man unexpectedly crushed him in a great enveloping hug. He released Edryd just as quickly, and as Krin pulled away, the Ascomanni captain did not appear afraid to show everyone that he had been crying.

"Logaeir told me that you did justice for her," Krin said. "I thank you for that."

"Where is Logaeir?" Edryd asked.

"He will be here before nightfall," answered a young woman keeping a vigil next to Irial's room.

Everyone turned to face her. "This is my daughter, Ruelle," said Krin, introducing her. Like Krin, she also appeared to have been crying, the strongly sun affected skin of her kind face streaked with tears. Edryd was a little surprised. He hadn't imagined Krin as a father.

"I looked to her as a sister," Ruelle said. "A great many of us did." This comment made Edryd think of Eithne, the young girl beside him now whom Irial had cared for as a true sister would.

Edryd took Eithne's hand, and together they entered Irial's room. She lay in the bed positioned as she had been the day before. Eithne placed her flowers atop her sister and stood beside the bed. She remained silent for a long while before turning away and running to her room, just ahead of the tears that she could no longer hold back.

Not knowing how to comfort Eithne, or even himself, Edryd pulled a chair over beside her door and waited. He wished that he too could hide somewhere. A part of him was glad that he was not known to many of these people, and especially glad that they did not know him as the Blood Prince, but he did feel like an intruder here, beside so many people that he did not recognize. It did not feel like the home he had known for the past little while. Krin pulled over another chair and sat down beside him.

"I knew her for longer than you did, and I will miss her, but I know how you felt about Irial. We could all see it," he said.

Edryd was taken aback. Krin was speaking of something Edryd had hardly admitted to himself, but it didn't matter any longer. It was not something to hide. "She did not return those feelings," Edryd said. He couldn't think why she should have.

"She did care for you," Krin said. "She held you in the highest possible regard. I think though, that maybe, she thought that you were a little too young."

Edryd would have done almost anything to change the subject, but Krin wasn't the sort to cooperate, and the man was drunk.

"I was supposed to protect her," Edryd said, choking back tears.

"You did everything you could," Krin said, grabbing a hold of Edryd's shoulder. "You did everything that anyone could."

His friend was trying to help, but it was not working. "None of this would have happened if I hadn't come here," said Edryd.

"No, none of this would have happened," Krin agreed. "This island would still be under the control of demons and criminals, and my people would be facing the threat of starvation in the winter, persisting on the margin of an ever dwindling supply of food, if you had not come here. Without help from you and your men, our attack yesterday would never have succeeded."

"I was not responsible for any of that," Edryd protested.

"And neither were you responsible for what happened to Irial. That it might not have happened had you never come to An Innis, does not make it your fault."

Edryd understood the truth in Krin's words, but he wasn't prepared to accept it. He wasn't going to be able to forgive himself so easily.

"If you need anything, if you ever need anything, you only have to ask," Krin said, grabbing Edryd's shoulder once more in his broad hand. He gave Edryd a solid reassuring nudge, before releasing his grip and walking away, leaving Edryd to sort through his grief.

Edryd realized how selfish he was being. He had been directly responsible for a handful of deaths himself yesterday, but hundreds more had also died, all of them in some way under the name of the Blood Prince. Edryd had much more to answer for than just his failure to protect Irial. There would be other people here who were mourning the deaths of people that they had loved, and many more than that had been hurt. One of those people had been Ruach, injured performing a duty Edryd should have been there to do himself. He was here now, recovering.

Feeling a guilt that came from not having given thought to Ruach since arriving at the cottage, Edryd rose and walked the short distance to his old room. His friend was sleeping peacefully on the bed as Edryd entered. Ludin Kar, who continued to attend to him, slept too, slumped over in his chair and resting his head on a table beside the bed. Edryd remembered now where he had heard the man's name before. Ludin Kar was the author of the book that Irial had borrowed from Uleth about the Sigil Order. The man was Aelsian's friend. That might prove useful in the days to come. Edryd brought a chair in, and grateful for a reason to break away from the people gathered in the open hall, he closed the door behind him, and waited for evening.

Logaeir did come, along with dozens of others, as darkness fell. Eithne and Edryd walked behind as Irial was placed upon the pyre by a group of women, some of them young and some of them old. Everyone then watched as Irial's body was consumed in an enormous column of fire and smoke that seemingly towered to an impossible height, reaching straight out into the stars of the night sky. Edryd saw Uleth then, staring at the pyre, with tears falling from his eyes. What Edryd saw might only be an image, but he knew that the pain in those eyes was something real. Uleth did not look back at Edryd, who continued to look on with the strange feeling that that he might not ever see this man again.

In the morning, the ashes would be placed in the cavity that had been created out of two great stones which supported an even larger monolith that rested flatly atop them. The structure looked something like a giant table. Earth and stone would then be piled up in a mound around the grave, covering the stones over entirely. It was the sort of tribute afforded only to a person of great status.

As people began to break away and leave, Edryd realized he had given no thought to where he would go now. He couldn't bear to think of sleeping in the cottage. Logaeir approached and solved the matter before Edryd could begin to worry over it.

"Aelsian has arranged rooms for you and Eithne aboard the *Interdiction*," Logaeir said. "You should head there tonight. It will be as safe a place as can be found for the two of you, and it will be a good place to sort things out in the days to come as well. I will meet with you there tomorrow."

Edryd didn't normally like to accept any of Logaeir's suggestions, but he was not about to argue with this one. There was nothing but sympathy and sorrow in the Ascomanni strategist's eyes, and Edryd knew that he had misjudged this man. It wasn't that he had been wrong in any of his conclusions about Logaeir, but Edryd had not tried to understand the depths behind the facade that Logaeir presented on the surface, and he been too slow to forgive him. Logaeir would never be someone in whom he could completely trust, but he was a loyal ally and friend.

They gathered a few of Irial's things and a few articles that belonged to Eithne, and walked together on through the night, enjoying the silence and the stars that shone brightly in the sky. When Eithne grew tired, worn out by the turmoil of the day, Edryd carried her over the remainder of the distance to the harbor. Aelsian was asleep when they arrived, but his men showed them to their rooms aboard the ship.

Eildach was still holding out, but a sort of normalcy had developed quickly within a few short days. Men and women, and even entire families from the settlements near the Ascomanni encampment, had begun to flow in, many of them returning to a home they had been forced to flee years ago. Order was kept under the banner of the Blood Prince. On this particular subject, seated at a table in the great room aboard the *Interdiction*, Edryd and Logaeir were having a heated argument that was being ineffectively mediated by Aelsian. Logaeir was losing the argument.

"They won't follow me," Logaeir said again, but somehow his objections were just not getting through.

"They are already following you," Edryd said, making the obvious point. "Barely any of them have any idea what I look like. If we keep it that way, when I leave, it won't undermine you. With the Sigil Corps soldiers backing you up, no one will question it. You could even go on pretending to be the Blood Prince."

"The Hand of the Blood Prince," Logaeir said. It was as far as he was prepared to go.

Edryd tried to shift his chair, but it wouldn't move. It was locked in place, as was the table and most of the other chairs around it. He found Logaeir's latest proposal to be even more alarming than the idea of allowing the man to continue impersonating him as he had done more than once before. Edryd had an unpleasant mental image in his mind of one of his hands moving about of its own volition, doing all sorts of things he wouldn't want it to do and dragging the rest of his body along behind it.

"The Regent of An Innis, and leader of the Ascomanni," Edryd offered instead. He wanted Logaeir to assume more responsibility and act under his own name and reputation instead of falsely pretending that he was carrying out Edryd's wishes. Logaeir seemed to consider this. The suggestion might possibly even have appealed to Logaeir on some level, but the man did not like to be out in front. He preferred to pull the strings, rather than be the puppet.

"Alright, but it is to be understood that you are the rightful ruler of the island, and the King of the Ascomanni. I merely speak and act on your behalf," Logaeir said.

"No," Edryd said, rejecting the suggestion but offering a modification. "You speak on your own behalf, but you have my support."

Logaeir wasn't pleased. He would have preferred to make Edryd stay here, at least for a little while, and failing that, he wanted to represent himself as the being an extension of the Blood Prince's will, but he seemed to accept that Edryd's current offer was as much as he was going to be able to bargain for.

Edryd, for his part, was pretty certain that Logaeir was going to call himself the Hand of the Blood Prince regardless of anything Edryd might do to try and stop him. Having reached an understanding, Logaeir took his leave from the two other men, muttering something under his breath.

"I'm going to make one last trip into An Innis to say a few goodbyes," Edryd said to Aelsian. "I will be back in a couple of hours."

"We'll be ready to leave when you return," Aelsian promised.

Edryd felt a twinge of guilt as he passed his cabin. Eithne was inside, which was pretty awkward all around and had forced him to sleep outside the door, but this was where she felt safe. The cabin Aelsian had given to her had been given back to the Officer she would have otherwise been displacing. Edryd knew she would want to come with him into town, but it was impractical and still too dangerous.

He made as direct a path as he could to Uleth's home. Edryd didn't know what he hoped to find, apart from Uleth, but he was determined to seek the man out. He thought he had come to the wrong place when he arrived at the heavy wooden door, which hung open now on its hinges. The garden looked the same as ever, with robust growths of carefully cultivated plants, but the home was in complete disrepair. It did not look as though anyone lived there. Edryd could see gaps in some of the walls where the structure was falling down. Surely more than this had to have been real. Edryd stepped inside the open doorway. The hallways were filled with rot and mold.

Edryd turned into the library. This room appeared to have been well sheltered from the elements and contained numerous shelves of books. A young man, Edryd supposed he must have been one of the Ascomanni, was packing books into a couple of folded cloths. Edryd feared that the library was being looted, but the young man seemed untroubled and did not act at all like someone caught in an act of theft. He explained to Edryd when he was asked, that he had been paid to move all of the books to the palace. Edryd left then, and rejected the idea of looking for Uleth at the palace or anywhere else. He somehow knew that he would not be able to find the man. Edryd turned instead onto a path that would take him to the Broken Oath. The inn wasn't far away.

He didn't have a good reason to be going there. Edryd didn't know Greven especially well, or anyone else that he might be likely to see inside, or at least not enough that they warranted a formal farewell. He realized as he walked that he had just needed to see the rapid improvements that were taking place, made quite plain by the number of shops that were opening up and the bustle of people moving about. An Innis was a different place, and it did Edryd good to think that his choices had contributed to and brought about things other than just suffering and death.

Edryd stepped inside the Broken Oath. The structure itself and the furnishings inside it had not been changed, but it did not feel like the same place. It was busier than ever and was serving a more varied collection of customers. There were crowds throughout, which made the one exceptional bare spot incredibly obvious. The patrons of the inn were keeping a healthy distance from the man in black robes who was sitting against the back wall.

Edryd felt sick. He hadn't seen his former teacher since the night of the attack, and he hadn't expected to see him now either. Seoras watched him enter, apparently having waited far longer than he would have liked and clearly angry that Edryd had declined his invitation to meet him near the ruins. Edryd walked past Seoras without acknowledging him, passing him on his way towards the inn's back door. Without a word, Seoras stood and followed Edryd out.

Standing with his back to the inn, Edryd surveyed the wreckage of the well in the middle of the courtyard. He wondered when someone would get around to repairing the damage he had caused while fighting with Cecht and Hagan that first night in An Innis. There were a handful of people behind the inn, but nothing compared to the number of people inside or the groups out in the street in front. Edryd couldn't trust that their presence would afford any protection from an angry shaper of the dark.

"You have no regard," Seoras said from behind Edryd.

Edryd couldn't understand why Seoras could think that he would, but he didn't say so. He was about to find out what the man wanted.

"Let's take this somewhere else," Seoras said. This somewhere else, his voice seemed to imply, was going to be a suitable place for a fight, a parting duel that could well leave one or both of them dead. Edryd had been carrying the sigil sword at his side for a few days now, having kept it close from the moment Seoras had returned it to him, but in that time it had exhibited no unusual attributes. There hadn't, however, been any occasions to put it to the test. It might well aid him only when there was a need, or it might continue to remain a simple piece of metal when it mattered most. Either way, Edryd could see that an occasion had come which would settle that question.

They walked together in silence, working their way towards the estate that had recently been restored to Giric Tolvanes. It was the place where Seoras had lived while training men, Edryd among them, to bend flows of pure æther to their will. Seoras had never had a more frustrating student than Edryd, and he wasn't ever likely to have another anything like him.

As they neared the property, Edryd saw that the gates had been pulled down. Seoras had been right when he had predicted that Tolvanes would have trouble holding onto the place on his own.

"What happened?" Edryd asked.

"Tolvanes was among those who once participated in the profits gained from enslaving the most vulnerable citizens of An Innis," Seoras explained. "When the Ascomanni attacked, there was a reckoning for people like him."

Edryd took this to mean the old man was most likely dead, but he didn't try to confirm it. He kept quiet as they walked into the practice yard. The place was empty and deserted despite the fact that it was clearly a valuable property. The years Seoras had spent here, housing draugar and training thralls, had established the type of reputation that would keep people away for a while.

On the assumption that Seoras was about to initiate a fight, Edryd began to make preparations. He strained to concentrate all of his focus on measuring the shifting currents of the dark and differentiating between the patterns that he could perceive. He could feel the sigil sword belted in place at his side. It was not quite cooperating, but it felt ready, as if it were cautiously aware of all that took place. There was something else unusual. Something he really ought to have noticed before. He was having trouble picking out the normally obvious pattern that Seoras generated. It was there, but it was indistinct, confused, and unstable.

Seoras noted the surprise on Edryd's face. "I showed you this once before," he said, calling to mind the time Seoras had hidden himself while he listened as Edryd spoke to Ruach outside the cottage. "I have made improvements. Though it is not the equal of your shrouding, and it is nowhere near close to what I need it to be, it isn't bad at all if you consider how little I had to go on," he boasted.

"I don't understand. Is this what you wanted me to see?"

"It would have been if I could make it work, in which case I would have wanted you to not see it," Seoras answered. "I'm asking you to show me how to do this correctly."

"Why would I, even if I could?" Edryd asked. "You could have helped me when I came to you, but you did nothing."

"I need you to teach me," Seoras said, ignoring the uncomfortable question. "I am tethered. I cannot escape him if you do not help."

"Just as you tied your leash around me," Edryd said, making the point that he had no sympathy. He did not care much right now who this master was that so troubled Seoras.

Seoras was surprised. "I did try", he admitted, "but I failed to create the link."

"No," Edryd insisted. "I felt every emotion that flowed through your head. Believe me when I tell you it worked."

Seoras was no longer surprised; he was dumbfounded. The intervention of the shroud had ensured that the link had only functioned in one direction. He looked anxious then too, frightened upon learning how much Edryd might know of him and worried that his darkest secrets had been compromised.

"Then you understand how my master can use the link to trace me," Seoras said. "I cannot hide from him without your help. I am sure that only it can shield me."

For the sake of ending all of this, if not for the pitiable state of fear this man was living in, Edryd was almost willing to do what Seoras was asking. "Would you believe that I don't know how it is done, that it is something caused by the sigil sword?" Asking this as a question, instead of stating it directly, did not make the explanation any more persuasive, but then Edryd did not actually know if it was the truth.

Seoras didn't seem to immediately dismiss the idea, but eventually he rejected it. "The sword is a focus, not a living object, Edryd," the shaper lectured. "It can only enhance your ability, in no sense can it actually shape."

Edryd felt certain that this couldn't be entirely correct. It did not match some of his experiences with the weapon. Seoras had to be at least partly right though. The shroud had remained in place long after Edryd had become separated from the sword. At most, the sword induced him to shape the concealment and worked to maintain it, but it could not be the actual source. It was an interesting thought, but this wasn't going to be something he was going to solve so simply.

"This is all beside the point," Seoras said. "I need this as a shield against my master. You are going to teach it to me."

"No," Edryd said, shaking his head.

Seoras was not ready to give up. "You can't say no. I will do whatever you ask, I will become your apprentice," he begged. The part about becoming Edryd's apprentice was spoken as if it were some enticement, but it was in fact what Seoras truly wanted, more even than the means to shut out his master. Seoras seemed to be overestimating Edryd in a truly dangerous way.

"No," Edryd insisted once more. He might have explained it in terms of his simple ignorance on the subjects Seoras wanted to be trained in, but instead Edryd said, "This shouldn't come as a surprise, but I don't quite like you, Seoras. I certainly cannot trust you, and I do not believe that I could ever teach you anything."

Edryd saw something then that he hadn't thought possible. Exposed for just a moment by the harsh words, a severe sadness and pain could be seen in the shaper's eyes. Edryd had come to believe that the man did not have any emotions that were not some form of anger, and had judged him to possess little or no capacity to be hurt by anything.

The momentary reaction did not take long to metamorphose into deep offense and from there into the raw anger with which Edryd was more familiar. Edryd felt fortunate that his link with Seoras had been severed, certain that the force of this man's anger would have been enough to almost knock him down. He was much too close to Seoras. Edryd retreated as quickly as he could, relying on the previously established correlation that distance meant safety where Seoras was concerned.

The sigil blade was in his hands now, and Edryd stopped backing up in response to some prompting that urged him to stand and face the shaper. Something opened inside Edryd again, but this time he couldn't have felt less prepared for it, lacking the sense of calm and expanded consciousness he had possessed leading up to his fight in the palace. Edryd understood this much, he could once again, for what would now be the second time in his life, consciously touch and shape the dark.

Edryd was not the only one filled with power. Seoras didn't even bother to draw his weapon. His entire body erupted in undulant flows of black flame. In contrast, Edryd appeared quite ordinary in all respects, and the same was true for the sigil sword. Edryd had no white flames with which to combat the black ones, and no idea what to do. He recalled then something Seoras had once said of himself, that he had 'always been especially good with fire.' Aware that he strengthened Seoras just by being near him, it seemed like an obvious idea to run as far and as fast as he could, but something continued to press him to stand firm, while at the same time giving the seemingly contradicting warning that even the briefest contact with those flames could incinerate him.

Edryd did not know for sure before doing it that it would even be possible, but he compressed his own aura. He had done the opposite before when he had confronted Aodra, straining the demonic construct that had been holding her and forcing it beyond its limits. This was no more difficult to do and had a much more immediate effect. The black flames around Seoras shrank back, decreasing in intensity until they extended only a small distance.

Seoras gasped as if air had been taken from his lungs, betraying a reaction to the power that was being forcibly pulled from his grasp. The flames may have become smaller, but they persisted, and Edryd was certain that they were no less dangerous. It was however more realistic now to believe that he might be able to avoid them.

"You are unwilling to allow me equal footing?" Seoras asked.

"We were never equal in anything," Edryd answered. Though this meant something different to Edryd than it did to his former teacher, it was truth from just about any perspective. Edryd was not a good judge of his own strength. Seoras was. The shaper knew just how big the difference in pure ability was. Seoras, however, had a deep knowledge of what he was doing and could exploit an enormous gap in understanding. Edryd comprehended this difference here much better than Seoras did. It was with these thoughts in mind that as they began the fight, each man was convinced he was overmatched and believed he had little hope of surviving against the other.

Seoras drew his long thin sword with his left hand, its reach not much less than that of the sigil blade. He would have immediately launched into an offensive flurry, but Edryd forestalled this by initiating a shaped attack of his own. Dark flames danced on his blade as Seoras blocked and absorbed the powerful attack. As the blades deflected off of the point of contact, Seoras returned the strike, delivering the energy he had absorbed from Edryd's attack in addition to further infused forces of his own. The sigil sword held up under these forces without being reinforced, as no other weapon could have.

They traded several blows in this manner, the accumulating power growing with each exchange. This could not continue, it would soon be more than either of them could handle. Edryd altered the sequence, recognizing that there was no sense in handing Seoras so much power to work with. He declined the opportunity for a counterstrike after blocking one of Seoras's attacks. Instead Edryd took hold of the accrued power, retaining it within the sigil blade. The ancient weapon was well suited for this, having an immense capacity to store such energies.

The master shaper, surprised by what Edryd had done, began to back away. He had been building to an attack that he was certain could not be blocked, and giving Edryd, by only a small degree, more credit than was due, he was impressed that his ultimate design had been so thoroughly anticipated and so easily frustrated. This generous interpretation of Edryd's intuitive discernment, made Seoras cautious.

Understanding little of what had motivated his teacher to pause, Edryd still appreciated that things were going well for him to this point. He didn't have a plan, but he didn't want to give the dark shaper more time to think. Edryd began to attack, applying everything he knew as a trained swordsman, executing swift skilled strokes, but imbuing none of them with added speed or momentum as a shaper would have done.

This too caught Seoras by surprise, having expected that Edryd would try to overwhelm him, but he soon began to adjust. His opponent might be holding back, but that didn't mean he had to. The speed and strength of his counters forced Edryd to back off, rebalancing the combat. Edryd was superior at anticipating Seoras and had mastered absorbing the shaped impacts, but he was reluctant to take any risks.

As the fight wore on, Edryd developed the beginnings of a very flawed concept. If he could keep a tight defense, Seoras would begin to tire from shaping such powerful strikes. His strategy failed for multiple reasons. Seoras was growing stronger instead of weaker as the battle progressed, and Edryd was increasingly concerned that his defense was not adequate. A single mistake would be fatal.

Edryd remained convinced that there was little to be gained by shaping his attacks, but he began to look for an opening, and when he found one he rushed a simple exploratory attack. Seoras shifted his stance and brought his sword up to knock the attack away, expecting that he would brush it aside, but something unexpected happened just as the blades collided. Edryd's sword barely changed course. Seoras felt as if he had struck against a dense iron pillar that had been firmly rooted into the ground, and his shaped attack was completely ineffective against it.

It felt strange to Edryd as well. It was not something he had done himself. It was as if the sigil blade were growing heavy just before the point of impact without slowing down, the corresponding momentum increasing as the weight changed and returning to normal only after the contact. It had put Seoras off balance. There was nothing unusual when Edryd struck again, or the time after that, but with his next strike the technique repeated itself. It then began to happen again at irregular intervals, becoming increasingly frequent but still random in sequence.

Edryd couldn't predict when it would happen, and neither could Seoras, which made it impossible for the shaper to react quickly enough to respond appropriately. Seoras inevitably mishandled some of these attacks, one of which in particular pushed an ineffective parry far away from center, nearly knocking the shaper's weapon from his hand. His guard had been blown open.

Drawing on the dark and imitating a move he had observed Seoras repeat many times before, Edryd stepped in with a speed that matched that of the master shaper, putting Seoras into the striking range of the sigil blade. At that moment, Edryd's side erupted with intense searing pain. Seoras held something in his right hand, his off hand. It was the bronzed hilt of an ancient sword. There was no blade, just a long strip of what seemed to be nothing, neither darkness nor light, just an impossible void. Somehow this all made perfect sense to Edryd. There had always been something off about the style of combat Seoras used, and now Edryd understood what it was. The man fought with an aggressive style that made use of two weapons, and Edryd was seeing it now, for the first time.

Edryd altered the target of his strike, swinging down almost blindly, but trusting that the trajectory was right. The sigil blade came alive with white light as it struck the hilt of Seoras's arcane weapon just above his hand, expending all the energies absorbed during the fight and shattering the object into thousands of pieces.

Seoras had sensed the immense release of energy and had only barely managed to ward against it in time. It saved the shaper's hand and his arm, but it could do little more than that. He was blown back several yards where he fell to the ground, stunned and barely conscious. Edryd had been pushed away as well but he had managed to keep his feet. His body had been further from the event, and he had been more prepared for it. Frantically, Edryd felt at his side with his free hand. He pulled his shirt away from where he was certain he had been pierced, but there was no wound, and no cut in the fabric of his clothing.

The pain he had felt was gone but the memory remained. He could find no physical injury. It seemed that he had destroyed the dark weapon before it could completely form, but it had done damage, even if there was no visible evidence. Edryd felt like he was bleeding, despite the absence of a wound, as though he were in the process of slowly losing vital energies which sustained his existence. He allowed his aura to decompress, achieving a natural stable balance, at which point he felt an almost delirious relief when the aural seepage ceased. This was an injury that no doctor could treat. Edryd would have to pray that it would heal on its own and be careful until it did.

Edryd walked over to Seoras, who was breathing painfully, his bright slender sword a few feet away on the ground. Defying a prediction made weeks earlier, Edryd once again had an opportunity to end the man's life. Edryd used the sigil blade, bringing it down decisively to destroy Seoras's weapon on the ground, something that was now simple to accomplish while it was not actively being reinforced by its owner. Edryd warily examined his fallen master. Life was returning to the man's eyes. His recovery disconcerted Edryd a great deal, but what surprised him most was that as Seoras became increasingly aware of himself, he seemed content, as if this is what he had expected would happen all along, and he was ready to die.

"If you will not give me your help, you should kill me," said Seoras.

Edryd could not believe Seoras was still begging for his sympathies. "I will put it to you once more, why would I want to help you? You did nothing for me, when I asked."

"You didn't need help," Seoras said, brushing the question away and looking uncomfortable, whether from lying defenseless on the ground, or as a result of what he had been asked, Edryd could not tell.

"I was fighting a draugr, of course I needed help," Edryd said, his patience growing thin. "You said you were prevented. What could have possibly prevented you? What could have been more important? Did Irial and Eithne mean nothing to you?"

"Eithne is my daughter," Seoras answered.

Edryd didn't believe it at first. He didn't want to. He could see the resemblance though, the blue eyes and dark black hair. She had also inherited her father's power.

"They would have killed her," Seoras said. "You can't know how grateful I am."

Edryd tried to put it all out of his mind, unable to handle the sudden need to reexamine everything that had happened. In that moment, if anything, he hated Seoras more than ever. Seoras had never been a father to Eithne. Edryd didn't try to comprehend the danger it would have caused for Eithne if Seoras had ever done so.

"You repay me for protecting her, by trying to kill me?" Edryd asked. He had no reason to forgive this man for anything, and the knowledge that Seoras was Eithne's father, absolved the shaper of nothing where Edryd was concerned.

"I wanted to see," Seoras said while rising to a seated position, but losing his concentration as he did so, he was unable to complete the thought. The man didn't want to die, he had just expected to, and maybe felt that he deserved it.

"What did you want to see?" Edryd asked, as he helped Seoras to his feet, prompting him to finish the thought.

"I wanted to see a sigil knight," answered Seoras.

"I am not a sigil knight," Edryd said. He had made this protest to others before.

"No, you're not, but you are the closest thing I am ever likely to find."

Edryd wondered why this was so important to Seoras. "Did you have to try to kill me just for that?" Edryd asked.

"Apparently I did. Nothing less has ever been enough to persuade you to show even the smallest measure of your power."

It wasn't worth trying to explain, and Edryd knew he needed to hide from Seoras just how helpless he would be without the sigil sword. Better to play the part Seoras had set for him.

"You must understand why it is that I cannot trust you," Edryd repeated again, with only a slight softening of the reproachful tone he had used before. "I am not a sigil knight, but you are the furthest thing from," Edryd continued. "You are corrupted and dark, and you are unworthy of a sigil blade." He could see from the shaper's reaction, one of shame and failure, that Seoras knew this already. Edryd guessed that Seoras must have tried to use the weapon after he had collected it from where it had been left near Esivh Rhol on the day of the attack. He had returned it to Edryd only once he discovered that he could not use it himself.

"There is nothing I can offer you," Edryd continued. "You are filled with too much anger and too much hatred. Knowing that, it would be wrong of me to give what you have asked."

"I will change," Seoras said. There was determination behind his words.

"You will have to prove that you have," Edryd replied. "Find and master a sigil blade of your own, and then I will agree to help you."

It was an unachievable task—a deliberately impossible demand—unreasonably presented as the only condition under which Edryd would ever consider the desperate shaper's request. Seoras must have understood this, but he took hope from the direction it gave him anyway. His reaction caused Edryd to feel guilty. It shouldn't have, he was being far more forgiving to Seoras than the dark man could possibly have ever deserved, but Edryd felt incredibly false playing at being some wise man of power whose dictates were a worthy guide for the other man's life.

But there was something he could do to make up for occupying Seoras with a foolish hope on which to waste the rest of his life. Edryd began to shape. It was a pattern equal to the most complex and powerful thing Edryd knew. He surrounded Seoras with a shroud, constructed so that it was fed by the dark shaper's own connection to the dark.

"This will not last," Edryd warned. "It will shield you from your master for a few days at most. If you can't figure out how to maintain it before it is gone, or make one of your own, it will be lost to you. Do not seek me out. I will see to it that Eithne remains safe."

Without any further explanation, Edryd turned, leaving a grateful Seoras behind in the stupor of his own stunned silence.

"Wait," Seoras called out, before Edryd could leave the grounds of the estate. "You need to listen to what I have to tell you."

Edryd turned to face Seoras once more. "Who is this master of yours?" he asked. Edryd supposed that he really ought to have been curious about at least that much.

"I won't speak his name. He would hear it," Seoras said, a bit of inner torment raising the pitch of his voice as he spoke.

"Ulensorl," Edryd guessed, and as soon as he said the name it was a guess no longer. The shaper's reaction, more than confirmed the truth.

"It is not safe to speak that name," Seoras said. "It will draw his attentions, and he has many servants to carry out his will."

"You and the draugar would be chief among them?"

"Yes, but there are more; many, many more."

"And are you are going to tell me who they are?" Edryd asked.

"Those that matter most, yes," Seoras agreed. "The King of Nar Edor conspired with him, and together they tried to use Beodred to bring about your grandfather's death and the fall of House Edorin. My master also found others in your kingdom, including your brother, who agreed to destroy you, men who shared his desire to bring about the end of the Sigil Corps. He bears a grudge against the Sigil Order of old. He is searching for you now. He will use you if he can, and kill you if he cannot."

It was too much for Edryd to take in, that a dark sorcerer responsible for the cataclysm that destroyed the Sigil Order, was still alive some five hundred years later, and actively searching for the last descendant of his ancient enemies. "He may try," Edryd said, sounding more confident than he felt. "From what you are telling me, he failed in everything you have described. He will fail again." Edryd said all of this slowly, careful to present a front that he was unaffected by any fears born from the information Seoras had just disclosed.

Seoras certainly must have had much more to tell, and Edryd should have stayed to learn all that he could, but he was having a hard time keeping up the pretense that he knew what he was doing, so he turned around and left without speaking another word. Seoras was, as a result of receiving such dismissive treatment, left with a much stronger impression of his former pupil. He stood silently admiring Edryd's courage as they parted ways, feeling a devotion to this young man, and a hope that he had not known for many years.

As soon as Edryd was beyond the property walls and safely around the corner, he picked up his pace. It was time to be gone, and if he never saw Seoras again, he would count himself a fortunate man.

Aelsian was waiting for him when he returned to the *Interdiction*. "Are we ready to go?" he asked.

"Not yet," Edryd said. "I have to speak with Eithne."

Aelsian gave Edryd a puzzled look. "Surely there will be time to talk as we travel to Ossia?"

"I'm not coming," Edryd explained.

The navarch didn't like this. He didn't try to ask Edryd why he had made this sudden decision, but he put forward the most powerful argument that could be made against it. "You cannot do this to Eithne," he said. "After what she has been through, she doesn't feel safe. She won't even leave your room. You cannot leave her. She doesn't trust another soul on this ship."

"That is why I have to speak with her," Edryd said, feeling truly guilty about the whole thing. "You will take care of her. I know I can trust you to do that."

Looking displeased, Aelsian assented. "I don't suppose you can tell me what is so important that you would do this?"

"I have business in Nar Edor," Edryd answered, without elaborating any further. This was as much of a surprise to Aelsian as anything Edryd could have said. He knew that Edryd had no desire to ever return to his home.

Edryd wasted no time reaching the room aboard the *Interdiction* that Aelsian had provided for him. Eithne was inside, reading a small white book by the light that came in through a rounded window. It was the book Irial had borrowed from Uleth, the book written by Aelsian's friend Ludin Kar. They had retrieved this and some of Eithne's belongings from the cottage, along with a few pieces of Irial's simple jewelry that Eithne was keeping in a box.

Edryd removed his coat and hung it beside the door before taking a seat near Eithne. "You are going to go on to Ossia ahead of me," Edryd said. Eithne looked upset, but she didn't complain. "You can trust Aelsian. He is my friend and he manages my home. You are going to be safe there, and I will come as soon as I can." Edryd did not tell her about Seoras. He couldn't. Not now and perhaps not ever.

Eithne handed him the book. It was special to her. It was memories of her sister, and stories of an older time that she had read through many times. "I'm keeping the one you had, with the Huldra and the Ældisir in it, but I want you to have Irial's book," she said.

Edryd accepted it a little too casually, thinking that Irial's book really should have been returned to Uleth. "That is one of my treasures," she said, reprimanding him. "You have to take good care of it."

He assured her that he would, but Eithne did not seem satisfied. He caught her staring at his coat, the one she had used as a blanket in the palace. Edryd knew what she wanted. She had admired his pins more than once. Edryd removed his coat from the peg it rested on and returned to his chair. He did not need any of the emblems. He was not a part of the Sigil Corps any longer so he did not need the symbols that marked his rank, and he had chosen not to embrace any of his family names, so he did not need his family crests.

"You can choose one," he said, turning up the collar on the coat. Eithne picked out a silver pin, on which a raven was represented in settings of polished black opal stones, which reflected every possible color within their dark depths. These precious stones surrounded a blue black sapphire that formed the bird's eye. It matched Eithne's features well and he supposed that is why she had chosen it. Though Edryd did not realize it, excluding the sigil blade, this pin was beyond any measure, the most valuable thing in his possession. It was the emblem of House Elduryn and proof of his bloodline. Because of the rarity of the black opals, there was no chance it could have ever been convincingly simulated.

"That is the symbol of my father's house," Edryd said, "House Elduryn."

Eithne beamed with pleasure, and it eased his guilt to know that it could be a comfort to her.

"You can wear it if you want," he said, encouraging her. "As far as anyone will know, you are my sister, Eithne Elduryn."

"I never had a family name," Eithne said excitedly, grabbing her own coat and moving the pin around the collar of the cloak, trying to find the best position for it.

Eithne hugged him. "I will keep this for you until you come back," she said. "I will protect it, and wait."

Edryd's heart was heavy as he left the *Interdiction*. He felt like he was doing something wrong, but the things he had just learned from Seoras had made the decision for him. He had to return to Nar Edor. Edryd walked back towards the Broken Oath. He would find someone there to take him where he needed to go.

Epilogue

Edryd recognized no one. The two men serving food and drink to the customers were new, and the innkeeper, Greven, of whom it could be inferred from the constant sounds issuing from the kitchen and his being too busy to make an appearance, was clearly in need of all the help he could get. The inn was filled with far too many customers, none of whom appeared to be paying for their meals, and the space was more crowded than Edryd could recall having ever seen it.

Thinking only this morning that there was a need for several new public houses competing for business with the Broken Oath, Edryd had predicted a surge in the innkeeper's business prospects, but he had not expected this. Edryd pushed his way in, and of necessity, was not delicate about moving people aside. At this moment, there were no other establishments in which he was more likely to find a ship's captain in need of a way to regain his ship.

There were a few injured or otherwise defeated men concentrated at certain tables. These servants of the harbormasters had surrendered their weapons and suffered the removal of any symbols on their uniforms, but their former loyalties could be identified by what was left of the tattered coats which they still wore. As for the rest, they consisted of deck hands and sailors mixed in with tradesmen and common townspeople, all of whom were wearing looks which expressed how uncertain they felt about their fates.

The reason behind this sweating assemblage of men and women was a puzzle that was soon solved. Edryd learned from the frequent complaints circulating through the room that the Ascomanni had seized every last store of food in the town. If you wanted to eat, anything at all, there were only two options: Ascomanni controlled areas where food was readily available, or Greven's Inn.

Those who had been on the wrong side of the fighting generally chose the latter option. In either case, the food was controlled and supplied by the Ascomanni, but here at least you did not have to eat it in the company of people who had just attacked and killed a considerable portion of the island's population.

Of those who were here, the majority appeared to be affiliated in some way with the ships crews that had been employed by the harbormasters. Displaced by the Ascomanni from their ships, on which some of them had previously been accustomed to rely as a place to sleep, they were now competing for space in some of the worst of the towns formerly abandoned buildings, eating food that was distributed at the inn each evening, and fretting over the dearth of ways in which to leave the island.

It was as well that Edryd did not know anyone here. That only meant it would not be unreasonable to expect to go unrecognized, and he could hope that he would be soon forgotten once he left. There could be few who knew of him as Edryd, and more importantly, there would certainly be none that would know him as Aisen, The Blood Prince.

Edryd crossed the room a few times before finding the object of his search, realizing only when he saw him, who it was that he had sought. Leaning forward over his table with his head buried in his arms, sat an idle looking man in expensive clothes. Advancing in years and exhibiting numerous strands of grey in his dark black hair, he fit a description, previously given to Edryd by the former thrall Hedryn, of the captain of the ship which had brought the draugar to An Innis.

Edryd put a hand on the shoulder of the man who sat opposite. The surprised man turned with a fierce objection to this touch, but one look at the sword belted at Edryd's side and the unfaltering look in his visitor's eyes, recommended an obvious action to the sailor. He surrendered his seat and left without either of them speaking a word.

"You're Captain Pedrin Eksar," said Edryd, after settling into the vacated chair.

Pedrin looked up upon hearing these words. He had a short sharp nose and a round face, somewhat soft in appearance owing to an excess of weight that he carried on his frame.

"And you're some random clod who I don't know from anywhere," Pedrin replied.

"Now that we have gotten through those formalities," said Edryd, "we have things to discuss."

Pedrin gave a dismissive shrug, and buried his head back in his arms.

"You are the captain of the *Wraith*," Edryd said.

Pedrin looked up then, and in a brief moment of curiosity, began to wonder who this person was and how it was that he knew him. "Was, the captain of the *Wraith*," he said, correcting Edryd. "She's in Ascomanni hands now, and I don't see clear to how I'm ever likely to get her back."

"Ah, but I do, if you care to listen," said Edryd.

Pedrin buried his head back into his arms once more. Clearly, he did not care to listen.

Edryd continued anyway. "I can get your ship released, but I will need a captain and a crew to sail her. It doesn't necessarily have to be you or your crew, but it might as well be."

"Not interested," said Pedrin Eksar, his voice muffled by his coat, no longer bothering to look up.

"You don't believe me?"

"And why should I?" said Pedrin, who was now sitting up straight for the first time. "And if I did believe you, not that I do, but if I did, what makes you think I would want you anywhere near my ship?"

"You have had far worse passengers than I," said Edryd, "and it is of my doing, that you are no longer troubled by them."

Pedrin was now fully attentive. He began to look carefully at the stranger, narrowing his right eye slightly as he studied Edryd's face. "You're the Elduryn boy," he finally said, "the one my masters came here to find. I won't ask what happened to them, but I won't thank you for it either."

"Perhaps you believe now that I can give you back your ship," said Edryd, declining to confirm Pedrin's guess, but seeming to endorse its accuracy by not disputing it either.

"Aye, I do believe you could," said Pedrin, "but I know better than to think that you would be doing so out of the kindness of your heart. I rather expect I would be simply exchanging my old masters for a new one."

"Look at it as trading up," said Edryd. He had meant this as a simple joke, but Pedrin brightened visibly as the comment struck at an idea somewhere in his head. Pedrin managed to collect his composure, and his expression changed so quickly, to one of disinterest, that Edryd almost doubted that he had witnessed that short moment of enthusiasm.

"I can't say your proposal is entirely unwelcome, but let's hear the entire thing out before I say any more," Pedrin said.

"I need to get to a certain place, to which I have learned from Hedryn, you have been several times before," Edryd explained.

Edryd's meaning was not quite clear to Pedrin, but he better understood now how it was that Edryd knew about him, and he felt that he knew now for certain who it was that sat across the table. Pedrin had seen Hedryn yesterday, and in a conversation with the thrall had learned what had happened to Áledhuir and Aodra and the other two thralls. They had been killed by this man. Pedrin could hardly have been anything other than impressed.

"This place I've been to, several times before as you put it," said Pedrin, "supposing you gave this place a name, what would it be?"

"I mean to keep that information strictly known only to myself until we are underway," Edryd said, refusing to answer Pedrin's inquiry.

It was Pedrin's instinct to negotiate, and settle upon the best possible terms, but his needs were unequal to Edryd's, and so was the position from which he bargained. Worse, Edryd clearly knew what his advantages were. "What would you have me do?" Pedrin said, resigned to accept whatever the man asked.

"Have your crew ready, and gather them near the northernmost pier. Hedryn and I will meet you there as soon as it is dark."

***

Eivendr walked the dark halls of Eidstadt's royal palace. He had chosen this late hour to avoid being seen, but the wisdom of that idea had been called into question when he discovered what he more reasonably ought to have already known. It was impossible for a king to go about entirely unnoticed. Two servants, and at least that many guards, had all observed him when he passed down the lighted hallways connected to the several rooms which served as his royal living quarters. They had no doubt been made curious by the sight of their monarch wandering about at such an unusual hour.

Thankfully, all of the remaining passageways he had taken since had been completely deserted. More than once he made wrong turns in the dark, and Eivendr had long since grown tired in the process, but he was getting nearer to his destination. Stumbling into some hidden obstruction in the dark, Eivendr formed a series of silent curses to his lips. Were it of any possible beneficial effect, Eivendr would have directed a string of impolite denunciations against the dark thrall, known only by the name Hedryn, who had brought the news that had inspired this trip. But as Eivendr was alone, and as he wished it to remain that way, he wisely suppressed the urge to shout these imprecations down the empty hallway.

Every last bargain he had ever made with these dark men had been a bad one, and nothing ever worked out the way it had been planned. Their information had never been wrong, and not once had they failed to fulfill the terms of any promise, but when things settled out he had ever found his position weakened by the results of the partnership, having profited but very little from their support. It was for this reason that he had sent them away many years ago, and he had seen little of them since.

But this time there had been nothing asked of him. Hedryn had come, he said, only to share a piece of intelligence. Eivendr had listened, believing that there could be no harm in doing so, and received two pieces of information, which if verified would be of incredible consequence, and the details of which, Eivendr could not ignore.

Stepping carefully along the wall, Eivendr progressed onward in the direction of Eidstadt's great library, his way illuminated by nothing more than faint moonlight reaching in through the windows. He arrived so abruptly that he almost questioned whether he was there when he reached the end of his journey. It all looked so different in the dark.

Stopping at a brazier that stood outside the library doors, Eivendr removed a small pottery lamp and a stoppered vial of oil from his pocket. Filling the lamp with a liberal quantity of the fuel from the vial, he then soaked a linen wick as well, and proceeded to ignite it using the smoking coals from the brazier. This created a small but steady flame that he would need in order to complete his task.

Eivendr pulled open one of the doors and contemplated the idea of taking a rest in one of the many chairs positioned around an enormous table which filled the space that stood before him, but he rejected the idea. He was too anxious to delay his purpose a moment longer than was necessary.

The documents he sought were buried in an archive room in the back recesses of the library. How Hedryn had learned about these records, he had not said, but he had been specific about the exact room in which they were stored and the name of the collection in which they were bundled.

The papers, with which Eivendr was so concerned, were the confessions of a ranking general of the attacking raiders, who had been found and captured hiding not far from Eidstadt in the weeks following the fall of Beodred's forces a little more than twenty years ago. The man's name had been Deneg, and the results of his interrogation had been written down. These records included a list of crimes which the raider had either witnessed or committed himself.

Among those crimes was listed a story, extracted under what pressures, who could now say, that recounted the abuse of Duke Kyreth Edorin's daughter by Deneg himself. It could be guessed that this confession might even be the original source of all the rumors about Aisen's having been fathered by one of Beodred's men.

Eivendr suspected that the contents of this document, of which he had just learned the existence, were entirely false. He had investigated such claims in the past and found credible confirmed evidence that Kyreth's daughter had never, at any point, been in the hands of or otherwise captured by anyone from the Rendish alliance that had attacked Nar Edor's Port City. She could reliably be accounted for by many witnesses as having been safely sheltered within the confines of Alsegate Castle throughout the three days of fighting.

Though the story had to have been false, this did not mean that the document recording Deneg's confession was of no value to Eivendr. There were ways he could use the prisoner's statements to undermine the position of the men of the Sigil Corps who claimed to be fighting in support of Aisen's lordship over the lands and property of House Edorin.

But not all of the information obtained from Deneg, as it had been represented to him by Hedryn, had been false. There was one record in particular which Eivendr knew most assuredly for the truth, for it involved Eivendr himself. It revealed his role, identified as the King of Nar Edor, in receiving a sum of money from Beodred's forces under the promise that he would give Beodred seven days in which to lay waste to the lands around Nar Edor's thriving Port City, for which the only additional compensation Eivendr had demanded, was the death of Duke Kyreth Edorin.

It was the one great evil deed of Eivendr's life, and like all of the bargains he had ever made with those men of Hedryn's kind, who possessed dark powers and secrets which they offered seemingly for so little, it ended badly. Aedan Elduryn had somehow anticipated the attack long in advance and protected the life of his lord, Duke Kyreth Edorin. In an incredible and improbable reversal, Aedan broke the Rendish alliance apart, killed its leader, Beodred, and in the battles aftermath helped Kyreth found the Sigil Corps. House Edorin had then become more powerful than ever.

Eivendr had harbored from the time of this great mistake, a hidden shame that ate away at him even now. If anyone were to ever discover what he had done, inviting an army of foreigners to destroy a part of his own kingdom, he would be deposed immediately, and his name would survive his eventual public execution as a byword of betrayal and deceit. Eivendr saw those consequences clearly. This prisoner's confessions could destroy him, and according to Hedryn, Lord Aisen had learned of its existence and would soon have allies in Eidstadt searching it out.

It was this dreaded document, designs upon the destruction of which had occupied some corner of every thought that surfaced in his head following the improvements in his knowledge regarding its contents, and the fear of its disclosure, that drew Eivendr to this place. Until he learned the names of the jailors to whom this man had confessed, and the ruinous words were burned in the flames of his lamp, Eivendr knew that he would find no rest.

Eivendr could trust no one with this. He had to eliminate the evidence himself so that no one, not even his most trusted allies, would ever learn the truth about what he had done. He could not bear to imagine what they might think of him if they did.

It was therefore a great comfort to see that the entire library was darkened, empty, and silent. The rooms that comprised this space, in which so many important books and documents were stored, filled a large part of an entire wing of Eivendr's palace. He reached the archive that had been indicated by the thrall only after a long, hesitating journey through confusing corridors of books kept upon wooden shelves which were supported within stone alcoves built into the many walls of the silent repository.

When at last he entered the room he sought, Eivendr found the light from his small lamp to be insufficient for his search. There were bundled papers stacked upon each other on every shelf and in every recess that could be found in the four corners of the simple space. There were no windows to admit what little light could be gotten from the moon, and owing to the risks posed by the stacks of papers stored here, there were no torches to light, nor any place for a fire.

It began to seem hopeless until Eivendr found a couple of rush lights, leaning upright in a corner beside a thin open ended iron cylinder perforated with hundreds of small holes. Taking up one of the dried rushes, which had been stripped down to the pith and soaked in grease, Eivendr lit an end with his lamp and dropped it into the iron container, where it began to cast light into the room through the empty spaces in the wall of the cylinder. It gave off more light than his lamp, but it would not be very practical to drag around. Encouraged in a small degree by this success, Eivendr began to inspect the nearest stack of papers.

Hope quickly became frustration. It was easier now to scan the piles of paper, but reading them was another thing entirely. He cursed his aging eyes, which in these dim conditions could not read the words scrawled on the documents.

The irresolvable worries which so weakened his heart and troubled his mind, grew more imposing to Eivendr as he began to realize how difficult this would be. It occurred to him that he would need to return during the day, when there was more light, and this line of thought pushed him into a mild panic.

If he left now, it would be discovered that someone had been here. Ashes from the rush light would give him away. Even with more light, finding the documents he sought would take more time than he had. Someone would uncover his strange attempt to investigate, and then they would learn why. He was quite beyond being rational and reasoned and saw everything in terms of the most unlikely and worst possible outcomes.

Noticing how excited his breathing had become, Eivendr forced himself to calm down. He took care to stand perfectly still until his breathing became more controlled, and he continued to do so until each inward and outward breath ceased to make sound. In this silence, he first heard the respirations of another man.

Initially frozen in a moment of terror, Eivendr was soon moved by his fear of discovery to cast about trying to locate the threat. He had thought the room had been empty when he had entered, and it seemed certain that no one could have come in unnoticed since, but Eivendr could still hear the breathing of the other man.

He had to look about twice before he saw the figure in the shadows. The more prominent features of this enemies face were outlined in the dim fiery glare of the rush light. At first, Eivendr found that his eyes seemed to lose track of the other man, but this strange feeling did not last. The face was familiar.

The man had a deep sun weathered complexion and dark hair. The light seemed to catch in his eyes, which looked like smoldering coals from a spent fire, and his stare pronounced a judgment which was informed of every dark deed that Eivendr had ever done. King Eivendr could have been no more surprised, or any more frightened, if it had been some terrifying creature of a dark realm come to claim his life.

"You might be more pleased to see me," Edryd said. "I worked ever so hard to arrange this meeting."

A pronounced terror began in Eivendr's shoulders and stuttered down his back.

"You look like you need to sit down," Edryd said. His tone was casual. It was almost friendly in the way that it seemed to express real worry and concern, but Eivendr took no comfort. He knew that he was about to die

Word regarding the fall of An Innis had reached Nar Edor two days earlier, and everyone knew that the Blood Prince would soon bring the violence he had wrought on that island, along with his Army of Ascomanni warriors, into the heart of Nar Edor to do battle with Eivendr. But they had gotten it wrong. He was already here.

"You have it?" Eivendr concluded. His mind was still obsessed with the secret that he had come here to destroy.

"Think on it a moment, Eivendr," Edryd said. "Just think about it all, and you will figure it out."

"How did you get here?" Eivendr said, in no condition to reason anything out at the moment. "You shouldn't have gotten here so quickly. How, how is it you can be here?"

"I came here on the *Wraith*, with Hedryn and Captain Eksar, men you already know well enough," Edryd explained. He then waited patiently for Eivendr to absorb what he had said.

Things began to fall into place for Eivendr. Somehow, Lord Aisen was now allied with the very men who had once sought his destruction. Under what circumstances they had come together, Eivendr could not possibly guess, but he could see that they were now united. "You had Hedryn lure me here with that story of Deneg's confession," Eivendr said, understanding how completely foolish he had been. "Was there ever even such a man as Deneg?"

"There is," said Edryd, who seemed to be amused by the question. "And he was once a captain among Beodred's men, but he has since become a low ranking bureaucrat on the island of An Innis. Or he was one at any rate. He's just recently become unemployed."

Eivendr did not like the look on the other man's face. Aisen just kept grinning as if he thought his king would have found all of this funny. "You know what I meant," Eivendr said. He was still frightened, but increasingly, he was just feeling confused.

"The one you are worried about is a fictional invention. Hedryn made him up," Edryd admitted. "The records of his confessions, obviously, were false as well."

Eivendr swore silently to himself, cursing his own stupidity.

"Sit down. Relax for a moment," Edryd urged.

"I do not dare hope that you have come for any other purpose than to kill me," Eivendr said, "and you think that I ought to relax?"

"It's true," Edryd said, "I might be here for that reason. But that is a very important might. For the moment at least, there is still more than one possible outcome."

It didn't seem to make sense, but the idea that Aisen was offering some narrow chance to escape a just and overdue punishment, only made Eivendr feel even more afraid. He decided that he would sit down. He was frightened, and tired, and he needed to rest.

It occurred to Eivendr that there was a reason he was not dead yet. "What do you want from me?" Eivendr asked. "I trust there is something you hoped to achieve, some purpose to all of this."

"There are several of them," answered Edryd, "and I will tell you their names."

Eivendr, correctly assuming this reference to have meant the vassal lords of House Edorin, began at once to distance himself from the men who had plotted Aisen's death. "I had absolutely nothing to do with any of that," Eivendr insisted.

"I believe you, Eivendr," said Edryd, "and even if I were inclined to doubt it, as indeed I would be, I know from Hedryn that you had no part in the plot."

The king began to speak more rapidly, further protesting his innocence. "Then you also know that I favored you in the succession. Hedryn will confirm it. I refused when they asked me to support your brother. I wanted you to inherit."

"Hedryn did tell me that. But your reasons for favoring me deserve to be explored. Was it not your opinion that you preferred me as being least popular of the two of us? Is it not true that you thought I would be easier to control and more dependent upon your support?"

"That," Eivendr said, "would be a mischaracterization."

Edryd looked at his king askance, reproving Eivendr for his efforts to dispute what they both knew had been a completely accurate description of the king's reasoning at the time.

"And what does it matter? You had my support!" Eivendr said with irritation. He was unaccustomed to being subjected to such disapproval and judgment, and he did not enjoy being put in a position where he needed to defend himself.

"As grateful as I am for your past support," Edryd said, after letting his king's question remain unanswered for a while, "what concerns me now is what you did after the attempt on my life. You harbored the men who betrayed me, and lent your sympathies to their lies."

Eivendr had no answer for this accusation. He had begun to fear Aisen from the moment he had heard the news of the slaughter in the Edorin family crypts. He had also become convinced that Aisen's allies in the Sigil Order were a threat, and most important of all, he had recognized an opportunity to expand his own strength. Seeing a chance to put the great Port City, which Duke Kyreth Edorin had founded, under Royal control, and put an ally of his own in Aisen's place on the throne of Alsegate, Eivendr had used the lies of Aisen's enemies to raise an army for the purpose of accomplishing his own selfish ends. He would have denied this to anyone else, but he knew that Aisen could see through him.

"What would you have me do," said Eivendr with as much humility as he could manage, "to make it right?"

"You will arrest the men who conspired against me. You will try them for treason. And you will see to it that they are all found guilty," said Edryd.

Observing how calm Aisen had been as he had spoken these words, Eivendr was sure now that he was right to be in fear of him, and began to esteem this enemy with an ever growing level of respect. Eivendr would have accepted the conditions immediately, if he had not sensed that Aisen had more to ask.

"You will announce in the morning that you have brokered an agreement with me to guarantee the safety of Nar Edor from an Ascomanni invasion, and that I have promised to never return to these shores. House Edorin lands and properties will, however, remain under my control."

These additions to Aisen's demands were so far contrary to what Eivendr had expected that for a long while he could not understand what it was that he had been asked. But Aisen was more than patient in repeating himself, two more times, so that Eivendr came to eventually understand. He would have to give up his designs on taking control of the port city, but Eivendr could hardly find anything else that he did not favor in this bargain, and as a result, he viewed the entire proposal with extreme suspicion.

"And how can I be certain that you will hold to your word. How do I know that you will not return one day to oppose me?"

"Because you will no longer be the King of Nar Edor, and so I will have no cause to do so," Edryd said, using this answer to introduce his final demand.

It took a moment to sink in, but when it did, Eivendr was enraged.

"If you wish to remove me from my throne, you will not find me willing," said Eivendr. "You can kill me if you wish, but nothing short of that will end my reign. I am old already, and can think of worse ways to die."

"I can think of worse ways too, Eivendr, be assured of that," said Edryd, a spark of anger appearing in his eyes, and his voice betraying the suppressed anger which he felt towards his king. It existed only for a moment, but it had clearly been there.

"I'm sorry," said Eivendr, without knowing what it was he had just apologized for, and feeling all of his proud defiance wither away.

"Sorry for what?" said Edryd. "You yourself say that you have had my interests at heart and have at no time caused me any harm. Perhaps you are sorry for something you did to someone else, then?"

King Eivendr recognized the weakly concealed derision in these words, and trembled in apprehension as he began to discern where the conversation was headed. Knowing that his tormenter was about to answer his own question, Eivendr remained quiet.

"Deneg and his confessions do not exist, but the events around which that story was built, are rooted in the truth. You may not have been involved on the attempt on my life, but you orchestrated an attempt on the life of my grandfather, and in the process, hundreds of innocent men and women died. It seems to me that the people of Nar Edor ought to know what kind of man you are. Once they do, I won't need to kill you, they will do it for me."

King Eivendr dropped his head and buried his face in his hands. Every word Aisen had spoken to him was true, and he did not doubt that this man, the terrible Blood Prince, had evidence to prove all of it, or failing this, that he possessed the necessary powers to persuade others of the truth of these claims.

Edryd could read in his king's reaction and in his hesitation to respond, a great deal more than Eivendr could ever have revealed in words. He decided it was time to condense everything for King Eivendr by placing it all into one simple abstraction. "Your choice is a simple one. You can either be a monarch who knew when it was time to pass his authority to another, living the remainder of his days in honor and respect while being celebrated for preserving the safety of his country, or... you can be a dead villain."

The king, forced to confront his crime, began to cry miserably, motivated in part by his shame, but equally by the mercy being offered to him, which he in no way deserved. "Please, promise me you will never tell anyone," said Eivendr. "I couldn't bear it to be known. Kill me if you think it is right, but let me be remembered as a good king."

"Give me no cause to ever regret it, and I will carry your secret to the grave," promised Edryd. He could not forgive Eivendr for the things he had done, but against every expectation he had carried into this confrontation, or any that he could have ever imagined, Edryd felt within himself a touch of sympathy for the old man. Eivendr had been, almost, very nearly, a semblance of a good King. There had been forty years of peace in Nar Edor under his reign, during which his secret attempt to bring about the death of Kyreth Edorin, a friend who had all but placed him on the throne, had been the only remarkable stain.

"How can you possibly forgive me?" said Eivendr, unable to comprehend being pardoned by the man known as the Blood Prince.

"I left Nar Edor to prevent bloodshed," answered Edryd. "And I have come back for the same reason. Your abdication, and my absence, will prevent a war."

"You are so like your grandfather," said Eivendr. "He could have sought the throne himself, but he supported a weaker man instead, in the interest of preserving the peace across Nar Edor."

"And you repaid that loyal service with betrayal," said Edryd. "But you have now a chance at some redemption. Relinquish the throne in favor of your nephew."

"Holdrem?" said Eivendr in surprise. Eivendr had two sons, neither of whom were legitimate claimants to the throne. They were misbegotten children born by different mistresses that Eivendr had favored at one time or another, and they were both of them profligate men of privilege who had never seen battle. As these children were widely considered a discredit to Eivendr's name, it was assumed that they would be passed over as successors, but Eivendr would not have guessed that his only nephew would have been favored by Aisen. It might not have been the choice that Eivendr himself would have made, but Holdrem was unquestionably a strong ally of the king's household, and had already sided with his effort to take House Edorin's lands.

"Don't imagine that because he spent a term of service in the Sigil Corps, that my nephew would ever be your puppet," said Eivendr, assuming that this is what Aisen wished for. "He has a strong sense of honor and would never submit to you. Unlike me, he carries no sins which you could use to control him."

"We did both serve together in the same company," said Edryd, "so I know him well. What you say of him is true, and that, more than anything else, recommends him for this purpose."

"You consider him to be a friend," said Eivendr, more clearly grasping things, and yet misapprehending entirely Aisen's actual intentions. "You believe that you can influence him."

"It is because he would not be under influence, neither yours nor mine, that I would choose him," said Edryd, correcting King Eivendr. "If I were to take control of this country, I would be an even worse ruler than you were. Nar Edor needs a strong king, but it must be one with neither blood nor the stains of betrayal on his hands."

Again, Eivendr saw in Aisen's character, an undefinable combination of human qualities that the king much admired, and had once regarded so jealously, that it had driven him to try to bring down Aisen's grandfather. It wasn't a chance for Eivendr to set things right. He would never be able to do that. But Aisen was setting things right for him, and all Eivendr needed to do was to listen and accept what was being asked.

"You are wrong," said Eivendr. "You would make the greatest king this country has ever seen." The king meant these words. The presence exuded by the Blood Prince felt like a tangible thing to King Eivendr, and he was, as he had never once been before in his life, in a state of awe. In that moment, Eivendr felt more strongly than ever that he deserved death at this man's hands, and almost wished that Aisen would deliver that long delayed justice.

The vindictive emotions which Aisen had until that moment mainly suppressed throughout the course of the conversation, ceased to exist. It was replaced with a desolate sense of sorrow so strong that Eivendr could feel its influence in the air between them. Edryd stretched an arm across the table and rested it heavily upon his king's shoulder.

This affected Eivendr in the way that such personal contact sometimes does. The pressure from the other man's hand awoke a sense of connection in Eivendr, and as if at the lifting of an unseen barrier, Eivendr's awareness expanded through the world around them. This sensation felt more an illusion, than anything real, and it was not without precedent, for he had as most people do at one time or another, felt such things before. But what he experienced next, he could find no past familiar ground for. He began to glimpse a vision of the future. He saw Nar Edor laid to waste in a conflict between the nobility on one side, and Aisen and the combined forces of the Sigil Corps and the Ascomanni on the other. This future began with Eivendr's own death at Aisen's hand. What followed were wars of conquest, begun first in this country, but soon spreading to other lands.

"This cannot be my future," cried Eivendr, tearing himself free from Aisen's grasp.

"It isn't your future," was Edryd's pained reply. "It is mine, in a world where you do not have one."

"Surely it can be stopped," said Eivendr. "This must never happen!"

Edryd's response was calm and reassuring. "It need never happen," he answered.

"I will do everything you have asked," Eivendr said, in an expression more sincere than any he had ever made in his life.

"I know that you will," said Edryd. His words were not expressive of mere faith in his king's promise, they carried with them such a feeling of immense relief that Eivendr knew something had changed, and it had changed for the better. He desired then to see what he supposed Aisen could see, but he was too afraid to wish to truly do so.

As Edryd left his king, he felt content and at peace in a way that had eluded him for a long while. On his journey here, he had been tortured with vengeful thoughts and the desire to act on them had been strong. Now, his soul was instead overflowing with gratitude that it had not been necessary to kill this defenseless old man. It felt like stepping out of the darkness and into a warm spring light which began the process of healing some of the scars which had begun to mar his mind.

For Eivendr's part, the experience had been no less profound. He felt an ease and freedom in his heart which he had not known in more than twenty years, and awakened within him was a bond of loyalty to this man who had spared him from judgment, which no power in this world would ever break.

*****

If you enjoyed reading The Sigil Blade, I hope that you will read the free short story, The Blood Prince. In appreciation for your support, it is available as a free download through most major e-book retailers.

Thanks!
Jeff Wilson

About the Author

A writer of science fiction and fantasy novels, Jeff Wilson is the author of the Archon Sigil Trilogy. Jeff fell in love with both fantasy and science fiction at an early age, and inspired by worlds built in the imaginations of others, he began to create worlds of his own. The decision to write about the heroes and demons populating these worlds was slow in coming, but after spending years reworking and refining his ideas, the words demanded expression.

Encouraged and assisted by a small group of fans, which included his brother, and his younger sister and her husband, Jeff completed work on his first short story, The Blood Prince. He has now also completed work on his first full length novel, The Sigil Blade, and has begun work on the second book in the series, The Sigil Knight.

Connect With the Author

Website: JeffWilsonBooks.com
Email: archon@jeffwilsonbooks.com
Facebook: facebook.com/archonsigiltrilogy
Twitter: @jeffwilsonbooks

Pronunciation Guide

Aed Seoras AYD say-OR-uhs
Aelsian AYL-see-yun
Aisen EYE-zen
Áledhuir al-ED-hewr
Alsegate ayls-GAYT
An Innis ahn IN-iss
Aodra AY-oh-druh

Beodred BAY-oh-dred
Beonen bay-uh-nen

Cecht sekt

Deneg DEN-ehg
Domiria doh-MIRR-ee-uh

Edorin eh-DOR-in
Edryd EHD-ruhd
Eidstadt EYED-staht
Eithne EYETH-nee
Eivendr EYE-vin-dur
Elduryn el-DURE-in
Esivh Rhol eh-SIV rohl

Feyd Gerlin fayd GEHR-lin

Giric Tolvanes GEER-ik tohl-VAYNZ
Greven GREH-vin

Hagan HAY-gun
Herja HERR-juh

Irial IRR-ee-yul

Irminsul EER-mihn-sool
Ivor EYE-vor

Kedwyn Saivelle KEHD-win SY-vel
Kyreth Edorin KY-reth eh-DOR-in

Ledrin LED-rin
Lineue LIHN-yoo-ay
Logaeir loh-GAIR
Ludin Kar LOO-din kar

Morven Tevair MOR-ven TEH-vair

Neysim Els NAY-sim els

Oren OR-in
Ossia OH-see-uh

Pedrin Eksar PEH-drin EHK-sar

Ruach ROO-ahkh

Sarel Krin SERR-il krin
Seridor SERR-ih-dor
Seym - saym
Sidrin Eildach SID-rin EYEL-dahk

Ulensorl OO-lin-sorl

Vannin VAN-in
Vidreigard VID-reh-gard

Eithne's Spiced Chicken Dumplings

2 Cups of chicken (shreaded into small pieces)
1 Large White Onion (minced)
1 Large Leek (minced)
1 cup of bread crumbs
2 Large Eggs
1/4 cup butter
2 tsp ground cinnamon
1 tsp nutmeg
1/2 tsp Ginger
1/2 tsp clove
5 Cups of chicken broth or chicken stock

Add 1/4 cup of butter to the pan. Add minced leeks and onion and sauté over medium heat until tender. Remove 1/2 of mixture to a bowl, and remove remaining mixture from heat.

When cool, add the cooked chicken to the bowl with the cooked leeks and onions. Add bread crumbs. Add cinnamon, nutmeg, ginger, and cloves. Add eggs and combine mixture, incorporating all of the ingredients in this step. Form into dumplings about one inch in diameter. Set aside on a plate.

Return remaining sautéed leeks and onions to heat. Add the chicken broth. Bring ingredients to a low simmer for approximately 5 minutes and add salt and pepper to taste. Gently ladle the formed dumplings into the pot. Add water or additional chicken broth if needed to ensure the dumplings are covered. Cook for 15 minutes.

Serve with a robust bread, and your preference of soft cheese. Simple sliced baguettes with bree work well.

Serves 2 to 4

<u>Acknowledgements</u>

I began writing when I was young, strictly for my own personal enjoyment. I continued to write as I grew older to give form and expression to the ideas that roll around inside my head. Inspired by history (especially the kind which is now only poorly remembered) and a need to explore the concepts that fire my imagination, I began to build stories. Considering my creative efforts an intensely personal process, I was selective in sharing it with others.

And that is where I would still be now if it were not for two very important people.

The first is my brother, who loves so many of the same things I do, but has more passion and feeling than I could hope to have. Where I could be characterized by restraint, introversion, and at times by a tendency to remain disconnected from others, my brother has the kind of warmth that reaches through walls, encourages friendship, and inspires me to reach for greater things. We have spent thousands of hours together discussing our stories. His influence is found throughout my work, lending a vibrant quality to my writing that it would not otherwise have.

My little sister, whose enthusiasm and encouragement have ever been sources on which I can rely for motivation when I become discouraged, and confidence when I have felt doubt, is the second. I owe her an incredible debt for all of the things she has done to inspire me to write, improve, and ultimately finish this novel, and I am truly grateful for the incredible passion she has shown for introducing my work to others.

With their encouragement, I shared this story with an expanding group of interested fans. In doing so, I have been on the receiving end of so much generous assistance that I cannot help but feel inadequate in expressing my appreciation to the many people—including friends, family and sometimes perfect strangers—who have given me advice, feedback, and material support. Deserving of particular mention, major contributions were made by my cousin Staci. Her expert work as the editor on the final draft of this book led to numerous improvements, elevating the quality of the narrative and the flow of the text.

I thank you for buying a copy of my book, and I am especially grateful to those of you who took the time, in some form or another, to share your impressions of the book. Your support affirms the simple purpose for which I write—expressing thoughts, feelings, and ideas that inspire me, in the hope that they will inspire you in turn.

20892934R00244

Made in the USA
San Bernardino, CA
27 April 2015